Praise for
The Art of Losing Yourself

"Once again Ganshert holds us spellbound in a beautiful story of endurance and hope—offering no easy answers but the irresistible light of Christ to guide us. And what characters! Real, heartbroken, warm, and seeking. Within them we meet our friends, our family, ourselves. I thoroughly enjoyed this and, as always, eagerly await her next."

—KATHERINE REAY, author of *Lizzy and Jane* and *Dear Mr. Knightley*

"*The Art of Losing Yourself* highlights Katie Ganshert's vivid prose as it brims with reality that will challenge and change you with every turn of the page. Ganshert is not afraid to write raw, to wrestle with the things that test our faith and, if we are willing, draw us closer to God."

—BETH K. VOGT, author of *Somebody Like You,* one of the *Publisher's Weekly* Best Books of 2014

"Katie Ganshert's poignant novel hits deep emotional chords as the characters battle to a place of healing through a haze of pain. As someone who has experienced the deep pain of miscarriage, I could so easily relate to Carmen's journey. Carmen's story emphasizes what I learned: the pain and broken relationships can be healed. While plumbing deep waters, this is a story of resounding hope and discovery. I highly recommend it!"

—CARA PUTMAN, award-winning author of *Shadowed by Grace* and *Where Treetops Glisten*

"This book will have readers lost in its pages for hours, journeying along with two sisters in a rich, emotionally-charged tale of second chances, restoration, and finding hope—and love—when it seems perpetually out of sight."

—BETSY ST. AMANT, author of *All's Fair in Love and Cupcakes*

"Sitting down with a Katie Ganshert novel is like talking with a trusted friend. It's something to look forward to, knowing the conversation won't disappoint and you'll be the better for it at the end. *The Art of Losing Yourself* is a poignant tale of estrangement, loss, and grief, and the joy that comes in discovering you are indeed loved. In her classic tell-it-like-is style, Ganshert's complex characters step off the page and invite you in. Their journeys are difficult but relatable, and we're sucked along for the ride, rooting for them the whole way. And when the last page is turned, we are left with a smile and the contented sigh that comes at the conclusion of every wonderful read."

—CATHERINE WEST, award-winning author of *Yesterday's Tomorrow*

"Katie Ganshert will sweep you into another world in *The Art of Losing Yourself.* I loved this book! The journey Katie's characters take is raw, beautiful, and honest, and the prose is lovely."

—CINDY WOODSMALL, author of *A Love Undone*

"In *The Art of Losing Yourself,* Katie Ganshert has woven a sensitive story of hope and healing for our modern world. The empathy with which Ganshert explores the complexity of the human heart is so authentic and the depth of emotion so real, I was brought to tears more than once. Sisters, daughters, and mothers alike will find themselves moved by this book."

—KRISTY CAMBRON, author of *The Butterfly and the Violin* and *A Sparrow in Terezin*

"Wounded, heart-tugging characters. Beautiful prose. An emotional journey that holds the reader captive. Katie Ganshert has such a way of tapping into those raw, vulnerable places with her characters, and *The Art of Losing Yourself* is no exception. I love the thread of hope and unabashed honesty weaving through this story of loss and letting go."

—MELISSA TAGG, author of *From the Start*

"With a keen attention to detail and a unique voice, Katie Ganshert has woven a poignant and powerful story in *The Art of Losing Yourself.* Universal themes, charged and realistic emotions, and characters readers will easily relate to make this story a standout."

—COURTNEY WALSH, author of *Paper Hearts* and the *New York Times* e-book bestseller *A Sweethaven Summer*

"*The Art of Losing Yourself* took my breath away with its ability to portray the complex facets of human relationships in such a realistic yet tender way. Ganshert's writing creates a prism of perspectives into the lives of characters as deeply flawed as they are endearing. Carmen's and Gracie's stories made me laugh, made me cry, and made me *think*—and that's my definition of a perfect novel."

—DEBORAH RANEY, author of *The Face of the Earth* and the Chicory Inn Novels series

THE ART
of
LOSING
YOURSELF

BOOKS BY KATIE GANSHERT

Wildflowers from Winter

Wishing on Willows

A Broken Kind of Beautiful

THE ART
of
LOSING
YOURSELF

A NOVEL

KATIE
GANSHERT

Author of *A Broken Kind of Beautiful*

WATERBROOK
PRESS

THE ART OF LOSING YOURSELF
PUBLISHED BY WATERBROOK PRESS
12265 Oracle Boulevard, Suite 200
Colorado Springs, Colorado 80921

Scripture quotations and paraphrases are taken from the following versions: The Holy Bible, English Standard Version, copyright © 2001 by Crossway Bibles, a division of Good News Publishers. Used by permission. All rights reserved. The King James Version. The Holy Bible, New International Version®, NIV®. Copyright © 1973, 1978, 1984 by Biblica Inc.™ Used by permission of Zondervan. All rights reserved worldwide. www.zondervan.com.

The characters and events in this book are fictional, and any resemblance to actual persons or events is coincidental.

Trade Paperback ISBN 978-1-60142-592-8
eBook ISBN 978-1-60142-593-5

Cover design by Kelly L. Howard; cover photography by Seth Goldfarb

Published in the United States by WaterBrook Multnomah, an imprint of the Crown Publishing Group, a division of Penguin Random House LLC, New York.

WATERBROOK and its deer colophon are registered trademarks of Penguin Random House LLC.

Library of Congress Cataloging-in-Publication Data
Ganshert, Katie.
    The art of losing yourself : a novel / Katie Ganshert. — First Edition.
        pages ; cm
    ISBN 978-1-60142-592-8 (paperback) — ISBN 978-1-60142-593-5 (electronic)
    I. Title.
    PS3607.A56A89 2015
    813'.6—dc23

                                    2014043264

Printed in the United States of America
2015—First Edition

10 9 8 7 6 5 4 3 2 1

For Salima, my brave, brave, brave little girl.
Being your mother is one of the greatest honors I will ever
be blessed with on this side of eternity. Come what may,
God's writing a grand story for your life.

The hand of the LORD was upon me, and he brought me out by the Spirit of the LORD and set me in the middle of a valley; it was full of bones. He led me back and forth among them, and I saw a great many bones on the floor of the valley, bones that were very dry. He asked me, "Son of man, can these bones live?"

—EZEKIEL 37:1–3

Prologue

CARMEN

The nurse rolled me down a hallway and through a door where my husband waited on a chair pushed into one corner of the small recovery room. He stood as soon as we entered.

"She's pretty groggy, but she's awake. She has to be up and walking before y'all can go."

"Is she in any pain?" Ben asked.

I closed my eyes, feigning sleep.

"She shouldn't be."

The door closed.

Ben came to my bedside and wrapped my cold, lifeless hand in his strong grip, as if the tighter he held, the closer I'd stay. But it was too late. I was already gone.

When the nurse returned, Ben stepped back. She gently shook my shoulder, encouraged me to sit, then stand, then walk across the room. And just like that, they released me—as if getting up and walking meant I was all better now.

Ben hovered as we made our way outside, his stare heating the side of my face more intensely than the Florida sun. He hadn't stopped looking at me since the nurse rolled me into that room. I had yet to look at him. He opened my car door. I eased inside, pulled the seat belt across my chest, and stared straight ahead with dry eyes and an empty heart. As soon as he turned the key in the ignition, Christian music filled the car.

Like a viper, my hand struck the power button.

We drove in silence.

Unable to get warm, I wrapped my arms around my middle and watched the palm trees whiz past the window in streaks of vibrant green. Ben white-knuckled the steering wheel, darting glances at me every time we hit a red light. When he pulled into the driveway of our home, neither of us moved. We sat in the screaming silence while I drifted further and further away—out into a sea of drowning hopes.

"Carmen." An entire army of emotions marched inside the confines of my name, desperation leading the way.

A better wife might have met her husband halfway, might have even offered him some reassurances—a glance, a hand squeeze, some sign that all would be well. I could do nothing but gaze at the pink blossoms on the crepe myrtle in our front lawn. New life.

How ironic.

Ben reached across the console and set his hand on my knee. "Tell me what to do. Tell me how to make this better."

Something feral clawed its way up my throat. A baby would make this better. Give me a *baby*.

Ben and I did everything right. We did things God's way. So why wasn't this happening? Why did this continue to happen? But I swallowed the wild thing down and moved my leg.

His hand slid onto the seat—bereft and alone.

GRACIE

When you grew up in a small town like New Hope, Texas, obscurity was a luxury that didn't exist. I was the daughter of Evelyn Fisher, a woman known for two things: making frequent visits to the corner liquor store and baptizing herself in the creek every other Sunday.

My little-girl self would sit on the tire swing beneath our oak tree, my big toe tracing circles in the dirt, and watch as my mother crossed herself in the name of the Father, the Son, and the Holy Ghost before walking out into the water that bordered our backyard. I remembered being more puzzled by the crossing than the actual baptizing. Back then, we went to a Baptist church where folks didn't do that sort of thing.

"You can take the girl out of the Catholic, but you can't take the Catholic out of the girl," she'd say.

"I don't know what that means."

"It means old habits die hard, Gracie-bug."

That, I understood. Because as often as she emptied her bottles into the sink and dunked herself in that creek, the liquor cabinet never remained empty for long. Needless to say, we were odd ducks in New Hope, and the oddest ducks of all at our church. Not so much because Mama carried a rosary in her purse, or cried during the sermons, or crossed herself during the benediction, but because she drank, and according to our pastor, drinking was the same as dancing with the devil.

One Sunday, as she headed toward our small house, soaking wet from head to toe, I stopped my tire spinning and squinted at her through the afternoon brightness. "Why do you dunk yourself into the creek like that?"

She paused, as if noticing me for the first time. That happened a lot—her forgetting I was around. Usually I had to go and get into some real trouble in order to remind her. Mama brought her hand up to her forehead like a visor. "To be made new, baby girl."

Eventually, she gave up on the baptizing and decided on rehab instead. I was at the end of fourth grade when she dropped me off at my father's for three months. When she finally picked me up, all of our belongings were crammed into the back of our rusty station wagon. We left New Hope behind and drove east to the town of Apalachicola, Florida. My mother got a job as a waitress and I went to school at Franklin High. No more church. No more creek-dunking. The one thing that hadn't changed? Mama's dance with the devil.

At the sound of my alarm, I experienced a wave of two diametrically opposed emotions. Relief, because this was my final year of high school at Franklin. And dread, because this was only the first day.

I slapped my phone into silence and picked up the mood ring on my night-stand; its stone was the color of stormy sky. I didn't actually believe it could read my mood, but I found it beneath a Laffy Taffy wrapper in one of the many roadside ditches I delittered over the summer. It was actually a nice ring, made with legit silver—not like those cheesy five-dollar ones you find at chintzy stores like Claire's. Plus, it fit. So I cleaned it off and stuck it in my pocket. My single, solitary treasure from a summer filled with trash.

Muffled conversation filtered through the sliver of space between the worn carpet and my bedroom door—a female-male exchange about a water main breaking in downtown Tallahassee. Mom was either (a) already awake watch-ing the news or (b) passed out on the couch from the night before with the TV still on. If I had any money to bet, I'd put it all on option b.

I pressed my thumb over the mood ring's stone and pictured violet—a color that meant happy, relaxed, free. I knew because last spring I'd found this behemoth paperback titled *The Meaning of Color* at Downtown Books and read it in a single day. I removed my thumb from the stone and took a peek. The amber color of a cat's eye stared back at me—mixed emotions.

Maybe the ring worked after all.

With a resigned sigh, I kicked off the tangle of sheets covering my legs and poked my head outside the door. The TV cast a celestial glow on my mother, who lay sprawled on the couch, one arm flung over her head. Dead to the world.

One hundred eighty days . . . one hundred eighty days . . . one hundred eighty days . . .

This became my mantra as I brushed my teeth, rinsed my face, lined my eyes with liquid liner, and dressed in a simple tee, frayed jeans, and a pair of combat boots I had purchased at a consignment shop back when I still had money. Thanks to Chris Nanning and my bad decision and the fat judge with a chronic scowl, my bank account had been wiped clean. I checked my reflection onc last timc.

The faded postcard I kept wedged in the corner of my dresser mirror had come loose. I pulled it all the way out and flipped it over. The invitation on the back was equally faded but sharp and clear in my mind. It was the only place where my company wasn't just tolerated but requested. Desired, even. If the evidence wasn't there, staring me in the face, I'd probably chalk the memories up to a serious case of wishful thinking.

I wedged the card back into place and tucked a strand of coal-colored hair behind my ear. It didn't stay. Two days ago, in a moment of impulsivity, I chopped off my hair and dyed it black. At the time, the change had felt bold, symbolic even, like a thumbing of my nose at the student body, which would undoubtedly be whispering behind my back extra loud on the first day of school. The new do was my message to them that I didn't care what anyone said or thought.

If only that were true.

In the kitchen, an empty bottle of wine stood at attention on the counter; another lay tipped on its side in the basin of the sink. I grabbed a strawberry Pop-Tart from one of the cupboards and glanced at the clock. Seven forty-five.

"Mom!" I turned on the faucet and slurped in a drink from the running water, then snagged my school bag from the back of a chair in the dining room. "It's time to go."

She mumbled something incoherent.

I picked up the remote from the coffee table and shut off the female news anchor. "You need to get ready."

She wiped at a string of drool and rolled over. Even with the smudged mascara, the tangled mat of hair, and the angry red crease running the length of her cheek, she managed to pull off beautiful. Too bad for me, I took after my father.

"I'm gonna be late for school. And you're gonna be late for work."

"Too tired," she croaked.

More like too hung over.

Heat stirred in my chest. I took a deep breath and exhaled. I had no idea how many more times she could be late before she got the ax, but my mother's tardiness wasn't my problem. It would only become my problem if I stayed here. Her boss might extend some grace; Principal Best (a name too ironic for words), on the other hand, would not. I dug inside her purse and grabbed her keys.

One hundred eighty days . . . one hundred eighty days . . . one hundred eighty days . . .

GRACIE

First period was physical education. Dodge ball. Hurray. I leaned against the wall while foam balls whizzed back and forth across the gym. The boys did most of the throwing. The girls did most of the shrieking. My gym teacher, who stood out of bounds midcourt, spotted me listening to my iPod and crooked his finger, beckoning me to come. I pretended not to see him. He joined me by the wall and held out his hand. "You know better, Gracie."

Reluctantly, I slapped the iPod onto his palm.

"You can collect this at the end of the day," he said, just as a foam ball pegged him in the back of the head.

"Sorry, Coach!" Kyle Marcello, one of Franklin High School's cockiest and most meatheaded linebackers, called from the other side of the court. "I was aiming for Fisher."

Coach resumed his position at midcourt, my iPod tucked away in the pocket of his shorts. Yuck. I wasn't sure I wanted it back anymore. Kyle caught my eye, then pantomimed swinging a baseball bat with a teasing smirk on his face.

I rolled my eyes.

One hundred eighty days . . . one hundred eighty days . . .

Second period was an upperclassman elective, Introduction to Philosophy, my guidance counselor forced upon me. *"You are a smart girl, Gracie. Your ACT scores are proof. This will be a good class for you."* When I picked apart her reasoning, the counselor said she saw this as more evidence that I was, indeed, well suited for the class. Never mind the fact that the teacher, short, bald, turtle-faced Mr. Burrelson, reeked of Ben-Gay and sported an eternal string of white spittle that stretched between his upper and lower lips whenever he talked. I stared at it while he handed out textbooks, *The Philosophical Journey: An Interactive Approach,* and droned on and on and on about class expectations.

His soupy eyes lit up when he talked about the importance of analysis and debate. He lost what little student attention he had left when he started throwing out fancy terminology like "ethical decision making" and "moral permissibility versus moral necessity." I fiddled with my mood ring, making the color change from yellow to peridot, and made predictions on how many inches Mr. Burrelson's spittle string could stretch before breaking apart.

As soon as the bell rang, I gathered my things and headed into the bathroom. On my way out of the stall, Chelsea Paxton, an overweight girl in my class, walked in. Chelsea was an outcast, like me. Ever since I arrived in fifth grade, I watched her try everything under the sun to fit in. So far with little success. More often than not, she looked like a kicked puppy, which was why I offered her a smile when we passed each other. Even though she was desperate to fit in with the people I loathed, I couldn't help but feel sorry for her.

Chelsea smiled back, then disappeared into the last stall.

I had worked a couple dollops of soap into a foamy lather when the scene took a decided nosedive. Two of the school's biggest clichés—Sadie Hall and her trusty sidekick, Jenna Smith—entered the room. As soon as Sadie spotted me, she gave me a slow, critical once-over. "Nice hair."

"Nice face."

A pinkish hue blossomed across her cheeks.

A toilet flushed.

I probably should have warned Chelsea to stay put. Sadie and Jenna were relentless when it came to her. They attacked her in person, they attacked her on social media, they attacked her via text messages. What was worse? She never stood up for herself and the teachers did nothing to stop it. I rinsed away the soap as Chelsea appeared. She said a breathless hello to Thing One and Thing Two, then turned on the faucet.

Jenna started making gagging noises.

Chelsea stared down into the sink.

I pressed my lips together.

"It reeks in here," Jenna said.

I tore off a ream of paper towels. *Stay out of it, Gracie. You can't afford to get into any more trouble.*

With her head still down, Chelsea moved past Sadie to dry her hands.

Sadie coughed and fanned her hand in front of her nose.

"What is your problem?" The words jumped out of my mouth before I could stop them, echoing inside the cavernous bathroom. Apparently, I wasn't as smart as my guidance counselor thought.

"*My* problem? I'm not the one who doesn't know how to bathe." Sadie gave Chelsea a disgusted look up and down. "It's the first day of school. She's not even trying."

"And some people try way too hard."

"Excuse me?"

"Is that one bottle of foundation on your face, or two?"

Sadie closed the gap between us, completely disregarding my personal bubble. We stood nose to nose. "Why don't you do us all a favor and grow your bangs a little longer? That way nobody will have to look at your ugly face. I know Chris would appreciate it."

My hands took on a mind of their own.

One second they dangled by my sides, the next they shoved Sadie away, hard enough that she stumbled back. Her expression was one of such shock that I laughed. I wasn't sure anyone had ever dared to push Sadie before. Her face twisted into a mask of ugly. She lunged at me, and somehow, we were wrestling on the floor in the girls' bathroom on the first day of school. Sadie's sharp nails dug into my neck. I balled my hand into a fist and connected with her mouth. She yanked my hair. I kneed her in the stomach. Jenna and Chelsea shrieked. The bell for third period rang. And a teacher pried us apart.

My chest heaved.

Sadie's lip bled.

So much for staying out of it.

Three uncomfortable chairs lined the windowed wall of the school office. I sat in one. Sadie sat in another, arms crossed, facing as far away from me as possible, like I had cooties or something. I stretched my legs out in front of me and tapped the toes of my boots together. Sadie scowled at my feet. I began to tap to Beethoven's Fifth, humming the tune under my breath. "Dun dun dun, duuuun. Dun dun dun, duuuun."

Sadie scowled harder. "You're such a freak."

The secretary answered the phone and clacked away on her keyboard, ignoring us both.

A half hour earlier, she had called our mothers and kindly asked if they could drive to school. Meanwhile Principal Best invited the two witnesses—

Chelsea and Jenna—into his office. Maybe if he had called Chelsea in first, alone, I would have stood a chance. But Chelsea and Jenna together? That sealed my fate. I may have stuck up for Chelsea, but Chelsea would never, ever stick up for me. Not in front of Jenna.

By the time Principal Best opened his door and dismissed the pair to class, Mrs. Hall had arrived. She was an adult-sized version of Sadie, only with age lines bracketing her mouth and no swollen lip. She was head of the PTA and beloved by all the teachers at Franklin, and although I expected the full brunt of her disapproving stare, she pinned her displeasure on Sadie. A small piece of vindication. Then Principal Best gave Mrs. Hall a friendly handshake and proceeded to apologize for the inconvenience. Actually apologize. Sadie's Mom might have been willing to give me the benefit of the doubt. Principal Best was not.

He invited mother and daughter into his office.

I resumed my boot tapping.

An hour and twenty minutes had passed since our bathroom kerfuffle. An hour and ten since the secretary called my mother. As if realizing this at the same time as I did, she looked up from her computer. "No sign of Mom yet?"

I shook my head. Nope. Zero sign. Nor would there be. I took her car. And she was probably still passed out on the couch. I touched the scratches along my neck and grimaced at the sting. Principal Best's door muffled the sound of laughter—one voice baritone, the other more feminine. There was more talking, and then the door opened. As soon as Sadie and her mother took their leave, Best cleared his throat with a loud, guttural sound.

I guess that was as close to an invitation as I was going to get. I stood, fully prepared to fight this battle solo, when the office door swooped open and in walked my mother, of all people, dressed in black slacks and a white blouse, her hair no longer a matted tangle, but pulled back into a mass of curls at the nape of her neck. Nobody would notice the pallor behind her makeup, the slight tremor of her fingers. Those were things noticeable only if you knew to look for them. Most people didn't know to look, and Mom was an expert at hiding her problems from the world.

"I'm sorry I'm so late. Gracie borrowed my car this morning. One of my co-workers had to give me a ride." As soon as her attention landed on my neck scratches, her eyes widened. "What happened?"

Principal Best swept his hand inside his office. No friendly handshake. No apology. Not for us. "We can talk inside."

Mom and I sat in a pair of chairs facing the front of Best's desk while he took the swivel chair behind. He leaned back in his seat with his fingers steepled in front of his chin, staring at me while Mom stared at him. It was like this long, boring game of Chicken. "Gracie, would you mind telling your mother what happened?" he finally prompted.

I looked at him through my bangs. "Does it matter if I do?"

"Gracie," Mom scolded.

"I'm speaking to a biased jury." I motioned to Principal Best, sitting there in his chair all puffed up like a peacock. The guy had a serious case of short-man syndrome. "His mind is already made up. Jenna's testimony dug my grave, and Sadie's buried my casket." I'm sure Best's set-in-stone opinion of me grabbed a shovel and kicked in. If I'd learned anything from my mother it was that we were all creatures of predictability. Our worlds were most comfortable when we saw what we wanted to see. And when it came to me, Best wanted to see the worst.

"I'm really sorry about this," Mom said. "I don't know what's gotten into her lately."

Principal Best drummed his steepled fingers together. "You're right about one thing, Gracie. Our actions do form an impression. Whether you think it's fair or not, past behavior does have a bearing on what a person believes in the present."

"So you admit this isn't a fair trial?"

"You have a history of violence and lying. Miss Hall, on the other hand, has never once been in trouble at this school."

"Sadie Hall is a bully. You should see the way she treats Chelsea."

"If that's true, why didn't Chelsea say anything about it in my office?"

"Because Chelsea's afraid of her. And you called Chelsea in with Jenna." Seriously. How moronic could one guy get? "Since she wouldn't stand up for herself in the bathroom, I decided to do it for her. What is it you preach to us at the beginning of every school year? Bystanders are every bit as guilty as the bullies themselves?"

Principal Best's ears turned pink.

"My behavior was morally permissible, if not morally necessary. Just ask Mr. Burrelson if you don't believe me."

"Your behavior was unacceptable. We do not tolerate fighting in this school."

Mom massaged the bridge of her nose and shook her head. She looked tired, fed up, exactly like the mother of a delinquent would look. And as the small man behind the desk relayed the very lopsided account of what happened in the bathroom, she only looked more and more so.

The story, of course, was one of innocent Sadie, who complimented my hair, only to be viciously attacked by wild and out-of-control Gracie. The scratch on my neck was self-defense on Sadie's part. The cut on Sadie's lip was unacceptable aggression on my part. Jenna spun the tale. Chelsea didn't contradict it. By the time Principal Best finished, Mom had turned into a wilted begonia.

"None of that was true," I said.

"Sadie didn't compliment your hair?"

"She was being sarcastic."

"And you didn't push her first?"

"She was making gagging noises at Chelsea."

Principal Best ignored me and spoke to Mom. "Given Gracie's prior infractions, we are left with no other option but a three-day suspension. We will see Gracie on Monday." If he had a gavel, I'm sure he would have pounded it. "I hope we can start fresh then."

A puff of laughter escaped through my nose.

Mom gave me a sharp look.

Seriously though—a fresh start? Did she not hear anything he said? There would be no fresh starts here, especially not with him, especially not for me. His mind was made up. So why even try?

GRACIE

The front door of our small house opened and slammed shut just as I managed to loosen the lid on the jar of spaghetti sauce. Mom was home. And judging by the sound of the door, she was no happier with me now than she had been when she dropped me off at home after our fun little meeting with Principal Best.

I turned on one of the burners. It clicked, clicked, clicked, then flamed to life. I twisted the knob to high, dumped the Prego into a saucepan, and set it over the burner. I was digging through the back of the pantry for a box of pasta when Mom walked into the kitchen and opened the fridge. My hand connected with something promising. I pulled out a package of rigatoni.

Mom grabbed a wine glass from one of the cupboards and filled it from a box of Franzia—the giant size she purchased from Costco. I dumped the rigatoni into a large pot, steam rising from the water while the Prego in the saucepan began to bubble. I stared, hypnotized by the way the orange sauce spit hissing droplets of red onto the stovetop. In Chinese culture, red symbolized purity, but almost everywhere else, the color was associated with passion or anger. The warm color of orange, on the other hand, was supposed to stimulate conversation. How appropriate, then, that as Mom drained her wine glass and poured herself another, the orange exploded, leaving beads of red in its wake.

Neither of us said a word.

Once the pasta reached al dente, I dumped it into a colander, mixed the Prego with the noodles, served myself a bowl, and headed out to the living room—away from my mother and her cheap wine. As much as her silence crawled under my skin, I preferred it to lecturing. I wanted to serve my sentence and move on. There were worse punishments than suspension. I settled onto the couch, found a rerun of *The Big Bang Theory,* and dug in.

On my fourth bite, Mom sat on the other end of the couch, wine glass in hand. I glanced at her from the corner of my eye, wishing she would finish her wine in the kitchen. On my sixth bite, she reached for the remote and turned off the TV.

I stopped chewing.

"I think you need to go live with your father."

The rigatoni turned into drywall. My mother hated my father. Had even used me against him in the past. And now she wanted to ship me off to go live with him? I forced the lump of food down my throat and glared.

She set her glass on the coffee table and rubbed circles into her temples. Resignation had replaced the anger she brought with her into the kitchen. "I called him today."

I scrambled off the couch. "You what?"

She looked up at me, exhaustion in her eyes. "As much as I might not like him, your father is better at asserting his authority than I am and it's obvious that's what you need right now. He said he's willing to take you for a few months."

"I'm not going."

"It's already been decided."

"You never even asked me."

"I don't have to ask you. I'm your mother."

My anger boiled over—thicker and redder than the Prego. She was barely a mother. "I told you I didn't start that fight in the bathroom."

"Gracie, you have a track record." She resumed her temple kneading. "And I don't know what to do anymore. Your sister was never like this."

I grabbed her glass off the coffee table and hurled it toward the wall. It shattered with a burst of red and bled down the paint.

Mom didn't move. She didn't speak. She didn't react at all. She just sat there like a statue, all remnant of color draining from her face.

"I'm not going to Dad's." Before she could argue, I walked to my bedroom and slammed the door.

When I moved to Apalachicola in fifth grade, I had a teacher who would spread her arms wide after we recited the Pledge of Allegiance every morning and declare, "Boys and girls, the world is your oyster!" She was a thin-faced woman named Mrs. Dulane, and although I wasn't sure what she meant by the words, they sounded nice. Hopeful, even. Seeing as Mom and I had just moved to the oyster capital of Florida—they sounded appropriate too.

Until my eleventh birthday, when I begged my mother to take me to Boss Oyster, a restaurant on the south end of Water Street that served the town's seafood of choice seventeen different ways. I remembered the sense of building anticipation as we waited for our food. What, exactly, would my world taste like? Imagine my displeasure when the waiter brought out a tray of half-shelled goobers. It took several whispered threats from my mother before I put one in my mouth. The slimy, chewy texture turned my nose wrinkle into a full-throttle gag. After that first experience, I didn't care about the sixteen other ways in which oysters could be made—I vowed never to eat one again.

On the drive home, I told Mom about Mrs. Dulane's ritualistic morning declaration. She laughed and explained that oysters made pearls. The saying originated with Shakespeare, she told me, as if that settled everything. What she didn't tell me, and what I later found out on my own thanks to Google, was that very few oysters made pearls in the wild. Most pearls were the result of someone forcing an irritant inside the poor shell.

Needless to say, I no longer found Mrs. Dulane's words nice or hopeful. She was basically telling twenty-five impressionable fifth graders that our worlds would contain the equivalent of gross food or inescapable irritants. Those were our choices.

Six years later and irony of all ironies, it turned out that *I* was the irritant.

My earliest memories were those of fighting—my mom and dad fighting, my mom and her parents fighting, my dad and stepmom fighting. Always about me. I was over it, which was why I started throwing toiletries and clothes into my duffel bag as soon as I slammed my door shut. I wasn't going to my father's, but I sure wasn't staying here either, an irritant forced into my mother's oyster world.

When I finished packing, I sat on the edge of my bed, listening as the microwave hummed and beeped. The faucet in the kitchen ran. A cupboard door opened and closed. The TV resumed its droning—first with the six o'clock news, then with some show I didn't recognize. I waited until darkness fell, the television went off, and the floor creaked with my mother's footsteps.

Once all signs of life outside my room ceased, I removed the postcard wedged in the corner of my dresser mirror and stepped into the hallway, my duffel bag strapped over my shoulder. I tiptoed into the living room. Mom hadn't cleaned up the broken glass or the stain of red wine running down the wall. My half-eaten bowl of pasta remained on the coffee table.

As quietly as possible, I made a peanut butter and jelly sandwich, grabbed a can of Mountain Dew from the refrigerator and all the cash from Mom's purse, and stepped out into the night. I considered taking Mom's car, but that would guarantee she'd come after me. So instead, I walked south on Hickory Street while eating my sandwich. Once I reached Avenue E, I cracked open my Mountain Dew and headed west.

A few cars passed, but nobody stopped or slowed. I took the last swig of my drink, kept an eye out for the next available trash can, and continued onward, attempting to ignore the duffel bag strap digging into my shoulder and the way my baggage grew heavier with every passing block. I kept walking, away from my mother and all of her dysfunction.

Once I reached the outskirts of town and headlights approached from behind, I stuck out my thumb. The car pulled to a stop on the shoulder of the road several yards ahead. Rust had eaten away half of the bumper and something like cellophane covered one of the back door windows. There was a soft sound of a latch as the trunk popped open.

I didn't give myself time to chicken out. I didn't consider what could happen if the person behind the wheel was a maniac. I checked to make sure there were no drugs or dead bodies in the trunk, then tossed my duffel bag inside and climbed into the passenger seat.

Country twang and cigarette smoke filled the car. A woman with leathery skin and long, straight hair the color of flint sat behind the wheel. "Where you headed?"

"A few miles west of Navarre Beach on Route 399."

The lady pursed her lips. "You buy me a pack of smokes and fill up my tank and I'll get you in the general vicinity."

I pulled the seat belt across my lap. "Deal."

Nodding, she shifted the car into drive and hit the gas.

My mother used to search for fresh starts in the creek waters of New Hope, Texas. I grasped for mine in a cloud of cigarette smoke on a stretch of Florida highway, a faded postcard clutched in my hand.

CARMEN

The summer between third and fourth grade, I developed an obsession with Mary Poppins. I watched the movie on repeat—over and over and over again until I knew every line by heart. There was this one scene at the beginning of the film where Bert entertained a crowd with a slightly spastic song and dance. The wind shifted and he fell into this odd, trance-like state. *"Wind's in the east, mist comin' in . . . Like somethin' is brewin', and 'bout to begin . . . Can't put me finger on what lies in store . . . But I feel what's to 'appen, all 'appened before . . ."*

I've often thought how convenient it would be if this happened in real life. If change would announce itself before arriving. At least then, we could brace for it beforehand. But change did not confer with the wind or the mist. It often came when we least expected it, which made its beginning difficult to pinpoint. For the Banks family, change began when Mary Poppins floated in on her umbrella after all the other nannies blew away. For me, I believe, it began with a mental breakdown in a Toys "R" Us parking lot.

I took a deep breath.

I can do this.

I simply needed to walk into the store, print a list, pick the first item, smile at the cashier, and leave. No reason to think. No reason to browse. No reason to imagine what might never be. I checked my reflection in the rearview mirror, ran my fingers beneath my eyes, and tucked a strand of wavy hair behind my ear. Despite straightening it earlier, Florida's humidity always managed to coax out my natural curl.

Hitching my purse strap over my shoulder, I stepped out into the muggy air and headed toward the front doors of Toys "R" Us, peering once or twice at the cloud-dotted sky—big, bright, sharply defined pillows outlined by a blanket of blue. They were the kind of clouds my dad and I used to spend hours looking at when I was a little girl. The kind of clouds Mary Poppins sat on while powdering her nose during the opening credits.

The doors slid open with a blast of cool air and the heels of my tan pumps went from clunking to clicking as they hit composite tile. I veered right, toward the Babies "R" Us portion of the store, where a friendly faced woman in a purple-collared shirt stood behind a counter.

"Is this where I print out a registry?" I asked.

"Sure is. What's the last name of the registrant?"

"Dolten. D-o-l-t-e-n. First name is Katy with a y." Katy was a good friend from church, one I should be happy for. Correction—one I *was* happy for. Truly. The problem wasn't my lack of happiness; it was the inescapably deep pang that accompanied it.

I waited as the lady typed the name into the computer, printed out the list, and handed it over, recognition seeping into the chocolate brown of her irises.

In different circumstances, I might have stuck around and talked about the weather. People liked when I did that. Today, however, I was on a mission. I thanked her for her help, then scanned the first page of the registry. Everything was already purchased. I shuffled to the second page. Then the third.

What in the world?

Not until the fourth did I find a few unpurchased items—all inexpensive and unrelated. A Philips Avent BPA-Free soothie pacifier, Safety First Sleepy Baby nail clippers, a bulb syringe, bathtub stacky cups, and a Diaper Genie refill. I flipped to the fifth and final page, hoping for something bigger, like a bathtub or a baby carrier. Something that would require visiting one aisle, and one aisle alone. I found nothing but more miscellaneous odds and ends.

I moved my finger down the list until I found the aisle number for the pacifier, then made my way to the right place. Tunnel vision. That was the key to survival. I didn't look at the adorable baby clothes surrounding me on all sides. I didn't look at the happy mothers with their adorable children looking at the adorable baby clothes surrounding me on all sides. I didn't think about how desperately I wanted to be one of those mothers.

With my shoulders pulled back, I convinced myself that it would happen. Maybe not in the conventional way I had imagined when Ben and I got married, but that didn't matter now. What mattered was that as of last week, we officially took our place on the adoption waiting list. After all the classes and the required reading, after all the frantic cleaning to prepare for the home visits, after fingerprinting and background checks, credit reports, references, never-ending paperwork, and a substantial chunk of money, I'd finally put the finishing touches on our portfolio and sent it off to our agency's social worker. One day soon, I'd join the Mother Club and that deep, inescapable ache would let go of my heart and melt away.

I marched down an aisle, picked up the pacifier, then turned down another aisle for the nail clippers and syringe. I managed five items altogether before my hands were officially full. Time for checkout. Halfway there, someone called my name.

"Carmen?"

Mandy approached from a distance, dressed in yoga pants, a Blue Angels T-shirt, and a baseball cap with Just Do It stitched above the brim. She waved enthusiastically as she closed the gap between us. "I thought that was you!"

I swallowed a groan.

Mandy Thom was the president of the Bay Breeze High School booster club. She had three sons. Her eldest played quarterback for the University of Central Florida. Her middle son was Ben's first-string tight end. The last time we'd seen each other had been during the booster club's annual spring trivia night—a fund-raising event that brought in the entire town of Bay Breeze. Mandy put Ben and me at her table, which meant I spent the evening listening to her flirt with Ben and gush about what a cute couple we were and when were we going to give her some gorgeous Hart babies to coo over already?

She meant well. She really did. That didn't, however, make the urge to run away from her any less real.

"How are you?" She wrapped her arm around my neck and gave me a squeeze. "Can you believe another season is upon us? I'm so excited I could just cry." Mandy's thick southern accent turned words like *cry* into two syllables.

"Ben's been hard at work, that's for sure."

"Of course he has. It's Coach Hart." She gave me that knowing look of hers and waggled her eyebrows. The booster moms were very open about their affection for Ben. "That husband of yours is too good to be true, I'm telling you. The way he loves those boys? And this year's lineup? He's gonna be the first coach at Bay Breeze to win back-to-back state championships. I just know he will."

I fumbled the pacifier.

Mandy picked it up off the floor and handed it over with wide eyes. During last spring's trivia night, I told her about our adoption. As soon as she asked me how much the baby was going to cost, I knew it'd been a mistake. "Oh my heavens, does this mean what I think it means? Are congratulations in order?"

"Oh, no. These are gifts for a friend." I took back the pacifier and tightened my grip on the Diaper Genie refill. "We're, um, still waiting."

"Bless your heart. Y'all have been waiting so long."

"Well, technically, we haven't." According to our social worker, once on the waiting list, some couples were matched with a child within months. Others waited years. The possibility of the latter made me feel like a dried-out husk. "Not nearly as long as some couples, anyway."

"So how does that work—y'all just have to wait until some woman picks you off a list?"

"Basically."

Mandy looked horrified.

I crept toward the nearest cash register, eager to get away.

"That must be so hard. How much control do y'all have in the process? I mean, do y'all even know what kind of baby you're gonna get?"

"A human one, I hope."

She laughed and swatted my arm. "You know, I was thinking about you a couple weeks ago."

"Oh?" I stepped up to an open lane and dumped my items onto the conveyer belt.

Mandy pushed her cart behind me, even though there was at least one open register to the left. "I was having lunch with one of my cousins. There's a woman from her church who adopted recently. Do you know it took them three tries? The second time, they actually had a sweet baby girl for two weeks, and then the birth mom changed her mind and they had to give her back. Isn't that just awful?"

Yes, it was. My worst nightmare, in fact. So nice of her to bring it up.

She seemed to realize her snafu, because she rushed on to explain that the woman had a six-month-old boy now and they were all as happy as clams. All the pain had been worth it. God had a plan. His timing had been perfect.

I pressed my lips together and nodded.

"Twenty-seven fifty-six, ma'am," the cashier said.

I removed my billfold from my purse and slid my credit card through the

machine. I scrawled my signature, careful to keep my strained smile in place.
She means well . . . She means well . . . She means well . . .

The cashier handed me my bag and the receipt.

"I'm so tickled that we ran into each other, Carmen. Please tell Coach Hart that I say hello, and I'll see you tomorrow night. First game of the season." Mandy raised her fist into the air. "Go Sting Rays!"

"Yep, go Sting Rays." I gave my own fist an awkward pump, said my good-bye, and hurried outside, frantic for a proper breath. I wasn't sure at what point the air inside Toys R Us grew too thick to breathe. Mandy's words had brought in a high tide of what-ifs. What if we were never chosen? What if we went through the same thing Mandy's cousin's church friend went through? What if Ben and I were doomed to forever be in this place we'd found ourselves, with no hope of getting out? I tried my hardest to shut the questions off.

God had a plan . . .

It was something I believed once, a long time ago. But now?

My hand settled over the flatness of my stomach, even as I attempted to keep the memories away. But they were stubborn, intrusive things, dredging up handfuls of doubt I was so sick of holding. Once upon a time, I naively thought God would bless Ben and me for doing life His way. Yet there I sat in the driver's seat, a bag of baby items resting in my lap, with nothing but aching arms and an empty house.

A ray of sunlight broke through the clouds and reflected off a parking sign straight ahead: For Expectant Mothers.

My composure snapped.

Without warning, without forethought, I shifted into drive and hit the gas, a wild scream tearing up my throat. My car lurched forward and rammed into the metal post. The sign remained standing. Its resiliency blistered all reason. I threw my car into reverse, backed up, and ran into it again, flooring the gas until a loud crunch rent the air.

I blinked several times with the steering wheel gripped in my hands. Then I rose up in my seat. A stork carrying a bundled baby was taking a nosedive toward the cement.

5

CARMEN

I couldn't let go of the steering wheel. All I could do was stare at the damaged sign bent beneath my bumper with wide eyes and a dry mouth and trembling hands.

A mother-child duo walked past my car. I could feel the woman staring into my window. I sank lower into my seat, wishing I had Mandy Thom's Nike hat. After they passed, I dared a peek. Her young son gawked at me over his shoulder as his mother dragged him inside, away from the crazy lady behind the steering wheel.

I reversed so my car no longer sat on top of the sign, and for a brief moment, I considered driving away. The parking lot was mostly deserted. I could make a run for it. But even if my conscience would have allowed it, the surveillance cameras up above put that plan to death. They had no doubt caught my battle with the sign on tape and, most likely, my license plate number too. There was no escaping. I would have to go inside and confess.

I stared toward the store, listening to the occasional jet engine overhead, considering the implications of what I had just done. The adoption process was an incredibly invasive one. Over the past several months, our entire lives had been sifted like water through a sieve, all to ensure that Ben and I were fit to be parents. If the store manager decided to press charges, I would have a police record. And then what?

I rested my forehead on the steering wheel and shook my head—back and forth, back and forth—until knuckles rapped against my window.

A man with a square jaw and silver hair looked down at me through the glass. Judging by his apparel, he was the store manager. I stepped into the humidity with my heart in my throat.

"Ma'am, are you all right?" He leaned back on his heels to take a good look at my bumper and the sign. When his attention returned to me, his brow went from furrowed confusion to raised surprise. "Well, I'll be. You're Carmen Hart with Channel Three News. I'd recognize you anywhere."

I swallowed, unsure what to say. I knew how I typically responded. A big smile, a friendly handshake, followed up with some banter about the weather. This, however, was not a typical situation.

"You're my favorite weather girl since Stacy Pine back in the eighties. You don't even know it, but you join the missus and me every weekday morning for breakfast."

The manager was a fan. I could have fainted with relief. Instead, I leaned toward him with a conspiratorial wink. "For future reference, I take cream with my coffee."

He chuckled and stuck out his hand. "Dale Benson."

"It's a pleasure to meet you, Mr. Benson," I said, giving his hand a shake.

"Mighty fine pleasure, indeed." And then, as if remembering the reason why we were meeting, he surveyed the bent sign once again. "If you don't mind me asking, Mrs. Hart, how exactly did this happen?"

"I, uh . . ." A nervous laugh bubbled up my throat. I what? Dale might be a fan, but what if that backfired? What if he went home and told his wife and she decided to post about the odd encounter on Facebook? I didn't just represent myself; I represented the entire news station. I was a public figure and public figures did not mess up, at least not publicly. "I am really, really sorry about this. I'm not exactly sure what happened, but I am fully prepared to write you a check covering all damages."

Dale scratched his temple.

I held my breath and begged God for a break. One measly little break.

He tucked his thumbs into the waistline of his pants. "Well, I don't see any reason to call in a report to the police station over a dented sign. Or any reason to have you pay for anything when we have some extras in our warehouse. I think the important thing here is that nobody got hurt. You're not hurt, are you?"

"No, I'm not hurt. Are you sure you don't want me to write you a check?"

"How about this? You give me an autograph and we'll call it even." The manager smiled. "It's the missus' birthday on Saturday. I think she'd be pleased as punch if I stuck your autograph inside her birthday card."

I wanted to place my hands on both sides of Dale Benson's cheeks and plant a big wet kiss in the center of his forehead. Instead, I searched inside my purse for one of my business cards, swirled my name in black pen across the

back, and laughed when Dale said he'd "see" me tomorrow morning. By the
time I got back into my dented car and drove away, my entire body was
shaking.

Thank You, Lord.

It was the first expression of gratitude I'd offered Him in a long, long time.
I had no idea the offering was premature.

I picked up a playing card from the deck, slid it in between an eight of clubs
and a nine of hearts, and discarded a king, even though I suspected Aunt Ingrid had at least one.

Every day after work, I drove to the Pine Ridge Continuing Care Retirement Facility to visit with my great-aunt. We played Gin Rummy 500 on her
good days, War on her bad. Hearts in the dining hall with friends on her ex-
ceptional days, which were fewer and farther between.

She looked at me over the top of her hand, paused for dramatic effect, then
picked up the king, laid it with two others, and discarded her final card
facedown.

I smiled. Aunt Ingrid was having a good day. All things considered, so was
I. I still couldn't believe the store manager let me off the hook so easily. The
entire ordeal had restored some of my faith in God's grace. Maybe He hadn't
forgotten about me after all.

Ingrid counted her points. I counted mine, then added both to our running totals while she shuffled the deck and dealt with the proficiency of a
cardsharp.

"How've you been sleeping?" I asked, picking up my cards one at a time.

She harrumphed, whether at the question or the way I collected my hand,
I wasn't sure. According to Aunt Ingrid, a card player wasn't supposed to pick
up her cards until the full hand was dealt. I'd never been very good at waiting.
"Last night I dreamt that Gerald bought me a rhinoceros."

Chuckling, I moved an ace of spades next to its accompanying king.

"There was this giant box under the Christmas tree that kept moving.
Gerald told me to open it, and when I did, I found a full-grown rhino with a
wreath around its horn. It started singing 'God Rest Ye Merry, Gentlemen.'"

"The rhino?"

"No, the wreath." She dealt my final card and started arranging her hand. I couldn't help noticing the thinness of her wrists. It wasn't enough that dementia was stealing her mind; osteoporosis was eating her bones. "It was the most bizarre thing."

"Dreams can be that way."

"It's the first one I've had in a long time. I miss them."

I thought about my recurring nightmare as of late. I wouldn't have minded some dreamless sleep. I drew a card, laid down three jacks, and discarded a five.

Ingrid muttered something about a lucky deal. "I woke up thinking about Christmas."

"Yeah?"

She discarded a two. "And how nice it will be celebrating at The Treasure Chest."

I looked up from my hand. We hadn't had a Christmas party at The Treasure Chest since her husband, Gerald, died four years ago. In fact, Dad and I had to close down the family-run motel and board it up last April when the manager quit. It had been incredibly depressing to see the place I'd loved so much in such a run-down condition.

"Remember the Christmas parties we used to throw when you were a kid? Gerald would dress up as Santa Claus, and you and your cousins would nearly wet your pants with excitement."

I smiled a nostalgic smile. "What about the Christmas Dad surprised me with a guinea pig?"

"How that little devil ended up in Mrs. Pennington's shower, I have no idea."

My smile grew wider. Mrs. Pennington had sprinted out of her room faster than I'd ever seen a woman run. After my Christmas pet had been safely returned to its cage, Aunt Ingrid spent a solid hour assuring Mrs. Pennington that The Treasure Chest did not have unusually large mice. "Or the time Ben tried making Dad's eggnog?"

Ingrid put her hands on top of her dark hair and let out a hoot. "That recipe called for two pints of rum, and he used quarts instead! I think my Scot of a husband was the only one who enjoyed it."

"And that Irishman in room 4." I shook my head. "Ben felt awful."

Aunt Ingrid's coffee-colored eyes twinkled with an entire labyrinth of memory. One I wished I could crawl inside and live in again. "Well," she said, "it was an honest mistake for our cabana boy to make."

Cabana Boy.

The two words nudged up against my affection, as if attempting to rouse it from a deep and abiding slumber. How long had it been since I'd thought about that nickname?

6

CARMEN

My car idled at the intersection of Bayou and Ninth while thoughts of The Treasure Chest churned in my mind. Over the past several months, life's circumstances had strong-armed my affinity toward the place into hibernation. I had relegated the motel and its fate to a mental holding room—the space for all the things I would deal with later. Reminiscing with my aunt, though, had stirred that affinity awake, wiggling loose a whole host of memories. One in particular stood apart from the rest—the time Aunt Ingrid had warned me to be on the lookout for the new cabana boy.

I had responded with a snort of laughter. "Cabana boy?"

She wiped down the surface of the front desk with a Pine Sol–dampened rag. Over the past three years, I'd entertained two distinct identities—from September through May I was the overachieving meteorology major at the University of Virginia, determined to learn everything I could about the tempestuous atmosphere as though it could be tamed; and from June through August, I was Aunt Ingrid's free-spirited, right-hand gal, with a sunburn on my nose and flip-flops on my feet. In all my years at The Treasure Chest, Ingrid had never once required a cabana boy.

"I hired him for you." She wagged her eyebrows at me over her shoulder, then disappeared into the back room.

She hired him for me?

What was that supposed to mean? The question lingered as I answered the phone, took reservations, and fielded inquiries from guests wanting to know where to eat the best seafood or shop for the best antiques or golf the best putt-putt courses. It wasn't until my shift neared its end that Aunt Ingrid's words made any sense at all.

I was in the back, moving a load of sheets from the washer to the dryer, when the front door opened. I threw in a few dryer sheets, hurried into the office, and came to an abrupt stop. A man stood in front of the desk—tall and broad-shouldered with a surfer's tan and an Ivy League haircut, the color of which could be brown or blond, depending on how the sun hit it.

"Welcome to The Treasure Chest," I said, using the extra-friendly voice I reserved for motel guests. It came out sounding so unnaturally high that I had to clear my throat. "Are you, um, checking in?"

One corner of his mouth quirked. "Ingrid sent me in here to fix the dryer."

"The dryer? But the dryer's not . . ." Cue the mental light bulb. "You're the cabana boy."

"Cabana boy?" He donned a lopsided grin and a furrowed brow at the same time. He wore both distractingly well.

"My aunt tells me we hired a cabana boy. I'm assuming you're him?"

He set his elbow on the front desk. "I'm no cabana boy."

I forced my feet to move forward, momentarily sidetracked by the blueness of his eyes—bright like sapphire without a hint of anything else, not a speck of green or gray or even lighter blue. Not even the nose-to-the-grindstone Carmen could have resisted them. "Okay then, who are you?"

"Ben," he said, offering his hand, "summer maintenance man."

I slipped mine into his—his palm the perfect combination of rough and warm. "Carmen, summer guest service representative."

"And famous niece."

"Famous?"

"Ingrid talks about you a lot. I've only been here a week and I think I could have a go at writing your biography."

I cringed. "Sorry."

"Don't be."

"I think she's trying to play matchmaker."

"Wanna make it easy on her?"

A few butterflies took flight in my stomach. Cabana Boy was flirting with me.

He winked. "So, the dryer?"

"Not broken."

"I had my suspicions."

"Really?"

"Your aunt had a definite gleam in her eye when she sent me in here to check it out. I'm getting pretty good at figuring out when she's up to something." He gave the desktop a few light taps and leaned closer. "Carmen, summer guest service representative, it has been a pleasure."

A car honked, wrenching me from the nine-year-old memory. The same smile that had puckered my cheeks then puckered my cheeks now. The car honked again.

I made a quick decision and headed south on Ninth, away from the auto repair shop on Summit Boulevard, toward the Pensacola Bay Bridge instead. Twenty minutes later, I pulled into the parking lot of Bay Breeze High School, not entirely sure why. After checking in at the front office and saying hello to several familiar faces, I put on a visitor's badge and headed toward Ben's classroom in the basement.

Most people assumed he taught physical education, since his favorite and most time-consuming role was head varsity football coach. But Ben taught Ceramics and Sculpture 1 and 2, two of the school's most popular electives. We even had a pottery wheel in our basement. Once upon a time, Ben used to give me personal lessons. He would joke that we were channeling our inner *Ghost.* I would laugh and call him a cheeseball while he sat behind me. But in truth, I thought my husband was a thousand times sexier than Patrick Swayze, especially when he brushed spine-tingling kisses along the side of my neck.

As soon as I pushed through the double doors at the bottom of the stairwell, the smell of chlorine and sawdust greeted me. Ben's classroom was located across from the pool and up the hall from shop class. School had started on Monday and already a layer of dust decorated his floor and students worked busily on what appeared to be coffee mugs.

Ben stood with his back to me at one of the high tables, still broad shouldered and narrow waisted, wearing work boots, tan Levis, and a casual button-up shirt cuffed to his elbows. One of the girls at the table noticed me in the doorway and said something to him. He turned around and cocked his head, then met me where I stood. I wasn't in the habit of showing up at his classroom in the middle of the school day.

"Hey." His brow furrowed with the greeting, a question sprouting in his eyes. I often forgot how striking his eyes were in their blueness. But not today. Not after reliving the Cabana Boy memory. "What are you doing here?"

"Can I talk to you for a second?"

"Is everything okay?" He set his hand on the small of my back and led me out into the hallway, away from the unwelcome attention of his pupils. "Did the social worker call?"

Oh, Ben thinks . . .

My heart contracted. He thought I'd come with good news to share. He thought I'd come because a birth mother had chosen us. He thought our wait was over, that we somehow flew through the process in record timing. The hopeful look in his eye had me regretting my decision to come. "No, she didn't call."

"Oh." He curled his hand around the back of his neck. "So why are you here?"

Because I missed him? I missed us? I had a memory that resurrected feelings I hadn't felt in much, much too long?

Ben raised his eyebrows, waiting.

"I ran into a sign."

"A sign?"

"Earlier this morning. In the Toys R Us parking lot."

"How did you run into a sign?" The condescension in his voice was audible enough to set me on edge, faint enough to make any defensive words on my part unreasonable. Ben had this delicate, frustrating balance down to an art form, and I was pretty sure he didn't realize it.

"It was for expectant mothers."

He scratched the stubble underneath his chin. Ben shaved three times a week, never enough length in between for a full beard, but long enough for thick scruff. "So . . . is there something you need me to do?"

"No."

"Then why did you come here to tell me?"

"I don't know, Ben." Maybe I didn't want to have the conversation later. Maybe all the reminiscing with Aunt Ingrid had made me nostalgic. Or maybe some part of me, deep down, no matter how much I balked or prickled, really did want Ben to do something.

"Is the car damaged?"

"There's a dent in the front bumper."

"How bad?"

"We'll probably need to get it replaced."

His jaw tightened.

I pressed my lips together to keep from screaming.

We stood there in the hallway—he and I—all the tension in the world between us, and I couldn't help but wonder how we got here. To this place of constant misses. I thought about that ancient Chinese proverb often quoted on the cusp of a long endeavor: The journey of a thousand miles begins with one step. People associated it with inspiring journeys, worthwhile journeys. But the thing was, it was every bit as true for the accidental, unfortunate ones.

My phone chirped inside my purse. I fished it out and said hello, thankful for the distraction.

"Carmen, it's Dad."

"Dad?" He didn't usually call in the middle of the workday, not without some sort of provocation. "Is everything okay?"

"Not exactly. A dispatcher from the Escambia County sheriff's department called me. Apparently, somebody reported a trespasser at The Treasure Chest."

"A trespasser?"

Ben leaned closer, trying to tune into the conversation.

"They sent a deputy to check things out. I guess she found signs of a break-in. They need someone to drive out there to secure the property. Do you think you could go?"

"Yeah, sure. I can do that." After the conversation I was having with Ben, some time at my old stomping ground sounded like the perfect way to recalibrate. Besides, I was long overdue for a visit.

"Thanks, sweetie." He paused on the other end, then filled the empty space with a sigh. "You know, we're going to have to decide what to do with the place soon."

His words, though softly spoken, stretched a seam of longing stitched inside my chest.

CARMEN

I could almost feel the seam splitting apart as I drove across the Bob Sikes Bridge, heading eastbound on a stretch of two-lane highway called County Road 399. Resort hotels and high-rise condominiums shrunk in size and grandeur and frequency the farther I drove away from the tourist hub that was Pensacola Beach, eventually giving way to a breathtaking view of emerald waters and white sand, dotted with sea oats and yucca and scrubby growth.

The Treasure Chest, formerly known as La Tresor Motel, was established in 1939 by my great-grandfather, Frank Sideris, with the financial backing of his good friend, Charles Darrow, whose invention of the game Monopoly earned him millions during our nation's worst depression. Back then, the motel had been the first of its kind on Santa Rosa Island, ushering in an era of roadside hospitality. When Frank passed on, he left the motel to his youngest daughter, who happened to be my aunt Ingrid. She loved the place every bit as much as he did and made it her life's breath to see it thrive. Now, however, The Treasure Chest was a dying breed, no longer just the first, but also the last of its kind on Santa Rosa Island.

Ten minutes from Navarre Beach with more high-rises ahead in the distance, I spotted the motel sign growing up from the side of the road, its neon lights darkened now for months. During prime tourist season, no less. As I turned into the parking lot, vacant except for a lone police cruiser, the seam of longing split apart completely. Aunt Ingrid's pride and joy looked much more like a rent-by-the-hour establishment than the family-friendly resting stop it had always been. The once-charming art-deco-meets-vintage-1960s thirteen-unit motel, complete with neon and chrome accents, sat abandoned and derelict on what must have been an incredibly valuable chunk of real estate.

How had this happened?

I thought about the past four years—Gerald's unexpected death, helping Aunt Ingrid through her grief, assuming her forgetfulness would ebb with time, noticing instead that it was only getting worse. The doctor's diagnosis, moving her into Pine Ridge, getting her adjusted to life at the care facility, all while dealing with my own secret losses. I had made a promise to Aunt Ingrid that I would look after her baby, but over the past two and a half years, I'd barely been out here at all.

I stepped out into the balmy air and nodded hello to the woman standing by her police cruiser. Beneath her deputy's hat, she had a mass of freckles on her face and wore her carrot-red hair in a long braid down her back. "Deputy Ernst," she said, extending her arm. "You're the proprietor's daughter?"

"I'm the proprietor's great-niece. My father's her nephew, as well as her power of attorney." Which technically put him in charge of the property. "He lives in Gainesville, so he asked me to come in his place." I surveyed the units forming a U around the drained, kidney-shaped pool, installed for vacationers who'd rather swim in water uninfested with sharks and jellyfish. "He said something about a break-in?"

Deputy Ernst nodded. "A tourist taking a run along the beach called in the report this morning. He saw someone lurking on the property, thought it was suspicious. So he gave our precinct a call. Whoever it was isn't around anymore, but I think they left some things behind."

"Some things?"

She motioned for me to follow her.

As we approached the entrance to the front office, something inside of me wilted. Boards had been rent loose. Windows had been broken. At some point, vandals had spray-painted crass words along the stucco facade. The offensive artwork dribbled onto the glass block surrounding the office doors.

"I grew up in Mobile," Deputy Ernst said. "Every summer my family would pile into the van and drive along the coast until we got to my meemaw's house in Rosewood. We'd stop at places like this along the way. We even stopped here a handful of times."

Aunt Íngrid would love the deputy's story.

"Most of the mom-and-pop motels we used to stay at lost the battle to those boys over there." She nodded a mile or so east, to a skyline that towered with hotels lining Navarre Beach. They crept closer with each passing year. "It's a shame to see this one so beat up."

She nudged the front office door open with her foot. We stepped inside, our shoes crunching over bits of debris and glass, and a small gasp tumbled from my lips. "Did the trespasser do this?"

"I'm not sure. The graffiti isn't fresh. I'm willing to bet that was the result of some bored teenagers over the summer. The rest, though, I can't tell."

Whoever it had been took extra care to ruin the little that remained inside, smashing an old-fashioned rotary phone, a couple of chairs, and the framed art on the walls, including the vintage monopoly board signed by Charles Darrow himself. Thankfully, they must not have known who the man was, because they left it behind.

A string of desperation threaded itself around my mess of emotions, pulling them together in a bundle more pathetic than the motel. It wasn't so much the vandalism that had me shaken as much as what was underneath the vandalism— the signs of neglect, of erosion, of slowly falling into disrepair. Thick layers of dust on all the surfaces, grime on the unbroken windows, the worn carpet and the cobwebs and the peeling paint. All of it hit too close to home.

"I think whoever broke in must have been squatting here for a while." Deputy Ernst led the way toward the hospitality room, which would have been empty except for a blanket and a pillow off in the far corner. "We have a lot of drifters in the area. Vagabonds passing through from one town to the next, holing up wherever they can find shelter. But I'm not so sure this is the case here."

"Why not?"

The deputy stopped in front of a duffel bag and crouched beside it. "It's clothes, mostly. Nothing too unusual. But then I found this." She handed me a postcard.

I recognized it immediately. They used to sit in a stack on the check-in desk during my summer college years. I flipped the postcard over. A note had been written on the back in Aunt Ingrid's loopy scrawl.

See you next summer, Gracie. You bring your sass. I'll bring the cookies.

"You don't happen to know this Gracie, do you?"

"As a matter of fact, I do." I looked up from the handwriting. "She's my sister."

GRACIE

I crouched behind a firebush beside the pool shed as a navy-blue Kia Optima with a dented front fender pulled up beside the police cruiser and out stepped Evelyn Fisher 2.0—a younger, sober version of my mother, with the same curly brown hair, the same wide-set eyes, the same delicate nose and fair skin. Flawlessly wrapped in a white blouse, pale-pink skirt, and matching pumps. Carmen Hart, a walking billboard for perfection.

She and the redheaded cop chatted awhile before disappearing inside. I pressed my knees together. I had to pee. Bad. But I couldn't leave. I had to stay and make sure they didn't confiscate my duffel bag. Apart from going back to Apalachicola (which I would not do), it contained everything I owned, including my dead cell phone and the measly three dollars I had left of Mom's purse money.

My stomach let out an angry growl. Over the past few days I had subsisted on the food I bought at the gas station near Navarre Beach. It had been a four-mile round trip in the glaring Florida heat. I had returned to The Treasure Chest, soaking with sweat and burnt to a crisp. If I didn't die of starvation, I'd probably die of melanoma.

The deputy with the long red braid moseyed back outside with Carmen right behind her. She had my duffel bag! I crouched farther behind the bush, trying to decide if I should come out from my hiding place, because I needed that bag, or if I should stay hidden, because cops and I didn't have the best track record.

The two exchanged some words. Then Officer Red climbed into her cruiser and drove away. Carmen brought her hand to her forehead like a visor and did a slow three-sixty, searching, I presumed, for the owner of the bag. I deliberated. When I came here, reuniting with my sister had never ever been a part of the plan. Sure, I understood our paths would cross from time to time, but that didn't mean I had to talk to her. Now, however, I wasn't sure I had much of a choice. I couldn't let her take my duffel bag.

She opened the back door of her Optima and set the bag inside.

I stepped out from the firebush and made my way toward the parking lot. My lack of food must have made me exceptionally light on my feet, because Carmen didn't notice me until she turned around and I was basically right there and she about jumped out of her pretty pink pumps. She clutched her hand to her chest and nearly fell through her opened door into the backseat of her car.

I let her catch her breath.

"Gracie, what in the world are you doing here?" she finally asked.

"Getting my bag."

She looked around, like maybe I brought some friends, then returned her attention to me—dirty, sweaty, sunburned, greasy-haired, ash-tray smelling, famished, needing-to-pee me. "How long have you been here?"

"Three days, give or take."

"Three days!" Carmen's eyes went all kinds of buggy. "Does Mom know?"

"If I had to take a guess, I'd say no."

She stared at me for a moment longer, then pulled a purse from her car and fumbled around inside of it until she drew out a cell phone and started punching numbers.

"What—you're calling the police on me?"

"No, I'm not going to call the police. I'm calling our mother. She has to be worried sick." She stuck her thumbnail between her top and bottom teeth and pressed the phone against her ear. "How did you even get here?"

"I hitchhiked."

Her eyes went buggy again. "You hitchhiked?"

"Save yourself the aneurysm. I have no plans to do it again." Of all the hitchhiking stories out there, mine was undoubtedly lame. I wasn't robbed or held at gunpoint or anything dramatic like that. But after four hours of listening to Deborah tell crass jokes about her ex-boyfriends while smoking her way through a pack of Marlboro Lights, I would have preferred gunpoint.

The only thing that had kept me in that smelly car was the thought of this motel. I had imagined a welcoming hug from Ingrid. I had imagined a warm meal and a hot shower and a comfortable bed. I'd imagined staying indefinitely, doing whatever odd jobs needed doing in exchange for a room. Maybe it wasn't a glamorous fresh start, but it was the only one I wanted. Instead, I got this—a boarded-up, vandalized motel with no air conditioning, no electricity, no running water, no bathroom, no food.

"I really love what you've done with the place," I said, motioning toward the rat hole before us. "It's taken on a whole new feel since my last visit."

Carmen hung up the phone.

"You're not going to leave a message?"

"Gracie, please tell me what's going on."

"Why don't you tell me what's going on. Where's your aunt Ingrid?"

"We had to move her into a care facility a few years ago."

"Why?"

"She has dementia."

"And that's it—Ingrid gets sick so you leave The Treasure Chest to fend for itself?" It was so typical Carmen that it wasn't even funny. She'd done the same thing to me. The only surprise was that I thought she actually cared about the motel.

"We hired a manager who turned out not to be such a good manager. We had to close the place down last spring. Then, apparently, someone decided to damage the property."

"Don't look at me."

Carmen cocked her head, like my comment and the quick way in which I said it couldn't have been more interesting. I rolled my eyes and tried to step past her to get my bag, but she moved in front of me. "Why don't you come to my house?"

"Thanks, but I'd rather stick a needle in my eye."

"I can't let you stay here."

I crossed my arms and concentrated on not wetting myself. "Can I please have my bag?"

"Come on, Gracie. At least let me feed you some lunch."

My stomach let loose a traitorous growl. As much as I hated it, I really didn't have a choice. I was out of food and I was sick of peeing on the beach. My big plan for a fresh start turned out to be one giant flop. "Fine. But I have to go do something first."

"Gracie."

"It'll just take a second." My bladder had zero concept of patience, and one last trip to the beach wouldn't kill me. Although going home with her might.

Thanks to all the practice, it didn't take long. And just like that, I was in her car reluctantly snapping the seat belt across my lap.

Neither of us said anything on the drive. Carmen left her radio off. And it was too hot to roll down the windows. So I sat there glorying in the cool blast of the air conditioner on my fried skin while she kept darting glances my way.

"When did you color your hair?" she finally asked.

"Last week."

She tapped the steering wheel. "What happened to your neck?"

I touched the scratches. Over the past couple days, they had turned into scabs. "Sadie Hall fights like her gender."

Carmen shifted uncomfortably in her seat. I could tell she didn't know how to take me. Not many people did. After my bad choice at the end of last school year, I was forced to see a counselor for "anger issues." The counselor was a young woman who hung her shiny new counseling certification proudly on her wall. She had called my behavior a defense mechanism. "You push people away so you won't be the one rejected," she had said, looking overly excited about her revelation. I'd asked her if she wanted a gold star.

Carmen turned down a street called Magnolia Avenue and pulled into a driveway. Turned out, she lived in a human-sized Barbie dollhouse. Complete with pale-blue siding and white shutters, double-hung windows, and a deep-set front porch with a small gabled balcony off the second floor. The inside was every bit as postcard-perfect as the outside—all spotless floors and shiny surfaces and *Better Homes and Gardens* magazine.

I dropped my duffel bag by the door and took a few steps inside the foyer, examining the large framed picture of gorgeous Carmen and her gorgeous groom on their gorgeous wedding day, gazing lovingly into one another's gorgeous eyes. It was enough to wake up my gag reflex. I ran my finger along the frame of the photograph and brought it away without a speck of dust. "Your house is freakishly clean."

"Thanks?"

"It wasn't a compliment."

With a sigh she picked up my bag and led me up a carpeted staircase, into a wide hallway. The entire upstairs smelled like dryer sheets and lavender. Carmen set the duffel in the first room on the left—a spacious bedroom with buttery walls, a matching dresser and nightstand, a full-length mirror in one corner, and a four-poster queen-sized bed with a snow-white down comforter and plush pillows. Sunlight filtered in from the large window, making everything look extra sparkly. "The bathroom is across the hall. Towels are in the linen closet. I'll go make us some lunch."

"Aye, aye," I said with a salute.

As soon as she left, I shut the door and plopped onto the bed. The mattress gave a few jostles, then stilled as I kicked off my boots.

A canvas hung over the dresser, painted with the words *Behold, I make all things new. –Revelation 21:5* in bold font. They reminded me of my life in New Hope, Texas, and my mother's semimonthly dips in the creek. But all the baptizing never made a bit of difference. Mom was the same person before she was wet and the same person after.

I guess being made new was an illusion.

9

CARMEN

I held the phone to my ear as I gathered a smorgasbord of food from the refrigerator—carrot sticks, ranch dip, hummus, grapes, pretzels, all the trimmings for sandwiches. I still couldn't believe Gracie was here, in my house, or that I'd found her there, at The Treasure Chest, or that she looked like such a homeless person. Or that her accusation left such a lasting sting.

"And that's it—Ingrid gets sick so you leave The Treasure Chest to fend for itself?"

Yes, that was exactly what I'd done.

The ringing continued. Mom didn't answer.

I removed a couple plates from the cupboard and dialed her work number at the bank. A young man informed me that Evelyn Fisher had not come in today. I drummed my fingers on the counter and tried her cell a third time. She had to be worried. Her teenage daughter had run away from home three days ago. I couldn't believe she hadn't called me yet.

She finally answered on the fourth ring, her voice so croaked I double-checked the clock on the stove. "Mom?"

There was a pause on the other end. "Gracie, is that you?"

"No, it's not Gracie. It's Carmen." I opened the sliding-glass door and slipped outside onto the back patio.

"Carmen?" It was only my name, but the sloppy way she strung the two syllables together dredged up an entire host of unpleasant memories. Drunk before noon. Unbelievable.

"Do you know where Gracie is right now?" I asked.

"Gracie?"

"Yes, Mom, Gracie. Your seventeen-year-old daughter."

"I don't know. She won't answer her phone."

"So that's it? You call. She doesn't answer. And you go about your day like it's not a big deal?"

"What else do you want me to do?"

"Call the police!"

"I'm not going to involve the police. Gracie's a big girl. If she wants to run away from home, then it's not my problem."

"Actually Mom, it is your problem. You're her mother." The fact that she got to wear that title—a woman who'd rather go on a bender than search for her own daughter—rankled with injustice. I took a deep breath and expelled my rising exasperation. "In case you want to know, I found Gracie squatting at The Treasure Chest."

"The Treasure Chest?"

"Yes. And apparently, she hitchhiked."

I waited for something—concern, embarrassment, relief. Even some confusion would have sufficed. Anything was better than nothing. "Mom?"

"Where's she now?"

"I brought her home with me." I glanced over my shoulder into the kitchen. "She's upstairs taking a shower."

"Do you mind if she stays?"

"What?"

"She doesn't listen to me, Carmen. She's completely out of control. Last May, she was arrested for criminal mischief." Mom hiccuped. "She had to go to court and do community service. The judge said she was lucky she was a minor. A few weeks ago, I found a bag of pot in the pocket of her jeans when I was doing the wash. And on her first day back to school, she got suspended for starting a fight in the girls' bathroom."

Gracie had been arrested?

"I don't know what to do with her anymore. You were never like this as a kid."

That was because I'd taken the opposite track, trying my hardest to supersede Mary Poppins's "practically perfect in every way" status by being completely perfect in every way. As long as everybody was complimenting me, they never noticed her. Family dysfunction at its finest.

"I—I need a break. Give me a few days and I'll come get her. I promise."

Judging by the slur of her words, she needed a lot more than a break. I wasn't, however, about to point that out over the phone, especially not when she was so inebriated. I shook my head. Ben and I were in no position to take on a troubled teenager for a few days, but what other choice did I have? Troubled or not, Gracie was my sister and she needed my help.

She came into the kitchen wearing black jeans with a series of tears running up the front of each leg, an oversized T-shirt that said *Bazinga,* and bare feet. The faint scent of strawberry shampoo replaced the cigarette smell that had clung to her hair in my car.

"How was your shower?" I asked, pasting on my best smile.

"Wet."

I laughed a little, then opened the refrigerator. "Can I get you something to drink? We have water, milk. Nestea. Cranberry juice."

"Any beer?"

I poked my head around the refrigerator door.

"Not funny? No sense of humor in this house? Okay, then. Water it is."

I handed her a bottle.

Gracie slid onto one of the stools with one foot tucked beneath her, her opposite knee drawn up to her chest. She snagged a piece of deli meat and rolled it into a tube before taking a bite.

"If there's something else you want to eat, you're more than welcome to rummage through the refrigerator or the pantry." I took a few grapes from the bowl, more for an excuse to have something to do than any real desire to eat them. "I got ahold of Mom."

She finished her turkey roll and spun another slice. "And?"

"And if it's okay, I'd like you to stay here for a few days."

"You would or Mom would?"

When I didn't answer, Gracie scoffed.

I shuffled my fruit from one hand to the next, searching for something to say. The longer the silence stretched, the more awkward everything started to feel. "So . . . how have you been doing lately?"

Gracie stopped chewing and stared at me like I was the world's biggest idiot. At that moment, I probably was. "Just dandy."

"Mom said something about community service over the summer?"

She dunked a pretzel into the ranch dip and popped it into her mouth.

Stubborn determination sprouted like one of Jack's beans. If Gracie was going to play the role of brick wall, then I'd take up my sledgehammer. Call it one of my fundamental flaws, but the harder it was to get something, the more I wanted it. Right now, I wanted to make some progress with my sister. "What happened?"

"I became well acquainted with litter."

My phone buzzed on the counter. My friend Natalie Jane's number lit up the screen, probably wanting to invite me to CrossFit. I sent the call to voice mail. "I don't mean what happened during community service. I mean why did you have to do community service in the first place?"

She rolled up her third slice of meat.

"Gracie?"

Nothing.

I inhaled slowly and decided to try a different track. "Why did you run away?"

"Because our mother wanted to dump me at my dad's."

"And you don't want to stay with your dad?" I didn't know Gracie's father very well, but it seemed like a better option than living with an alcoholic parent.

She rolled her eyes. "I'm not getting into this with you."

"Getting into what?"

"Family dynamics."

I set the grapes on the counter. One rolled off and fell onto the floor. "How long has she been off the wagon?"

Gracie looked up from her meat roll. "Do you remember how old you were the last time she went to rehab?"

"Twenty-two." The answer came quickly. It had been the summer I met Ben. When Mom called from the rehab facility, I'd been both shocked— because I didn't know she was drinking again—and relieved, because if she was at rehab, then she and Gracie wouldn't be visiting me at The Treasure Chest in July. I'd have all that time with Ben.

"Well then. Take the age you are now. Subtract twenty-two. Add a month." Gracie grabbed a handful of pretzels. "And you have your answer."

I opened my mouth, but before I could think of anything to say, Gracie slid off the stool and walked out of the room.

My phone buzzed a second time against the counter. This time it wasn't Natalie. It was my dad. He asked about The Treasure Chest. I told him the bizarre story that had unfolded since last we talked, starting with the tragic condition of The Chest, followed by the duffel bag and ending with Gracie in my house. "I locked the place up when we left, but I'm not sure what to do about the broken windows. Deputy Ernst said we should board them up again, which I can do tomorrow if you want."

"I think it's time, Carmen."

I squeezed my eyes shut, not wanting to hear what he was about to say. The second he put the motel on the market would be the second some developer bulldozed it to the ground and replaced it with another overpriced "you've seen one you've seen them all" luxury hotel. "Dad, it's part of the family."

"Sweetie, I'm a tenured professor with no intentions of retiring into the motel business. Last I checked, your uncle Patrick has no intentions either. You've chosen your career path. Your cousins have chosen theirs. And as much as I hate to say it, Aunt Ingrid isn't coming back. It's time to put the motel up for sale."

The finality with which he spoke the words punched a hole in my chest. The Treasure Chest was a piece of me, a piece of me and Ben as a couple. If Dad had his way, it would become nothing but rubble.

10

CARMEN

I brushed my teeth, willing the irritation that had gathered over the course of dinner to go away. It refused. Somehow, my husband got my acerbic sister to smile. She told him she hated football. He laughed, and then they spent the rest of dinner swapping hitchhiking stories. I had to remind myself that he dealt with teenagers every day. He knew how to communicate with them. Even the surly ones.

I spit in the sink, rinsed my mouth, and padded into the bedroom. Ben sat on the edge of the bed fiddling with his phone. My own showed two more missed calls from Natalie. I'd have to remember to call her tomorrow. For now, I pulled back the comforter and slid in between the sheets. Ben and I should probably talk about Gracie. At least more than the spurts of conversation we'd had in between dinner preparation and dinner cleanup. But I wasn't in the mood. And besides, the clock on my nightstand read 8:30, an hour and a half past my bedtime. Early to bed, early to rise—a by-product of my occupation. "Could you shut off the light on your way out?"

Without looking up from his phone, Ben stood, shut off the light, and instead of leaving, sat on the bed, leaning against his side of the headboard, stretching his legs in front of him.

He usually watched football on Thursday nights. "You're staying?"

"I'm not going to watch TV alone downstairs with Gracie."

And there it was. His aggravation had come out to play. "She's my sister."

"She's seventeen."

"What did you want me to do, Ben? Leave her at The Treasure Chest?"

He sighed. "It's been a long day, Carmen. I don't want to argue about this."

Of course not. Conflict-avoidant Ben. He never wanted to argue about anything. Well, too late. I was itching for an argument. "I'm sorry for inconveniencing you tonight with family obligations. But it just so happens, I didn't have the best day either."

I turned onto my side and blinked into the darkness. The longer I waited, the more I seethed. Was he really not going to say anything? If I turned around right now, would he be back to his phone—adjusting his fantasy football roster or watching video clips on ESPN? The very thought, and the likelihood of the possibility, left me feeling horrendously alone.

"I'm sorry," he finally said.

The softness of his voice reminded me of that Proverb my father often quoted when I was a child—"A soft answer turns away wrath, but a harsh word stirs up anger." Only it didn't turn away my wrath so much as increase my irritation.

"Are you upset about Gracie?" Ben asked.

Gracie. My mom. Her inability to quit drinking. The run-down state of the motel I grew up loving. My sister's unshakable accusation. Waiting for the social worker to call with news that our wait was finally over. The sense of obligation that had risen throughout the course of the night. All of it gnawed at me. "I think she should stay here longer than a few days."

"What do you mean?"

"I mean my mom's off the wagon and Gracie needs some stability in her life. We could enroll her at Bay Breeze."

"What about her father?"

"She doesn't want to stay with her father. It's why she ran away in the first place."

I braced myself for more questions. Some commentary or pushback. Surely he had all three to offer. Instead, he gave me nothing. Silence. As much as I wanted him to agree without qualms, I knew this was a lot to ask. So I waited while Ben processed. And the longer I waited, the more I wanted to convince him that this was a good idea. That Gracie needed me. But I kept quiet, until finally, Ben let out a resigned sigh. "If you feel like it's something you have to do."

"I do." I rolled onto my back and curled my arm over the top of my head, thinking about the postcard Deputy Ernst had showed me. Of all the places Gracie could have gone, why the motel? What did the place mean to her? "My dad wants to sell The Treasure Chest."

Ben looked down at me.

I wanted him to object. To cry foul. To hate the idea as much as I hated it.

"You knew it couldn't sit like that forever."

"Yes, but I didn't think that meant we had to sell it."

"What did you think it meant?"

"I don't know. Maybe we could fix it up and get it running again."

"Carmen." He gave me this look, like my suggestion was nonsense.

"What?"

"I have a job. You have a job. We have a house. And now a teenager to take care of. When would we ever have the time to fix up a motel?"

In my recurring nightmare, I forgot how to swim. Water crashed around me, rising higher as I thrashed and gulped and sputtered. *Help! Somebody help!* But nobody ever did. A whole host of people stood on dry ground, smiling at me as I flailed.

"Well done," their smiles seemed to say. "You're doing great."

The water rose over my chin.

Cold water filled my lungs.

With a sharp intake of breath, my eyelids snapped open. Ben stared at me through the dark, his face stretched with alarm. I sat up, trying to gain my bearings. I wasn't drowning. I was in bed. It had been a dream. One I'd had before, only this was the first time I'd woken Ben up with it.

"Were you having a nightmare?" he asked.

I pushed a tangle of curls from my eyes and nodded.

"Do you want to talk about it?"

I set my hand on the space of bed between us. Back in college, I had a psych professor who spent an entire lecture talking about muscle memory and how practice didn't make perfect, it made permanent. According to research, muscle memory was one of the hardest things to undo. I wanted to tell Ben what plagued me in the night. I didn't want to shut him out. But after years of curling in on myself, practicing this posture of survival, I wasn't sure I knew how to unfold anymore. And before I could say anything anyway, the clock struck two and the alarm on my cell phone began buzzing.

"It's okay," I said. "You can go back to sleep."

After I finished getting ready, I stopped in front of the closed door of Gracie's new bedroom. It had become an odd sort of ritual—staring into this dark, empty room, wondering if it would always remain dark and empty. The first night Ben and I moved in, furniture yet to be delivered, we sat in here shoulder to shoulder, sharing a root beer, dreaming about what color we would paint the walls—pink or blue? I guessed blue. Ben was adamant on pink. We had talked late into the night, giggling over ridiculous names we would never use, wondering if the baby would have Ben's double-jointed thumbs or my curly hair. I had been struck then by two things. My husband was glowing with paternal joy and I couldn't wait to have his baby. Two weeks later, I had my first miscarriage.

We painted the walls cream.

My sister turned over in bed.

I took a step back.

The room was no longer empty. It was full of anger.

11

CARMEN

Like always, I was one of the first to arrive at the station. I shuffled into the break room to start a pot of coffee, turned on the lights to the studio, and prepared to predict the future. That's what weather forecasting was, after all. A task made especially difficult by a fickle atmosphere.

My job left no room for error. The information I gathered had to be absolutely accurate. The slightest misinterpretation of the weather's initial conditions could quickly lead to giant inaccuracies in the forecast—ones we'd hear about from unhappy viewers later. I was meticulous about checking radars, satellites, automatic weather stations, and every other bit of relevant data supplied by the National Oceanic and Atmospheric Administration supercomputer in Maryland.

Usually, I spent the first hour nursing my second cup of coffee while poring over the data. By the time I moved on from data collecting to data analyzing, my producer's heels would *click-click-click* into the studio. This morning, however, she arrived seconds after I settled into my station. The sound of her caught me off guard.

"You're here early," I said.

"Yes, well, we need to talk."

I braced myself for her strategizing. How can we get more viewers? What aren't we doing that our competitor is doing? She usually snapped her fingers when she asked these types of questions, like the sharp sound would elicit better, faster answers. Instead, Nancy called me into her office.

The request was every bit as odd as her early arrival. The two oddities combined had my heartbeat accelerating. My mind scrambled about for an explanation as I followed her through the studio and eased into one of her office chairs.

Nancy sat down behind her desk. "I assume you know what this is about."

"No, I'm afraid I don't."

"The video."

"What video?"

Nancy swiveled her computer monitor so it faced me. A YouTube video came to life of a little boy waving at the camera. And then, *crunch!* The sound of metal hitting metal. The little boy spun toward the noise. The image jostled, then refocused. My stomach dropped to the floor. It was my car—in the Toys R Us parking lot. Reversing, then slamming into a sign. The shot of my profile was crystal clear. And positively deranged.

I blanched. So far, 15,753 views.

"One of our viewers posted that to our station's Facebook page yesterday, wanting to know if the woman in the video was Carmen Hart from Channel Three News. It's being shared all over social media. Unless you have a doppelganger, it's definitely you behind the wheel. What I don't understand is why. What would cause you to do something so out of character?"

My pulse thrummed wildly in my ears. My mouth hung open, desert dry. I couldn't answer Nancy and I couldn't look away from the screen. The number of hits had already grown by seven, and it was three in the morning.

Nancy waited for an unusually long time. When it became apparent that I couldn't—or wouldn't—answer, she waved her hand in the air as if to shoo the question aside. "I don't know what caused you to behave in such a manner, but you are a public figure. You represent our station."

This was Nancy's credo. It had been ever since they hired me several years ago.

"I spoke with our executive producer about how best to handle the situation. We both agreed it wise for you to take some time off."

"What?"

"You have a lot of PTO, Carmen. I don't even remember the last time you called in sick. Some time off would be good for you. Maybe you and Ben can take a vacation. Get away for a few weeks. Relax or regroup or whatever you need to do to come back well rested."

"A few weeks? But—but I don't need a few weeks."

"It's not a request." Nancy folded her hands over the top of her desk. "We need to let this storm pass, and we believe it's best if you're off the air while it does."

She continued talking.

I processed snippets of her monologue here and there. Something about lying low. Letting the station handle things. The weekend meteorologist ready and willing to fill in while I was away. At some point, the sound in my ears turned to ringing. I couldn't stop staring at the frozen YouTube video on Nancy's computer screen.

The hits continued to climb.

I got lost once as a kid when I was eight years old. Dad and I were at the Florida State Fair in Tampa, wandering around Cracker Country—a living history museum on the fairgrounds. One second he was beside me. The next he was gone. I walked around the Okahumpka Train Depot with this growing sense of dread, calling my father's name. It had been a terrible feeling. It must have been for him too, because when he found me, he pulled me into such a crushing hug that I could barely breathe.

Now, as I drove up and down the coast of Escambia Bay on an eleven-mile stretch of scenic highway, my phone blowing up with text messages from Natalie, I felt that same way. Everything was falling apart. There was an incriminating video of me spreading like the flu. I'd been suspended from work. Dad wanted to sell The Treasure Chest. And I had a hostile houseguest. My car coasted past the oaks and magnolias surrounding the bridge over Bayou Texar, along giant bluffs that served as the highest point along Florida's coastline. But the vantage point brought no clarity. All I could see was that video. It played on repeat in my mind's eye until the sun rose over the horizon and the needle on my gas gauge dipped toward *E*.

Yesterday I'd foolishly thought God had given me a break with the nice store manager. Somehow that break had turned into a giant disaster: my mental breakdown caught on video for all to see. What would happen if someone from our adoption agency saw it? The very thought spun my emotions into an F5 tornado. A very ugly part of myself had gone public and I couldn't hide it. I wasn't put-together Carmen Hart, beloved weather girl on Channel Three News. I wasn't Coach Hart's pretty, smiling wife who hosted team dinners and chatted with the booster club. I was the deranged woman ramming into a sign for expectant mothers.

I felt lost, in desperate need of something familiar.

Playing cards with Aunt Ingrid seemed like a good idea, so instead of driving home I headed to Pine Ridge, where I made my way to my aunt's room on the second floor. I spotted Rayanna stepping into the hallway with a bundle of sheets in her arms. She was my favorite of Aunt Ingrid's nurses—a hefty African American woman with hair cut short against her scalp, a pair of gold studs I wasn't sure ever left her earlobes, and a pronounced gap between her front teeth. Whenever she laughed, she reminded me of that song from Mary Poppins, the one Uncle Albert sang when he floated to the ceiling. *"Some people laugh through their teeth, goodness sakes. Hissing and fizzing like snakes."*

While it wasn't at all attractive to Mary's way of thinking, I found it endearing. Usually whenever she saw me coming, Rayanna's face would split into a large grin. Today, however, that grin did not come.

My sense of dread expanded. Rayanna had probably seen the video.

"Hey, girl." She shifted the bundle of sheets from one arm to the other. "You're here earlier than usual. No work today?"

"No work today." Or tomorrow. Or the next. What in the world was I going to do with myself? I held up a deck of cards. "Do you think Ingrid's up for a game?"

Rayanna frowned. "She's having a pretty rough morning."

I'd ask what triggered it, but nobody seemed to know the answer. Aunt Ingrid's brain had become as unpredictable as the weather. Her old self might show up from time to time, but at the end of the day, she was more lost than I was.

As if on cue, the unmistakable sound of Aunt Ingrid's yells filled the hallway.

Rayanna hurried after the shouting. I hurried after her, past the small entryway and living area, into my aunt's bedroom, where she huddled over a bowl of red Jell-O like it was the sole life raft in a chaotic sea.

A girl dressed in scrubs, who couldn't be much older than Gracie, tried consoling her.

"You stay away from my Jell-O, do you understand? I want you to stay away from it!"

The girl looked at Rayanna with wide eyes. "I thought she was finished, but the second I tried taking her tray she started freaking out."

Aunt Ingrid picked up her spoon and threw it. Actually threw it at the girl.

I watched the scene unfold with a sick feeling in my gut.

Rayanna moved into action, murmuring words of assurance while waving the young girl out of the room, asking her to get a new spoon. She left gladly.

"You don't have to worry one bit, Miss Ingrid. Nobody is going to take your Jell-O."

Slowly, Ingrid became less hysterical.

The girl poked her head in just long enough to hand me the new utensil, then left before anything else could be thrown at her.

I took a step toward Aunt Ingrid, holding out the spoon.

She looked at it like I was trying to give her a snake.

"Go on now, Ingrid. You can't eat Jell-O without a spoon," Rayanna said.

"Are you going to take my Jell-O too?" she asked me.

I shook my head. "I promise I won't."

Ingrid straightened her shirt, which had gone askew in the battle, and took my offering. "Not all things are worth saving, you know. But some are worth every ounce of fight you can throw at them." With all the dignity in the world, she took a few small bites of her dessert. "You just have to know the difference."

12

CARMEN

I followed Natalie past the exuberant student section of the Bay Breeze football stadium, where a row of shirtless boys, their torsos painted blue and gold, worked on riling up the crowd. We climbed the aluminum bleachers to a spot where we never sat—far upper left, away from the rest of the coaches' wives and booster moms. Usually we sat with them in the middle, but not tonight. Tonight, I hadn't even planned on coming. Not with that video circulating. But then Natalie showed up on my doorstep and forced me out of hiding.

Her husband coached with Ben. That's how we met—four years ago when Brandon took the job as defense coach so Ben could be promoted to head varsity. At the time, Brandon and Natalie had been new to Bay Breeze, Yankee transplants from Minnesota who still to this day elongated their *o's*. Natalie and I started off making small talk at banquets and team dinners and Friday-night games, which led to double dates, which led to us inviting them to church, which led to Natalie and me attending women's ministry events together, then hanging out all on our own.

When we first met, Natalie had been slightly overweight—a tired mom with three young children underfoot and a preteen in the throes of puberty. Then she saw a picture of herself on Facebook, looking, in her own words, "run-down and fat." She decided to join a gym and became one of CrossFit's biggest advocates. Her transformation had been something to behold.

"Everyone's staring," I mumbled, pulling the brim of my hat down lower.

"Nobody is staring," Natalie said, ushering Reese and Lainey up the stairs in front of her. "And if anyone says anything, make a joke. Trust me, the less embarrassed you act about it, the sooner everyone will move on to something else."

When we reached our little corner, she pulled out a few Barbie dolls for Lainey and handed Reese her iPhone. He was the youngest of her brood and the spitting image of his mother, only in little-boy form.

I squeezed in closest to the railing and tweaked Reese's knee. "How's kindergarten?"

He scrunched up his nose and gave me the universal hand signal for so-so. I laughed while he returned to his game.

Natalie stood on her tiptoes, craning her neck so she could look over the crowd toward the field. Her third-grader, Mason, leaned against the fence with a few of his buddies, finagling miniature footballs from one of the cheerleaders while the rest turned cartwheels and backflips on the track. As if sensing his mother's stare, Mason turned around and looked up into the bleachers. Natalie pointed to her eyes, which were crazy wide, then pointed to her son. He gave her a solemn nod. This was the first time Natalie had let him run around with his friends during the game. She'd told him at least three times in the van that if he thought twice about going under the bleachers or didn't check in every quarter, he'd spend the rest of football season playing Barbie dolls with Lainey.

Natalie was a good mom.

"He's so grown up," I said.

"Just don't let him hear you say it." Her attention moved to the student section, where one of the blue-painted boys flirted with Samantha, her oldest, officially a freshman in high school. Natalie and Brandon had done things the "hard" way. Pregnancy first, marriage second. It seemed to work for them.

"How long is Gracie staying?" Natalie asked.

Earlier today over the phone, I'd filled her in on the past forty-eight hours of my life. I started with my sign demolition in the Toys R Us parking lot and moved on to Gracie, the video, my forced leave of absence, the panic attacks I had whenever my phone rang—because what if it was the social worker calling?—Aunt Ingrid's disturbing fit, my crazy idea regarding The Treasure Chest, and the four-hundred-dollar bumper replacement.

"I'm not sure." I looked at Reese and Lainey in their own respective worlds, healthy, well-adjusted children because they had a mom and a dad who loved them. Gracie didn't have that. And as much as I wanted to rail against our mother for being so pathetically lousy at motherhood, I couldn't. Because that would mean I'd have to make an honest assessment of myself and sisterhood, and one thing had become glaringly clear over the course of the day. I'd been a giant failure in the sisterhood department. "Indefinitely, I guess."

"And Ben's okay with that?"

"He says he is."

"Brandon would have a cow. He doesn't even like having my parents at the house for a long weekend. I tell you what, that man's spiritual gifting is not hospitality."

"Ben doesn't know about the video. Or my job. Or my plans for The Treasure Chest."

Natalie raised her eyebrows in that knowing way of hers.

"I didn't want to unload it on him before the game." I would not be responsible for distracting my husband before the first game of the season.

"You don't think he already knows about the video?" Natalie asked.

"If he does, he hasn't said anything to me." Ben wasn't on social media, but his students were. Did my husband already know? And did that knowing bring him the same sense of dread it brought me? My attention wandered to the field, where Ben ran the offense through a series of pregame drills. He wore his royal-blue Sting Rays polo and his most serious game face. I really needed them to win tonight. Talking to him about these things would be much easier in the wake of victory.

The Sting Rays lost ten to fourteen. The opposing team and their fans went ballistic, jumping and cheering and hugging as if they'd won the Super Bowl. Our side of the stadium seemed to be in shock. Florida's 4A state champions had started the season with a loss to an unrated, mediocre team—on their home field, no less.

Natalie collected her two olders and we filed out into the parking lot, surrounded by grumbles that were all a different version of the same.

"They were overconfident."

"Every single one of them looked lost out there."

"They had their heads up their you-know-whats."

"Maybe this will be a much-needed wake-up call."

I found Ben's car, which he'd parked near the door where the players and coaches exited, and leaned against the hood. The night was muggy and extra thick with mosquitoes. High up above, mayflies and moths swarmed the lights.

Normally, Brandon and Ben and the other coaches would swing by Jake's Bar and Grill for a beer and I'd go home and crash. Tonight, however, we needed to talk.

The players began filing out, somber faced and saggy shouldered. They met moms and buddies and girlfriends who wrapped them in hugs or slapped them on the back or said things like, "Better now than later."

The coaches exited last.

Brandon headed to his family-laden van idling nearby, where Natalie stood outside. He wrapped his beefy arms around her waist and buried his face in the crook of her neck. I looked away from the gesture to Ben, who walked toward me with his thumb tucked beneath the strap of his bag, the glow of the stadium lights casting shadows along his jaw line. The idea of slipping my arms around his neck like Natalie had done with Brandon felt about as foreign as my father's astronomy books.

I wiped my sweaty palms on the back of my jean shorts. "Rough game."

"Worse than rough."

"Maybe this will give them a little kick in the butt."

"Yeah, maybe." He dragged his hands down the length of his face and released a long, drawn-out sigh. When his fingers no longer obstructed his view, his eyes flicked toward the top of my head. "Cute hat."

I gave the bill a self-conscious adjustment and mumbled a "thank you." I didn't typically wear hats, but I also didn't typically try to disguise myself from the public. "Are you going out with the guys?"

"Not tonight."

There was a moment of uncertain silence, and then . . .

"Do you want to grab a bite?"

"We need to talk."

We spoke at the same time.

And as soon as I processed Ben's words, I wished I could take mine back. "About anything in particular?" he asked.

Yes. But what we *needed* to talk about and what I *wanted* to talk about were two different things. I didn't want to bring up the video. Everything in me wanted to push it under the rug and hope Ben never heard about it. That, however, was impossible. I scanned the parking lot. Brandon and Natalie had already driven away. Most of the players had left. Nobody felt like loitering tonight. Me neither, but Ben was waiting, and if I didn't get it out now, I never would. "Did you hear anything about a video today?"

Judging by the way his eyebrows knitted together, I took that as a no.

"When I hit the sign yesterday, somebody captured it on their phone"—I looked down at my feet—"and posted the video on Facebook. A lot of people have seen it."

"Define a lot."

"Enough that my producer asked me to take a few weeks off work."

"Because you ran into a sign?"

"Because I reversed the car and ran back over the sign."

I waited for his reaction, wondering what it would be. Did he realize that my mistake could jeopardize all of the hard work we'd put into this adoption— the sweat and the tears and the financial stress? Did his heart thud with dread at the thought of our social worker being among one of the viewers?

Ben pushed out a breath. "Well, I guess this will give you a chance to spend more time with Gracie."

"Speaking of that . . ."

He cocked his head.

"There's something I'd like Gracie and me to do together."

"Like?"

"Fix up The Treasure Chest."

His countenance darkened. "I thought we talked about this."

"Ben, if I don't do something, the property will be purchased and the motel will be razed. I know you think that's inevitable, but I don't." And I couldn't let it happen. Aunt Ingrid said so herself. Some things were worth fighting for. The Treasure Chest was one of those things. "With this forced leave of absence, I'll have the time."

"The motel is going to take a lot longer than a few weeks to fix up. And what makes you think Gracie will even want to help?"

"There's a reason she went there. The place has to mean something to her." Not to mention the postcard from Ingrid that she'd kept all these years. I shifted my weight, my resolve strengthening. "I talked to my dad this afternoon. Aunt Ingrid has plenty in savings from Gerald's inheritance. It took a little convincing, but he agreed that there was nothing more Ingrid would want to spend her money on than this. It won't cost us anything."

"Are you expecting me to help you?"

The question made my teeth clench together. "I never asked for your help."

"What happens when you're finished?"

"I don't know."

"Do you plan on running it? Moving in?"

"I said I don't know!"

Ben rubbed his jaw and looked up at the sky, as if composure could be found in the stars. "I'm sorry, but we're not exactly in a position right now to take on the restoration of a motel."

"Why not?"

"*Why not?* Carmen, if we're going to work on anything, don't you think it should be our marriage?"

It was the first time Ben had ever hinted at the broken state that was *us,* but I was too hurt to grab the lifeline. Sadness spilled from the unstitched seam in my heart, pooling into a dense mass of longing. But longing for what—The Treasure Chest in its former glory? Ben and me without all this distance? A child to hold in my arms? The video to magically disappear so this expanding sense of dread would go away? Something—*anything*—that might show me God still cared? That He was up there at all?

Ben looked at me, waiting.

"I don't know what else you want me to say." I lifted my hands in a shrug, then let them clap against my thighs. "If I wait, The Treasure Chest will be gone." And everything we used to be along with it.

13

GRACIE

The town of Bay Breeze smelled like salt and citronella. I wandered past houses with manicured lawns and white picket fences, turning up and down roads at random until I found a bike trail off a street named Sand Castle Circle (seriously?). Mom had this phobia about bike trails in the evening—called them a breeding ground for hooligans (she actually used those words), but thanks to my snooping ways, I found a hunting knife in one of Carmen and Ben's junk drawers and tucked it into my boot before leaving.

Twilight ran its course and I ended up on a road with gas-lamp streetlights and brick walkways along a town square lined with small shops—Kirby's Antiques, a candy store called Sweeties, a hardware store, an art gallery, some restaurants, a couple cafés. The whole thing circled around a small park with wrought-iron benches, pink-blossoming crepe myrtles, and a gazebo. I felt like someone had plopped me straight in the center of a Hallmark movie set, only nobody had bothered to show up for work. The place was a ghost town.

I turned onto Dock Street, the air thick with brine. A collection of sea-weathered wood buildings hung over the water—tourist gift shops, another art gallery, some bar-and-grill eateries. The last of the sunlight slipped away. Swirls of oranges and pinks melted into blood red over the water until darkness stretched from one horizon to the next, and the faraway lights of the hotels lining Pensacola Beach twinkled across the bay.

Up ahead a lighted dock moored with boats reached out into the water. In Apalachicola, a town whose livelihood depended on the sea, the docks were forever lined with shrimp boats and oyster boats and fishermen. Here in Bay Breeze, the boats rocked alone. I shuffled toward the lights.

The football game had to have ended by now. Carmen and Ben were probably back in their Barbie dollhouse, discussing the problem that was me. Earlier today, Carmen had invited me to stay longer than a few days. She said she and Ben had discussed it and agreed it would be a good idea. I could enroll in Bay Breeze High School. I sat on the edge of the dock and pulled the knife from my boot. The plan had never been to stay with Carmen and her husband. I did not want to be one of her charity projects. But considering my financial status, my options were horribly limited. I dangled my feet above the water, opening and shutting the knife's blade, trying to figure out my next move, until the dock swayed with footsteps.

I jerked around, wielding the knife, heart racing.

A tall kid with muscular arms stopped and held his hands up like I was a cop with a gun who had just yelled "Freeze!" Even with my knife, I wouldn't stand a chance against him. Thankfully, he looked every bit as surprised by me as I was by him, which meant he hadn't followed me out here with bad intentions. Beneath the dock's lighting, I could make out a pair of ratty sneakers, faded jeans that hung low on his hips, a plain white undershirt, skin the color of rich caramel, and not much else.

"This is a first," he finally said.

"What is?"

"Running into an armed stranger in Bay Breeze."

I lowered the knife, but I didn't flip it shut. Thanks to the surprise arrival, adrenaline had my senses on high alert.

"Can I put my hands down?" he asked.

"I never told you to put them up."

He brought his arms down to his side and studied me across the length of space between us. "Mind if I join you?"

"It's a free dock."

I watched him warily as he approached and lowered himself beside me. He had full lips and a broad nose and curly eyelashes and he smelled like the air after a hard rain. As I stared, he smiled—a straight, white, deep-dimpled smile that had me shifting away. I didn't trust smiles that straight or white.

"So," he said, curling his fingers under the edge of the wood, "do you live around here?"

I hesitated, unsure whether or not to engage. "That's to be determined."

My answer seemed to amuse him. "What—you're scoping the place out before deciding?"

"Something like that."

"How old are you?"

I raised my chin. "How old do you think I am?"

His eyes, which were an earthy mixture of brown, green, and amber, moved from my boots, dangling over the water, up to my face. "Fifteen?"

I scoffed.

His smile widened. "Do you have a name?"

"Most people do."

"Are you gonna tell me what it is?"

"Do you always ask this many questions?"

"Only when I find knife-wielding girls on my dock."

I quirked one of my eyebrows. "*Your* dock?"

"Well, it's not technically mine."

"So what—it's *figuratively* yours?"

"Let's just say this dock and I are well acquainted." He nodded toward the second-to-last building, a ramshackle restaurant with a neon sign that said Jake's Bar and Grill. "My mom used to work at Jake's. For real, how old are you?"

"Seventeen."

"Isn't that a little young to be determining where you'll live?"

"Not when I'm on my own."

"Ah." He nodded, like he got me or something. His skin really was a beautiful color. Distractingly so. And his voice had this soothing cadence about it, like the gentle lapping of the water. "You ran away from home."

"I didn't run. I hitchhiked."

"Why?"

"Because I'm not much of a runner."

His smile came back. And his dimples along with it.

Waves from the bay gently rocked the boats as I waited for him to finish the third degree. When he didn't, I flipped the knife shut and returned it to my boot. "You didn't go to the football game tonight?"

He cocked his head. "Is it a problem if I did?"

"No—why?"

"Because you asked the question like you were disgusted with the possibility."

I shrugged. "It's a dumb sport."

"Yeah?"

"Dressing up in pads and putting on a helmet all for an excuse to run around hitting and tackling people? Come on, it's like a giant, overrated mating ritual."

"A mating ritual?"

"With all the chest bumping and fist pounding and strutting around like demigods just because one team gets a ball on the other side of a field more than the other? It's like a giant game of let's see whose is bigger."

The boy laughed—an appealing sound that boosted my confidence. Made me feel witty. He shook his head and massaged the palm of his hand. The word *Truth* was tattooed on the inside of his wrist.

"What's up with the tattoo?" I asked.

He rubbed his thumb over the black-inked word. "Truth is important."

I rolled my eyes.

"You disagree?"

"In the words of philosophy teachers everywhere, 'What is truth?'"

The penetrating way he looked at me made me want to fidget. "What do you think it is?"

"Most people would say it's subjective."

"I didn't ask what most people would say. I asked what you think."

I frowned at the water, my thoughts wandering to Mrs. Dulane's morning declarations in fifth grade. The canvas hanging in my new bedroom. My mother's creek dunking and the church services she dragged me to in Texas. The truth was, I didn't know. And this conversation was getting far too personal and strange for my taste. I let out a deep breath and pushed myself up to standing.

"No answer?" he asked, looking up at me.

"I think I've done enough philosophizing for one night." And without a wave good-bye or a look back, I made my way to land.

At some point during my encounter with Dr. Truth, Bay Breeze came back from the dead. A boy and a girl sat shoulder to shoulder on the open tailgate of a rusty truck parked along Dock Street, a group of teenagers goofed around on the grassy knoll in the center of the town square, and a whole bunch of cars squeezed themselves into a small parking lot beside a place called The Barbeque

Pit. My stomach rumbled at the thought of chicken wings, and Carmen had left me a ten-dollar bill for dinner. Had to be enough to appease the growling.

The twang of country music thickened the closer I got to the door. When I stepped inside, a few tables of teenagers stopped and stared. Without making eye contact with anyone, I walked past the gawkers and ordered a Coke and the spicy chicken wings to go. Fifteen minutes later, I was back on Magnolia Avenue with a white bag in hand.

Light filled every one of Ben and Carmen's first-floor windows.

Great.

As soon as I walked through the door, Carmen sprung up from the couch and pushed hair from her disoriented eyes. "Where have you been?"

I held up my bag and kicked off my boots. They thumped, one at a time, near the front closet doors. "Getting food."

"At ten thirty at night?"

I headed into the kitchen.

Carmen followed. "It would have been nice if you'd left a note. I've been worried sick."

I laughed.

"Why is that funny?"

"You, worrying about me. It's ironic." I pulled out a box of chicken wings from the bag. The spicy, sweet scent of buffalo sauce made my mouth water. Being here was never in the plan, but I had to admit—this was a whole lot better than falling asleep in a hot room on a hard floor with an empty stomach. "You never worried about me when I was being raised by an alcoholic."

Carmen frowned.

I didn't care. I would not feel guilty about her guilt. I wouldn't. I picked up a wing, took a bite, and nearly groaned over how good it tasted.

"I didn't know," Carmen said.

"That she drank?" I snorted. *Give me a break.*

"I didn't know how bad it was."

That was because she chose not to see. That was because seeing would have meant she had to do something about it. She stayed comfortably ignorant because anything else would have been an inconvenience, and heaven forbid Carmen's perfect life encounter an inconvenience. I ate the last of the meat off the wing and sucked the bone dry. She watched, looking a little repulsed. I licked my fingers and cracked open the Coke. My tongue was on fire.

"Would you like to come out to The Treasure Chest with me tomorrow?"

I took a loud slurp from the can. "You're returning me already?"

"No, I'm not returning you." She tucked a strand of hair behind her ear and smiled an overly enthusiastic smile. The kind that looked more nervous than happy. "I was hoping we could fix the place up. Get The Treasure Chest running again."

I blinked at her. "Why?"

"Because that's what Aunt Ingrid would want. And it's what I want too."

A worm of hope wiggled its way into my heart. I hated that worm. When you grow up with an alcoholic parent, you learn pretty quickly that hope leads to disappointment. Promises end up in a pile of broken pieces. And change never lasts. Carmen wanted to appease her guilt, and so this was her solution. I didn't have any confidence it would last longer than a couple weeks. I wiped my hands off on a paper towel, took a long swig of my drink, and set the empty can on the counter with a pronounced click. "No, thanks."

My answer, for whatever reason, made her expression flicker with confusion. She blinked at me. I blinked at her. A silent, blinking face-off. And then her lips thinned and she got this look I recognized. It was the same one I wore whenever anybody told me I couldn't do something. "What if I pay you for your time?"

My eyes narrowed. "You'd pay me?"

"You saw the place. I need the help."

"How much?"

"Eight dollars an hour."

"That's barely minimum wage."

"Fine. Ten."

I picked up another chicken wing. "What time do I start?"

Carmen smiled, like she'd won the victory. But the victory was mine. She was going to pay me ten bucks an hour to take back my plan A.

14

CARMEN

I stood in the pockmarked lot with a bucket of cleaning supplies in each hand
and my sister by my side, trying not to think too hard about the video that
threatened to go viral or my last-minute decision not to attend Katy's baby
shower. Natalie said I was being ridiculous. Nobody cared about the video. I
told her I wasn't canceling because of the video; I was canceling because of
Gracie and The Treasure Chest.

We were both lying.

Overhead, stratocumulus clouds broke apart blue sky. They hung in large,
low rows—their darkened underbellies all bark and no bite. People often saw
them and thought rain was on the way, but stratocumulus clouds rarely brought
rain, and if they did, it was usually nothing substantial. The ones above us had
released a teasing precipitation that came and went in the span of our drive
here, leaving the air heavier and more humid than it was before.

The sun made its way into a patch of blue. Gracie brought her hand up to
her forehead like a visor. I looked from my sister to the motel, trying to figure
out what it meant to her. I'd been convinced it meant something, but if that
was the case, why didn't she care to get it running again? Why did I have to
bribe her? At ten dollars an hour, no less.

"I used to love coming here when I was a little girl," I said, hoping the comment might elicit some sort of response since Gracie came as a little girl too.
Granted, one big appeal for me had been coming without my parents. Which
meant I didn't have to deal with a mother who drank too much or a father who
pretended she didn't. For a month every summer, I was free from the heavy
yoke of being me—perfect little Carmen, who was so pretty and so polite and
so good in school that surely nothing could be wrong at home. Gracie, on the
other hand, always came with Mom. I peeked at her from the corner of my eye.
"This place holds a lot of great memories."

She huffed. "Tell that to TripAdvisor."

I turned around to look at her all the way, a can of furniture polish clanking inside one of my buckets. "TripAdvisor?"

"I looked up some of the reviews on my phone while you were rounding up your arsenal of environment killers. There were a lot of complaints."

"About what?"

"Unidentifiable marks on bedspreads. Carpets that smelled like cat pee. Horrible customer service. One person said the water from the faucet was the color of tea, and I quote, 'I'd rather get stung by a large family of jellyfish than stay there again.' End quote."

"That's a little dramatic, don't you think?"

"I'm not the one who wrote it."

My sense of guilt grew, overtaking any positive feelings I'd mustered earlier in the morning. Guilt over not being there for Gracie and guilt over not checking in at the motel more often after we moved Aunt Ingrid into Pine Ridge. Like the weeds growing up from the cracks in the parking lot—unwanted, unappealing pests best pulled out by the roots. I wanted to make things right with The Treasure Chest. I wanted to make things right with Gracie. But she sure didn't make it easy. "I bet the older reviews were good."

"Who cares about old reviews if the current ones suck?"

"If something was once good, then it has the potential to be good again." The words were more for me than her.

Gracie, however, looked skeptical.

Taking a deep breath, I started toward the office, hoping Gracie would follow. She did, but not very enthusiastically. I unlocked the door and stepped inside. The same stale, unmoving heat that had greeted me and Deputy Ernst on Thursday greeted Gracie and me now. First thing Monday morning, I would call the utility company and turn everything back on. August in Florida meant we needed air conditioning. And if we were going to do any real deep cleaning, we'd need running water too. Even if it was tea-colored.

I handed her a garbage bag and a pair of gardening gloves. "Let's start in this room and see how far we get."

I put on a pair of gloves and started picking up the bigger chunks of glass, scattered bits of smashed rotary phone, and smaller parts of ruined chairs. I threw the glass into a cardboard box and the rest into a bag. The bigger parts of the chairs, I gathered into a pile outside. Most likely, we'd need to rent a Dumpster. If Gracie was right about the reviews, and the carpet in the rooms really did smell like cat pee, then it would have to go. I swept the remaining dust and debris from the floor into the dustpan, dumped the pile into Gracie's bag, tied them both up, then put them beside the broken chairs outside beneath the portico.

Sweat had soaked through my T-shirt, and Gracie's black bangs had plastered themselves to her forehead. We'd left the door open in an attempt to get some air flow, but it still felt like we were working inside a sauna. We took a break outside in the shade. Gracie and I gulped from the bottles of water we'd purchased at a gas station along the way.

"How did you sleep in there for three nights?" I asked, wiping beads of sweat from my forehead with my shirt sleeve.

"Uncomfortably."

A breeze swept in from the ocean and although it was muggy air, at least it was moving. I picked up a crowbar from one of the buckets. If we were going to keep working, I needed to pry some boards off the windows. I jammed the end of the crowbar beneath one of the plywood boards over an unbroken window to the left of the door.

Gracie leaned against a support beam and watched.

"Ben talked to the principal at Bay Breeze. He said they called to have your transcripts sent. You're all set to start on Monday." I gave the crowbar a few yanks and pried the board loose. "Maybe after we're done here we can grab a bite to eat and get some school supplies."

Gracie said nothing.

I set the board beside the garbage bags and got to work on another. "We could grab a slice of pizza at Bruno's. They have an excellent selection."

Still no response, so we returned inside. Gracie engaged in a halfhearted battle with the dust while I continued on the windows. I left the broken ones alone, but attacked the others with a bottle of Windex and a couple of rags in an attempt to get rid of both the stubborn grime from the glass and my growing frustration with my sister, until my muscles burned in protest.

Gracie batted at cobwebs in the corners of the room with a broom. They gathered on the bristles like a thick net and stuck to her fingers when she tried removing them. "So why don't you and Ben have any kids?"

The question stopped me mid-Windex spray.

It was a Gracie-fied version of *the* question. The one people usually asked with a little more tact and an expectant smile. *"When are you and Ben going to have kids?"* As if having a child was simply a matter of choice. I finished spraying and gave her the answer I gave everybody else. "We hope to someday."

If the video didn't mess everything up.

I glanced at my phone sitting on top of the now-cleaned front desk. Whenever it rang, my stomach cramped and my heart raced so quickly I got lightheaded. The video and its possible repercussions had placed an invisible thundercloud over my head. Thinking about it now made the muscles in my shoulders tighten and the air in the front office stuffier. "I'm, uh, going to start on the hospitality room."

Gracie went to work on another corner, stirring up a frenzy of dust motes.

I escaped into the adjoining room with cleaning supplies in hand. Up until the early sixties, the room was just another unit. But then Aunt Ingrid did some renovations, one of which involved transforming this particular unit into a gathering place for motel guests, something most motels lacked at the time. Thus, the hospitality room was born—not only a place to serve complimentary coffee and muffins, but a place to highlight the motel's rich and interesting history. It eventually became The Chest's most lucrative attraction.

Though empty now, the room had once brimmed with knickknacks. Gerald had handcrafted a large trophy case, only instead of putting trophies inside, Ingrid had lined the shelves with relevant memorabilia, most of them Monopoly related. She had covered two of the walls with framed photographs—black and whites of the motel when it was La Tresor Motel, an eight by ten of Frank Sideris shaking hands with Charles Darrow, and poignant pictures from the end of the Great Depression and World War II. Wall three became the wall of fame, highlighting all the celebrities who had stayed at or visited The Chest since its inception. And then my personal favorite, the fourth wall. A wall Ingrid invited guests to sign, doodle notes, scribble jokes, or scrawl their favorite quotes. She called it the wall of wisdom.

As a girl, I memorized nearly every single word, so that now, as an adult, I could quickly find my favorites.

Dead center: *Phillip Peppergree was here.* I liked the sound of his name so much I named my first and only cat after him.

Further to the left and up a bit: *John 3:16. Life.* For the longest time, I thought that was the person's name—Life. And what a funny name it was. Until I looked up the verse in Aunt Ingrid's Bible and realized it wasn't a name at all, but a statement.

A hand's width below: *Soul Mates, Helena and George, 1962.* I used to wonder if they were still alive, if they were still in love, if they had children or grandchildren.

Down to the right, so low as to almost be on the ground, was my childhood favorite: *Life is worth living as long as there's a laugh in it.* That used to be my absolute favorite quote from *Anne of Green Gables.* Whoever wrote it didn't leave a name, but one thing was obvious. We were kindred spirits. Now, as an adult, my mind recalled a much different line from Anne's story.

My life is a perfect graveyard of buried hopes.

I shook the words away, then pressed my hand over some obscure initials scrawled inside a tiny heart, right near the center next to Mr. Peppergree—*CB + WG.* A memory pulsed beneath my palm.

"We've only been on one date," I'd told Ben. And as amazing as that date had been, this was the wall of wisdom. Whatever a person wrote couldn't be taken back.

Ben had given me a disapproving look. "Aren't you a pessimist."

"I'm just saying, once you put us on the wall of wisdom, it's there forever."

Shaking his head, he drew a skinny, slightly lopsided heart—nothing feminine or bubbly about it. Everybody who would see it ever after would know it was a man's heart.

"I'm serious," I said. "You could be jinxing everything."

Ben brought the marker down to his side. "Okay then, how about a compromise?"

"What do you mean?"

Inside the heart, he scrawled the initials CB, and below that, WG, adding a plus sign in between.

I squinted at the letters. "Who's CB and WG?"

"Us."

"Those aren't our initials."

"Sure they are. Cabana Boy plus Weather Girl." He took my hand and pulled me toward him, making heat quiver in the depths of my stomach. He smelled irresistible—a masculine combination of soap and the subtlest hint of cologne. "That way, if you decide to get rid of me, nobody would be any wiser."

"I would," I said, a little too breathlessly. I couldn't fathom getting rid of him. Not in a million years.

He placed his hand on the small of my back. Ben's touch was electrifying. It did funny, funny things to my heart. And so far, no lips had been involved. Our first date had ended with a lingering hug. The kind that was so wonderful it made me ache, giving new meaning to the song "Hurts So Good."

"You know how I know we'll make it?"

"How?"

"Your aunt loves me." He grinned then—a devilishly delicious, cocky grin.

"You think you're so—"

Ben didn't let me finish. So suddenly I couldn't have anticipated it, he pressed my body against his and kissed me. The kind of kiss that had me gripping tightly to the cotton of his T-shirt, so certain was I that I'd float off the ground if I let go. Our very first kiss. In my favorite room, in front of my favorite wall at The Treasure Chest Motel.

Now, standing in the empty space, my fingers moved to my lips, and the memory slid away, replaced by a haunting thought. Most days, Aunt Ingrid didn't even remember Ben, let alone love him. So what did that mean for us?

15

GRACIE

The town whizzed past at a very steady thirty miles per hour. Carmen held the steering wheel at ten and two, making driving instructors everywhere proud. I sat in the passenger seat picking a cuticle, my mind fast-forwarding to lunch in the cafeteria and the utter awkwardness that would be finding a table. I hated high school. I hated that Carmen insisted on dropping me off like I was a little kid. And I hated the fact that I tried so hard to look like I wasn't trying so hard. I went through all three of my outfits this morning before settling on my favorite pair of skinny jeans—black and frayed—my go-to boots, and an Orange Crush T-shirt. Carmen took one look at me and said she would take me shopping later in the week. I took one look at her and scoffed. Something told me her taste and my taste were about as far apart as Santa Claus and penguins.

My cuticle burned. A pinprick of blood oozed from the tear. I stuck my finger in my mouth and sucked away the stinging, trying to ignore the insecurity swelling in my gut.

Carmen gave the steering wheel a couple taps with her thumb. "Are you nervous?"

I found another cuticle and got to work.

"Because it's okay if you are."

I could feel her peeking at me. She did that a lot. Like I was some sort of wild animal that might, at any moment, go ballistic and cause injury to myself or the people around me.

"When I had to change schools in sixth grade, I was so nervous on the first day."

A couple of teenagers in a Honda CR-V sped past us. Carmen flipped on her blinker and turned onto a street called De La Cruz Boulevard, lined mostly with residential houses and a few scattered businesses.

"Bay Breeze is a great high school, though. The teachers are really nice. I'm sure they'll make you feel welcome. And Ben's there if you need someone to talk to."

"I'm not nervous."

"Oh, okay. That's good."

I blinked at her through my bangs. This morning, when Ben had asked if I was coming, Carmen stepped in and insisted she was going to drive me. It was one of the few times I'd heard them talking to each other, and I'd been sleeping under their roof for four nights now. Something was definitely afoot. I had a strong suspicion that something was me—the perpetual irritant. "Is this going to be a morning ritual—you driving me to school like I'm five?"

"It's your first day." Carmen turned onto Breeze Street, which came to a T, at the center of which was Bay Breeze High School in all its glory—a sprawling brick building with a crowded parking lot and a large blue-and-gold sign in front that said Bay Breeze High School, Home of the Sting Rays.

"I've been getting to school without your help for years." On my first day of kindergarten, I walked myself to class and watched as all the mommies and daddies hugged my classmates good-bye. Carmen hadn't been there then, and I didn't need her here now. "So can you please do us both a favor and stop trying so hard?"

Her face paled.

A pang of guilt twisted my stomach, but I didn't have time to deal with it. We were officially in front of the main entrance, where kids mingled on the steps leading up to the double doors. Before Carmen could do something crazy like get out and walk me inside, I stepped into the morning heat and slammed the door shut.

After stopping in the front office to snag my schedule and listen to a miniature pep talk from my new guidance counselor, I found my landing place—locker 128. Hopefully the last high school locker I would ever have the displeasure of owning. I spun the dial combination and transferred the contents of my bag into the space while students milled around behind me. So far, I'd managed to avoid eye contact with all of them.

"Do you have everything you need?"

The familiar voice behind me belonged to Ben.

I shoved my backpack inside, grabbed a folder and a notebook, and slammed the locker shut. "Did Carmen send you to check on me?"

"No, I thought of that all on my own."

"I'm touched."

A small cluster of thick-necked boys walked past us, slapping Ben high-fives along the way. One would think—from their cocky swagger—that they'd won the game on Friday night.

"I can see they're still pretty upset about the big loss."

Ben smiled. "You know, Gracie, for some reason people around here tend to like me."

"You have them fooled, huh?"

His smile grew. "Feel free to name drop if you think it will help."

"I'll keep that in mind."

"I have practice after school, so I think Carmen's going to pick you up."

Oh dear Lord, no. "I can walk."

"Are you sure?"

"That I'd rather walk than be picked up from school? Yes."

"Okay. I'll give her a call and let her know." He told me that if I needed anything—anything at all—his classroom was in the basement, across from the swimming pool, and that I shouldn't hesitate to come visit. He had no idea how tempted I was to visit him during lunch. He gave my shoulder a squeeze, then made his way out of the locker bay. Several groups of girls stared after him. I wondered if Carmen knew how popular her husband was at school.

I tucked the folder and notebook under my arm and began the task of finding first period. Five minutes and a couple wrong turns later, I found my destination: Debate and Ethics with a teacher named Reyas. My new guidance counselor had informed me that it was as close to my Franklin High philosophy elective as they could find. Inside the classroom, the tables were arranged in the shape of a U with only a few students occupying the chairs. One of the kids—a lanky, blond-haired boy—eyed me in the doorway.

"Boo."

I jumped—like legitimately jumped—and spun around, fully prepared to sock whoever just booed in my ear. But all the fight swirled away in an aftershock of confusion. Under the fluorescent lighting his skin was more creamed coffee than caramel, but there was no mistaking it. It was Dr. Truth—the boy from the dock. Right there in front of me.

"Good thing you don't have your knife. I think I might have been stabbed." He stepped inside the classroom, allowing a couple of students to file past us.

"What are you doing here?" I asked.

"This is my class."

I blinked, positive I would wake up at any moment and have to start the whole dreadful morning routine over again. I mean, seriously. What were the chances of this boy having the same first-period class as I did? It wasn't even a rhetorical question. I honestly wanted to know.

He motioned for me to walk ahead. "After you."

I took an empty seat at one of the tables in the back.

He snagged the chair beside me, flipped it around, and sat with his long legs straddling the backrest. "So you decided to stay?"

"What?"

"Last time we talked, staying in Bay Breeze was TBD."

"Oh, yeah." I swallowed, still plenty shocked that this boy was sitting beside me. I'd replayed our dock visit a few times over the weekend, trying to guess his age. I decided he was probably in high school and acknowledged the fact that at some point our paths might cross again. I just never imagined they'd cross so quickly. "For now."

"For now," he repeated.

I scanned the room. Every single student stared at me like I was a fish in a bowl.

Dr. Truth leaned toward my ear. "Don't worry. They're looking at me, not you."

"Sure they are."

The bell rang. A few stragglers hurried inside, filling the remaining seats. Reyas, it turned out, was a Hispanic woman with black-framed glasses and dark, shiny hair. She sat at her computer and took roll call. Two names in, she called out the name Eli and the boy beside me lifted his arm into the air.

I set my elbow on the table. "Eli, huh?"

"Do you approve?"

I checked him out—from his ratty sneakers, to the casual way he draped his arm over the back of his chair, to his beautiful skin and his multicolored eyes. "You don't look like an Eli."

"No?"

I shook my head.

"Do I look like an Elias? Because that's what my birth certificate says. Elias Dante Banks, to be precise."

Elias. Now that was a good name. *"Crowds and Power."*

"Huh?"

"It's a book by Elias Canetti. It helped win him the Nobel Prize in Literature in 1981." It took me an entire month to get through it, but I was glad that I did. The guy was sardonic and funny and rambling and profound all at the same time. "It's also Walt Disney's middle name."

Elias was smiling at me.

"What?"

"Do you know this much about names as a rule, or should I feel special?"

"I'm weird with trivia." My brain had this way of retaining random facts with little to no effort on my part.

"Gracie Fisher?" Reyas pushed her glasses up the bridge of her nose and did a quick search of the room before finding me.

The fish bowl got smaller.

Heat crept into my cheeks.

"Welcome to Debate and Ethics, Gracie." She held out a tattered textbook.

When I returned with it to my seat, Elias was smiling at me again.

I narrowed my eyes at him. "What?"

"Nothing." He tucked his smile safely away into one corner of his mouth—the only evidence of its existence the dimple in his left cheek. "Gracie Fisher. It's a good name."

⌒‿

"So Gracie Fisher, is the mystery gone?" Elias asked, walking with me out into the hallway.

I bit back a smile. I didn't tend to be easily charmed, but there was something about this Elias Banks that set me at ease. He wasn't like every other high school boy I knew. Case in point? Just now in class, Reyas had started a debate about the pros and cons of minimum wage. Elias argued for, so naturally, I argued against. I blew him out of the water. Only instead of getting defensive or embarrassed or threatened, he had smiled at me the entire time, like my ability to formulate articulate arguments impressed him. "What mystery?"

"Me and you, not knowing each other's names."

I shrugged. "It's not like it was going to last. Nothing ever does."

"Now *that* deserves an emphatic objection. Some things last."

"Like?"

Before he could respond, a girl—tan, bottle blond, petite—interrupted our conversation like I wasn't there at all. She stepped between us and gave Elias a side hug, fitting perfectly beneath his arm. "Rough game on Friday, but at least you looked good out there."

"Thank you."

And my forehead scrunched into wrinkles, slow-motion like. *Rough game on Friday? You looked good out there?* "Wait a second—you're on the football team?"

The girl acknowledged me for the first time, her attention moving upward from my boots to my hair. She wasn't very subtle about the checkout. "He's not just on the football team. He's the star of the football team."

Eli brushed off the comment.

A sudden and mysterious bad taste filled my mouth.

"Oh, come on," Blondie said to him. "You're the reason the team won state last year and you know it. Anyway, as your official rally girl, I wanted to say good game." She reached up on her tiptoes to kiss Eli's cheek, patted his flat abs, and flounced away.

I watched her go, the bad taste growing more pronounced by the millisecond. Elias Banks had a rally girl. And my classmates in Debate and Ethics? They really weren't staring at me. They'd been staring at Eli—the stud player on the state champ football team making nice with the weird new girl.

"You're wrinkling your nose," he said.

"You're a liar."

He raised his eyebrows. "How am I a liar?"

"You never told me you were a football player."

"You never asked."

"That's another lie. On the dock, I asked if you went to the football game."

"And if I remember correctly, I never said I didn't."

"That's because you hedged. And then you let me go on and on about the sport being a mating ritual." He had even laughed, which I'd found refreshing at the time. Now, though, I felt hoodwinked. Like he'd been laughing at me, not with me.

"Withholding the truth isn't the same as lying."

"Says the boy with the word *Truth* tattooed on his wrist."

This made him grin. "Do you want me to walk you to your next class? The layout here can be a little confusing."

"Thanks, but I think I'm capable of finding a classroom on my own."

I was fifteen minutes late to second period.

16

GRACIE

Droning chatter filled the cafeteria, broken apart by an occasional screech or burst of laughter. I stood off to the side with a frozen Snickers bar and a can of Mountain Dew in hand, telling myself to get it over with. Inhaling a deep breath—sustenance for my cowardly soul—I made a straight path toward an empty table in the back. I didn't look right or left. I didn't walk too fast or too slow. And I didn't exhale until I was sitting in a seat, my back turned to the commotion.

The worst was over.

I put one foot onto the chair and stuck a pair of earbuds into my ears—universal code for *leave me alone*. With Fiamma Fumana playing in my ear, I used my teeth to tear open my Snickers and started reading my not-so-new copy of *Slaughterhouse-Five* (assigned reading from my very new English teacher). The Celtic Italian techno added a slightly frantic sense of immediacy to the reading experience. I finished off my bar and was settling into the story when the chair beside me scooted out from the table. I looked down at a pair of sneakers so well worn they reminded me of the book in my hand.

I didn't have to look up. It was Eli—the lying football player.

He turned the chair around and sat the same way he sat in first period. I looked around the cafeteria. I swear, the entire student body was watching, the least subtle of which was a table full of big, bulky boys. Not at me, the new girl. But at him, sitting with the new girl. I considered continuing on with my music and my fiction, but he seemed prepared to stay for the long haul. The quicker I addressed him, the quicker I could dismiss him. I held my spot in the book with my finger and removed my earbuds. "Can I help you?"

"Gracie Allen."

"That's not my name."

"No, but it is the name of a famous comedian. She was married to George Burns. I guess they were a pretty hilarious duo." He wiggled his phone at me.

"Not as impressive, I admit, since I had to use Google, but it is a piece of trivia about your name."

"Cute."

"Come on. Are you really going to write me off because I'm a football player?"

"No. I'm going to write you off because you lied." And maybe also because he was a football player.

"I thought we already discussed this. I omitted. Omission is not the same as lying. Although I'm sure if we had a debate about it right now, you'd convince me otherwise."

"I will not be flattered."

"Look, I didn't tell you I played football because you made it pretty clear off the bat that you had issues with the sport. I didn't want something as insignificant as that skewing your opinion of me."

"Why does my opinion matter?" It wasn't like he had a shortage of worshipers. The guy had his own personal rally girl, for crying out loud. So what exactly was he trying to prove with me? "Do you see me as a pity project or something?"

"Are you always this cynical?"

"It's better than being naive."

"You aren't a pity project." His attention wandered to the wrapper and can in front of me. "Even if a Snickers bar and Mountain Dew for lunch is a little pitiful."

"It was a Snickers *ice cream* bar. And it's been the least pitiful part of my day."

This earned me one of his grins. I wanted to tell him to put his dimples away; they were no good here. He tipped his chair to lean closer to the table. Closer to me. "I think we should be friends."

"Why?"

"Because I find you interesting."

"Well, that's sweet, but I don't make friends with football players."

"Why not?"

"I find them to be cliché."

Something flashed in the amber-green-brown of his irises, and for one uncensored moment, he dropped the grin.

An intriguing reaction, one I couldn't let lure me in. Eli might offer his friendship. I, on the other hand, had to refuse. It was best if I kept my life in Bay Breeze as uncomplicated as possible. Especially when I had no idea what the future held. At the moment, my life was in a state of major flux. Friendship was the last thing I needed. I opened up *Slaughterhouse-Five* and resumed my reading, hoping Eli would get the hint and leave.

"You know what *I* don't like?" he asked.

"Rejection?"

"Bigots."

My book came down. "I'm not a bigot."

"Bigot, a person who hates or refuses to accept the members of a particular group. Thank you, Webster."

"That's an odd definition to have memorized."

"Not when you're part of a minority."

I stared at him for a couple seconds, doing my best impression of bored, but his accusation scratched a nerve. I considered myself a lot of things, but bigot had never been among them.

"You're jumping to conclusions about my whole person based on one tiny facet of Elias Banks. Which is too bad, because if you actually got to know me, you'd find out I'm about as far away from cliché as a person can get." And with that, he stood, put his hand on the back of my chair, and leaned toward my ear. "Enjoy your book, Gracie Fisher."

I watched him walk away, a tiny puddle of regret slopping around in my gut. But then he joined the table full of big bulky boys and the puddle evaporated. Slipping my earbuds back into place, I pushed Eli's accusation away and returned to Vonnegut's masterpiece, thankful for the perspective the story offered. I ate alone at lunch. And then there was poor Billy Pilgrim. Life could always be worse.

CARMEN

Rayanna suggested Aunt Ingrid and I play our card game in the dining hall. It took half an hour of her encouragement before she was able to convince Ingrid, a self-proclaimed extrovert, to leave her room. Now we sat in the dining hall, Ingrid skittish, me deflated, laying cards down on the tablecloth in a game of War. The longer we played, the more she seemed to settle. I, however, remained disheartened. Maybe later I'd call Natalie and take her up on her CrossFit invite. Perhaps the exercise would chase away the lethargy.

Thanks to Alice, one of Ingrid's friends who joined us now and then for an increasingly rare game of Hearts, piano music played in the background. I laid down a nine of diamonds. Ingrid laid down a ten of clubs.

"Did you know I used to beat your husband in this game?" she asked, raking the cards into her pile. "Gerald thought I should let the boys win whenever we played games, but not me. Losing teaches a person character."

She wasn't talking about Ben. She was talking about Henry, my father. At the moment, Aunt Ingrid thought I was Evelyn, my alcoholic, irresponsible mother. Instead of correcting her, I played along. This was what her doctors recommended. Aunt Ingrid flipped over a six of spades from the top of her stack. I laid down a queen. She frowned.

"Character," I reminded, taking the cards.

This made her smile.

My phone vibrated on the table, making my heart skip a beat, but it was an 800 number. Not our social worker. I sent the telemarketer to voice mail as Alice started a new song on the piano and Earl approached from across the hall. A jolly old man with a white beard, Earl reminded me of a malnourished Santa Claus. He had a weak heart but a keen mind, and he loved to socialize. With his tuft of wispy white hair exposed, he twisted his hat in his hands and stopped in front of our table.

"Morning, Carmen." He gave my aunt a friendly nod. "Ingrid."

A polite but unsettled smile trembled across Ingrid's lips. Earl was one of

her first friends here in her new home, but today, he was a stranger. Her attention slid to me. I could see the cry for help in her eyes. The fact that she couldn't
remember him, yet he knew her, unnerved her. Ingrid had always been good
with names and faces. At times I wondered if she had a photographic memory.
A guest could come for as short as a single night, then return a year later and
somehow Aunt Ingrid would remember them.

"Ingrid, this is Earl."

"Oh, it's a pleasure to meet you, Earl." She stuck out her thin hand and the
two shook. "Are you enjoying your stay?"

Earl didn't skip a beat. "Yes, very much, thank you."

"I'm so glad."

Twisting his hat, he gave us another nod and left us to continue our game.

Aunt Ingrid watched him go, looking relieved at his departure, then turned
over another card. "So tell me more about this Gracie."

I had brought Gracie into the conversation several hands ago, secretly hoping the familiar name might strike the right synapse in her brain and bring my
aunt Ingrid back. I wanted to know what she had to say about my sister. The
two of them must have had some sort of relationship I'd overlooked. The postcard was proof. But it hadn't worked, and since my mother had no half sisters,
or any sisters at all, I acted as though Gracie were the troubled daughter of a
friend, staying with us while her mother took a vacation. "She has all these
walls up. I keep trying to climb over them, but she won't let me."

"Why do you want to climb over them?"

"I don't know." I flipped another card. "I guess I was hoping she wouldn't
just get *through* our time together, but that she might actually enjoy it."

"Sometimes getting through is the only thing a person can do." Aunt Ingrid perked up. "Hey, that rhymed."

"But how do I show her that I'm here for her?" Driving her to school had
been a monumental fail, and Ben had already called to let me know that Gracie
didn't want to be picked up. "How can I do that if she keeps shutting me out?"

"With a lot of patience."

Patience. I was really starting to loathe that word.

Ingrid flipped a seven of hearts.

I flipped a seven of spades.

My aunt's face lit up with excitement.

I laid three cards facedown, then flipped the fourth faceup—a nine.

Aunt Ingrid did the same, only instead of flipping a fourth card, she folded up the corner and took a peek. I expected her tried-and-true poker face. Instead, her excitement turned into pure glee as she turned over a nine. Double war. That rarely happened. We laid down three more cards, then at the same time, we flipped. I had a two. She had a jack. With a victorious cackle, she scooped her bounty into a pile significantly larger than mine.

"Did you know Henry went through a sullen phase in his teen years?"

"Really?" I had a hard time picturing my father being sullen, even as a teenager.

"Latent grief, I think, over his parents' death."

I nodded. When my dad was seven, his parents died in a car accident. Just like that, he and his brother were orphaned. My aunt didn't hesitate to take the boys in as her own. Maybe that was another reason I wanted to be there for Gracie. It was no less than Aunt Ingrid would have done if she were in my situation.

"And a healthy dose of resentment toward the motel. It's not easy, you know, living here. It's a lot like living on a farm. The job's never done. My dad used to say that some people are born with the business in their blood, and some people aren't. I was born with it. My brothers and sisters weren't. Neither were Henry or Patrick."

This wasn't the first time I'd heard Ingrid express such sentiment. In fact, I grew up hearing her say that the motel was in my blood too. It was one of the things that made our relationship so special. We had shared a deep and abiding love for The Treasure Chest. It was a love I'd neglected for far too long. I straightened my meager pile of cards into a thin stack, fighting the urge to tell Aunt Ingrid about my plans—that for the first time in four years, we would celebrate Christmas at The Chest like old times. I was bound and determined to have it fixed up enough for that. But if I shared this now, I'd be rewarded with nothing but confusion. No, my news would have to wait. "So what did you and Gerald do?"

"All we could do—we helped him get through it, not over it." She flipped over an ace. "Because there some things in life we aren't meant to get over."

My phone buzzed.

And that invisible thundercloud looming over my head? It clapped with thunder. Because this time, our social worker's number lit up the screen.

I vented my frustration on the poor window frames of the motel's main office, fully realizing, as I tore out perfectly fine windows, that I was being illogical. Installing new ones wasn't a wise financial decision. At the moment, however, I didn't care. In a storm of so much bad, I needed to see something good. And right now that good was bringing this place back to life. I jammed the crowbar into the wedge between window frame and wall and started yanking with every ounce of strength I had.

"I. Am. Not. Crazy!"

The frame cracked loose.

A lump rose in my throat. I swallowed it down and blinked the stinging from my eyes. How many tears had I shed over my losses? What good had any of those tears done? I was still here, in this place of longing. I began attacking the opposite side of the same window frame, replaying the things our social worker had said.

Taken off the waiting list.

A mental status evaluation and mandatory counseling appointment for me.

A mandatory counseling appointment for Ben.

A mandatory counseling appointment for both of us.

"To re-evaluate," she had said. *"To make sure . . ."*

The unfairness of it burned, fanning a fire of desperation inside my soul. It wasn't fair, these hoops we had to jump through. It wasn't fair that one tiny slip could cost so much. It wasn't fair that women all across the globe could do drugs and drink alcohol and beat their kids and still be mothers. It wasn't fair that I had to sit with some therapist while he mentally poked and prodded my life. It wasn't fair that I had to go home and tell Ben, or that so much had changed between us, or that the one thing I was convinced would fix our problems remained so impossibly out of reach.

"Life isn't fair!"

Screaming the words left me feeling no better. So I grunted and tugged and even kicked at the windows until I reached the final one in the back room, where the commercial washer and dryer were located. The vandals had already rent the plywood board loose, giving me a clear view outside.

A bead of sweat rolled down my temple. I wiped it away, looking toward the pool, the ache in my muscles becoming an ache in my heart. If I were to close my eyes, I'd be able to see the memory and its accompanying setting. Not an empty, kidney-shaped hole with rust stains crawling up the sides, but a sparkling clean pool with oiled guests lying on white chaise lounges and a doughy kid with lemon-yellow hair jumping into the water.

I couldn't remember his name—Tommy or Tony or Timmy, something with a *T*—but I could see him doing his running leap, tucking his knees up to his chest and curling his arms around his knees, yelling, "Cannonball!" while he sailed through the air and splashed into the water, soaking Ben's boat shoes as he finished reading the chlorine levels.

He had taken a quick step back and bumped into the woman behind him. I'd secretly been referring to her as Barbie. With her long legs and impossibly small waist and disproportionately large chest, the name was a natural fit. She and two of her friends had stopped at The Chest on their way to Destin. She got one good look at Ben, decided to stay a couple extra days, and had been shadowing him around the grounds ever since.

Anyway, he had bumped her and she had stumbled—a little dramatically, in my opinion—ensuring that he would wrap his arm around her waist to keep her upright. The sight of her bikini-clad body in his arms twisted me up with jealousy. I quickly looked away, scolding myself for the silly feeling. At that point, nothing had gone on between Ben and me but some harmless flirting. I certainly had no claim on him, especially since I was going back to the University of Virginia at the end of the summer and he would begin his first year of teaching and coaching at Bay Breeze in the fall.

I had sprayed the window and scrubbed it clean, then moved on to the windows in the hospitality room, when the desk bell dinged. I stuffed the rag into the pocket of my Capri pants and headed into the front office.

Ben stood up front, a teasing smile curling up the corners of his mouth, his skin an even bronzer tan than when we'd first met two weeks ago.

"That bell's supposed to be for guests," I said.

"I was checking to make sure it worked."

I frowned. Flirty McFlirterson would not charm me today, not when I had witnessed his hands on Barbie's bare skin seconds earlier. I headed back into the hospitality room to finish the windows.

Ben followed. "Are you upset with me for ringing the bell?"

"I don't care about the bell. I'm trying to get my work done." I sprayed one of the windows with Windex. Blue droplets hit the pane and dribbled clear down the glass.

"Well, I need a break. It's a scorcher out there."

"Maybe you should take a dip in the pool. I'm sure Barbie would love it."

"Who?"

"Sorry. Rachel, or whatever her name is." I didn't dare turn my back on my cleaning to observe Ben's face when I pointed out the fact that I'd noticed the girl's attention. Whether my jealousy entertained or annoyed or baffled him, I couldn't say. I was too busy wiping the window clean and moving onto the last. I could say, though, that when he joined me near the trophy case, he looked amused.

"I have a hypothetical question for you."

I raised my eyebrows—invitation for him to proceed.

"What would you say makes a great first date?"

No, I shouldn't have been jealous, but I definitely wasn't going to help him woo Barbie. I sprayed down the glass on the trophy case and resumed my wiping. "I don't know. Dinner and a movie?"

Ben scoffed.

I stopped my work. "What's wrong with dinner and a movie?"

"Nothing, I just expected something more original from you."

"I'm sorry, but my idea of a great first date is probably not the typical woman's idea of a great first date."

Ben crossed his arms and leaned against the wall. "See, now I'm intrigued."

"A picnic in a boat, watching the clouds."

"You mean the stars?"

"No, I mean the clouds." The stars belonged to my dad. The clouds belonged to me. "They're fascinating."

His bluer-than-blue eyes twinkled and his lips practically puckered with the effort of biting back a smile. "Fascinating?"

"You're making fun of me."

"No, I'm not. I swear. I want to know why you find the clouds so fascinating."

I thought back to little-kid Carmen, the girl who could sit on that pool deck outside and gaze up at the sky for hours. "When I was younger, I thought the clouds were like a crystal ball."

Ben leaned in a little. It made my heart go *bump*. He had this way of making me feel like I was the most interesting person on the face of the planet. What I couldn't figure out was whether he made every other girl feel that way too.

"If I could learn how to read them, then I'd always know if good weather or bad weather was on the way."

"Carmen, the fortune-teller."

"Yeah, well, reading the clouds isn't as straightforward as I thought. They like to change. But that only makes them all the more captivating." All of a sudden, I was keenly aware of the lack of space between Ben's body and mine. Heat climbed up my neck as I cleared my throat and took a step back.

Ben didn't move. "Will there be clouds tomorrow?"

"Lots of them." I picked up the spray bottle and turned toward the supply closet in the back room to put the Windex away. Something told me Barbie would find cloud-watching boring, so my confession caused no harm.

"Carmen?"

I stopped in the doorway.

"Will you look at clouds with me?"

I turned around.

Ben wore that smile of his.

My eyes slowly narrowed. "Are you asking me on a date?"

He placed his hand against his chest. "In the smoothest way I know how."

And that was that.

The next day, Ben borrowed a boat from one of his buddies and took me out on the water. We ate peanut-butter-and-jelly sandwiches and drank bottles of lemonade and watched the clouds change shape as they rolled across the sky.

18

CARMEN

With the sun sinking into the west, I pulled into the driveway beside Ben's car. The clock on the dashboard read 7:45. I never meant to stay so long at The Treasure Chest, but one window led to another, and before I knew it, I was at Lowe's, figuring out how to remove spray paint from stucco. In the moment, the escape had felt necessary, as though my sanity hinged upon it.

Now, however, I realized that not only had I left Gracie alone after her first day of school, I'd left Ben on his own with Gracie. I imagined him coming home from practice to my absence and Gracie's presence. Having to fend for themselves for dinner with no note or explanation from me. They deserved better.

I stepped outside to the chirping of crickets and katydids. My shoes barely made a sound as I headed up the walkway. Inside, the house smelled like pizza. And not just any pizza, but Bruno's signature five-cheese shrimp scampi thin crust—a longstanding favorite of mine. My stomach let out a low grumble. The phone call from our social worker had stolen my appetite, which meant the last meal I ate was a boiled egg for breakfast.

Gracie sat on the couch with one knee pulled up to her chest, flipping through the channels on the television with a can of sour-cream-and-onion Pringles in her lap. She didn't look at me when I closed the door and she didn't look at me while I slipped off my shoes and set them in the closet.

I stepped farther inside. "Hey."

She acknowledged me with a grunt.

"How was your first day of school?"

"Uneventful."

"Did you get something to eat for dinner?"

"Ben ordered pizza. There's leftovers in the kitchen."

"Do you know where he is?"

She reached inside the can of Pringles. "Out back."

In the garage. AKA, his man cave.

I stood in the entryway contemplating my options. I could grab some pizza and go upstairs, shower, change into my pajamas, and drift off to sleep without telling Ben about the new hoops we had to jump through. Another day come and gone with the gaping chasm between us. Or I could try something novel and attempt to bridge it. I could go outside and tell him about the phone call and all the accompanying feelings that came with it.

Perhaps it was the memories resurrected while working at the motel—of a Ben who took me out on his buddy's boat to look at the clouds and wrote our fake initials inside a heart on the wall of wisdom. Or maybe it was the realization that eventually, Gracie would notice if my husband and I never talked. I had no idea why the second option became so urgent. All that mattered was that for the first time in a long time, I was determined to break this pill-bug posture. I took a step toward the kitchen.

"Were you at The Treasure Chest?" Gracie's question stopped me.

I turned around.

She kept her catatonic gaze pinned to the TV.

"Yes."

Her eyebrows twitched—a reaction that came and went so quickly I didn't have time to translate its meaning. Gracie seemed to hate every second she was with me on Saturday cleaning up the front office. I had no reason to believe she would want to go out with me today, not when she was on such a mission to avoid me.

"I didn't think you'd want to come," I said.

"I could use the money."

I paused there for a bit, unsure where to step with Gracie Fisher. It seemed everything I said was the wrong thing to say. "I'm going out tomorrow if you want to help me install some new windows."

She fished out a thin stack of chips from the can. "Sure."

It couldn't be considered progress. Not really. Yet as I headed into the kitchen, I felt the smallest sliver of accomplishment. It fueled my resolve. Until I saw the bouquet of flowers and completely stalled out.

A dozen yellow roses had been carefully arranged inside a vase beside the Bruno's pizza box on the counter. For one panicked moment, I thought I'd forgotten our anniversary. But no, that had come and gone this past July. I removed the small card propped inside the bouquet and opened it.

Thought these might brighten your day. Yours, Ben

I touched one of the stems. Buried my nose in the petals and inhaled the scent. Ben used to buy me flowers all the time. He'd bring them home from work or send bouquets to the station for no reason at all. Somewhere along the line, he'd fallen out of the practice. Seeing them here, abandoned and alone in the silent kitchen, squeezed my heart. I wasn't the only one trying to bridge the chasm tonight. Ben had bought me a bouquet of my favorite flowers and a box of my favorite pizza, but I hadn't been here to receive them.

I opened the sliding-glass door and stepped out onto the patio. I walked through the grass in my bare feet, toward an unattached two-car garage that Ben took over almost immediately after we moved in. I knocked tentatively on the side door, but with Van Halen playing so loudly from the opened window, I doubted he would have heard even if I'd banged. I pushed the door open.

My husband lay back on the bench press, sans shirt. As soon as he spotted me in the doorway, the weights clanked and he sat upright, beads of sweat trickling between his pecs. At thirty-two, he was no longer as chiseled as he'd been in his early twenties, but any woman with two eyes would appreciate his physique. He picked up a controller and Van Halen stopped.

The sudden quiet echoed.

My hands fidgeted—first with the hem of my shirt, then with the tendrils of hair that escaped from my ponytail. "Thank you for the flowers."

"Yep."

His curt response and the hard set of his jaw took a nasty slice at my sails. I didn't want him to be upset. "You're mad?"

"It would have been nice to know you weren't planning on being home tonight."

He was right. I messed up. I knew I messed up. So why was it so hard to squeeze out an apology? "I'm sorry."

"Were you at the motel?"

"Yes."

"So is this how it's going to be from now on? You working out there while I'm here alone with your *teenage* sister?"

"Time got away from me." And I had to go. After that phone call, I could barely breathe. Being there had given me my breath back. "I promise it won't happen again."

Ben ran his hands down his face.

It was a worn-down motion. An "I'm tired of this" motion. And you know what? So was I. Weary to the bone.

"Our social worker called."

His body snapped to attention—a world of anticipation flooding his eyes—and in that infinitesimal unguarded blip of a moment, he showed me a glimpse of a heart I rarely saw anymore. Ben wanted to be a daddy. "And?"

"And we have to see a counselor."

"A counselor? But I thought we were done with all that stuff."

"She saw the video." The words escaped devoid of emotion. In the wake of Ben's disappointment, I had no more left to expend. "I guess when something like this happens, protocol is to take the couple off the waiting list until they can reevaluate the situation."

"So we have to see a counselor?"

"Once individually. And once together."

"Then what?"

"Then the counselor writes up a report and, hopefully, we get back on the list." The whole thing had me feeling like a naughty little girl, desperate to show Santa I deserved so much more than a lump of coal. When Ben said nothing, I started to turn away, back to the katydids outside.

"Carmen."

I stopped, a swell of desperation rising in my throat. If only he could find a way to break the dam that kept me from confiding in him. I closed my eyes. Wished a wish. Prayed a prayer. I didn't know anymore.

"We're having team dinner here on Thursday."

"*This* Thursday?"

"Some of the moms cornered me about it tonight at practice. I couldn't say no."

Yes, he could have. But I was hardly in a position to say so tonight. I had no right to feel annoyed, but I couldn't help it. Team dinners were exhausting. Not only would I have fifty-plus teenage boys milling about my house and yard, plus coaches and booster moms, I would have to play the part of hostess. Which wouldn't be a huge deal if I wasn't so mortified about the video.

Ben lay back on the bench.

I guess we were done.

I barely got two steps out the door before the sounds of Van Halen resumed.

I bypassed the pizza and headed straight for the shower, tucked myself into bed, buried my face in my pillow, and muffled the sound of my tears. They changed nothing, but they came anyway. Somewhere around eleven, Ben slipped between the sheets. I could smell the faint scent of his shampoo. He lay there for a moment, breathing into the silence, then ever so quietly, barely even a whisper, "Are you awake?"

I didn't move. I didn't speak. I remained curled on my side, eyes long dry, blinking into the darkness as he set his hand on my hip, a touch so gentle it would never wake me. His palm was warm, but my heart was cold.

19

GRACIE

"And there goes another fifteen minutes of my life I'll never get back," I said, lengthening and shortening the measuring tape in my hands.

So far, Carmen and I had watched four YouTube videos about window installation on her phone. And so far, the only step I understood was numero uno—measure the height and width of each window frame. Everything beyond that was pretty much Mandarin.

Carmen stared at her phone screen with her thumbnail wedged between her teeth. "Maybe we should hire someone to install them."

I could have told her that three videos ago.

A gust of wind slapped at the plastic sheeting covering the space where a window used to be. The material gave me flashbacks of my time with chain-smoking Deborah.

"Do you want to tackle the pool instead?" she asked.

"Sure."

The pool did not require a fifteen-minute tutorial on YouTube, just a strong stomach, some heavy-duty gloves, and if available, a nose plug. After months of being drained with no tarp for a cover, the kidney-shaped hole had served as a natural garbage dump, collecting an impressively diverse ecosystem of moldy debris. We climbed inside—Carmen armed with a push broom, me with a trash bag—and began ripping the ecosystem apart.

I stuffed my bag with soggy trash and bits of rotten plant matter, trying not to get too nostalgic about my summertime community service ditch-cleaning adventures, while a distracted Carmen pushed the too-small-to-pick-up debris into a pile in the middle. Gone was the overly enthusiastic woman from Saturday. Gone was the desperate woman from yesterday's first-day-of-school drop-off. All that existed now was lifeless Carmen—a woman who looked like she wanted to be anywhere but here. Apparently, her attention span for the renovation project was about as long as my pinky toe.

Wind rippled my trash bag and whipped strings of hair into my face. It blew in from the ocean, tossing big, rolling waves onto the beach. A man jogged into the chaotic water with a surfboard. Farther beyond that, a small girl combed the sand. When I was a kid, Ingrid paid me a nickel for every seashell I could find. I used to wake up early in the morning and fill an entire bag full, then count them carefully while I sat at this very pool soaking my feet in the water. After I finished, she'd ask me to clean off the sand and pour them in the vases inside each of the rooms. She used to tell me she was lucky to have such a hard worker on her payroll.

I glanced at Carmen and stuffed a soggy palm branch inside my bag. "How's your aunt?"

She swept the last of the debris into her growing pile, carefully avoiding eye contact. "Not very good."

I helped her scoop the filth into my trash bag, trying to picture the clever, energetic woman I remembered without her wits. If it wasn't so depressing I'd appreciate the irony. The one person who actually enjoyed my presence, or at least seemed to, had officially lost her marbles. "So she has Alzheimer's or something?

"It's an undiagnosed form of dementia."

I tied up the trash bag, trapping the disgusting ecosystem inside its new home.

"You know, if you ever want to come visit her with me, you're more than welcome. I'm sure she'd love to see you."

"I doubt she'd remember me."

"If she's having a good day she would."

I pictured walking to her room. Standing there all awkwardly while she either recognized me or didn't. Uncomfortable for me, sure. But a hundred times more uncomfortable for her. The entire scenario made me shudder on her behalf.

Carmen's phone dinged, like our time was up. She pulled it out from her back pocket and checked the screen. A crease worked its way between her eyebrows as she pressed the phone to her ear. "Mom?"

Funny how one syllable could make my stomach clench into such a tight fist.

"Yes, Gracie's fine. I told you she's staying with me. Don't you remember?" Carmen's eyes met mine before quickly looking away. I left eight days ago. As far as I knew, this was the first time Mom had bothered to call.

Carmen climbed out of the pool, out of earshot. I hoisted myself up onto the ledge and let my feet dangle over the side while my sister paced near the weed-infested courtyard for a couple minutes. When she returned, she held out the phone. "Mom wants to talk."

I lifted my hands and leaned away from the offering. "No way."

Carmen hesitated, then brought the phone back to her ear. "Mom, Gracie doesn't want to talk right now." She nodded. Murmured an "uh-huh" and an "ah-huh," then hung up and sat down beside me.

Another guest of wind blew at us.

"Did she have a nice bender?" My question tasted like the contents in my trash bag.

Carmen massaged the bridge of her nose, a mannerism so much like our mother I had a hard time stomaching it. "She said she woke up in an abandoned parking lot this morning, without any clue where she was or where you were. I guess she lost her job at the bank a couple days ago."

The nasty taste got nastier. I pushed up into standing. "Do you have a power washer in the pool shed?"

"Gracie . . ."

"What?"

"She feels awful."

"I'm sure some Advil and a glass of wine will solve that problem."

"She called to say she was going to check into rehab. She wants you to call her when you're ready."

I crossed my arms and shook my head.

"Can't you give her another chance?"

I looked my sister directly in the eyes. "Some people don't deserve another chance."

Not when they'd already used up so many.

⌒

I people-watched from the top of the staircase with my iPod turned to low. Coaches, booster moms, and football players hung out in Carmen's clean home. There was one in particular who kept drawing my interest—Eli Banks, the growing enigma. After I insulted him in the cafeteria, I expected animosity. Nobody I knew responded well to insult, especially bigheaded football players. And while he did make a point to challenge me in Debate and Ethics, my arguments seemed to amuse him more than trigger his hostility. Then there'd been Wednesday, when I dropped my books on my way out into the hallway. Instead of walking on my stuff, or past my stuff, he bent over and picked up my stuff.

I couldn't figure the guy out.

I exhaled a long breath that lifted my bangs from my eyes and spotted Carmen, smiling and laughing and conversing as though she hadn't been crying in the bathroom an hour ago or venting to a woman named Natalie on the phone about some embarrassing YouTube video five minutes before the first guest arrived. She set her hand on Ben's forearm and laughed at something he said. Her phoniness scratched like nails on a chalkboard. Ben glanced up at my spot in the shadows, as if sensing the waves of judgment rolling off of me. He excused himself from the conversation and came to the bottom of the staircase.

"You know you can come down here and join the party, right?"

"You know I'd rather eat nails, right?"

Ben laughed. "Bruno's lasagna is hard to pass up."

"I'm good." At least I would be once he returned to the conversation he left behind. His presence at the bottom of the stairs was gathering unwanted attention, and I really didn't want Eli to see me sitting up here spying. I snuck a quick look in his direction and realized it was too late. He was already making his way over.

I dropped my attention to my lap and twisted my mood ring around my finger. The stone had been the color of coal ever since I woke up. It usually changed color at least once. Apparently not today. Today it remained black—the absorption of all color. If only it would absorb me.

"Gracie?" Eli stood next to Ben, a plate of lasagna and garlic bread in hand, looking every bit as shocked as I'd felt that first day of school when he booed in my ear.

I gave him a lame, dispassionate wave.

"What are you doing here?"

"Gracie's my sister-in-law," Ben said. "You two have already met?"

"We have first period together."

"Good, maybe you can convince her to come down." Ben clapped Eli on the shoulder and returned to the adults.

Eli climbed the stairs and sat next to me, bringing with him a steam cloud of garlic and oregano. "Coach's wife is your sister?"

I tapped my nose.

His left dimple flashed. "Is this where you live?"

"Don't think I've missed the irony."

Eli shook his head, his right dimple joining his left. I resented how cute they looked together. He motioned to the cacophony below. "This must be your worst nightmare."

"It's pretty close."

He continued his head shaking and took a few bites of lasagna, then set his plate off to the side, plastic fork still in hand. I found myself distracted by his Truth tattoo. Now that I thought about it, he never told me what the word meant to him, other than the nebulous *truth is important*. "So if you are so against the sport of football, why did you come here to live?"

"Because my mom's a drunk." I watched for his reaction, expecting one of two things: shock or pity.

He stuck his fork in his mouth and wiped the tongs clean. The awareness this brought of his lips, full and more inviting than I cared to admit, had my attention returning to my black-as-night ring.

"So is my dad," he said.

I jerked my head up. "Seriously?"

"It's not something I'd joke about."

We sat without speaking for a moment while I processed his confession. "She checked into rehab today," I finally said.

"That's good."

"It's her third time." And somehow I didn't think it was going to be a charm.

"Three's better than zero."

I quirked one of my eyebrows.

"Hey, if she's been to rehab three times, that means she's trying."

My mouth opened, but nothing came out. I'd always seen Mom's inability to stick to sobriety as a sign of weakness, further proof that she didn't care enough. And here this boy flipped her stints in rehab inside out, holding them up to the light so that I had to at least consider them another way.

"My dad's never bothered with rehab. At least not that I know of."

"He's not part of your life?"

"Not since I was two."

I almost apologized. But I kept the *I'm sorry* tucked inside my throat. I had a feeling he didn't want my sympathy any more than I wanted his.

"My father—he's about as cliché as a person can get." He gave me a pointed look when he said it, as if making sure I remembered the word I tossed out so casually at lunch on Monday.

"How so?"

"He's not just an absentee father, he's a black absentee father."

"Wait a minute." Eli accused *me* of being a bigot, and now he was going to go and say something like that? "That's a bigoted statement."

"It's not bigoted. It's the truth. A white man abandons his kid and he's a deadbeat father. A black man abandons his kid and it's all about his color."

I narrowed my eyes. "That's not true."

"Says the naive white girl." He gave me a teasing nudge. "I'm not saying it's fair, but it's definitely true."

As much as I wanted to argue, give our society a little more credit, it wasn't my place. Like Eli said, I was white, and when it came to things like white privilege, it wasn't the white people who noticed it. "So it's just you and your mom, then?"

"Thankfully. My dad was a violent drunk."

He was making my own mother sound more and more saintly by the second.

"You don't have to look so sorry for me. My mom—she's great. Works harder than anybody else I know. And I'm not lacking in male role models. I have Coach Hart. And I have Pastor Zeke, who's a better dad to me than the majority of real fathers out there."

"Who's Pastor Zeke?"

"Ezekiel Raymond Johnson the Third. He's the pastor at the church my mom and I go to. It's called The Cross. Maybe you can meet him sometime."

I made a face. "I'm not very religious."

"Neither is Pastor Zeke."

Before I could process what that was supposed to mean, one of the bulky boys called up the stairs. "Hey, Eli! Coach Jane and I made a bet. He thinks Coach Hart can catch more passes in a row than you. We're moving this party into the backyard."

"Well, Gracie Fisher, it was nice talking." Eli pulled himself up by the banister and tossed me a wink. "You coming to the game tomorrow night?"

"Not on your life."

With a chuckle, he headed down the stairs and joined his teammates. It wasn't until they were all outside that I noticed my grin.

CARMEN

I sat across from a woman who held too much power in her hands. Her name was Dr. Sue Rafferty. From the list of recommendations provided by our adoption agency, hers was the shortest wait time for an appointment. So here I was, staring into the sharply lined face of a woman who looked much more like a boarding school headmistress than a therapist, especially with her pepper-colored hair pulled back into such a severe bun.

"How do you feel about being at a counselor's office today?" she asked.

"A little nervous."

"Have you ever seen a counselor before?"

"No."

"I'm sure it must feel strange, talking to someone you don't know about such personal things. But rest assured, this is a safe place. Anything we discuss today is confidential."

I recalled the release form I was asked to sign upon arriving, giving Dr. Sue Rafferty permission to send the summary of her report on to my social worker. It didn't feel safe or confidential.

"Unless, of course, you report any abuse to a minor or elder, or you threaten to hurt someone." Dr. Rafferty grasped her clipboard with both hands. The questionnaire I'd filled out in the waiting room was clipped to the front. It asked questions like: *Do you have a history of violence?* and *Have you or anybody in your family suffered from a mental breakdown?* "Why don't we start with the video?"

"Okay."

"Do you mind telling me what happened?"

"I ran into a sign in the Toys R Us parking lot."

"Why were you there—at Toys R Us?"

"I was buying a baby shower gift for a friend."

She scribbled a note on her paper. "And how did that make you feel?"

"Fine."

She looked up from her notes.

"A little jealous, I guess. Sad, maybe." I shifted in the seat, extracting some squeaks from the leather. "Listen, Dr. Rafferty, I understand that this is protocol and you have to make sure I'm mentally sound, but please believe me when I say this isn't my typical behavior. I've had plenty of pregnant friends. I don't break down every time I need to buy someone a baby gift."

"So what made this time different?"

"I guess I was having a weak moment. I promise it won't happen again."

Dr. Rafferty studied me with a poker face that would have made Aunt Ingrid proud. "Moments of weakness are bound to happen. I'm afraid it's a side effect of being human."

I tucked a strand of carefully straightened hair behind my ear and looked down at my tan pumps. I'd worn newly pressed, light-khaki dress pants and a Persian-green silk top with matching earrings. I may have overdressed a tad.

"What matters is how we cope in our moments of weakness."

"Yes, well, I don't typically run into parking signs when I'm feeling weak."

"What do you typically do?"

I grappled for a response. I had my Sunday school answer at the ready, standing at the very tip of my tongue. *I hand my weakness over to the Lord, of course. After all, God doesn't give us more than we can handle.* But I wasn't even sure what that meant anymore. "I have a really great friend named Natalie. She's a good listener."

Dr. Rafferty scribbled another note.

"And there's Ben," I blurted, heat rising up my neck and spreading into my cheeks. I probably should have mentioned Ben first.

"How are you doing in light of the video?"

"Fine." Disgraced. Humiliated. Terribly self-conscious about going out in public. Working double time to prove to acquaintances and strangers alike that I had my life together. "Work wanted me to take some time off, understandably, so I'm renovating a motel that's been in my family for years. Have you heard of The Treasure Chest?"

Dr. Rafferty shook her head. "I'm fairly new to the area."

"Well, I'm fixing it up with my sister, Gracie." For the past two and a half weeks, Gracie had been accompanying me out to the motel after school. We worked together for two to three hours, then came home to have dinner with

Ben. We hadn't made any sisterly breakthroughs. Gracie still communicated in grunts and shrugs. But she seemed to be settling into life at Bay Breeze okay. She was certainly better off now than she'd been when I found her. That had to say something about my capabilities. Not only was I taking on a major motel renovation project, I was raising a teenager in the midst of it. "My sister is actually living with us for a while. Gracie's seventeen. Ben and I have her enrolled in school at Bay Breeze. She's doing well."

No bathroom brawls or arrests, anyway.

"Sounds like you have a lot on your plate."

"Not really. I mean, it's not overwhelming or anything."

She jotted more notes. "Why don't you tell me why you and Ben decided to adopt?"

I bit my lip. It was a loaded question that came with multiple answers. I decided to go with the simplest. "We want to be parents."

"Why?"

The question took me off guard. Why did anyone want to be parents? "Isn't that usually the plan—go to college, get married, start a family?"

"Not for everyone."

I pulled at my sleeves.

"Why is being a parent so important to you?"

"Because it's important to Ben." The answer escaped before I could think. Before I could filter. Before I could take it back. I think it shocked me more than it shocked Dr. Rafferty.

I stepped into the cool lobby air of Pine Ridge and spotted Rayanna at the front desk chatting with the woman behind it. When she saw me, her face split with that gap-toothed grin of hers, only something about it looked bigger than usual. "Guess who asked to visit the dining hall this morning?"

My spirits lifted. After my mandatory counseling session, which had ended with a mental status evaluation that made me feel certifiably insane, I could use a smile. "Really?"

"She's there now. And I think she might be up for a game of Hearts."

Forget lifting, my spirits soared altogether. I'd been carrying the news about Christmas at The Chest in my pocket for almost three weeks now, eager to pull it out and hand it to my aunt. But all we'd had were a handful of War days. My eagerness to tell her grew hotter to hold by the day. I made quick work of signing in, gave Rayanna's forearm a grateful squeeze, as if she were somehow responsible for the state of Ingrid's mind, and hurried toward the sound of dining hall chatter.

Elderly people filled the room. No piano music today, which made the chitchat more pronounced. It was a lot like a junior high cafeteria, really, with group conversations trending toward one of two topics. Who was dating whom and the edibility of the food. I found Ingrid sitting at one of the round tables near the back, conversing with Earl and another of her friends, Dorothy.

Earl and Dorothy couldn't be more unalike if they tried. Rare was the day Earl wasn't in the dining hall, playing chess or Mancala with anyone he could snag—a nurse, fellow resident, high school kids visiting for a service project, or me on Ingrid's especially horrid days. As far as I knew, Earl didn't have any family—at least none that visited.

Then there was Dorothy, a cantankerous, shriveled old woman who wore a cannula and wheeled around an oxygen tank because she suffered from something called chronic obstructive pulmonary disease. On Ingrid's first day at Pine Ridge, every time Ben pounded a nail into the wall to hang a picture, Dorothy, with her TV blaring, would whack the wall back at him from the other side. Finally Ingrid went over and asked what was wrong. "The guy with the hammer, that's what's wrong." Ingrid liked her immediately. Unlike Earl, Dorothy had a constant stream of visitors.

Earl saw me approaching first. He didn't stop waving until I maneuvered around the tables and stood in front of theirs. I could tell he was every bit as excited to have Ingrid back as I was. I gave my aunt a tight hug, and Earl too, but I knew better than to extend the affection to Dorothy. She didn't do hugs. So I waved to her, a gesture she shooed away.

"These two are debating the carbohydrate-to-protein ratio served in our meals," Ingrid said with an eye roll.

I took the fourth seat at the table, using every ounce of willpower I had to keep from blurting out the news about Christmas at The Chest. "Oh, really?"

"I think all the fiber is what gives Alice her gas problem," Earl said.

Alice was Ingrid's third friend and missing from the group today. She was a little old woman—the archetypal grandmother with a mind that was also slipping away. Her presence in the dining hall was as scattered as Ingrid's.

Dorothy shook her head. "IBS gives Alice her gas problem."

I bit the inside of my cheek to keep from smiling and dug through my purse until I found the deck of cards and held them up in the air. "Anybody up for a game of Hearts?"

Ingrid raised her hand.

Dorothy shooed at me again, then let out a great big hacking cough, the kind that sounded as though she was expelling a lung. If I hadn't known any better, I might have been alarmed. But chronic bronchitis was part of her COPD. According to Ingrid, Dorothy was once a chain smoker. Forced to quit against her will, her moods turned irritable. Occasionally, I caught a whiff of cigarette smoke in her hair. She must have found a way to sneak cigarettes inside, past the nurses and her never-ending family.

"Come on, Dorth, I'll make you a deal," Earl said above her wheezing. "If you play Hearts today, I won't bother you about Connect Four tomorrow."

When Dorothy regained control of her body, she gave Earl a beady stare. "Fine."

I slipped the cards from the case and began shuffling, my news growing hotter by the second. With one eye on Ingrid, I passed out the cards—thirteen to everyone—then picked up my hand and started organizing. I slid a pair of clubs and the nasty queen of spades facedown to Earl. "I've been out to The Treasure Chest quite a bit," I said as casually as I could, picking up the three cards passed to me.

"How's the old girl doing?" Ingrid asked.

"She's looking good." Better, at least. So far Gracie and I had managed to clean out the front office, the back room, the supply closet, and the hospitality room. We'd removed the vulgar graffiti from the front and had new windows installed. Despite Gracie's lack of conversational skills, my time there was quickly becoming my favorite part of the day, and I suspected hers too. Her scowl, at least, disappeared.

Earl took the first trick and led the next with a five of diamonds.

"I don't even know how long it's been since I've seen the place," Ingrid said. "I hate that I can't seem to keep track of the time anymore."

Dorothy took the second trick, then threw out an ace. "That's what calendars are for."

Earl furrowed his brow—not at Dorothy's words, but at her lead.

"I asked Nurse Ray the date the other day and she told me September 14. Mid-September? I have no idea how it got to be mid-September. The whole thing gave me a nightmare. It was the strangest nightmare too. I was on the beach searching for seashells. Nurse Ray was there and she kept yelling at me to put the shells down and get out in the water for a swim. Then all of a sudden a riptide was dragging me away, and no matter how hard I swam, I couldn't get back to the shore. There were sharks and everything." Ingrid shuddered. "I've never been so happy to wake up in all my life."

I laid a ten and jiggled my leg, searching for a way to get the conversation back on track.

"You know," Earl quipped, "you'll never escape a riptide by fighting against the current. I learned about it on the Travel Channel. Seems counterintuitive, doesn't it? But many people have drowned fighting the current."

"You're supposed to swim parallel with the shore," Ingrid said.

Earl smiled. "Precisely."

"I'll keep that in mind," Dorothy said dryly, "the next time I take a dip in the ocean."

"So, Christmas!" Never mind subtlety. It was getting me nowhere. I beamed at my aunt. "You ready to celebrate out at The Treasure Chest this year?"

"Am I ready?" She pressed her bony hand against her sternum, tears welling in her eyes. "That would be the best Christmas present I could ask for. I'd die a happy woman."

Some tears might have welled in mine too.

"You're not dying anytime soon," Dorothy said. "Now play a card."

Ingrid tossed out an off-suit heart.

"No diamonds?" Earl asked.

"No diamonds," she replied.

Dorothy scooped in the cards and laid the ace of hearts.

Earl slapped the table. "I knew it, you're shooting the moon!"

She smirked, then convulsed with another round of hacking coughs.

When the worst of it passed, Ingrid sighed. It was as if my news had lit her up from the inside out. I could almost see the joy shining from her pores. "You should have seen the Christmas parties Gerald and I used to throw back in the day. The whole family would come—Patrick and his wife and their two kids, Genevieve and little Beau. Henry and Evelyn and Carmen. Gerald's two sisters and their families, not to mention the motel guests. We'd put up a giant tree and have tinsel everywhere! I'd even make homemade baklava, one of the only Greek foods my picky Scot of a husband enjoyed."

A whole slew of memories rose up in the wake of her reminiscing, just like they did the last time. Only this time, I couldn't have wiped the smile from my face if I'd tried.

"That sounds like a slice of heaven, Ingrid," Earl said. "The best kind of Christmas there could be."

"You should come!"

Ingrid's invitation ripped me from my reveries. It was going to be enough work taking her out for the day. I couldn't imagine bringing Earl too, especially with his heart condition.

"You and Dorothy, both." Ingrid reached across the table and squeezed Earl's hand. "Maybe Alice can even join us."

Oh, dear.

Now Earl's pores shone with joy too. "What do you say, Dorth?"

"I'm not going to any motel on Christmas. If I had my say, I'd go nowhere on Christmas." Dorothy examined her cards, then laid the queen of hearts. "And here my family's already prattling on about two separate parties! As if one isn't torture enough."

"Torture?" Ingrid waved her finger at Dorothy, like a mother reprimanding a sullen child. "Christmas is the best holiday of the year."

"Christmas is for the kids." She stopped short of saying bah humbug.

"Christmas is about the Christ, which makes it for everyone," Ingrid said.

"Don't start talking religion at me."

Ingrid opened her mouth to say more, but Earl tapped the table. A timely distraction. "I'd be honored to join you for Christmas, Ingrid. Absolutely honored."

So, Earl was in. What was one more, really? Nobody should be alone for Christmas, especially not somebody as jolly as St. Nick himself.

I looked around the table. We had reached the final trick of the game.

Each of us held one last card. Dorothy had been leading the entire time. If she won, she would have shot the moon, landing the rest of us with twenty-six points. She stared at Earl, then laid down the jack of clubs. I knew exactly what Earl had left. I was the one who had slid it to him in the beginning of the game, after all. But his face revealed nothing. Ingrid laid a seven. I laid a diamond. Earl paused, for dramatic effect, then with a hoot, he laid the queen.

"The Black Maria foils your plans, Dorth!" He scooped up the trick, chuckling away, happily accepting his thirteen points for the sake of our zero.

21

GRACIE

Ever since my mother told Carmen she was checking herself into rehab, a number with an 850 area code lit up my phone screen every night at 6:30 p.m. And Carmen had turned into a parrot. *Squawk! Have you talked to Mom yet? Squawk! You should really talk to Mom.* It took everything in me not to stuff a cracker in her mouth and tell her to shut it. I leaned against the headboard of my bed for two more rings before swiping the screen and saying hello.

"Gracie?" Her voice came out in a gush of shock and relief.

I rolled my eyes.

"I'm so glad you answered." She let out a shaky breath, as if waiting for me to fill the silence. I had nothing to say. "How are you doing?"

"Fine."

"Carmen said you're enrolled at Ben's school?"

Yep.

"Are you enjoying your new classes?"

"Sure."

"Have you made any new friends?"

"Not really."

"Are you behaving yourself for Carmen and Ben?"

"I have to go."

"Gracie, wait . . ."

I stared at that canvas with the Bible verse about Jesus making all things new while she sniffled on the other end. I didn't like when my mother cried. Her tears were manipulative and weak. I wanted to tell her to suck it up. She wasn't a victim. And I was all out of sympathy.

"I—I love you. You know that, right?"

"Sure, Mom. I'll talk to you later." I dropped my phone into my lap and rested my head against the wall as it muffled Ben and Carmen's voices in the other room. The sound reminded me of Charlie Brown's teacher—"waa-waa-waa." I didn't pay much attention until the words *The Treasure Chest* broke through the gibberish.

I got up on my knees and pressed my ear against the wall.

"You go back on Monday," Ben said.

"I know."

"How are you going to have time to do both?"

"I'm done every day at ten. I can go to The Chest after I get off work."

During the day. While I was at school.

I sank down onto the mattress and picked up the postcard on my night-stand. Once again, Carmen was leaving me out of her plans. I didn't know why it surprised me.

My hand throbbed. I had spent the entire afternoon and evening filling out job applications. I started at the end of Dock Street at the Hot Dog Hut, a restaurant with a giant shark head protruding over the door like an awning. Then I made my way down the street and around the town square, careful not to miss any possible places of employment. I doubted Carmen would let me drop out of school to work at The Treasure Chest with her during the day, which basically meant I was out of a job.

I stood in front of the last place along the square, the restaurant I'd been intentionally avoiding all night: The Barbeque Pit. Country twang escaped from the door every time another football player walked inside. As the unofficial gathering spot for Ben's football team, it wasn't exactly my first pick. But since it was one of Bay Breeze's busiest restaurants, I'd be dumb to pass it up.

Go in, fill out an application, and reward yourself with a bag of Funyuns.

By the time I got home, Carmen would be asleep and Ben would be in the garage out back, which would leave me with the TV all to myself. I could watch reruns of old-school sitcoms. *The Cosby Show* played four times in a row starting at eleven on TBS.

Shaking out the cramps in my hand, I walked inside to the tangy smell of barbeque and the twangy voice of some dude singing about his sexy farmer's tan. Apparently, our ideas of sexy were vastly different.

Most of the booths were lined with kids my age—lots of big, bulky boys and other less bulky boys I vaguely recognized from school. Elias sat at one, spinning quarters on the table with a few others. As if sensing my presence, his eyes lifted from the spinning quarters and met mine. I looked away, made a beeline for the counter, and asked the woman behind it for an application. She handed one over and I sat on one of the barstools and began filling in the boxes with my back to the majority of my peers. My hair blocked the rest.

"Looking for a job?"

I stopped my pen scratching and swiveled around. It wasn't Elias. It was the blond, lanky boy from Debate and Ethics. His name was Parker. And while I sometimes got the impression that he liked hearing himself talk, I had to admit that he was impressively smart. Elias, I could beat in a debate. Parker and I pretty much went head to head. I could never tell if I impressed him or irritated him. Probably both.

"It's Gracie, right?"

Whatever. Parker knew my name.

He sat in the stool beside me. "Can I ask you a question?"

"It's a free country."

He scooted his stool closer to mine. "Why don't I ever see you outside of school?"

"You're seeing me now."

"You know what I mean."

I wondered how I should fill in the boxes of availability. Whatever I checked meant time away from helping Carmen at The Treasure Chest. While I wish I could have said *Forget you, you're on your own now,* I couldn't. I liked being there. I liked fixing the place up. Even if it was with my sister. I decided to leave them all blank and see what the manager came up with—if he or she even offered me the job. "Probably because I don't hang out where you hang out."

"That's too bad."

The lady who gave me the application rang up a harassed-looking mother with four kids, then raised her eyebrows at whomever stood next in line.

"Can I get a refill, please?"

I swiveled my stool around in the opposite direction. Elias tipped his chin at me, then shifted his attention to Parker.

"Hey, Eli," Parker said. "I was just about to invite Gracie to a party I'm having on Saturday night. My parents are out of town. You should come too."

He handed me an actual business card, on the back of which was scrawled his name, number, and address. "Starts at seven." And with that, he left—back to whichever table he came from.

I turned the card over. It belonged to his father, who, according to the card, had his own law firm. I knew because it was called Zkotsky & Schmidt Legal Office, and Reyas was always calling Parker Mr. Zkotsky.

The waitress set Elias's freshly topped drink on the counter.

"You gonna go?" he asked.

"I don't know. Are you?"

"It's not really my scene." He took a pull of Coca-Cola from his straw, then scratched his earlobe. "In the spirit of speaking truth?"

I folded my arms on top of my application. This, I had to hear.

"I'd stay clear of Parker. He's kind of a jerk."

"Duly noted."

He glanced at the sheet of paper beneath my elbows and tapped the counter. "I hope you get the job." With a wink, he picked up his glass and returned to his booth.

I finished the application, handed it over, and made a fast exit, stopping at a gas station and grabbing a bag of Funyuns on the way home. I reread the address on the back of the business card. I'd done enough wandering around Bay Breeze to know that the house was in one of the wealthier neighborhoods. No surprise, if Parker's dad was a hotshot lawyer. I slid the card into my back pocket and cut across Ben and Carmen's front lawn, encouraged by the darkened windows.

When I stepped inside, though, Ben sat up from the couch, his hair springing from the back of his head. The TV cast a glow into the room. On the screen, a white-and-red team played a purple-and-gold team. Thursday Night Football.

"Hey," he said.

"Hi."

"Did you find a job?"

I shrugged. If I didn't, nobody could say it was for lack of effort.

"The game's a blowout." He nodded toward the football players. "TV's yours if you want it."

"It's fine."

Ben ran his hand down the back of his hair. "I talked to Reyas in the teacher's lounge today."

My shoulders tensed. An ingrained reaction. One of my guardians mentioned talking to one of my teachers and my hackles were going to go up. This time, however, I was pretty sure I knew what Reyas talked to Ben about. Because Reyas herself cornered me after class, giving me no choice but to listen as she turned into a living, breathing billboard for the debate team.

"She says you're one heck of a debater."

I kicked off my boots. I wasn't typically one for class participation, but somehow Reyas made keeping quiet a virtual impossibility. Plus, there were Parker and Elias to argue with.

"Do you think you'll go out for the team?" he asked.

"I'm not much of a joiner."

"Well, maybe you should start. Reyas doesn't go into recruiting mode unless she's highly impressed with whoever she's recruiting."

I lifted my shoulder like it was no big deal, but Ben's words expanded like this strange pocket of warmth in the center of my chest. Other than Ingrid and her seashells, nobody had recruited me for anything.

Stop. Turn around. It's not too late. These were the commands my brain gave my feet. These were the commands my feet ignored. They kept walking toward my first-period classroom, only it was the end of the day. Stupid, stupid feet. The loud chatter filtering into the hallway had me stutter stepping. It was the kind of noise created by twenty, thirty kids, easily. Yet when I reached the door, there were only seven. Six boys. One girl. Five were gathered around the table up front—talking over one another, arguing, laughing, passing around papers, and typing onto laptops.

One I recognized more than the others—Parker Zkotsky. I should have known he'd be on the debate team. He twirled a pen around his thumb with his feet crossed on top of the table. "The NSA targets the wrong people," he practically yelled.

"We know, but that can't be our only negative contention," said the one and only girl, pushing Parker's shoes off the table. He almost toppled back in his chair, but caught himself at the last second. Everyone laughed as Parker put all four chair legs on the ground.

On the other side of the room, the two students not at the table stood on either side of Reyas. She held her chin and nodded at nothing in particular while one talked with his hands and the other pointed at a sheet of paper.

This was nothing like debate class.

In debate class, Parker, Elias, and I were the only ones who talked. Here, everyone talked. Loudly. My feet started to back-pedal, finally catching on to what my brain already knew. I didn't belong. But before I could back-pedal out of view, Reyas looked up from her carpet, nodding. "You came!"

The room went quiet.

Reyas intercepted me at the door, pulled me into the classroom, and introduced me to everyone but Parker, whom I already knew. By the time I met the last student, I had forgotten the names of the first, second, and third.

"I'm working with my policy guys right now." Reyas hitched her thumb toward the two boys standing off to the side. "Policy is a whole different ball game. Kids who do it are kids who've been doing debate since junior high. Don't worry." She cupped my shoulder with an alarmingly firm grip. "You won't do policy. You'll do public forum debate, which is the structure we follow in class. Gathering evidence. Building your case. Et cetera, et cetera."

I wanted to tell her that I wasn't doing anything. I was only there to get her off my back.

"Kimmy," Reyas said.

The girl, who wore her hair in a low, tight ponytail, looked up from her laptop. Her attention flicked briefly toward my black hair, then down to my equally black boots.

Reyas motioned for her to join us, then cupped her shoulder too. We were both trapped. "This is the student I was telling you about—Gracie Fisher. I think the pair of you would make a strong team. Kim's been doing debate since freshman year, but her partner graduated last year. Trust me, with Kimmy, you're in excellent hands." She looked from me to the girl. "Gracie hasn't done debate, but don't hold that against her, all right? This girl is brilliant at countering and refuting arguments. Just ask Parker."

"It's very annoying," he said, not really looking annoyed at all.

My stomach did a reluctant flip. Parker was cute. And while he wasn't totally my type, he was a lot closer than Elias was. I should focus on Parker. Not the star football player.

"Why don't you introduce Gracie to this month's resolutions? You can spend some time showing her the ropes. I need to get back to my policy boys. We have an important tournament tomorrow." Reyas released our shoulders and left us to it.

Kimmy stared at me.

I stared at Kimmy. Unlike Elias's honey caramel, her skin was Elmer's glue white with a yellowish hue. I was beginning to wonder if she'd ever been outside.

"You've never done debate before?" she asked.

I hated the way her question stirred up feelings of inadequacy. It was on the tip of my tongue to tell her that Reyas went out of her way to recruit me, but I shrugged instead. "Unless you count Debate and Ethics class."

Judging by her face, she didn't count it. "So it's safe to say you've never been to any camps either?"

"Zero camps."

She let out a long sigh. "I think I can get you caught up if you're as good as Reyas says."

I raised my eyebrow. *If?*

"Just so you know what you're getting yourself into on the front end, I'm going to win state this year. Which means I need a competent, committed partner. Last year was a complete four-two screw. It was completely bogus. We didn't even reach the out-rounds."

"Get over it, Kimmy," Parker called from the table.

"The judges were horrendous and you know it." The slight tinge in her cheeks told me she was either mad at Parker or had a crush on him. "Anyway, our first tournament is in two weeks and right now, we're building a case for this month's resolution—The Benefits of Domestic Surveillance Outweigh the Harm. Are you familiar with the NSA?"

"Vaguely."

"Then we have a lot of work to do." She fished out a thick stack of papers, bound together by a large rubber band, from the backpack hanging off her chair. "I eat, drink, and sleep research. Non-tournament Saturdays will be our biggest workdays. I hope you're prepared to spend hours at the library."

"You shouldn't underestimate the benefits of Vitamin D."

Parker laughed.

Kimmy didn't even blink. She handed over her giant stack of bound papers. It was heavier than half my textbooks. "This is called a brief. It's our starting point for every case."

"I know what a brief is," I mumbled.

"Kimmy's anal about printing the briefs out," Parker said.

"I like to highlight."

"And kill trees."

"And wear red power suits," another boy added.

She turned to face her teasers head-on. "Don't knock the red power suit. It intimidates my opponents."

"It intimidates us." Parker winked at me when he said it.

Kimmy shook her head. I wanted to ask what she'd do if I didn't stick around. I was looking for a job and hopefully helping at The Treasure Chest on Saturdays. How could I possibly offer Kimmy the kind of commitment she was looking for when I was still cautiously pursuing plan A while putting together a plan B?

"You'll want to start reading through the brief," she said. "I'll keep researching while you catch up."

Kimmy reclaimed her seat next to Parker. He slid his hand across the back of her chair. "You coming to the party tomorrow night?" he asked me.

"Maybe."

"You should make that maybe into a yes."

"Can we please get back to work?" Kimmy slapped Parker's hand away from the back of her chair. "You can flirt all you want *after* practice is over."

He smiled at me, then saluted at Kimmy.

I found a seat at one of the empty tables and flipped through the brief, reading but not comprehending the words. I was too busy eavesdropping on the fast-paced conversation up front, reluctantly stimulated by the atmosphere in the room—an odd mixture of camaraderie and antagonism. I had to push my tongue against the roof of my mouth to keep from joining in. At quarter past four, once Reyas was finished with her policy boys, she perched on the edge of her desk and asked the team to tell me more about debate.

Talk turned to weekend tournaments—debate's life blood, it would seem.

"The cafeteria between rounds is pandemonium," Parker said.

"Four hundred kids talking over one another. Wrappers and food on the floor."

"Everyone looking up last-minute information on their laptops and phones."

"Some teams bring their own printers."

"Some kids speed-read to the walls."

"We like to make allies so we can figure out our opponents' weaknesses."

"It's like *Survivor*," Kimmy said. "Only smarter."

I leaned forward in my seat, soaking up the words and painting the scene in my mind.

22

GRACIE

"Idle hands are the devil's playground." The pastor back in New Hope loved that saying. He would quote it to me and the other kids in the congregation after the service ended, always in the context of helping out around the house. At the time, I didn't know what it meant. I just knew that a playground sounded much more preferable than the stiff wooden benches at church. Now, however, I get it. Because if I'd had something to do, I wouldn't have ended up here on the dock on a Friday night, keeping an eye out for Elias.

I had no idea if my encounter with him here three weeks ago was a fluke, or if he came after every game. Part of me wanted it to be a fluke. This growing infatuation I was developing for a boy who was not only the star athlete of my new high school but also a self-proclaimed Christian needed to end. The similarities to Chris Nanning should have sent me running in the opposite direction. But another part of me wanted Elias to come. Because maybe if he came, he'd do or say something that would prove he was like every other high school boy out there and my infatuation would fizzle and die. Or maybe I just really wanted to tell someone about the debate team.

Last night, I told Ben the truth when I said I wasn't a joiner—especially not when it involved a bunch of high expectations from Reyas and a partner as intense as Kimmy. Even so, I couldn't deny the fact that I'd spent the last three hours in my room, highlighting and memorizing that brief, formulating so many arguments for and against domestic surveillance that I could probably take on Parker.

The dock creaked with footsteps.

I twisted around.

Sure enough, Elias stood beneath the lights. "No knife this time?"

Heat rushed into my cheeks. I turned back toward the water, feeling like the world's most pathetic loser. It couldn't have been any more obvious that I came here to see him. "Har, har."

He joined me at the end of the dock. "So what's up, Fisher, you stalking me now?"

"You wish."

"Hey, I told you this was my dock. You knew I'd be here." He nudged me with his shoulder. "Does this mean we're friends?"

I wrinkled my nose.

He laughed.

The amount of pleasure this gave me set off major alarms in my head.

"Did you find a job?" he asked.

"Yes, actually. The theater on the square." I'd received a call from the manager earlier in the evening. I was an official employee of Bay Breeze's one and only cinema—a vintage theater that was big enough to show three movies at a time. With its chrome accents and 1960s feel, the place reminded me a lot of the motel, except without the mold and mildew. "My first shift's tomorrow night."

"Nicely done."

A wave rolled in from the bay, lapping at the dock beneath us. I tucked my hands beneath my knees and looked down at our feet, which swung back and forth like pendulums over the water.

"I heard you tried out for the debate team."

I jerked my head up. "From who?"

"Parker. He was hanging out in the high school parking lot before the game. He said you went to practice today."

"I didn't *try* out. I was just checking it out."

"What did you think?"

I shrugged, wondering what Elias would say if I told him the actual truth—that deep down, the debate team sounded like fun, but even deeper down, I was afraid to put myself out there. Would the captain of the football team even understand something like that?

"Look, Gracie. I'm not a big fan of Parker, but Zkotsky aside, you'd be really great at it."

I gave him a skeptical look.

"I'm in debate class with you, remember? Half the time, I don't even think Reyas knows how to argue with you."

"Yeah, but class is easy. There's no pressure there." The second I stood in front of a debate tournament judge next to my partner in her red power suit, I'd probably choke. And I wasn't about to show Reyas or Kimmy or anyone else what I already knew: I was a screwup. It was my area of specialty. Elias had football. Apart from that whacked-out YouTube video, Carmen had being perfect. And I had screwing up.

"Pressure is something you get used to."

Easy for him to say.

"My mom did debate in high school," he said.

"Really?"

"It's why I signed up for the class. When she was our age, she wanted to be a civil rights attorney."

Somehow, I had a feeling that dream never came to fruition. Not many civil rights attorneys worked at places like Jake's on the side. "And . . . ?"

"She's a nurse."

"What got in her way?"

"Me."

A mosquito landed on my knuckle. I slapped it dead. I knew all about getting in the way. "How old was she when she got pregnant?"

"Twenty. Halfway through her undergrad. Her parents were paying her way. Super proud. But then she met my dad, who can turn on the charm pretty thick when he wants to."

So could Elias, but I didn't think he'd appreciate the comparison.

"Anyway, one thing led to another. She let him talk her out of her convictions. She got pregnant. And her parents cut her off. School took a backseat after that."

"They cut her off for getting pregnant?" Sounded a little archaic to me.

"Not for getting pregnant. For getting pregnant with a black man's child."

Even more archaic. "That's incredibly racist."

"Unfortunately, my dad didn't help convince them that their racism was wrong."

"And your grandparents now?"

"Largely uninvolved. I can count on my left hand the number of times I've seen them. They're polite enough. Kinda stiff. A little boring. I never liked visiting them as a kid."

Same with me. I'd met my dad's parents a few times, and while they were nice, I always felt awkward at their house. My mom's parents were a different story. She didn't let me see them. Ever. They tried to get involved in my life when I was younger and we lived in Texas, but Mom had forbidden it. "So your mom became a nurse?"

"She worked double shifts as a waitress so she could pay her way through nursing school and keep me fed, which wasn't easy, seeing how much I can eat. She's kind of heroic." His attention shifted from the bay to me. "You remind me of her sometimes."

I laughed. "How so?"

"Well, for one, you're both too smart for you own good." He gave me another nudge with his shoulder. "And you're both tough. She had to be, being a single mom. Putting herself through college. Making a life for us. She hates asking for help, but thankfully, Pastor Zeke doesn't need to be asked. And he doesn't take no for an answer."

"That Pastor Zeke sounds like a decent guy."

"He's everything my dad isn't." Moonlight reflected off the dark water and cast alluring shadows along Elias's face. It made him look ethereally beautiful, like an African Caucasian god of perfection. "Speaking of parents, how's your mom doing?"

I shrugged. "I guess she's still in rehab."

"That's good."

"If you say so."

"And *your* dad—where does he fit in the picture?"

I stuck my tongue in between the sliver of space between my first and second premolars. It was a spot in constant need of flossing. "He's a military guy. Did a couple tours in Iraq after I was born. When he finally came home, he and my mom tried to make it work, but it was a no-go. They divorced and he's remarried with a nice house, two kids, and a dog. I'm welcome there, but I don't really fit in."

"I'm sorry."

A mourning dove crooned into the night—a sad, haunting sound.

It wasn't like my dad ever beat me or my mom or anything, but they had fought. A lot. Mostly about me. I shrugged, like none of it mattered, and attempted to tuck my bangs behind my ear. They fell back into my face, but not before our gazes connected.

"You have really beautiful eyes."

His words were like a warm egg cracked over my head. The sensation trickling over me was both unsettling and distracting.

"You shouldn't hide them."

23

CARMEN

When a woman has had as many miscarriages as I have, with no children to help her forget, there are too many depressing anniversaries in a year. Not just the day of the actual loss, but due dates too. I never set out to remember them. In fact, I set out to actively forget them. A few I was able to let pass without notice, but not this one. This one stuck out more than all the rest, an inevitable turning point in our journey.

I picked up my barely touched plate and Ben's mostly empty one, both messy with remnants of fish taco, and brought them into the kitchen. Thanks to Gracie's new job at the theater, it was just Ben and me. Normally, Gracie's presence added more tension to dinner. Tonight, her absence screamed. Of all the evenings she had to be gone, why this one—on the anniversary of my third miscarriage? It might seem odd that my third was the one I remembered most vividly. You would think it would be my first. But not so. With the first and the second, I still had hope. My trust in God was shaken but not shattered. Besides, the percentage of women who had three consecutive miscarriages, my doctor had said, was very small. So when I became a part of that very small percentage, something more than my baby died. By the time I had my fourth, and then my fifth and sixth, the shock and the pain had turned dull.

I used a fork to scrape the remnants of food off the plates and fed them to our garbage disposal. I wanted nothing more than to hurry up with the cleaning so I could climb between the covers of my bed and leave this day behind. I wasn't even sure Ben remembered. He hadn't brought it up. I flipped off the disposal, plugged the drain, and filled the basin of the sink with hot, sudsy water. Leaning my hips against the counter, I immersed my hands until my palms lay flat against the steel bottom.

I'm drowning.

Just like in my dream. I was drowning, and nobody even noticed. I kept waiting for God to throw me a life ring. So far He seemed content to watch me sink.

Ben walked into the kitchen behind me. I expected him to grab a drink from the fridge. Relax in the living room while watching ESPN or disappear into the garage to listen to music and throw some darts. Instead, he stayed, tapping his thumb mindlessly against the counter, staring at some spot on the ground with a furrow in his brow. When his eyes lifted and met mine, I turned back to the sink.

"How're things going at the motel?" he asked.

"Fine." It was more than fine, actually. Even with Gracie's sardonic commentary, the motel was the only place I felt like me anymore. I loved the sense of accomplishment and simplicity the manual labor brought. There, if I scrubbed a wall hard enough, it would start to look new. Nothing complicated or uncertain about it. I was mourning the loss of my time there come Monday, but what choice did I have? Quit work? I had a good job. And renovating the motel didn't pay the bills. I rinsed off plate one and set it on the rack.

"Brandon tells me you've been going to CrossFit with Natalie."

"A few times." During my forced leave of absence, my presence at Vitality Gym had been scattered at best. I had yet to drink the CrossFit Kool-Aid. My poor muscles refused to embrace something that caused so much pain. But Natalie was convinced I needed the endorphins, so she pestered me to come on a daily basis. Maybe she noticed I was sinking. Maybe CrossFit was her life ring.

"Are you liking it?" he asked.

"I no longer want to murder her while I'm doing it."

"Well, you look good." He smiled a faint smile, and in the upturned corners of his mouth, I saw a spark of the man I fell in love with. The man who used to make my heart do funny things. The man whose touch once set my skin on fire. "You always look good."

His compliment hung in the air between us, an electric thing I didn't want to touch. I set plate two beside plate one and began working on the silverware. He remained for a couple seconds longer, as if waiting for me to go next. Ask him about his day, perhaps. But I had no energy for pottery or football or teenagers. Sadly, I realized, I didn't have any energy for him. He let out a long sigh and exited the kitchen, leaving me alone with this chronic ache and a sad sliver of relief.

Then he returned with our glasses in hand. He brought them to the sink and dried the plates with a towel. "Did Gracie tell you she might join the debate team?"

I stopped mid fork scrub. "The debate team?"

He placed the plates into the cupboard. "I take that as a no?"

"She's going to join the debate team?" And she told Ben about it, but not me?

"The debate coach—Reyas?—she thinks Gracie's a natural. I guess she checked things out yesterday after school."

"So this Reyas talked to you about Gracie?"

"Yeah."

"And you didn't think I'd want to know?"

"You're upset because I didn't tell you about a passing comment some teacher made in the teacher's lounge?"

I set the silverware onto the rack. "I'm upset because I have no idea how Gracie's doing."

Ben chuckled, which meant he didn't hear the hurt in my voice. It had been three and a half weeks since Gracie arrived, and my sister was every bit as caustic toward me as she'd been when I found her living as a homeless person. In fact, her attitude toward me today while we worked on the motel had been the worst, and I had no idea what I did to deserve it.

"You spend all that time together at The Chest."

"Gracie isn't exactly a chatterbox." The harder I tried to engage in a conversation, the more terse her responses became. True phenomenon. If I made a point to ignore her while we worked, she ended up talking more. It was ridiculous, this game I was forced to play.

"She's just being a teenager. You can't take it personally." Ben finished drying the silverware, put it in the drawer, then came behind me and wrapped his arms around my waist. "Trust me, I work with them all day."

My posture stiffened.

He must not have noticed, because he pressed his lips against the sensitive spot behind my ear.

And all of a sudden, it made sense. Ben's small talk. His compliments. Helping with after-dinner cleanup. This wasn't about me or the date on the calendar; this was about him and his needs. His lips moved to my opposite ear.

I pulled away. "Ben."

"What?" he whispered.

"Gracie's going to be home soon."

"Gracie's working at the theater." He turned me around and tucked a strand of hair behind my ear. "I doubt she'll be home soon."

I leaned away. "Ben, seriously."

"Carmen, it's been a while."

I wanted to scream. At the top of my lungs, scream. I wanted to pick up a dish and chuck it against the wall. Wake him up and make him see me. Couldn't he understand that this was the last thing I felt like doing? On today of all days, did he really think sex was anywhere on my radar? "I have a headache."

My words might as well have been a heavy blanket over a fire. All traces of desire snuffed out from his eyes, replaced instead by a hardness I hated. He turned around. Opened the cupboard above the stove. Pulled out a bottle of ibuprofen and set it on the counter with a snap. Then he headed out into the garage, leaving me to stew in my guilt and resentment.

24

GRACIE

A zit-faced girl with a mouth full of braces smiled at me as I handed her change and a large tub of popcorn. She hurried into theater two where a cheesy romantic comedy played and left behind an empty lobby. Gus, a mop-haired kid two years older than I and also my trainer for the night, bobbed his head up and down like a human-sized bobblehead, making the ridiculous white sailor hat we were forced to wear as part of our work uniform go crooked on his head. "Great job. Great job. Do you have any questions so far?"

"Scoop popcorn into tub. Hand to customer. I think I got it."

"Got it. Good. Good."

I read a book once where the character had this condition called echolalia. It was a legit thing where he compulsively echoed the last word or two of whatever another person said. I was beginning to think Gus had a case of echolalia.

"Whenever there's a lull, I make sure to sweep up the floor, wipe off the counters, and restock the candy."

I grabbed a broom and swept the fallen popcorn into a pile, all under the watchful eye of bobbleheaded Gus. I gathered the pile of popcorn and debris into the dustpan, dumped it into the garbage, and wiped off the counter. As I was finishing restocking the candy in the display case, the same zit-faced girl from earlier came back to the counter, sans her popcorn tub. "Excuse me, but there are some girls in the front of the theater who keep throwing Skittles at the screen."

Gus bobbed his head, then turned to me. "I need to deal with this. Do you think you can manage manning the counter alone for a little while?"

"I think I can manage."

He gave me the thumbs up, marched ahead of the girl past the first set of double doors, then disappeared into the second set of double doors to go deal with the Skittle tossers. Theaters one and two played whatever was most popular at the box office. Right now, it was the cheesy rom-com and some high-action thriller that was all gunshots and screaming whenever somebody pushed open the door. According to Gus, those were the theaters that brought in the majority of customers.

The third and smallest theater—the reason I could tolerate the ridiculous hat—played reruns of the classics. Alfred Hitchcock films, black-and-white film noir, anything with Cary Grant, and a smattering of my favorite—timeless eighties movies. In exchange for one five-dollar bill, a person could get a small tub of popcorn, a small drink, and a seat in theater three. I thought that was a mighty fine deal.

I was stuffing a few more Sno-Caps inside the candy display case when one of the four front doors opened and my pulse hiccuped. Because it was Elias who walked inside. Two people shadowed him—a short, skinny boy with a sizable Afro and a gait like a penguin, thanks to the pants that kept sliding down his butt. And a girl. I didn't recognize either.

Elias came to the counter with a smile on his face. "Cute hat."

I snatched it off my head. "What are you doing here?"

"Came to see a movie. What else?"

I narrowed my eyes at him. He knew I was working tonight. I told him yesterday on the dock, when he told me I had beautiful eyes. He'd said nothing then about plans to see a movie.

"Gracie, meet Chanelle. Chanelle, meet my friend Gracie."

Chanelle, with no qualifier, had skin the color of melted chocolate and not a single blemish to be found, big light-brown eyes, and short, kinky curls held back from her face by a hot-pink headband. She looked like she should be on the cover of *Teen* magazine. And she was with Elias. She stuck her hands in the front pockets of a zip-up hoodie which was the same color as her headband. The word *Cutie* was written across the front in sparkly rhinestone letters. "Nice to finally meet you, Gracie."

Finally?

Elias hooked his muscular arm around the boy's scrawny neck. "And this is Chanelle's little brother, Sam."

Sam, who looked to be somewhere in the junior high range, squirmed out of Elias's headlock and patted his Afro. "Name's Samson. And I ain't little."

"You are when you stand next to Elias," Chanelle said.

My stomach twisted at the sound of that name on her lips. She called him Elias. I had no idea why it bothered me. I looked between them, trying to figure out what they were. I mean, if they were boyfriend and girlfriend, why the kid brother? But if they were just friends, then why didn't Elias put a qualifier in front of her name, like he had with mine?

"Chanelle and Samson live across the bay in Pensacola. Her family's been going to The Cross longer than I have."

So they went to church together.

Chanelle tipped her chin at me. "You should come to youth group sometime on a Wednesday night."

"Youth group isn't really my thing."

"Why not?"

My mind wandered to Chris Nanning and his buddies going to Fellowship of Christian Athletes during the week, then partying hard on the weekends. It was all a little too hypocritical for my taste. "I don't really like the people who go."

Chanelle's eyes widened a little.

Elias set his elbows on the counter and smiled. His dimples were extra deep tonight. "I told you she was honest."

My stomach twisted. *He told her?* So what, the two were talking about me?

"I need to take a leak." Samson held up his pants and waddled off to the rest room.

"Me too," Chanelle said. "But I prefer to call it 'using the rest room.' I'll take a popcorn and a lemonade." I didn't miss the way Chanelle's hand lingered on Elias's arm before she walked away.

Elias pulled three tickets from his wallet and slid them across the counter. They were for the third theater, which meant he had good taste. "Three popcorns, one lemonade, and two Dr Peppers."

I grabbed three of the small tubs and three small cups from their respective stacks next to the popcorn machine and attempted indifference. Elias showing up at the theater with a beautiful girl should not bother me. "Is this your first time seeing *Little Shop of Horrors?*"

"Yep."

"Get ready for a classic."

"It's good?"

"A giant singing plant that eats people?" I filled the tubs with popcorn. "What's not to like?"

He chuckled. "So how's the first day on the job?"

"Besides Gus, it's not too bad." I set the three popcorns on the counter, then went to work filling each cup with ice.

"Who's Gus?"

"My trainer for the evening. He's currently dealing with a Skittles emergency in theater two."

"Sounds serious."

"We don't take Skittles emergencies lightly here." I pushed the first cup beneath a fountain of lemonade.

"When do you get off?"

"After your movie's over. It's the last show for the night."

"Are you going to Parker's party afterward?"

"I don't know. Maybe." I waited to see if he was going to argue with me some more. Give me another warning. I fitted a lid over the lemonade and set the second cup beneath the Dr Pepper nozzle.

"I'm gonna ask you a question, even though I'm pretty sure I already know your answer."

This had my attention. "Okay."

"What's your opinion on high school dances?"

I looked at him over my shoulder. "You mean like homecoming?"

"Yes, like homecoming."

I turned my attention back to the soda fountain, a sickening feeling expanding in my gut. Was Elias really asking me to a dance when his date for the night was inside the ladies' room? Maybe he was more like Chris Nanning than I thought. I put lids over the Dr Pepper drinks and brought them to the counter. "Are you asking me to go?"

"Yes."

"With you?"

"Yes, with me." More dimples. "And Chanelle and a bunch of other kids too. A group of us from youth group all go together."

"Oh." Out of the corner of my eye, Samson pounded away on an old-school Pac-Man arcade game sitting outside theater one. His big sister exited the rest room and headed toward us. Still no sign of Gus. "Chanelle doesn't go to Bay Breeze."

"No, but neither do a lot of the kids at youth group. We've been going to each other's dances since freshman year. It's a fun time."

An image of me in one of those gaudy prom dresses, standing off in a corner while Elias and Chanelle slow danced to some equally gaudy boy band music—his large hands on her small waist, gazing into one another's eyes—made me nauseous. Not exactly my idea of a fun time.

"Is she going to come?" Chanelle asked.

I blinked away the image. Eli's maybe-date had returned, and apparently she already knew he was going to invite me.

"I'm not really a dance person," I said.

He smiled. "Just what kind of person are you, Gracie Fisher?"

Gus exited theater two looking harassed.

I shoved the hat back on my head.

Eli gave the counter a tap, like he didn't really care about the answer, then palmed two of the popcorns in one hand, two of the drinks in the other, and walked with Chanelle toward theater three, stopping at the Pac-Man game to hand Samson his movie treats. With one of his arms now free, he set his hand on the small of Chanelle's back and ushered her inside to see *Little Shop of Horrors*, leaving me with bobbleheaded Gus and a heart full of disappointment.

CARMEN

My eyes fluttered open. I blinked into the dark, disoriented, trying to figure out why I was awake. The red numbers on my bedside clock read 10:10. I'd only been sleeping half an hour, yet it felt like an entire night. I pushed myself up to sitting. Outside our bedroom window, light shone from the garage. Downstairs, there was rustling, then the creaking of steps. Gracie said her shift ended at ten. She must be home.

The thin strip of space between the carpet and the bottom of my bedroom door turned yellow. I leaned against the headboard, listening as a door closed, the toilet flushed, water ran through pipes, resolve rising up inside me. According to Natalie, the teenage years were proving to be way more challenging than the middle-of-the-night-feedings, spitup-everywhere years. Yet here I was, with a teenager on my hands. I had no idea why Gracie had been extra prickly at The Treasure Chest today. I just knew we were supposed to be progressing in our relationship, not regressing. But that was what today had felt like. One giant step back. Well, no more. I was determined to prove to myself and whomever else that I could do this.

I flung the covers off my legs, squinting as I opened the door, stepped out into the brightly lit hallway, and knocked on Gracie's open door.

She turned around with her backpack in hand and saw me standing in the doorway dressed in a tank top and matching pajama bottoms. The vent in the hallway breathed cool air onto my shoulders. Goose bumps marched up my arms. I drew a mental picture of my sister standing behind steel-reinforced walls and tried to figure out the best way to breach them.

"How was your first day of work?" I asked.

"Fine."

I scanned her room. A four-poster bed with a rumpled white comforter. Matching curtains. Nightstand, dresser, linen chest. Mostly bare walls except for a canvas with a verse from Revelation. Nothing about the space looked like Gracie at all. I tucked a strand of curly hair behind my ear. "You know, we can redecorate this room if you want. We could even paint the walls. It might be fun."

She lifted her shoulder, annoyance radiating from her pores and saturating the air.

The smart part of my brain knew that the easy solution would be returning to bed. The masochistic part of my brain had me standing my ground—halfway in the hall, halfway in Gracie's room. I was going to break through her animosity. "I hear you went out for debate."

She unzipped her backpack and dug for something in her bag. "I didn't *go out* for debate. Reyas wanted me to check it out, so I did."

"Did you like it?" Honestly, I couldn't see Gracie liking debate any more than I could see Ben coaching debate, but I wasn't about to say any of that out loud.

I stepped toward her, as if my closeness would force her to answer. The subtle way she shifted so that her back remained toward me did not go unnoticed. *"You can't take it personally."* Ben's words mocked me, because how could I not take it personally when she didn't act this way toward him? "Are you going to join the team?"

"Can't." She pulled out a notebook. "I have a job."

"Debate's more important than a high school job." The words sounded like I borrowed them straight from my father. Had I really forgotten what it was like to be a teenager? I shook my head and tried again. "Anyway, you have a job. I'm paying you to help me at The Treasure Chest. You're not going to ditch me, are you?"

Gracie huffed. "You're the one doing the ditching."

"Me?"

"I heard you talking to Ben. Starting on Monday, you're going to work at The Treasure Chest while I'm in school. Unless you're cool with me dropping out, I don't see how that will make me very much money."

"Gracie, we can still work at the motel together." Granted, it would be a little trickier. Gracie and I had been getting home after seven each weeknight. Now that I would be resuming my one o'clock wake-up calls, I couldn't afford to do that. Not without bags under my eyes on the camera. I needed to be in bed by seven, which meant dinner had to be at six, which meant I'd have to be home by five thirty, which meant I'd have to leave no later than five. Gracie didn't get home from school until three thirty, and it took a good half hour to get to The Treasure Chest. Weekday evenings were definitely out.

"When?" she asked.

"We have the weekends."

"Debate has tournaments every weekend."

"I'm sure we can figure something out." I gave her a weak smile. "Debate would look great on your college applications."

She looked at me like I didn't get it, like I was the most delusional person on the face of the planet. I probably was. Gracie had never given any indication that she was interested in college. She tossed her backpack on the bed and walked past me, out into the hallway.

"Are you going somewhere this late?" I called after her.

"Ten fifteen isn't late." She hurried down the stairs and walked out the front door.

25

GRACIE

Parker lived in a colonial mansion at the end of a cul-de-sac. Spotlights shone onto the home and cars leaked out of the driveway onto the street. It was nothing like the parties I went to in Apalachicola. Those were always in the basements of low-income houses or in the living rooms of seedy apartment complexes.

I'm not sure why I bothered knocking on the front door. The bass thumped so loudly it rattled the windows. When nobody answered, I pushed the door open and stepped inside to the house party to end all house parties. It seemed like the entire student body of Bay Breeze had squished themselves inside, either mingling or dancing or flirting, red plastic cups in hand. Surprisingly, the music wasn't half bad—some grunge band with a decent vocalist. Nobody noticed me standing in the doorway, and for a second I considered leaving. I sure didn't belong. But then I remembered Eli's hand on Chanelle's waist and I pushed my way through the crowd in search of Parker.

Once I pushed through the mosh pit of bodies in the great room, I found myself in a fancy kitchen—all stone flooring and marble countertops and stainless steel appliances.

"What's up, Gracie!"

I turned toward the sound of my name.

A pink-faced Parker leaned against the kitchen island with a couple girls by his side, his red cup raised in the air. "You looking for the beer?"

"Not really a fan of beer." Even though I had to yell over the music, I didn't think Parker heard much besides beer.

"Come on." He waved his hand sloppily in the air. "Follow me."

And so I did. We made our way through the kitchen, into a small living room, and through a sliding-glass door that led out to a giant double-story deck, where the music wasn't nearly as loud and two kegs sat on the edge of a patio table. An impressively long line of teenagers wound down the steps, onto the lower level of the deck, where there was a hot tub and, beside that in the manicured yard, a swimming pool. Both were filled with kids my age. Not too far from the kegs, a couple boys passed around a joint. Parker hooked his arm around the shorter kid and snagged it from his hand.

"Hey!" the kid said. If his red, half-opened eyes had anything to say about it, he'd had plenty of puffs already.

"Perks of being the host." Parker smiled a straight white smile with zero trace of dimple, took a deep inhale until the end of the joint burned orange, then held it out to me.

I hesitated.

"You came here to have some fun, right?" Parker held the joint higher.

I stared at the offering. It wasn't like I hadn't done it before. And if I wanted to forget about Dimple Face and his beautiful girlfriend (or whatever she was), this was the perfect opportunity. I took Parker's offering once, then again, and again. Until one joint became two and my eyelids grew heavy, my mouth dry. Time became jumbled and somehow I had a red cup in hand and the other two boys were no longer around.

I took a long drink, the foam tickling my upper lip.

"Did you bring your swimsuit?"

"Never."

Parker found this hilarious for some reason, and the more he laughed, the more I laughed. Turned out, I kind of liked him. He was at least better than football-playing, churchgoing, Chanelle-loving Eli Banks.

"Your eyes are beautiful."

Ugh. How had I actually fallen for such a line? I drained the rest of my cup. Parker filled it up and found us a spot near an unoccupied piece of banister. "So are you gonna join the debate team or what?"

I could feel the alcohol working its way through my veins, turning my teeth numb. "You know, I'm getting really sick of that question."

"Okay then, new question."

I took another drink.

"How does it feel being Banks's new project?"

"What do you mean?"

"He has this thing about the outcasts. Likes to take them under his wing. Turn them into upstanding Christian citizens."

The warmth in my belly turned cold.

"Me, on the other hand? I happen to believe in accepting people as they are. And I also happen to believe that you, in particular, are not interested in being an upstanding citizen."

"You would be correct." I drank my second cup.

Parker refilled it. Then again and again. As I drank, he talked. About what, I couldn't say, except that everything he said was funny. Parker Zkotsky amused me. At some point—I wasn't sure when or how—we were no longer leaning against the banister. We were sharing a chaise lounge and Parker wasn't talking anymore. His lips were on my neck and his body was on top of mine and I couldn't think straight enough to tell him to get off. The entire world spun. But it didn't really matter because somebody lifted him off for me. Whoosh, he was gone. Like he weighed the same as a gnat.

I squinted up at my rescuer. Of all the faces in the world, Elias's swam above me, and all I could do was put my hands on my stomach and laugh.

"C'mon." He took my arm and pulled me up into sitting. "I'm taking you home."

"Hey, you're not her dad," Parker said.

Elias shoved him. He stumbled and fell. A line of staring teenagers blurred in and out of focus as Elias pulled my arm around his neck and lifted me to standing. "I can't go home. My home's in Apalachicola."

He half led, half carried me through a house that was crazy and loud, out into the front yard, down the driveway, and into his car.

"Apalachicola." I kept saying the name. It felt funny on my lips.

He buckled my seat belt, climbed behind the wheel, and slammed his door shut.

"You better tell me if you're going to be sick."

I cupped my hand over my mouth. "Don't talk about it and I won't be."

Shaking his head, Elias pulled away from the curb. "And you accused me of being cliché."

CARMEN

"It's one o'clock in the morning."

Ben sat on the couch, his elbows on his knees, hair sticking up from his head, his eyelids drooping with sleep. My frantic pacing was probably the only thing keeping them from shutting altogether.

Me? I was well past the point of tired. In fact, my emotions had run the gamut and were currently stuck on a circuit that alternated between seething mad and worried sick—one second convinced Gracie was doing this out of spite, the next, positive she had been kidnapped by a psychopath or killed by a reckless driver. I tried her cell phone again but got shuffled to voice mail. "Why isn't she answering? And what are we supposed to do if she decides not to come home? At what point do we call the police?"

"Carmen, I'm sure she'll come home."

"But what if she doesn't?"

"Maybe we should go to bed. Get some sleep. She'll probably be back in the morning."

I was about to tell him there was no way I could sleep right now. Every single decibel of noise, every single reflection of light outside the window would have my eyes popping open. But then the doorbell rang and my frantic pacing stopped. Gracie wouldn't ring the doorbell. We'd given her a key. This thought had me turning panicked eyes on Ben, who slowly and calmly stood from the couch and opened the door. I braced myself for the police—whether bearing bad news or returning a juvenile delinquent, I wasn't sure. Instead, it was Eli Banks, the receiver of Ben's football team. He had his hand wrapped around Gracie's waist, and considering the way her head lolled to the side, I doubted she'd remain standing if he let go.

Every single ounce of worry vanished into smoke. All that remained was anger—red-hot, incredulous anger.

"Sorry about this, Coach."

Something about Eli's greeting made Gracie laugh. "Coach," she said, pushing away from him and stumbling into the foyer. She reeked of alcohol.

"Does your mom know where you are?" Ben asked.

"Yes sir. I wasn't at the party, but I knew Gracie was going. I wanted to check on her. And this"—he motioned his hand toward a slouched-over Gracie on the couch, who twirled a string of dark hair around and around her finger— "is what I found."

"Why don't you go be Chanelle's hero, *Eli*?" She half sneered, half slurred his name. "I don't need you to be mine."

Eli and Ben glanced at her, then back at each other.

"Thanks for bringing her home," Ben said.

"No problem. I'm sorry it's so late." He gave us both an apologetic shrug, then turned around and left.

"Hey, Eli?" Ben called.

He stopped halfway down the drive.

"You're a good kid, you know that?"

"You've said it before, sir." And with one final nod, he climbed into his car and reversed out of the driveway.

I rounded on Gracie, but she had ceased twirling her hair and was already snoring away. I was fully prepared to rattle her awake and give her a serious talking-to, but Ben took my elbow and put his finger to his lips.

"You can't think I'm letting her get away with this," I hissed.

He locked the front door and draped a blanket over Gracie. I wanted to tell him not to bother. After the worry this girl put me through tonight, I'd prefer to let her shiver. Ben flipped off the lights and gently led me up the stairs, into our bedroom. "We'll talk to her in the morning," he said. "Right now she needs to sleep it off."

"I can't believe her. She went out and got wasted? Ben—alcohol?" Gracie was a lot of things, but I never thought stupid was one of them. Surely she knew alcoholism ran in families.

Ben sat on the edge of our bed and pulled off his shirt. "Judging by the smell, I'd say it wasn't just alcohol."

"She can't do this. She can't live here and do whatever she wants." I shook my head, my frustration and helplessness swelling to the size of a hot-air balloon. "But the second I try to lay down the law, she'll run away. And there's nothing I can do about it. She's almost eighteen. She'll take off and I'll have failed at this entire thing."

"What *thing*?"

"Gracie being here. Under my care."

"If your sister's going to take off, that's not on your shoulders."

"Yes, it is."

"Carmen, what are you trying to prove with her?"

His question popped all the fight inside of me. I sank onto my side of the bed. What was I trying to prove? Why did this feel so absolutely important and so positively personal? I sank onto my side of the bed and shook my head. "I don't know. That I can be a mom?"

His expression softened.

I looked away from his sympathy. I didn't want it.

"I think the best thing we can do right now is get some sleep." He turned back the covers. "Let me try talking to her in the morning."

I let out a long breath and lay back against my pillow. I had prayed for a child of my own—a sweet, innocent baby who would giggle when I smiled and ask for my kisses. Instead, I got Gracie—a hostile, rebellious teenager who hated my guts.

26

GRACIE

My head felt like someone had burrowed inside my brain and was using a crowbar inside my skull in an attempt to break free. I clasped my forehead and creaked open one eye. A piercing light shone in through the windows and had me closing my one eye back up.

I rolled over like an old lady and lifted my head off the couch's armrest. If my neck muscles could talk, they would not have had happy words to say. I squinted into the brightness, the details of last night returning in fits and spurts. My shift at the theater. Eli and Chanelle. Going to the party. Talking to Parker and then . . .

I clamped my hand over my mouth.

Elias saw me and Parker making out. He dragged me to his car and he called me a cliché and now, I was here. On this couch in Carmen and Ben's living room, only I had no recollection of getting here. Did Eli have to carry me inside? Did I throw up in his car? If the rancid taste in my mouth was any indication, the outlook wasn't good. I pushed myself to sitting with a groan. The motion made the person inside my skull attempting a jailbreak more aggressive with the crowbar. I waited for the room to stop spinning and my stomach to stop rolling, then forced myself to stand.

I shuffled to the stairs, the boots on my feet two heavy anchors. I wanted them off, but there was no way I could manage it. I had to keep moving. That was the key. Clinging to the banister, I took one step at a time, desperate to reach my room before I ran into Carmen or Ben. If only my room didn't feel five hundred miles away.

God help me.

The intelligent part of my brain realized the absurdity of the prayer. Praying to God in the midst of a massive hangover, asking Him to get me to my room so I wouldn't have to face the consequences of coming home drunk and stoned the night before? Somehow, I didn't think God would approve.

Just as I crested the staircase landing, a freshly showered Carmen stepped out of the hallway bathroom. She stopped. I stopped. And a stare-off ensued. I braced myself for the lecture to end all lectures. Instead, her lips tightened into a thin line and, without saying a word, she disappeared into her bedroom with a towel in hand.

Huh. So maybe prayer worked after all.

I convinced my feet to get moving again, closed myself in my room, and collapsed onto the bed. A moment later, Ben and Carmen murmured and moved about in the hallway, getting ready for church, probably. They went every Sunday morning.

The front door opened and closed right before I fell into oblivion.

In my dream, a woodpecker pounded against my temple. *Tap-tap-tap, tap-tap-tap.* I batted it away, but it didn't budge. *Tap-tap-tap.* I tried again, but my hand hit nothing but air. I opened my eyes and the woodpecker was gone, but not the tapping and not the pain the tapping left behind. I pulled the pillow over my head. Ben and Carmen must be back from church, and she must be ready for her lecture now.

Tap-tap-tap.

"Go away!" I moaned the words into my pillow.

There was a pause. And then, "I come bearing gifts."

The voice belonged to Ben. I set my booted feet onto the floor and found the door.

He wasn't lying. He did have gifts—a bottled water and two ibuprofen, to be exact.

"My hero." The words came out like a croak. While Ben watched, I twisted the cap open, popped the pills in my mouth, and chased them down with gulps so greedy they sucked in the sides of the plastic water bottle.

"If you're here to tell me that I made a fool out of myself last night, don't bother." I knew that perfectly well all on my own. Seriously. Since when did I drink? Or make out with spoiled rich kids? The thought of me and Parker on the chaise lounge made the nausea in my stomach a hundred times worse. The thought of Eli seeing me and Parker had that nausea rising up in my throat.

"I know you've basically been on your own for the past seventeen years." Ben crossed his arms. "And I know you think you don't need a mom or a dad."

"Yep. I have those already." I finished off the water. I could drink four more and still be thirsty. "Didn't work out so well."

"I know you think you can take care of yourself."

"I can."

He dipped his chin and gave me a knowing look. A "yeah, you really took good care of yourself last night" kind of look. It had me taking a sudden interest in the carpet. He was right, of course, but I wasn't going to admit that out loud. "Here's the thing. Carmen and I aren't your parents. But you are staying in our house, and I think it's pretty reasonable to expect a little bit of respect and courtesy."

I rubbed my knuckles beneath my eyes. They came away smudged with black. I must have looked ravishing. "I can be courteous."

"To Carmen especially."

"Why *especially*?"

"Because she's my wife, for starters."

"She doesn't act like much of one."

"You should give her a break." His words cut with a sharpness I'd never heard before. It had me looking up from the carpet, at the hard set of his jaw and the fierce protectiveness glinting in his eyes. "You don't know what she's been through."

What she's been through?

I looked around the room, immaculately clean like the rest of Carmen's house, and the rest of Carmen's life. From my vantage point, she hadn't been through much. But I guess we all had our secrets.

"She's trying, Gracie. And despite what you think, she cares about you."

"She didn't care about me when I was a kid."

Ben leaned against the dresser, his arms still crossed. "You want my two cents?"

"Two cents doesn't buy much these days."

"You shouldn't let something that happened in the past stop you from having something that could be great in the present."

I twisted my lips to the side, waiting for him to finish.

But he didn't say anything more. Ben pushed off the dresser and left me alone with his two-penny thoughts. I lay back in bed and pulled the pillow over my face. Tomorrow I had to go to school, where I would face Parker and everybody who saw us at the party and worst of all, Elias. The thought made my stomach churn.

GRACIE

Time moved on and so did the gossip surrounding Parker's house party. It was a hot topic at school for a good week. Thankfully, most high school students had the attention span of a flea. The student body at Bay Breeze was no different. Not so fortunately, my attention span was decidedly more mature. No matter how hard I tried scrubbing that night from my memory, the details remained.

Needless to say, I didn't join the debate team. I avoided Elias like he had the bubonic plague. The homecoming dance came and went, and my new life in Bay Breeze fell into a predictable pattern. School, theater, sleep—five times over. Saturdays at The Treasure Chest. Sundays at the theater. Six-thirty phone calls from Mom in the evenings. Lather, rinse, repeat until October turned into November and I'd saved up enough money to purchase my very first car, a rust-eaten maroon Mitsubishi Mirage. Some dude in Pensacola listed it online for a thousand dollars. This morning I called him and talked him down to five hundred, so long as I agreed to pay in cash. I was going to take the bus across the bridge into Pensacola at four o'clock to pick it up.

Four o'clock couldn't come quickly enough.

My own set of wheels meant I could hit the road without hitchhiking. My own set of wheels meant I could drive out to The Treasure Chest without Carmen. It opened up an entire world of possibility. In my excitement, I forgot to eat breakfast and my stomach was staging a revolt. It snarled through the entirety of third and fourth period. When fourth period finally ended, I made a beeline to my locker, only to discover that breakfast wasn't the only thing I forgot. I left my wallet on the nightstand in my bedroom.

I slammed my locker shut and turned toward one of the stairwells, away from the cafeteria. I wasn't too proud to ask Ben to spot me some lunch money. Hopefully, he'd be in his classroom, not in the teachers' lounge.

I walked down the stairs and stepped out into the hallway. To my left, beyond floor-to-ceiling windows, students played water polo in the swimming pool. The swimming unit in my sixth-period gym class had started on Monday. Thankfully, it was only a week long. Today was the last day. As I approached, the sound of laughter came from Ben's classroom. And not just any laughing either, but a familiar nasal laugh that I basically couldn't stand.

I heard it way too much in fifth-period trigonometry.

When I reached Ben's door, I found him standing at a tall table off to the side where he broke apart a hunk of clay, slammed one half onto the surface, followed by the other, then kneaded the two hunks back together again. He wasn't alone. My least favorite teacher sat on a metal stool beside him, chattering in his ear.

Her name was Miss Henson. No relation to the creator of the Muppets, whose movie *The Muppets Take Manhattan* played in theater three all last week. I'd seen her flirting with Ben before, mostly in the hallways, more often now that the regular football season had given way to playoffs and nobody would shut up about Coach Hart and the team. *Would he or wouldn't he bring home another state title for the Sting Rays?* All the attention gave Henson more opportunity to gush and giggle and touch him. He was always polite. And she was always pathetic.

Miss Henson tilted her head back and laughed, and as she came forward in her laughter, she not only showed off her cleavage, she set her hand on Ben's forearm and left it there for a few seconds longer than appropriate.

I cleared my throat. Loudly.

Miss Henson hopped up from the stool like the metal had turned into a stove burner. Her smile melted away, leaving behind the face of a guilty person, as if I'd caught her doing a striptease instead of sitting on a stool fully clothed. "Hi, Gracie," she said.

Ben looked up from his clay and spotted me in the doorway. "Hey. Come on in."

"I don't want to interrupt anything."

My trig teacher's face turned the color of her pretty pink lipstick.

Ben didn't seem to pick up on my innuendo. "I appreciate the update, Jill."

She replied with an awkward nod-smile combo, ran her fingers through her hair, then walked out of the room. Ben resumed breaking apart his clay, slamming the two parts onto the table, then kneading them together with this faraway look in his eye.

"What are you doing?" I asked, snagging one of the stools.

"It's called wedging." He repeated the break-slam-knead process. "Before you start a project, you always have to condition the clay. Right now, it has a lot of air bubbles." Break-slam-knead. Break-slam-knead. "If I don't work them out, whatever I make on the pottery wheel will blow up in the kiln."

"Poor clay." It looked like a violent, painful kind of process.

"It's for its own good." As soon as he said it, he got that faraway look again. The man was surprisingly subdued, considering all the hype surrounding tonight's game. If the team won, their next stop was Orlando for the state championship in the beginning of December, and the Sting Rays were playing the third-ranked team in the state—the Franklin Seahawks—to get there.

"So what was Miss Henson doing in here?" I asked.

Ben brought his hunk of clay to the pottery wheel. "Giving me her weekly report."

"For what?"

"How my players are doing in math."

"You're not that naive, are you?" I'd been around for a while now. He was a favorite at Bay Breeze, not just with his players, but with the girls too—pupils and teachers alike.

He ignored the question and pumped a lever on the wheel with his foot that made it spin, dipped his hands into a bucket of water, and began shaping the hunk of clay. Clearly the man didn't want to discuss the state of his female-flirting discernment.

Around me, the room was mostly dusty gray, but there were some shelves next to a kiln that housed a collection of student projects—all glazed in shiny earthen blues and greens and dark reds. In no time at all, Ben's creation on the wheel was a perfectly symmetrical vase with a teardrop-shaped body, long neck, and a lip that flared wide.

"That's impressive."

"I do teach this stuff, you know," he said with a wry smile.

"Why don't you ever use that pottery wheel downstairs in the basement?" I spotted it the first time I did a load of laundry. An abandoned pottery wheel shoved off to the side, collecting dust.

He let the wheel come to a stop. "I don't have much time anymore. Not with a state title to uphold."

My stomach let loose an embarrassingly loud growl.

Ben raised one of his eyebrows. "You better feed that thing."

"I forgot my wallet at home."

"Ah. So that's why you're here."

"Any chance I could borrow five bucks? I promise I'll pay you back as soon as I have my wallet on me. I've got a five-dollar bill waiting for you in there."

Ben washed the wet clay from his hands in the sink, dried them on the front of his apron, and slipped his wallet from the back pocket of his jeans. He removed a crisp five-dollar bill and held it out to me.

When I grabbed it, his grip tightened so I couldn't take it.

"Gracie?"

"What?"

"It's just five bucks."

"Hey, five bucks will get you a movie in theater three, along with popcorn and a drink."

Ben released the bill. "I don't think I'll have time for a movie anytime soon."

I folded the five in half. "Maybe you should make the time. Ask your wife on a date or something." I mean, I was no marriage expert, but a date seemed like a logical, healthy thing for a marital relationship.

He slid his hands into his pockets and let out a long sigh. "I'm not sure she'd accept."

Miss Henson plopped the stack of papers on her desk at the front of the room just as the fifth-period bell rang. "I think many of you will need to retake this one."

Students made a mad dash for their tests. In zero hurry to get to gym class for the swim unit, I waited for the herd to clear. Then I made my way up to the desk and snagged the lone test with my name scrawled at the top. *A-*.

"I really wish you'd apply the same effort in class as you do on your exams."

"I don't apply any effort on my exams."

Miss Henson pursed her lips. Gone was her nasally laugh and her fake smile. She didn't need it—not when Ben wasn't around. She had even closed up another button on her blouse, verifying that she'd *un*done that same button for my brother-in-law. Gross.

"Would you mind closing my door on your way out? Every single year Mr. O'Ryan brings in those foul-smelling goats for some agricultural project for his honors biology class." She picked up a red gel pen and scooted closer to her desk. "It can't be sanitary."

She muttered something under her breath about a traumatic event from her childhood involving a goat, a petting zoo, and her brand-new My Little Pony backpack.

I tossed my test into the trash can, stepped out into the hallway, and slammed her door behind me. Some last-minute stragglers passed by, their sneakers squeaking against linoleum, disappearing into classrooms until the hallway was empty and the sixth-period bell rang.

A goat bleated into the silence.

I peeked inside O'Ryan's classroom, located directly across from Henson's.

Two goats stood in the back, tethered to a chair near a door that led outside to the teachers' parking lot. One of them bleated again and stared at me with doleful eyes. I didn't speak goat, but it sure seemed like the little guy was pleading for an adventure.

28

CARMEN

"How would you say you handle conflict?" Dr. Rafferty sat in the leather chair across from Ben and me on the sofa.

"We don't fight very often," I said.

"But when you do?"

"We talk through it." I looked at Ben, waiting for him to affirm my answer with a nod so Dr. Rafferty could jot down a note about the mature way we handled conflict. But what I found instead was the strangest expression on his face, like he was lost in a world I'd never been to. I couldn't tell if he was thinking about tonight's game or the phony answer I'd just given Dr. Rafferty. Once upon a time, I had only to glance his way and I could read every thought on his mind. At what point had that changed?

Dr. Rafferty asked Ben the same question.

I watched my husband as he answered, trying to see him as she saw him. He'd come to the appointment freshly shaved, dressed in a nice pair of slacks and his royal-blue Bay Breeze polo, which made his impossibly blue eyes even bluer. He was fit and broad shouldered and sat beside me in this easy, confident way that was totally and completely Ben.

Tonight the team had its final playoff game. If they won, they'd be off to Orlando. If they lost, the season would be over. Ben had zipped over here right after school. Getting these final appointments scheduled had been a disaster. Because of a short-lived stomach bug, Ben had to cancel his first appointment, which had already been scheduled later than I would have liked. He finally met with the counselor in mid-October and then Dr. Rafferty got appendicitis, of all things. By the time she returned to work, Ben had entered playoff season, a chaotic land where his schedule and Dr. Rafferty's refused to cooperate.

I called our social worker to ask if we could have our final appointment with a different counselor, but she said no, not unless we redid our individual appointments. There was no way I was redoing anything. So here Ben was, before the biggest game of the season thus far, answering incredibly personal questions about our marriage. He had arrived a little late. Some crazy nonsense about a missing goat and a teacher's car.

I stuck my sweaty hands beneath my knees to keep from fidgeting. I just wanted this nightmare to be over. I wanted Dr. Rafferty to write up her report and deem us worthy so our social worker would put us back on the "good" list. She had to be close to finished. We'd been answering questions for forty minutes.

"And you, Carmen?"

I blinked several times. "I'm sorry, what was that?"

"Do you feel like you and Ben can share your grief?"

I could feel Ben watching me. Waiting for my answer. And all of a sudden, I was back in our old car after that third miscarriage with Ben beside me, asking what he could do to make it better. He'd wanted me to share my grief then, but I couldn't. Because if I shared my grief with him, then he'd share his with me, and I wasn't strong enough to hold his, not when I could barely hold my own. "Yes, of course."

The counselor wrote a note on her clipboard.

After we finished and Dr. Rafferty had promised to get her report to our social worker as soon as possible, Ben and I walked together out of the office into the sunlight, our hands close but not touching. I wanted to tell him I was sorry. For lying in that office. For pretending everything was okay when we both knew it wasn't. I wanted to promise him that it would be. All of this was for the purpose of getting better again. Once we had a baby in our arms, we could leave this desert wasteland of a season behind. I would be me again, and we could go back to the way we were before this chronic, debilitating ache had taken over my heart. But when we stopped in front of his car and I looked up into his haunted eyes, all I could manage was a faint, "Good luck tonight."

GRACIE

My manager gave me the night off. "Go enjoy the game," he said with a smile. Like he was doing me some sort of favor. Well, I had no intention of enjoying a football game. I considered driving my new car into Pensacola to explore, but then I remembered the cost of filling up my equally new gas tank and decided to drive around Bay Breeze instead, keeping as far away from the stadium lights as possible. Tonight the Sting Rays were playing the Franklin Seahawks, the team from my old school. Whoever won would advance to the state championship game in the beginning of December.

My mood was a melancholy gray, my ring a soft blush pink, which supposedly meant thoughtful. Both shoes fit. My mind kept spinning around Chris Nanning and his clichéd cheerleading fan club—Sadie Hall and Jenna Smith. All three of them were here in Bay Breeze. They were at the stadium right now, facing off with Elias and Ben.

I parked my Mitsubishi on Dock Street, shuffled past the shark-headed Hot Dog Hut, and ended on the dock, hands shoved in the pockets of my jacket, wondering how different life would be if I hadn't used the bathroom that first day of school back in Apalachicola. If I wouldn't have used the rest room, I wouldn't have felt compelled to stick up for Chelsea Paxton and I wouldn't have gotten into a fight with Sadie and I wouldn't have been suspended. I wouldn't have fought with Mom and she wouldn't have threatened to send me to Dad's and I wouldn't be here.

How odd, the chain of events that were set in motion because of a full bladder.

I lay back against the warped wood, dangled my legs off the dock, and gazed up into the nighttime sky, made darker by clouds that blocked the stars and the moon, thinking on the deeper things of life. I was almost positive I believed in God. I just wasn't sure what kind of God. Was He like a puppeteer who manipulated my bladder so I would go to the bathroom at that exact moment, knowing what would transpire? Did He orchestrate the entire thing so I would end up here, at this very moment, for some unknown reason?

Or was He more like the bystanders Principal Best talked about in his bullying unit, passive observers who neither joined nor prevented? I swung my feet like pendulums over the water, waffling back and forth, coming up with new possibilities, as dark clouds rolled across an even darker sky and footsteps sounded behind me.

I sat up with my heart thud-thudding inside my chest. I didn't turn around. By now, the football game would have ended. Elias had come to his dock.

His footsteps stopped beside me. "No work tonight?"

"My boss thought I might want to watch the game."

Elias lowered himself into sitting. He wore a hunter-green beanie and looked cuter than any boy had a right to look. "Your boss must not know you very well."

A nippy breeze blew in over the water, fluttering wisps of hair into my face. I peeled some strands away from my lips, waiting for my heart to settle. It felt like a bunch of giant white elephants stood in line behind us, all of them named Parker's Party. The two of us hadn't had a real conversation since my drunken escapade. Parker's suggestion that I was no more than one of Elias's projects flitted to mind. It took a good bit of effort to push it away. "So . . . ?"

"So what?"

I rolled my eyes. "Did you make it to the state finals?"

"We did."

The news brought a twinge of satisfaction. It was kind of fun, imagining Chris and his meatheaded friends on the somber bus ride back to Apalachicola. "I'm glad."

"Since when are you glad about us winning a football game?"

"Since you played the Franklin Seahawks."

"Ah." He nodded slowly at the sea. "No love for your alma mater, huh?"

"Zero." Before he could ask why, I turned to look at him. "Why do you come here after games?"

"I told you. My mom used to work at Jake's."

"I don't mean how you found this place. I mean, what is it you do here, exactly?"

"Brainstorm ways I can beat you in debate class."

"Har, har."

Elias smiled. "I don't know. I guess I come because it's a good place to talk to God."

I quirked my eyebrow. "Does He talk back?"

"Sometimes."

"Audibly?"

"No, not audibly." He patted his chest. "He talks here."

I must have looked skeptical because Elias cocked his head. "Is that hard to believe?"

"I'm just trying to figure out what that sounds like. I mean, how do you know it's God talking and not just your conscience?"

"Who's to say our conscience isn't one of the ways He talks to us?"

I squinted at the boy beside me. Our conversation was getting a little theologically heavy for a Friday night. That seemed to happen a lot with him. "I heard you signed with Mississippi State."

"You heard correct."

"Ben thinks you'll go pro in two years."

"Nah."

"Elias Banks is doubting himself? Now that is a first."

"Oh, I'm not doubting myself. I could go pro in two years." He said this with a teasingly cocky grin. "I just don't want to."

"Yeah, right."

"You think I'm lying?"

"You're telling me that if you had the opportunity to play in the NFL, you'd say no?"

Elias traced a large X over his chest. "Cross my heart and hope to die. I'll even stick a needle in my eye if you want."

"Gross."

He gave me a friendly nudge. It felt good, joking around with him again. "I'm being for real. What you said that first night here on this dock—about football being overrated? I happen to agree with you."

I eyed him suspiciously. He was the star athlete on the state's best team. He couldn't be serious.

"Look, it's a fun sport. I enjoy being on the field, but at the end of the day, it's a means to an end."

"What end? Becoming famous and filthy rich?"

"More like getting a full-ride scholarship. Football's my ticket to a higher education. I'd like to do something with my life besides get concussions."

I shook my head. "If you have a chance to go pro, you won't turn it down."

"Okay, Miss Confident, how about we make a bet?" He stuck out his hand. "A hundred bucks says I never go pro. If in four years, I'm drafted, I'll pay up. If not, you pay up."

"We won't even know each other in four years."

"Sure we will."

The simple sincerity of his response had my gray mood warming a little. I slid my hand in his big one and as we shook, I couldn't help but notice that beneath the dock lighting, Elias's eyes looked extra green tonight. According to *The Meaning of Color,* green represented peace and stability. At the moment, I could understand why.

Elias let go.

I wiped my palms along my jeans.

"Have any fun plans for Thanksgiving?" he asked.

I groaned and lay back against the dock. A patch of clouds broke apart around a pale sliver of a moon. "My mom invited Carmen and me to the rehab facility."

"You gonna go?"

"Carmen thinks we are."

"You don't want to check on your mom? See how she's holding up?"

"Oh, I know how she's holding up. For now, at least." The last time I answered her 6:30 p.m. phone call, she was all sunshine and roses, like life had turned colorful again. As if the last seventeen years didn't matter, because she was all better now. I'd give her two weeks post rehab before she fell off the wagon again. "Do you think it's weird that Carmen and Ben aren't spending Thanksgiving together?"

"Coach Hart's not going with you?"

"I don't think so." I overheard them arguing through the walls last night. Something about him wanting to spend the holiday with his family in New Orleans and her not wanting to deal with his mother. That hadn't gone over too well. "What about you—do you have any Thanksgiving plans?"

"My mom and I always go to Pastor Zeke's. It's a fun time." Elias lay back beside me. "So what's the deal? Are you really not gonna come to the state finals?"

"Nope."

"Have you even seen a football game? Because it's not fair for you to hate on a sport you've never seen."

"Trust me, I've seen football games." The scathing words tumbled out before I could censor them, and in the tumbling, they felt much too revealing.

"Back in Apalachicola?"

I stared up at the sky, pleading the fifth.

"Come on, Gracie, there's a story here."

I twisted the ring on my finger. Around and around and around and around. With each spin, my mind changed. Tell Elias about Chris Nanning; don't tell Elias about Chris Nanning. When the clouds covered up the moon, I was on the "tell Elias about Chris" spin and decided to go for it. "The team you played tonight? I used to have a thing for the quarterback."

He turned his head. "Chris Nanning?"

"You know him?"

"I know *of* him."

"Last year, we had a couple classes together. I have no idea why, but I had a crush on him." I rolled my eyes at my own stupidity. "He invited me to his games, and despite my opinion of the sport, I actually went to a few. We started hanging out a little."

"And?"

"And I was flattered by his attention. It was the first time anybody had ever really given me any." My dad and Carmen certainly hadn't. The only time my mom ever did was when I was getting into trouble. Then along came Chris. "I thought the more I gave him, the more he'd like me. Turned out, the more I gave him, the less he cared."

Elias shifted beside me.

"Stupid, I know." I took a breath and continued. "He did the whole Fellowship of Christian Athletes thing. He did the whole partying thing too. Anyway, there was this one party last spring. I was a little . . . high. One thing led to another, and well, you know . . ." Heat rose in my cheeks, but I'd already gotten this far. Might as well get the whole thing out; let Elias judge me with *all* of the facts.

"That Monday at school, the whole student body knew about it, and Chris laughed at me like I was a big joke." I pulled my sleeves over my hands, feeling like a fool all over again. "For all my talk about clichés, it turns out that I'm the biggest one of them all: a stupid girl who lost her virginity to the stud football player, thinking he cared. What an idiot, right?"

I waited for Elias to say something about my confession. He had to be thinking plenty. The entire situation was much too similar to the one he rescued me from a couple months ago. The longer I waited, the quicker my heart raced.

"Gracie," he finally said, "Chris Nanning is the idiot. Not you."

And just like that, Elias Banks had my gray mood melting altogether. I folded my hands over my stomach. "Too bad the judge didn't agree."

"The judge?"

"I got a little angry. And Chris had such an obsession with his car."

Elias propped himself up on his elbows. "What did you do?"

"Blew off some steam with a baseball bat and a can of spray paint." Despite all the trouble my bad decision had caused, I couldn't help but smile. "It only cost me two thousand dollars in fines and one hundred twenty hours of community service."

One would think I'd have learned my lesson. At least where cars were concerned.

29

CARMEN

Temperatures on the Florida panhandle in November hovered near perfection, with highs in the midseventies and nighttime temps dipping into the upper fifties. At the moment, seventy-four degrees of sunshine warmed my back, bolstering my sense of accomplishment as Natalie and I walked up the stairs—renovations had officially moved to the second floor of The Treasure Chest.

All ten first-floor units were clean. With Gracie's help, I had washed the walls, polished the furniture, pulled up the carpet, and scrubbed the bathrooms. We pitched all ten moldy shower curtains and roughly half of the comforters. Thanks to copious amounts of Tide and stain remover, I was able to resuscitate eleven. The others were unsalvageable. But with plenty of extra bed sheets to go around, all of which we'd washed with bleach, none of the beds were completely naked.

Natalie and I reached the second-story landing and made our way to the biggest of the three apartments, where Ingrid had lived for the majority of her life. Natalie set the bucket of cleaning supplies on the ground. "I can't believe you and Gracie have tackled this entire place on your own."

"Not entirely on our own." I searched the key chain for the right key. "We had someone install the windows and replace the carpet."

"Have you decided what you're going to do with it yet?"

"Hopefully hire a manager. Get the place up and running again." I twisted the master key into the lock. The door creaked open and a wall of stench nearly knocked us both over.

We covered our mouths and noses and stepped back from the smell.

"Either someone cleaned the carpets with sour milk," Natalie said, "or there is a dead, decaying mouse in there."

"That smells like more than one dead, decaying mouse." I used the crook of my elbow to cover my nostrils and prodded the door open with my toe. With the shades drawn, all I could see was darkness. "I don't understand how it could have gotten that bad."

"It's the law of entropy. Without regular upkeep, things fall apart. Like my house."

"Your house is not falling apart."

"You only think that because I clean it before you come over. All month, Mason assured me he was cleaning the toilet in his and Reese's bathroom. When I checked yesterday, the thing was emitting toxic fumes. Little bugger had been lying to my face."

I stared at the half-open door. As much as I wished there was some reverse entropy button I could push, there wasn't. And since it was technically my mess to clean, I wasn't going to make Natalie do the dirty work. I took a giant gulp of air, then hurried inside, flung open the drapes while dust billowed like smoke, and attempted to open the windows. They refused to budge. By the time I managed to pry open two, my lungs were starving for oxygen.

I hurried outside and inhaled the clean, briny air while Natalie gave my shoulder an encouraging pat. "You're a brave, brave woman."

Once I restocked my blood stream with O_2, I slapped on a mask and stepped back in, this time armed with two cans of Febreze, and sprayed figure eights of mist into the room, my arms moving in slow circles like some sort of karate sensei. When the mist settled over the disgusting odor, I flipped on the light switch and Natalie stepped in behind me.

"Whoa."

Whoa was right. What I saw before me made me question the mental acuity of the manager Ingrid had hired. Honestly. The guests took better care of the motel rooms than this man took of his own living space. The place looked as though he invited a den of foxes to be his roommates. Even though he took his stuff and moved out, the aftermath remained. Multiple stains dotted the carpet. There was a hole in one of the walls, like he either punched it or ran something through it, but never bothered to fix it. Broken window screens. Busted trim. Naked electrical sockets and uncovered light fixtures. All made worse by the usual signs of neglect: layers of dust, cobwebs in the corners of the walls, grime on the windows.

We began a cursory check of each room, bracing ourselves for the worst. All were in serious disrepair, but thankfully, we only found one freshly dead mouse in a vent. Back in the living room, we did the only thing there was to do: dive in. We started at the top. Natalie removed cobwebs from the corners of the ceiling while I wiped away a thick layer of dust from the blades of the ceiling fan. We scrubbed the walls, the windows, and the window ledges.

Natalie removed the drapes. "I'm gonna go beat these outside." She gathered them over her arm and shot me a smile. "Unfortunately for my children, that is not the first time those words have escaped my mouth."

As she stepped out of the room, a bead of sweat trickled down my temple. I wiped it away with the short sleeve of my T-shirt, pulled the rubber gloves off my hands, and stared at the plastic-covered couch. I was positive I would find more unidentifiable stains upon removing it. Instead, I found memories. A whole slew of them awakened in the uncovering. I set my hand along the length of the blue-and-white striped backrest, recalling all the times Ben and I sat here on this couch watching the TV with an antenna sticking up from the box set like a pair of rabbit ears.

"Name something," the game show host had said inside the screen, "that costs more money if you have a daughter instead of a son."

"Weddings!" I shouted.

Ben and I were watching *Family Feud*. Richard Karn, better known as Al Borland from the sitcom *Home Improvement,* was the host. I liked him a lot better than the previous host, Louie Anderson. Richard turned to his left, deferring to a bearded guy dressed in an argyle sweater.

"Clothes!" the man declared.

Richard pointed the cards he held in his hand toward the game board. "Survey says . . ."

The second black rectangle flipped over with a ding, which meant the woman on Richard's right would get a chance.

"Weddings?" she squeaked.

The number one spot on the board flipped over. The woman's team started jumping up and down like they won the lottery. I turned to Ben, a smug smile on my face. I was good at *Family Feud*. He pointed the remote at the TV and switched it off.

"Hey, I was watching that."

He scratched the back of his head—a boyishly cute gesture that made me want to lean in and plant a kiss on his lips—then straightened his arm over the backrest of the couch. "What are we going to do?"

My smile slid away. He wasn't talking about what we were going to do right now, or what we were going to do later that night. He was asking *the* question—the one neither of us had touched since he wrote our sort-of initials on the wall of wisdom a month and a half ago. The time between then and now had been filled with laughter and stolen kisses, fun dates, and ceaseless flirting. When we walked, we held hands. When we sat, our legs touched. When we stood, Ben put his arm around my waist. And when we got moving again, his hand would touch the small of my back. It wasn't enough for us to be together, we had to be *touching* while being together. I would never get enough of this man beside me, and now he was asking *the* question.

I pulled my feet onto the couch and faced him with crossed legs. We might not have talked about it, but that didn't mean I hadn't thought about it. Oh, I had. Over and over again, every night after Ben and I pulled ourselves apart and said our "see you tomorrows," I lay in bed thinking about it. Praying about it. Begging God to make the decision an easy one.

His finger found my skin and traced feather-light circles on my shoulder. "We have to talk about what happens next."

I looked down into my lap. I didn't want to talk about what happened next. I wanted to keep each moment we had left unmarred by *next*.

"I'm in love with you, Carmen."

My heart took off, a million beats per second. I looked into eyes as blue as the ocean and as serious as a storm. More than anything, I wanted to tell him that I loved him too. So much at times that it was a physical ache. But what I said instead was the one thing I couldn't get past, no matter how often I rolled the various scenarios through my mind each night. God hadn't made the decision easy, but He had made it simple. "I'm leaving in a week."

"And I start practice in three days."

"So you're going to be busy with work. And I'm going to be at UVA finishing my senior year." I didn't see how it could work, with me in Virginia and him here in Florida. "I know how important coaching is to you, Ben. I hear the way you talk about football. It's not like you'll be able to get away on the weekends. And me, I'll be applying to grad schools and sending out résumés."

Somewhere in the middle of my speech, Ben had started to shake his head.

I picked at the hem of his cargo shorts. "Can't we just spend this last week together?"

"And then what—say good-bye? That's what you want to do?"

I bit my lip. Of course not. The thought of saying good-bye left a gaping hole in my chest, but what other option did we have? A tear gathered in my eye and spilled over.

Ben wiped the trail of moisture with the pad of his thumb.

I put my hand over his and leaned into his palm. Relishing the warmth. The calluses. The smell of his cologne, so subtle you had to be extra close to smell it. He curled his fingers around the back of my neck and drew me in for a kiss—so sweet at first it made the hole in my chest bigger, then growing in passion and urgency, as if everything we couldn't say or wouldn't say resided inside of it. By the time he pulled away, we both had to catch our breath.

Ben touched his forehead to mine. "People do long distance all the time."

"I know, but I don't know where I'll be after I graduate." Limiting myself to the Pensacola area would be putting every single egg in one very tiny basket. The chances of my getting a job here were minimal. I wasn't going to graduate with a degree and not use it. I pulled away from Ben's touch. If I had any hope of remaining practical, I needed some space. "I'll be applying everywhere. I could end up in California. And then what?"

He didn't have an answer.

"Ben, my roommate did long distance her entire freshman and sophomore years. She was always thinking about him, trying to get to him, organizing her entire schedule around phone calls and weekend visits. She was miserable. Her grades suffered." In exactly one week, carefree summer Carmen would return to the closet, and perfectionist, studious Carmen would come out to take her place. Carefree summer Carmen might be able to flit back to Bay Breeze every weekend, but perfectionist, studious Carmen could not. "I have to focus this year. *You* have to focus this year."

"What we have doesn't come around very often."

"I know, but if it's meant to be—"

Ben ran his hands down his face and groaned. Loudly.

"What?"

"Don't say that. I hate that. It's like the girl's version of 'It's not me; it's you.'"

I reached into his lap and took his hand, hating the hurt on his face. The hurt I was putting there. He felt rejected, I could tell. I wanted, more than anything, to kiss him, declare my undying love, tell him that we could try. But from my vantage point, that outlook would only lead to more heartache. "I can't do long distance."

"Can't, or won't?"

I didn't answer.

With a dullness in his expression, Ben pulled his hand from mine and pointed the remote back at the TV. Richard Karn stood with his arm around the bearded man in the argyle sweater for the bull's-eye round, the part of the show that usually had me shouting a stream of answers at the screen. This time, however, my heart wasn't in it. Of all Richard's categories, I couldn't think of a single answer.

"Drapes are officially beaten!" Natalie announced, breezing back into the room.

I let my hand slide off the back of the couch, away from the memory. Nine years wiser and I understood something I didn't back then. Distance was more than physical. Two people could live under the same roof, sleep in the same bed, with all the distance in the world between them.

"You okay?" Natalie asked.

I bit the inside of my cheek. I told Natalie a lot of things. She knew about my miscarriages. She knew about my frustrations with Gracie. She knew my concerns about Aunt Ingrid. She knew how I felt about my mother-in-law and her incessant, unsubtle hint dropping that she needed more grandchildren. My relationship with Ben, however, remained close to my chest. That particular hand felt too important to share.

My phone vibrated against the kitchen counter.

Saved by the bell.

I walked over and grabbed it. "It's the high school." I swiped the screen and said hello.

"Hello, Carmen, it's Mrs. Hershey."

Mrs. Hershey was the school secretary—a sweet gray-haired woman who always had a smile to offer and a bowl of Hershey's Kisses on her desk. Ben said she was retiring after the year. "Hi, Mrs. Hershey, is everything okay?"

"Well, I have Gracie here in the office. I'm afraid she's in a little bit of trouble."

I stuck the tip of my pinky nail between my teeth.

"I would have called Ben, but he's in the middle of class and I knew you were done with work for the day. Plus, you are listed as Gracie's primary contact. Do you think you can come in to speak with her guidance counselor? If you'd rather I talk to Ben, that's fine too."

"No, no. I can come. Do you mind telling me what she's in trouble for?"

Natalie furrowed her brow while Mrs. Hershey explained.

When she finished, I said "thank you," told her I'd be there in thirty minutes, and hung up the phone.

"What happened?"

"Apparently, my sister stole a goat."

CARMEN

The video on the screen went black as Gracie's guidance counselor, Mr. Vogel—a tall, stork-like man I'd made small talk with a few times over the years, mostly at Christmas parties or football concession stands—stopped the security camera footage. He sat with one ankle resting on a knee, his hands folded over his shin.

I looked from him to my sister, absolutely speechless.

When Gracie offered no explanation for the footage I'd just watched, Mr. Vogel uncrossed his leg and set both of his loafers on the floor. "The goat handler was beside himself with worry."

Gracie rolled her eyes. "I made sure the goat was fine."

"Gracie."

"What? The windows were down. I gave it some water."

I shook my head, unable to make sense of it. The whole thing was ridiculous. So ridiculous in fact, that if I hadn't seen the footage with my own eyes, I'm not sure I would have believed it. "What would possess you to put a goat in a teacher's car?"

"I don't know—boredom?"

"Gracie, this is a very serious offense." Mr. Vogel locked gazes with my sister. "The damage done to Miss Henson's car was minimal, but that's beside the point. School property was stolen and a teacher's car was broken into. Those offenses together should result in a two-week out-of-school suspension."

My eyes widened.

"And something like this would go on your transcript, along with, it would seem, myriad other infractions from your previous school."

My eyes widened further.

Gracie seemed unfazed by the whole thing.

"But"—Mr. Vogel held up his finger—"this is your first offense here at Bay Breeze, which means there is a certain amount of freedom at my disposal, and I happen to be a believer in second chances. Gracie, I think beneath that rough exterior is a young lady who wants to make better choices."

Gracie crossed her arms.

Mr. Vogel typed something on his keyboard. The printer on his credenza came to life and spat out a sheet of paper. He picked it up and handed it to my sister.

"What's this?" she asked.

"A list of extracurricular activities."

"Why are you giving it to me?"

"I've spoken with your teachers. Every single one believes that you have an enormous amount of potential. All agree that an extracurricular activity would be quite beneficial, especially if boredom is the culprit." Mr. Vogel recrossed his legs, this time clasping his hands over his knee. "Instead of the two-week suspension, I'm proposing that you pick one of these activities. You commit to whichever one you choose. As long as nothing like this happens again, we can forgo the suspension."

I nearly melted with relief. "And it wouldn't go on her transcript?"

"No, it wouldn't."

"Thank you, Mr. Vogel." I turned to my sister, urging her with my widening eyes to say "thank you" too. The offer was more than generous.

"So it's either a two-week suspension or join one of these?"

"That's correct."

"I'll take the suspension."

I came forward in my seat. "What?"

Mr. Vogel sighed. "All right then, if that's your decision, we will see you in December."

"See you then." And before I could object or even process her decision, Gracie stood up and walked out of the office.

I remained seated, stuck between two options. Apologize to Mr. Vogel on behalf of Gracie's behavior or rush out of the office and address her behavior. I motioned toward the door apologetically.

He extended his long arm. "By all means, go after her."

"Do you mind if I have that sheet?"

Mr. Vogel handed it to me. "If she changes her mind, please let me know."

"I will. Thank you."

By the time I reached the hallway, Gracie was already outside, walking down the steps toward the parking lot. I quickened my stride to close the gap she'd put between us and pushed through the front doors. "Gracie, wait a second!"

She stopped at the bottom of the cement steps and turned around.

"Have you lost your mind?"

She rattled her head a little, as if attempting to shake water out of her ear. "I'm pretty sure it's still in there."

"Mr. Vogel offered you an amazing deal."

"Right, and since he offered it to me, not to you, that means I have the freedom to accept or not. I chose not."

"A suspension will go on your transcript."

"I don't care about my transcript."

"Right now, maybe not. But that doesn't mean you won't care about it someday."

"Please don't start talking about college again."

I ran my hands back through my hair and shook my head, all the frustration and irritation I'd been stuffing away rising inside me, tangling with several other emotions that had nothing to do with my sister. "This can't keep happening."

"What do you mean?"

"Coming home wasted from parties? Stealing goats and putting them in teachers' cars? Enough is enough."

"I got drunk forever ago. You saw the footage—it was *one* goat and *one* car. Not plural. And please don't pretend like I'm the only one who was caught doing something incriminating on video." She raised pointed eyebrows at me.

The barb had my cheeks turning warm. The two of us had never talked about my embarrassing YouTube claim to fame. I shook my head, unwilling to get off point. "What in the world would possess you to put a goat in Miss Henson's car?"

"I don't like her."

"Okay, fine. Then don't like her. But that doesn't negate the fact that she's still your teacher, which means she deserves some respect."

Gracie laughed.

"I don't see why that's funny."

"Miss Henson does not deserve my respect. And if you knew what she was up to at lunch last Friday, she wouldn't have your respect either."

Her ominous words and the cryptic look she gave me while delivering them distracted me. "What was she doing at lunch?"

She turned to walk away, but I grabbed her elbow. "Tell me what she was doing at lunch on Friday, Gracie."

"Coming on to your husband."

I let go of her arm. "What?"

"I went to his class over lunch to borrow some money. He wasn't alone. Miss Henson was inside keeping him company, and she was awfully . . . cozy. It's not the first time I've seen her that way with him."

Warmth drained from my face.

She turned on her heels and walked to her not-so-new car, leaving me standing at the bottom of the staircase, a seed of suspicion planted in my heart.

31

CARMEN

"I have to pee," Gracie said.

I gritted my teeth. This was the third time she'd informed me of her situation, the first being thirty miles back on Interstate 10. I hunched over the steering wheel, gazing up at the line of towering cumulonimbus clouds and their impressive anvil-shaped crowns. We were driving parallel with the squall line, and it was closing in fast. I wanted to beat it to Tallahassee, but stopping for a bathroom break would almost certainly ensure we wouldn't. "Can you hold it?"

"Not without getting a bladder infection."

Gripping the wheel tighter, I flicked the blinker and took the first exit available—an unincorporated town called Potomac Springs that boasted a general store and a gas station. Unfortunately, the amenities were much farther from the interstate than I anticipated and I saw nothing resembling a town.

Gracie grumbled something at her window.

My muscles tightened. "Look, I know you're not happy about coming, but she's our mother. Don't you think we should offer our support?"

"Not particularly."

I ground my teeth. Ever since Gracie's stubborn, obstinate refusal to take Mr. Vogel's offer on Monday and our ensuing fight outside the school, wherein she accused a teacher of hitting on my husband, she had crawled under every last one of my nerves. For three months I'd tried making dents in her walls, and for three months I'd done nothing but fail. Apparently, I could no more pull Gracie from her sardonic, miserable moods than I could snap my finger and get myself a baby. "It's one day. Can we at least pretend to get along for Mom's sake?"

"Is it really for Mom's sake?"

I opened my mouth to ask what she meant, but Gracie pointed to a decrepit 7-Eleven up ahead, squatting all by itself on the side of the road. It had two gas pumps and an attached outdoor rest room. The place was the perfect setting for a horror flick. I pulled into the lot and stayed in the car with the doors locked while Gracie jogged inside, came out with a key attached to an empty milk jug, and let herself inside the rest room. I kept one eye on the clouds and scanned the radio for something better than static.

Come on, Gracie, hurry up.

Several fat drops hit my windshield. And then the sky officially unzipped. Rain fell like sheets and pounded the roof of my car. Squinting through the downpour, I was able to make out a blur that was Gracie sprinting through the rain. As soon as she climbed inside, her body convulsed with a violent shudder. "That was disgusting."

Lightning fissured the darkened sky overhead, followed by a blast of thunder that made us both jump. I pulled onto the road and drove toward the interstate, gripping the steering wheel with white knuckles.

Gracie clutched the console. "Shouldn't we pull over?"

I pressed the gas pedal. If we were going to wait out the storm, it was not going to be on the shoulder of some eerie, unpopulated road. We would get to the interstate and pull onto the shoulder and wait in the company of other vehicles. Another bolt of lightning ripped through the clouds. I leaned over the wheel and focused on my only reference point—the yellow dotted line in the center of the road—when a mass of gray darted into the path of my headlights.

Gracie shrieked.

I jerked the wheel. Slammed the brake.

The car whipped in a circle, then slid to a stop in the mud, thankfully not in the ditch.

Gracie and I stared at one another while the rain pounded the roof, our chests heaving in unison. "What was that?" she asked.

"I don't know. Some kind of animal."

I took a deep breath. Then another. Once my heart had settled into a somewhat regular rhythm, I set my hands back on the steering wheel and pressed the gas. The car gave a funny lurch and the wheels spun. I pressed the gas harder. The car remained sedentary. With a rising sense of panic, I pushed the gas all the way to the floor. The spinning wheels spit mud into the rain. The car didn't budge.

"We're stuck?"

"It seems that way." I picked up my phone to dial AAA, but it didn't have a signal, whether from the storm or the obscure location, I wasn't sure. I showed it to Gracie. She pulled out her phone too. Same thing.

My panic morphed to anger. We were stuck in the middle of nowhere in a torrential downpour all because my sister needed to use the rest room. "I told you not to drink that Mountain Dew."

Gracie's black-lined, sea-green eyes went a little buggy. "Are you kidding? You're blaming this on me?"

"If we hadn't pulled off the interstate, we wouldn't be stuck here."

"You're the one who dragged me along in the first place!"

"Gracie, she's our *mother* and she's *trying*."

"Give it a few days. She'll be back to her old self in no time."

"That's a great attitude to have."

"I'm being realistic."

"No, you're being cynical. You're being typical, pessimistic Gracie."

"It's better than being a giant hypocrite."

"Oh, and I suppose that's me, right? I'm the giant hypocrite. Please enlighten me. How am I a giant hypocrite?"

"Everything about you is fake. You only smile when people are looking. You only touch your husband when people are looking. You go to church every Sunday morning, and then you come home and you cry in the bathroom."

Her observation came like a sucker punch to the gut. It stole all my breath. Gracie heard me in the bathroom?

"You said The Treasure Chest was important to you, but you only care about things so long as they fit into your life. You abandoned The Treasure Chest back then just like you abandoned me back then."

"Gracie . . ."

"You have no idea what it's like living with her!" The words exploded from her mouth like a crack of thunder, puncturing the air inside the cab.

We breathed into the deafening silence while fog crawled up the windows.

My sister broke eye contact first. She turned away from me, but not before I caught her swiping discreetly at her eye.

"Gracie, I lived with her for twelve years."

"It wasn't the same. You were never alone with her. You had your dad to look after you. I had nobody. I was a burden to Mom. An inconvenience to my father. And absolutely nothing to you."

"That's not true."

"You are such a liar." Gracie shook her head. "And what makes it all worse, is that you *knew*. You knew I was being raised by an alcoholic mother, but you did nothing."

Her accusations were a paper shredder, slivering me into thin strips of guilt. I could have argued. I could have stated my case—that I thought she was sober, or at least relatively close to the wagon. But Gracie was right. Deep down, I'd known. It was simply more comfortable playing the fool. Dad decided he'd had enough when I was in seventh grade—the year before Gracie was born—and I was still so relieved to be far away from Mom, the dysfunction that marked our life and the exhausting work of trying to hide it, that I barely gave my sister a backward glance. I had no problem sacrificing my relationship with a baby for the sake of my newfound freedom. I condemned a little girl to a life I was desperate to escape, all so I wouldn't have to deal with it anymore.

Gracie reached for the door handle, like she couldn't stand being in the same car with me for one more second, then stepped out into the downpour.

I scrambled after her, the rain falling in such sheets I was soaked before I was all the way out. Mud slopped at my shoes like suction cups. I had to yell to be heard. "Come on, Gracie, get back in the car!"

She leaned against the hood with crossed arms. "No."

"I'm sorry, all right?"

"Do you think I want your lame apology? It means nothing."

I squinted through the cold downpour. Another bolt of lightning lit up the sky from one end to the other. "You're right. My sorry can't undo what's been done. I can't fix that hurt or make up for my cowardly behavior. But I'm trying *now*. I want to be here for you *now*." Raindrops dripped off my eyelashes and into my mouth. I blinked away the wet and stepped closer. "But I can't be here if you keep freezing me out at every turn."

She looked up from her crossed arms, her black hair plastered to the sides of her face, her eyeliner smearing black down her cheeks.

"I want to be the sister I should have been from the beginning, but I can't be unless you let me in a little." The heavy rain began to thin. The worst of the squall passed. I stared at Gracie and waited for her to decide. I couldn't do it for her. If I'd learned one thing over the past three months, it was that I couldn't help someone who didn't want the help. I couldn't force her to trust me. This was her choice.

She worried her lip.

The rain turned into a sprinkle.

"Do you have any cardboard?" she finally asked.

"What?"

"For the wheels. If we have something to wedge underneath them, maybe we can get ourselves unstuck."

It wasn't a clear answer, but it was a start.

I popped open the trunk and pulled out the box we'd been using to cart various items in and out of the motel. Together, we broke it open, tore it in half, and wedged one large square of cardboard beneath each front wheel. Gracie got behind the steering wheel while I stood behind the bumper and prepared to heave with all my might. She eased onto the gas and I pushed with every ounce of strength I had. She gunned the gas a little harder. The car shifted forward. The front tires caught on the cardboard. The back wheels kicked up a fountain of mud. And somehow, someway, the car lurched onto the road.

For a moment I stood there, staring.

Oh my goodness, we did it. We got the car unstuck.

Gracie climbed out, looking every bit as shocked as I did. We gaped at one another, both of us resembling drowned rats, and a sound came out of Gracie I'd never heard before. Laughter. Not sarcastic or cruel, but pure, delighted laughter. When I looked down at myself, I couldn't help but join in. I was splattered with mud from head to toe. We laughed and we laughed, so hard that soon we were doubled over with tears.

By the time we laid towels over the seats and were driving again, the laughter was long gone. But the feeling it left behind? That stayed. I merged onto the highway and snuck a sideways peek at my sister. "I've had six miscarriages."

Her head whipped around. So quick it seemed more reflex than willful choice.

"That's why I cry sometimes. In the bathroom."

Gracie gave me the smallest, subtlest of nods. And we were on our way.

32

GRACIE

When Mom hugged me, I noticed two things—she wasn't as skeletal as she'd been in August, and she smelled like cigarettes. Less blatantly than Deborah, but it was there in the folds of her hair. I guess exchanging one slow death for another was the thing to do in rehab. When she pulled away, tears swam in her eyes. "I am so, so happy you came."

Last night, Carmen and I arrived in Tallahassee mud covered and soaking wet, but relatively intact. We stayed in a cute mom-and-pop motel off Interstate 10, where we showered, ate pizza, and slept, and now here we were at the Fresh Start Rehabilitation Center. The two of us were still basically strangers, but I felt this softening toward her that I'd never felt before. I went to bed with the feeling last night and woke up with it still there this morning. I had no idea why—whether it was the result of getting the car unstuck together or if her confession aroused my sympathy or if the apology had made a difference after all. I only knew that years' worth of accumulated resentment had lost some of its edge.

It was a weird feeling.

Mom ushered us into the dining area and introduced us to all of her new friends, the most interesting of which was a conspiracy theorist named Jimmy. He looked like Jesus—at least the Americanized version on paintings inside churches—except Jimmy wore his beard in a ponytail and his hands trembled when he talked.

While Carmen and Mom chatted, Jimmy told me about the end of the world. He didn't know how it was going to happen, but he was adamant on when. Apparently yesterday, while taking a walk outside, he told God that if He would reveal when the world would end, Jimmy would know that God was real. And apparently, when Jimmy looked up at the sky, he found a cloud in the perfect shape of a three, which according to him, meant that as of today we all had two years, three hundred sixty-four days left until the apocalypse. I considered asking him why the three meant years instead of months or weeks or days, but he seemed so relaxed about all the time he had on his hands that I couldn't bring myself to rain on his delusional parade.

And besides, Mom wanted to show us her room. She kept up a constant stream of chatter the entire way there and the entire way back and didn't stop until the Thanksgiving meal was served. I filled my plate with turkey, stuffing, mashed potatoes, and cranberry sauce and smothered it all in gravy. The three of us sat at Jimmy's table, and he said a prayer that was, hands down, the most entertaining prayer I had ever heard in my life. When it was done, I stuffed my mouth with food, bracing myself for step nine. Mom could talk only so long and so fast before she ran out of things to say and finally got to where she was going.

"I feel better than I ever have. I really mean that." She cut off a bite of her turkey.

Carmen peeked at me while buttering a roll. "That's great, Mom."

I waited for Mom to keep going, but it seemed we had finally reached the lull.

She put the bite of turkey in her mouth, chewed, swallowed, and dabbed her lips with an orange-and-gold napkin that said Gobble Gobble. "Carmen, I'm sorry."

And here it was. Step nine: make direct amends with the people you have wronged. She may have been to official rehab only three times in her life, but that didn't mean she hadn't made multiple attempts to give up the bottle on her own. Hence, her baptisms. Not only did I have to watch her dunk herself into the creek every other Sunday, I also had the pleasure of experiencing step nine. Over. And over. And over.

Carmen must have been expecting it too, because she put down her fork and gave our mother the courtesy of full eye contact. Me? I looked down at my food. Step nine had lost its sincerity years ago.

"I'm sorry for not being the mother I should have been to you."

"It's okay. Really."

"Gracie?" Her voice quivered over my name.

I mixed cranberry sauce with mashed potato, enjoying the creamy white swirled with deep burgundy. Who knew a Thanksgiving feast could lend itself to creative art?

"I've failed you worst of all. I should be the mother in our relationship, and yet you've always had to take care of me. I know that isn't right. And I promise things will be different from now on." She reached across the table to squeeze my knuckles. "I'll be finished here in a week and we can have a fresh start."

"I don't want a fresh start."

"Gracie," Carmen mumbled.

I looked up from my plate—first at Carmen, then at Mom. I could tell my words had taken the wind out of Mom's sails. But I couldn't help it. The thought of returning to Chris Nanning and Sadie Hall and Principal Best and the deadbeats I used to eat lunch with was enough to make me shudder. Never mind the nights at home, waiting for Mom's dance with the devil to resume. The past three months had me forgetting a little what that had been like—the instability of each moment, the walking on eggshells. Sure, Ben and Carmen had their issues, but at least I never had to wonder if it was safe to ride with them in the car. At least I never came home to either of them passed out drunk on the couch. "I want to stay with Carmen."

I'm not sure who was more shocked by my announcement, Carmen or me.

"I guess that is something we can talk about." Mom folded her napkin in half, then in half again, and smoothed the creases out over her knee with hands that trembled like Jimmy's. "Now if you'll excuse me, I'm going to get some seconds."

Never mind the fact that she wasn't through with her firsts.

I watched her walk to the big table where the feast was spread.

"Gracie, she is trying," Carmen said.

"I wasn't trying to be rude."

"What were you trying to be then?"

"Honest."

Carmen looked skeptical. "You *want* to stay with me?"

"I get it, if you don't want me to." I kept my voice neutral, unattached. But inside, my heart tapped a quick SOS against my chest. I wanted to stay for a lot of reasons; The Treasure Chest and Elias were two very large ones.

"If that's true. If you're serious about staying . . ." She scraped her fork against remnants of green bean casserole. "I have a condition."

"What is it?"

"You have to take Mr. Vogel's deal."

"You mean join an extracurricular activity?"

"Yes."

My attention wandered to my mom. Jimmy was up getting seconds too, and it appeared by the enthusiastic way he gestured toward the ceiling with his hands that he was telling her the story about God's apocalyptic cloud message. As my mother smiled and nodded, I recalled something Elias had said a while ago, at the top of the staircase of Ben and Carmen's home.

"If she's been to rehab three times, that means she's trying."

Her past might be riddled with failure, and she would never win the award for world's best mom, but I did have to give her credit for getting back up again. For putting herself out there, even though she would most likely fail.

"So?" Carmen prompted.

I expelled a breath. "So I guess I'll need to see Mr. Vogel's list again."

Carmen smiled.

I returned to my potato-cranberry sauce mixing, slightly perplexed. Not only was Carmen letting me stay, she looked happy about it. Knowing how I'd been treating her these past few months, it didn't make much sense.

33

GRACIE

I sat at my lonely table in the back of the cafeteria with my boots propped on an empty chair, the hood of my hoodie pulled up over my hair, my ears plugged with earbuds, my mood bordering on morose. According to Mr. Vogel, I had until Monday to choose an extracurricular activity, and the only one I had any interest in joining was no longer an option. The debate team was preparing for districts, and Kimmy had found a partner months ago. My options were on the printed list in front of me.

I'd already crossed out all activities associated with sports, drama, and music. I would not be wearing any uniforms or performing on any stages. Or singing on any of them either. I may have enjoyed listening to music, but listening and doing were two very different things. And unless spray-painting Chris Nanning's car counted, I wasn't really into art either. That left me with newspaper, speech, and a smattering of clubs that all made my nose wrinkle. At some point in the middle of Delain's "Are You Done with Me," my sixth sense kicked in. I looked up from the sheet of paper and noticed that one of the empty seats at my table was no longer empty. Elias Banks seemed to have joined me for lunch, something he hadn't done since my first day of school.

I hid the list beneath the table and unplugged my ears, raising my eyebrows at the concoction of turkey, mashed potatoes, and gravy piled high on a slice of Wonder Bread on his tray. "Don't the lunch ladies know we're all sick of turkey by now?"

"I think it's leftovers." He gave me his dimpled smile. "So what's up, Fisher? You're extra mopey today."

"Mopey's the name of a dwarf."

"Dopey's the name of a dwarf. There are no Mopeys, to my knowledge. You should really get your Disney trivia straight." He stuck a forkful of turkey and gravy into his mouth, chased it down with a carton of two-percent milk, then nodded at the spot of the table beneath which I'd hidden my list. "What were you looking at just now?"

"Nothing." My answer came too quick.

"You do know that suspicious behavior only makes people more curious, don't you?"

I exhaled loudly. If I was going to join one of these things, people were going to find out. Might as well get it over with and tell him now. I handed him the list. "My options."

"For what?"

"An extracurricular activity."

He almost spit out his milk. "You *want* to join an extracurricular activity?"

"No, I don't *want* to. I'm being forced to against my will."

"By who?"

"Mr. Vogel and Carmen. The two are in cahoots."

"How exactly are they forcing you?"

"Remember the goat in Miss Henson's car?"

Elias's cheek pulled in with a smile. He set his fork on his tray and placed his elbows on the table, giving me his full, undivided attention. "I don't think anybody's forgetting that anytime soon."

"I may have had something to do with it."

His smile grew, but he placed his hand over his mouth so I couldn't see and shook his head. The twinkle in his eye, however, was impossible to hide. I don't think he completely disapproved.

"I guess Bay Breeze has security cameras, which I should have taken into consideration before I kidnapped the goat. Anyway, it was either suspension for two weeks or join an extracurricular."

"I would think you'd choose suspension."

"I did, hence my absence on Tuesday and Wednesday last week. But then there was this whole thing over Thanksgiving"—I twirled my hand in the air, not really wanting to go into the *thing* with Elias—"and I was coerced into changing my mind. Thus, the list."

He scanned it. "Hey, the academic bowl team's on here."

"You know what that is?"

"Yeah. They're really good. Even went to nationals last year. A good buddy from youth group is on the team."

"Youth group."

"You should come Wednesday night and meet him."

The invitation had Parker's niggling question from the party creeping to mind once again—*"How does it feel being Banks's new project?"* I batted it away. I was not going to let someone like Parker Zkotsky tarnish this thing between Elias and me, whatever it was. An invitation to youth group did not necessarily make me Elias's project. "I already told you. I don't like phonies."

"Meaning all kids who go to youth group are phonies?"

"A lot of them are."

"Please don't base your opinion on Christians off of some jerk like Chris Nanning."

"I'm not."

He quirked his eyebrow, because, yeah, right, I totally was. "You need to start seeing the person behind the stereotype."

"Meaning?"

"Meaning you wrote me off because of football, and now you're doing the same thing, only with youth group." He handed the list back. "I'm sure you don't like when people look at you and make assumptions."

"What assumptions would they make?"

His attention wandered from my boots on the empty seat all the way up to the hoodie pulled over my head. "That you're an angry emo chick."

I scoffed. "I am *not* emo."

"You wear black army boots. I have, on occasion, seen your fingernails painted black. You have black hair, listen to weird music, and wear a scowl half the time."

I slugged him in the arm.

He held up his hands and laughed. "Hey, I'm keeping it real."

"I'll have you know that the music I listen to is called techno fusion. It's not weird and it's definitely not emo."

"Sorry, techno fusion. My point is, I see the person behind the black hair and combat boots." He spread his hand over his chest. "Just like you're starting to see this person behind the football. Can't you do the same thing with youth group this Wednesday? Who knows, you might even make some friends."

"Friends, huh?" I'd never really done the whole friend thing before. Life was less complicated that way. But a lot lonelier too. I looked up at the ceiling and let out an exaggerated sigh. "Okay, fine. I'll come." I held up my finger. "But if I don't like it, you can't ask me again."

34

CARMEN

"Welcome to your first parent-teacher conferences!" Natalie extended her arm toward the entrance of Bay Breeze High School as though giving me a grand tour. She wore a hooded sweatshirt with the name of Samantha's dance studio on the front. "Are you brimming with excitement?"

"I had a dream last night that all of Gracie's teachers yelled at me."

Natalie snorted.

"I'm serious. Every single one of her teachers told me she brought a goat to class and then they proceeded to scream at me for allowing her to do such a thing." And when I walked into the bathroom to cry, I found Ben and Gracie's trig teacher making out in one of the stalls.

"I still can't believe she put an actual goat inside Miss Henson's car."

"Me either."

"It's kind of funny if you think about it."

"Natalie."

"Come on. A goat in her car?" Laughter bubbled from her mouth. She cupped her hand over the sound to trap the rest inside.

My lips twitched.

"Brandon said Miss Henson was screeching like a banshee in the parking lot and the goat was just standing there in her backseat, chewing on a seat belt."

Natalie and I looked at each other for a second or two, then burst into laughter. I collected myself first—and quickly. I couldn't be seen in hysterics about such a serious offense. I had to be the responsible adult. Especially now. "Ben and I are back on the waiting list."

"What!"

"The social worker from our agency called today. According to Dr. Rafferty, we are mentally sane. At least enough to be parents."

"Of course you are." Natalie wrapped me in a hug. "You only need ten percent sanity for something like parenthood. You and Ben are at least at twenty."

"Gee, thanks," I said, hugging her back. "So what should I expect?"

"With parenthood?"

"No, with the conferences."

"Eh. It's all pretty informal." She hooked her arm around mine, and the two of us headed inside. "You go to whichever classrooms you want. Wait in line, if there is a line. Sit, listen to what they say, ask your questions, and be on your merry way. At least that's how it went in junior high. I'm assuming it's the same here."

"Sounds simple enough."

"If I get bored, I plan on pulling my husband into a janitorial closet so I can have my way with him."

"Natalie."

"What? Football season needs to be over already. He's barely home. We women have needs too, you know." She gave me a nudge and a wink, as if we were co-conspirators in the needs department.

She had no idea.

"How was Thanksgiving?" she asked.

"Interesting."

"Yeah?"

Inside the locker bay, parents milled about in small pockets. Several noticed Natalie and me and made passing comments about the big game this Friday. We smiled and nodded and portrayed the appropriate level of enthusiasm while making a quick exit into the main hallway. "Want to join me for CrossFit tomorrow and tell me all about it?"

I waffled. I did more huffing and puffing than actual talking at CrossFit.

"Come on. It's been a couple weeks. Humor your best friend."

"Fine."

She beamed. "All right, I'm off to Spanish class. Samantha got a C on her last test. First C of the girl's life. You would have thought she broke both legs the way she was going on about it." She gave my arm an encouraging squeeze. "Good luck."

Once she was gone, I gazed toward Gracie's trig class with a heavy dose of morbid curiosity. But what did I expect to find? Ben's classroom was downstairs. Miss Henson's classroom was upstairs. There was no reason I would catch them together tonight. Still . . . I wouldn't mind seeing if she was as

pretty in person as she was in the picture on her Facebook profile. I inched in
the direction of Gracie's trig class, but practicality stopped me.

No, I didn't come here to check out Miss Henson.

I came to speak with all of Gracie's teachers.

The normal, sane thing to do would be to start in order. I went in search of
Gracie's first-period class with Mrs. Reyas like the good guardian I was determined to be. If only parent-teacher conferences weren't so discouraging. It was
all a slightly different version of the same. *Gracie does well on tests, but she doesn't*
apply herself in class. Her third-period English teacher seemed pretty offended
by the whole thing. By the time I reached fourth period, I did a lot of nodding
and "uh-huh"-ing, but very little listening. And I was too preoccupied with vi-
sions of a gorgeous blonde hitting on my husband. By the time I was finally on
my way to fifth-period trigonometry, my stomach had tied into knots. Gracie's
accusations aside, there was the whole goat thing to apologize for.

But then I saw something that had my rehearsed apology evaporating altogether. Ben, taking a drink from a water fountain right outside Gracie's trig
class. He wasn't alone. In plain and public view, the woman I recognized from
Facebook slid her hand up his arm and whispered something into his ear. I
stopped in the middle of the hallway.

Mine.

The possessive pronoun blared through me like the blast of a trumpet long
silent. Images of that woman and Ben cavorting in darkened hallways, her
hands on his hips, his lips on her skin, her body pressed up against a wall,
turned the trumpet blast into a siren's wail.

As Miss Henson returned to her classroom, I closed the gap between me
and my husband. "I need to speak with you."

Ben stopped.

Parents wandered past us, up and down the hallway. A few made eye contact with Ben and me and said hello. Ben returned the greeting. I was pretty
sure my greeting looked more like a grimace than a smile. "Somewhere pri-
vate," I added.

"Uh, we can go to my classroom."

I kept my lips pressed together as we walked. Gracie's accusation had
planted the seed. Miss Henson's touch had it germinating, and now my overac-
tive imagination watered the thing into a budding plant. By the time we reached

his classroom, my lips were mashed so tightly together, I felt like the tin man in need of his oil can.

Ben closed the door halfway. "What's up?"

"You tell me."

His eyebrows drew together.

"Is there something going on between you and Gracie's math teacher?"

"Me and Gracie's math teacher?" His expression went from confused to more confused. "What are you talking about?"

"Gracie told me that Miss Henson was in here over lunch."

"Okaaay." He drew out the word nice and long, obviously waiting for more.

"Gracie said she was coming on to you."

He ran his hands down his face. It wasn't so much an "I've been caught red-handed" gesture as it was an "are you kidding me" gesture. "Jill Henson likes to update me on how my players are doing in her class. Gracie came in during one of her weekly reports."

I stared at him. "Weekly reports?"

"Yes."

"Would you really tell me if it was something more?"

His countenance darkened. "I don't like what you're insinuating."

"I just saw her hands all over you." The intensity of my possessiveness had me wobbling off kilter. And somehow, relieved. Like my jealousy was proof that I still cared about Ben. "A woman doesn't touch a man like that unless she has feelings. And why were you up there in the first place, getting a drink from the fountain outside of her classroom?"

"I was in the teacher's lounge eating dinner. I have to pass her room to get down here. And I was thirsty." He shook his head. "I can't even believe we're having this conversation."

"Why not?"

"*Why not?* Come on, Carmen, do you honestly think I'm that kind of a man?"

Deep down, no. I didn't. Ben wasn't a cheater. I knew that. But it wasn't something I could admit. Not when the trumpet had awoken a monster inside of me. "I don't know."

"You don't know?"

"Sometimes it feels like we're strangers."

"Well, I haven't changed."

Meaning I had. Meaning this distance in our marriage was *my* fault.

"If you really don't know anymore, then let me spell it out for you." He stepped closer, his blue eyes blazing. Ben took my wrist and placed my palm against his chest. Warmth rippled beneath his hardened muscles and for one blip of a second, I knew what Natalie meant about needs. "I'm not interested in Jill Henson. The only woman I'm interested in is the one I married seven years ago."

His passion burned too hot to hold. Instead of leaning into it, I stepped away from it and watched as the fire in Ben's eyes fizzled into a hurt I couldn't soothe. Because I was hurt too. Hurt that he'd put the weight of our problems on my shoulders. Hurt that Gracie's trig teacher could so easily flirt with my husband when I didn't know how to anymore. So we stood there, he and I, lost in our own worlds of pain and perceived mistreatment, each waiting for the other person to apologize first, until there was a knock on his half-open door.

"Am I interrupting?" a woman asked, poking her head inside.

Ben turned to the woman with his hurt properly masked, inviting her all the way in with a wave. "No, not at all. Come on in."

She looked between us. "This is my daughter's all-time favorite class. She made me promise to meet Mr. Hart."

"That's nice to hear. What's your daughter's name?"

"Hannah Pierce."

Ben smiled a smile that made women like Miss Henson melt. Apparently, he had already compartmentalized our argument into a box marked *Later*. Or maybe *Never*. If only I could compartmentalize this so easily.

35

GRACIE

The second I stepped through the front door of The Cross, I pulled my sleeves over my hands and shot Elias an alarmed look, but he didn't seem to notice what I noticed, that I was a lone marshmallow in a sea of hot chocolate. Teenagers milled about the lobby area—talking, laughing, flirting. One girl looked Vietnamese, there was a boy who might be Mexican, and not a single slice of white bread.

I gave Elias a nudge. "Everybody's staring at me."

"Nah, they're staring at me."

Although it was the same line he fed me on my first day of school, this time I didn't think he was right. My pasty skin might as well have been a blinding white spotlight. Nerves pinged around inside my belly like a hyperactive game of pinball. But before I could tell Elias that I'd been afflicted with a sudden and debilitating headache, somebody wrapped me in a hug. "You came!"

I neither nodded nor hugged back. I was too stunned by the exuberant welcome.

When my assailant unhanded me, I almost didn't recognize Chanelle. She no longer had the short kinky curls she sported at the theater. Her hair hung in cute, wavy layers past her shoulders. She hugged Elias next. The sight of his arms wrapped around her small waist set off a really silly spark of jealousy. "I can't believe you got her to come."

"It was a minor miracle." Elias winked at me when he said it.

"I didn't know miracles were categorized," I said.

Chanelle wore black-and-purple skater shoes, skinny jeans, and a lime-green knitted top. If I tried wearing that color, I'd look like a ghost with the flu. Chanelle, however, pulled it off with dazzling success. And her hair wasn't the only thing that was different.

"Did you get a . . . ?"

She covered the small rhinestone in her left nostril with her fingers, a self-conscious maneuver. I couldn't imagine what she had to be self-conscious about. "My dad almost killed me."

"I think it looks good," Elias said.

Another spark of jealousy crackled, but I smothered it. It was a dumb emotion. Besides, Elias was right. It did look good. "I agree."

"You do?"

"It looks natural on you."

"I knew I liked you." She elbowed Elias. "Did I mention how much I like her?"

"You might have once or twice. Hey, is Malik here yet?"

Chanelle rose up on her tiptoes to search the crowd, then cupped her hand to the side of her mouth like a megaphone. "Yo, Malik!"

How a shout so loud could come out of a person so small, I wasn't sure. It had me shrinking into Elias's side. I waited for the entire room to stop and stare. Most didn't even bat an eye. The shout did the trick, though, because a second later, a boy parted through the crowd, wearing oversized glasses with thick, black frames, a pencil behind his ear, and red suspenders. He walked toward us with his hands cupped over his heart, a grin tucked into the corner of his mouth, and unmistakable swagger in his step. "To what do I owe the pleasure of being so boisterously harkened?"

Chanelle rolled her eyes. "Malik likes to talk fancy."

"I prefer vernacular of the poetic variety."

Elias laughed, and the two boys skinned palms before pulling each other in for a manly back thump. "I want to introduce you to my friend, Gracie Fisher."

"Gracie Fisher." Malik didn't just shake my hand, he sandwiched it between his palms and bowed his head. "It is my immense pleasure."

I managed a single-syllable "Hi." Was this kid for real?

"Eli has enlightened me of your interest in the academic bowl team."

I threw Elias a "thanks a lot" look. "*Potential* interest."

"Well, you should make that interest kinetic. We are competitively genial folk." The smile tucked in the corner of his mouth spread across his lips, like he knew he was being facetious. "For real, it's fun times. You should join us, or at least check things out. We're in need of an intelligent female."

"How do you know I'm intelligent?"

"A comrade of Elias can be nothing but intelligent."

I quickly discovered that Malik was for real. Everything he said was accompanied with an amused smile, like he was fully aware of his absurdity but could be no other way. According to Chanelle, he performed spoken-word poetry at some coffee shop in downtown Pensacola every Thursday night.

"We should go sometime," Elias said. "He's brilliant."

"My friend is generous with his hyperbole, but I'm grateful for the encouragement." Malik clasped his hands over his chest again. "Now if you'll excuse me, the lavatory beckons." He pointed at me as he backed toward the door. "Join us on Monday. I have a feeling you'll enjoy yourself, Gracie Fisher."

When the door closed behind him and I turned back toward Elias and Chanelle, they wore matching grins. "Welcome to the experience that is Malik," she said.

"Never a dull moment." Elias shifted his weight to look past me. "Hey, it's Pastor Zeke."

And without warning, Elias grabbed my hand and pulled me toward a man with a bald head and a body so large he could be a linebacker for the Miami Dolphins. He was slowly making his way through the crowd, stopping occasionally to chat. We reached him just as he was finishing up a conversation with the Vietnamese girl and two of her friends.

When he saw me, he clapped his hands together. "This must be Gracie Fisher."

I gave Elias another sideways look. "You know me?"

"Eli may have mentioned you a time or two." The deep rumble of Pastor Zeke's voice reminded me of Mufasa from *The Lion King.* "I hope these two are making you feel at home." He clasped his large hand over Elias's shoulder. "You ready for Friday?"

"Bags are packed. Team leaves tomorrow morning."

"The missus and I will be there, front and center. We're proud of you, son." He let go of Elias and turned his attention to me. "Worship begins in two minutes. I'll see you from the pulpit."

"I'm sure I'll be easy to find."

With his rumble of a chuckle, he moved on into the sanctuary.

Chanelle linked her arm around my elbow. "You ready?"

"For what?"

"This ain't your mama's youth group."

I had no idea what she meant until the music began.

Our breaths escaped in frozen puffs that disappeared into the night as The Cross's parking lot slowly emptied and Elias walked me to my car. After the singing ended and Pastor Zeke finished his message and students broke out into small groups with various leaders, Elias and I stayed in the lobby to chat with Malik and Chanelle and a few others. Well, Elias did the chatting. Me? I hadn't said much since I stepped into the sanctuary.

"So . . . ?" Elias asked, our arms swinging side by side.

"So?"

He took a few steps ahead of me, turned around, and started walking backward. "You've been pretty quiet."

I bit the inside of my cheek. Back at the church Mom and I went to in New Hope, we sang songs out of giant, dusty hymnals. I yawned through the sermons while people around me either checked their watches or battled with small kids in stiff pews. I didn't know what Sundays were like at The Cross, but Wednesday nights at least were far from anything I experienced at New Hope.

There had been clapping and dancing and, strangest of all, students who lifted their hands in the air. Both hands, straight up, their faces glowing with joy. And yet later I discovered that those same kids with hands lifted high had problems and baggage just like me. Absentee fathers. Broken relationships. Foreclosed homes. Death and abuse and loss and battles nobody saw. Yet when they sang, it was like none of those things mattered. They lost themselves in the music.

During the message, there were "amens" and "hallelujahs" and I couldn't find a single person playing a game or texting on a phone. After Pastor Zeke finished preaching on the stage, I joined Elias in a smaller group, where there were uncomfortably raw confessions and sincere encouragement, all wrapped up in the kind of prayer that made my arm hair stand on end.

The whole thing was a lot to process.

"Are you going to say anything?"

"Um . . ."

Elias reached my car first. He sat on the hood and propped his feet on the front bumper while stars sprinkled the sky overhead. "Um good, or um bad?"

I stopped in front of him. "Um, I like Chanelle?"

He smiled. "She's easy to like."

It was the truth. Despite the sparks of jealousy, despite our having very little in common, Chanelle set me at ease almost as much as Elias. She'd included me in the group without putting me on the spot and when she asked for my cell number at the end, she seemed one hundred percent sincere about wanting it. I wanted to ask Elias what the two of them were, exactly, but I had no idea how to do so without sounding ridiculous.

"Would you come again?"

I crossed my arms to ward off the chill. *Would I come again?* In truth, despite the warm welcome, I had felt awkward throughout the majority of the night. I stuck out in more ways than one. My skin color, it turned out, was the least conspicuous. "Pastor Zeke's message was interesting."

"It was a good one."

"Jesus and that Peter guy walking on water? Pretty cool stuff."

He peered at me through the night, a ghost of a smile haunting his lips. "I'd love to hear your opinion on the man of the hour."

"I kept hearing his voice echoing from the clouds. '*Simba, remember who you are.*'"

"What?"

"*The Lion King?* That scene where Simba sees his dad in the clouds after Rafiki made him look at his reflection in the water."

Elias set his elbows on his knees. He looked completely lost but also entertained.

"And you accused *me* of not knowing my Disney trivia." I shook my head. "Pastor Zeke could be a voice double for James Earl Jones."

"I wasn't talking about Pastor Zeke. I was talking about Jesus."

"You want to know my opinion on Jesus?"

"Humor me."

"Here is something humorous. Over Thanksgiving, I met this guy named Jimmy, who was convinced Jesus spoke to him in the clouds."

Elias chuckled. "You are fixated on these clouds."

"That wasn't me. That was Jimmy."

"For real, though," he said.

I twisted my lips to the side and searched my thoughts. Not for something humorous, but for something honest. What *did* I think about the man of the hour? "Carmen and Ben go to church, but it's just a thing they do. To my mom, I think Jesus was a crutch who never really helped her stand. And don't even get me started on Chris Nanning." I hooked my thumbs through the belt loops of my jeans. "But then there's you. You seem to take the whole Jesus thing pretty seriously. And despite what I may have thought in the beginning, you're not too bad of a guy."

"That's nice, but you're evading the question."

"Yeah?"

"I said I wanted *your* opinion on Jesus." He slid forward and set his ratty sneakers on the cement. "Who do you say He is, Gracie Fisher?"

"Honestly?"

"Always."

"I have no idea."

Elias's ghost of a smile materialized. "Since we're being honest, what if I told you that I really want you to come to the game on Friday?"

"Seven hours is a long way to drive for an overrated mating ritual."

"Come on, you're living with the coach. And you're friends with the star receiver. You have to come. I'll even let you wear my jersey."

"Your jersey, huh? How 1960s of you." I poked fun, but the offer had an alarming amount of pleasure spreading through my body.

36

GRACIE

The student body gathered in the parking lot early Thursday morning while the football team loaded onto a rented bus. Elias found me in the crowd and tipped his chin, a question in his eyes. Was I coming? I wrinkled my nose and shook my head. He laughed and stepped onto the bus, and the Bay Breeze Sting Rays hit the road to the hoots and cheers of my classmates.

Turns out my steely resolve was made more of tin foil. Intrigue won the battle.

Which was why, the next morning, I found myself in the back of a van with a freshman named Samantha Jane, her mom behind the wheel, and Carmen riding shotgun on our way to the Citrus Bowl Stadium in Orlando, Florida.

I was going to a football game.

Chanelle texted me when we were twenty minutes away: *r u coming?*

Biting my lip, I stared at her question until we reached the hotel. Once we were checked in, I responded with a simple yes.

Ten seconds later . . . *Yayayay!! u have 2 sit w/ussss!*

My adrenal glands kicked into action. Going to a football game was one thing. Going to youth group with Elias was one thing. Watching Elias play football while cheering him on with his youth group was another. But what was my other option—sitting with Carmen and Natalie and all the booster moms? Or worse, joining Samantha and her dancer friends in the Bay Breeze student section?

Where r u sitting?

She texted me the section and row and somehow, after grabbing burgers with my road-trip buddies, I was wandering through a stadium surrounded by a sea of blue and gold. It may have been over a year of no football, but I hadn't forgotten what the games were like. Make that game a state championship in a stadium designed for college, and the energy level was insane. As I made my way down section 132, Chanelle found me before I found her. I caught her waving enthusiastically from row twelve. She wrapped me in a hug when I arrived, her light-brown eyes wide and bright.

"Elias said there was no way you were coming!" She held onto my arms when she talked and hugged me again. "I'm so glad you changed your mind." She was wearing a blue-and-gold jersey with the number eighteen on it—Elias's number. He must have asked Chanelle to wear his jersey after I declined the offer—if his offer was even a serious one.

Over her shoulder I saw a guy who had painted his entire face blue with the same numbers painted on his cheeks in yellow as Chanelle wore on her person. I did a double take and realized it was Malik without his glasses. "Hey, Malik."

"Salutations, Gracie Fisher. You ready to cheer on our fearless friend?"

"I think so."

Chanelle held out a bag of Skittles, then poured some candy into my upturned palm. "Where are you staying?"

"Comfort Suites."

"So are we! Girls in one room, boys in the other. You should drive back with us tomorrow morning. It'll be fun."

I gave her a noncommittal nod and stuck a red Skittle in my mouth, trying to get a handle on things. It was all very weird—this moment. Standing in a football stadium, being so enthusiastically included. Things were starting to feel uncontained, like my decision to go to youth group had burst open a can of confetti that could not be closed up again.

The crowd broke out into cheers, and the marching band let loose an anthem song. The Bay Breeze Sting Rays ran out onto the field along with the cheerleaders. I caught myself standing up on my tiptoes, searching for number eighteen. He ran up in front, leading the pack.

Excitement flickered through my veins, and as the game progressed, that flicker grew into a seismic wave. Watching Elias in his element was more mesmerizing than it should have been. His movement was like art. I couldn't look away. When he scored a touchdown in the first quarter, I cheered with everyone else. When he scored another one in the third, I was practically jumping. And when the final quarter clock ticked down to ten seconds with the Sting Rays behind by two and Elias caught a pass that put the team within field goal distance, my heart thudded so fast and so hard I wondered if it was possible to experience oxygen overload.

The kicker took the field, only instead of watching him, I found Elias on the sidelines with his helmet off, standing beside Ben. Their matching expressions said it all. For all Elias's talk, he loved this sport. And for all his downplay, at this moment, right now, winning mattered. And since it mattered to him, it mattered to me. So much that my mouth went dry and my palms went sweaty and I didn't even care that Chanelle's nails were digging through the fleece of my jacket.

The center snapped the ball and the kicker started his approach. He let his foot fly. The ball soared through the air and sailed between the two uprights. I looked at the referee with wide eyes as he raised his arms over his head and every single person dressed in blue and gold went berserk.

"They won!" Chanelle yelled, still clutching my sleeve. "Two years in a row, they won state!"

The two of us jumped up and down like idiots, and somehow I was running onto the field with Malik and Chanelle and what must have been the entire student body. Chanelle found Elias first. She practically launched herself into his arms and he lifted her off the ground. When he put her back down, our eyes met over her shoulder. I took a quick step toward him. He took a quick step toward me. We didn't hug, but he did stare down at me with a set of dimples flashing deeper than I'd ever seen. "You came!"

I slid my hands into the back pockets of my jeans, my cheeks hot. This close in his football pads and uniform, Elias looked impossibly tall and athletic and irresistible.

"I can't believe you came."

"Yeah, well, I figured since I live with the coach and all . . ."

He pushed his hand through his hair, his eyes twinkling. My heart fluttering. It looked like he was going to say something, but then a teammate threw his arm around Elias's neck and dragged him away to celebrate. I watched them go. And in my line of vision, I spotted Carmen walking toward Ben. I couldn't see her face, since her back was to me. But I could see Ben's. His hat was askew and he wore a victorious smile, and he looked at his wife in this smoldering way that I was sure would make women all across Bay Breeze swoon. When Carmen reached him, he wrapped her in a hug and pressed his lips against hers. I was mesmerized all over again. In all my months with the Harts, this was the first time I'd seen them kiss.

CARMEN

"Who are you trying to race, girl?"

I wasn't sure. I only knew that between the post-state-champ sports broadcast on Channel Three and this morning's picture posted on the station's Facebook page, my muscles felt like sprinting. Far, far away. Logic, however, forced them to slow. Natalie wanted to run five miles. There was no way I could maintain this speed for that long a distance, even with a tsunami of chaotic emotions to expel.

"Did you see the picture on Facebook?" I asked.

"Of you and Ben smooching?"

I shook my head, not because she was wrong, but because the posting of the picture without my permission rubbed me the wrong way. The motion set my curly ponytail into a swing. We jogged down a short incline onto a bike path. In a little over a mile, we'd be running along the bay. Perhaps the gorgeous view would take my mind off my producer's antics.

"It's fabulous publicity," she had said earlier this morning. *"Viewers are eating it up. Way better for the station than that video in August."*

It wasn't enough that the station had to show footage of Ben and me kissing as part of the state-championship news story. No, Nancy had to go and post a picture too—of Ben and me standing in the middle of a green football field amongst his celebratory players, with Ben's arms wrapped around my waist, his lips pressed against mine. Last I saw, it had over three thousand likes and some five hundred comments. People gushing over the win, heralding Coach Hart for his hard work and dedication, and complimenting me for the cuteness that was us—me and Ben, Bay Breeze's sweethearts. One girl wrote: *U R so lucky! Coach Hart is hawt. <3* She wasn't alone in her sentiment.

"I'm sick of my personal life being on public display."

Natalie laughed. "I guess a career in acting is out, then? Do you ever look at those celebrity magazines? I saw one at the grocery store yesterday. Leonardo

DiCaprio was on the cover, standing next to a *urinal*. What is wrong with the paparazzi?"

"Anytime I go to the grocery store, I run into somebody who thinks they know me."

"You are on their television screens every morning. And they probably follow you on Twitter or something."

"Don't get me started on Twitter." Another one of Nancy's "suggestions," which were never really suggestions at all. The things I posted on Twitter weren't me. They were alter-ego Carmen. The one who lived in Happy Land with her happy husband. "Whatever happened to broadcast meteorology being about *broadcasting meteorology*?"

"I understand wanting some privacy, especially after the whole expectant-mothers sign demolition, but might I suggest something?"

"What?"

"You're overreacting?"

"Overreacting?"

"Carmen, it's a good picture. You and Ben look cute."

Yeah, and deliriously happy. But Ben and I weren't deliriously happy. And therein lay the crux of my ire. I was tired of feeding the illusion. I was tired of smiling for the camera. My smiles were counterfeit.

"So guess what I signed up for in January?" Natalie asked.

"What?"

"CPR class."

"Any particular reason?"

"You know how I've been miserable at home without Reese? Well, Brandon and I have been having these knock-down-drag-out fights about me working again. He's so old-fashioned. Anyway, the other day he pulls this idea out of thin air. I love kids. He loves having me at home. Why not start an in-home day care?"

"That'd be right up your alley."

"I know! Wanna join me?"

"With in-home day care?"

"No, the CPR class. It's a good skill to have."

Maybe Natalie was on to something. According to our social worker, some couples waited two years before they were chosen. The thought of waiting that long in this torturous purgatory made me want to crawl out of my skin. Perhaps adding *CPR certified* to our portfolio would snag the attention of a birth mother. "Sure, I'll join you."

"Perfect. I'll get you registered. Now catch me up. How are things going with Gracie?"

"We remain in this very odd, courteous twilight zone. And she joined the academic bowl team. She seems to like it so far, even if she would never say so."

I had told Natalie about getting stuck in the mud on the way to Tallahassee, the fight that ensued, and the deal we'd made at the rehabilitation facility. But I didn't tell her about Gracie's accusation—the one where she called me a hypocrite. Of all the words we exchanged, those were the ones that left the deepest impression. I didn't want them to be true anymore, but peeling off so many accumulated layers of persona was no easy thing. I was slightly terrified that once I peeled them all away, nothing would remain but a bag of dry bones. I forced my breathing into a Lamaze-type rhythm. "Hey, Natalie?"

"Yeah?"

"Have you and Brandon ever had marital problems?"

"Have you not been listening to a thing I've been saying lately? I wasn't kidding about the knock-down-drag-outs."

"Yeah, sure. You two argue." A lot, actually. But they touched a lot too. Poor Samantha had been mortified on more than one occasion. "I'm not talking about arguments. I'm talking about . . ." What was I talking about? How did I even begin to describe this thing we'd become?

"Are you and Ben okay?"

"I don't know."

Natalie slowed into a walk and took my arm so I had to slow too. "Carmen?"

It was on the tip of my tongue to tell her. All of it. From the very first moment I began pushing Ben away, to the giant wall that stood between us now— the one I yearned for him to claw through, even though I had no idea what I'd do if he did. I wanted to peel off the layers until they were nothing but a littered trail of metaphorical onion skin on the path behind us, but after years of holding my cards so closely, I couldn't get the details out. "We've hit a rough spot, I guess."

Natalie wrapped her arm around my shoulder and gave me a sympathetic squeeze. "You and Ben have been through a lot these last few months. You'll get through it, especially now that football season is over. You know how that is."

"Yeah, I do."

"All last week, I thought Brandon and I were going to rip each other's throats out. But we're okay now. Every marriage has dry patches."

I nodded, but I wasn't sure this was a dry patch so much as a dead one.

Natalie and I resumed our jogging and rounded a bend. The bay came into view in all its sparkling late-morning glory. It should have taken my breath away. Instead, I beheld the scene before me with a dispassion that shouldn't be. I attempted to pray, to speak words to God in my mind. All I could manage were two. They repeated in tune with my panting.

Lord, help . . . Lord, help . . . Lord, help . . .

For all I knew, I was speaking to the air.

38

GRACIE

I went Christmas shopping, hoping for a distraction. Maybe by the time I finished, the unease that had camped out in my stomach since Bay Breeze won state would finally take a hike. Unfortunately, I walked out of Kirby's Antiques feeling no better than when I entered. Turned out, I was pretty awful at picking out gifts.

So far I had browsed the used bookstore, Sweeties Candy Store, some clothing boutiques, the gift shops on Dock Street, a candle store, even this random rock emporium next to the Hot Dog Hut, where I found some pretty cool mood rings and seashell necklaces, but nothing that Ben or Carmen or my mother might like. I shuffled toward one of the iron benches and took a seat.

With Christmas less than two weeks away, town square had turned into a snowless version of the North Pole, with holly strung on the streetlights and wreaths on the back of each bench, even a Christmas tree in the center of the gazebo. A lady walked past it now with her yappy dog. As someone who lived in the South her entire life, I saw white Christmases only on postcards. But this year had been colder than usual, so maybe . . .

"Hey, Fisher!"

I turned toward the sound of my name. Elias strolled toward me through the park with his hands tucked inside the front pockets of his corduroy jacket, his hunter-green beanie on his head. My stomach did a loop-de-loop. He was starting to matter too much. Actually, everything was starting to matter too much—our friendship, The Treasure Chest, even the short time I'd spent on the academic bowl team. Maybe this explained the nerves. The world was a lot less worrisome when I didn't care.

"Catching some rays?"

I pointed at my face. "Does this look like the skin of a girl who can catch rays?"

He smiled. "What are you up to?"

"I was attempting to Christmas shop, but I failed miserably."

"How does one fail at Christmas shopping?"

"Everything I saw seemed so . . ."

"Let me guess." He cocked his head. "Cliché?"

"How'd you know?"

"Come on." He nodded for me to follow him.

"Come on *where?*"

"To a place that will solve all your Christmas shopping woes."

"I've been to every single place along this square and up and down Dock Street twice. I highly doubt you are going to solve my woes."

"Have you been to the General Store?"

"Bay Breeze has a general store?"

He gave the underside of my boot a soft kick and nodded again for me to follow.

So I did, past the Christmas tree in the gazebo, to the other side of the square. "If this is true, why have I never seen it?"

"Because it's off the beaten path."

Why a general store would be off the beaten path was beyond me. But Elias appeared to know exactly where he was headed, and since I was out of options, I continued after him past The Barbeque Pit. "What are you doing out and about?" I asked.

"Enjoying my first Saturday of freedom."

"No football practice."

His grin widened. "No football practice."

My attention dropped to his hand, which was no longer inside his pocket, but swinging casually by his side. The entire football team had not only been wearing their state championship rings but making a habit of holding their fists up toward one another in the hallways and the cafeteria while I gagged in their general direction. Some even wore two—last year's ring on the left hand, this year's ring on the right. Elias, however, wore neither. "So Mr. MVP, do you have a speech prepared for the big football banquet tonight?"

"I haven't been named MVP."

"We both know you will be."

"Then I'll wing it." He stepped past the yogurt shop and led me down a side street called Franklin Way. A block later, we reached the front of a building that looked like it came straight out of the 1800s. Elias stopped in front of the door and held out his arm like a male version of Vanna White. "Welcome to the General Store, Bay Breeze's hidden treasure. Let this be a fair warning. Once you step inside, every other convenience store will be ruined for you for the rest of your days."

I looked at him with heavily lidded eyes. "Are you done now?"

He opened the door to the sound of a bell jingle and waited for me to go first. Stepping inside this store was like stepping out of Dr. Emmett Brown's DeLorean straight into the nineteenth century—all brick walls and wood plank flooring and a whole counter full of old-fashioned candy. Black licorice, jawbreakers, bubblegum cigars, Necco Wafers.

Elias gave me a nudge. "Told you."

Indeed.

The place was even better than the hole-in-the-wall music store on Avenue D back in Apalachicola, and I spent more time in that store browsing through depreciated techno fusion CDs than I'd ever admit to anyone. I commenced wide-eyed browsing immediately.

It had a little bit of everything—food (a lot of local sauces and spices), soaps, cookware, gardening tools, kerosene lamps, and a random variety of novelty toys. I held up a Magic Eight Ball. In fourth grade, I had a friend who bought one at a garage sale. We used to sit on her bed after school and ask the toy random, silly questions until her mother discovered it and threw the ball in the trash. Her daughter would not play with toys that encouraged fortune-telling, she had said. "I can't believe they have these!"

Elias stepped behind me. "What is it?"

"You don't know what a Magic Eight Ball is?"

"I know what an eight ball is, but I've never seen one this big and I wasn't aware that some were magical."

I rolled my eyes. "Is Elias Banks completely lame for not knowing what you are?" I shook the ball, then flipped it over. A luminescent blue triangle with the words *Signs point to yes* floated in the display. I let out a burst of laughter and showed it to him.

He narrowed his eyes at me, then leaned over my shoulder. "Am I totally awesome for showing Gracie Fisher this General Store?"

I shook, then flipped. A new blue triangle appeared in the display: *Ask again later.*

"What kind of bogus answer is that?" He took the ball from my hand and gave it a rattle.

I held up an Erector set. "What do you think—a good gift for Ben?"

"I loved those as a kid. I think my mom sold my old one in a garage sale."

"Nerd."

Grinning, he returned the Magic Eight Ball to the shelf.

I wandered down the aisle with Elias close behind, passing Lincoln Logs, a Radio Flyer wagon, Etch A Sketches, Hula-Hoops. The place was like a labyrinth of eccentricity. I had officially found my happy place. I turned down a new aisle and continued my roaming.

"How about these?" Elias said, holding up a tin. "Everybody loves moon pies."

"Add some RC Cola and you have yourself some esculent perfection."

"Esculent?"

"Edible."

Elias shook his head. "Malik is rubbing off on you."

Indeed he was. I'd spent three after-school practices with him checking out the academic bowl team, and already my vocabulary had improved. I even downloaded a dictionary app on my phone so I could look up definitions of words as soon as he said them. I liked predicting how many words I would have to look up beforehand. It had become a fun game.

I stopped in front of a selection of teas. "What are your plans for Christmas?"

"My mom and I will go to church on Christmas Eve."

I pulled the lid off a canister and inhaled the scent of mint and rosemary. "And?"

"And that's it. She has to work Christmas Day, so we don't really get a chance to plan anything fancy. Pastor Zeke and his wife head to Alabama to spend the holiday with one of their daughters."

"You and your mom should come to The Treasure Chest after church." The invitation popped out before I could suck it back in. It turned my cheeks warm. I couldn't believe I just invited Elias and his mother to our family

Christmas gathering. He had to think I was weird. Or desperate. Or who knows what. "I mean, if you wanted to stop by, you could. But there's no pressure or anything."

"Christmas at The Treasure Chest with you?" He came beside me and smelled the tea too. "That doesn't sound half bad."

39

CARMEN

I drove to The Treasure Chest at nine thirty on a Saturday night without a valid reason as to why. After tonight's football banquet, I changed into comfy pants, popped a bag of kettle corn, and plunked myself on the couch to watch some Netflix when the motel's neon sign came into my head and refused to leave. My brain decided that I needed to make sure the sign worked tonight. Not tomorrow afternoon after church, but now. My stubborn, illogical desire to ruin a perfectly fine night of vegetating on the couch made absolutely no sense.

Until I turned into the pitch-black parking lot and discovered a familiar vehicle parked in the beam of my headlights—a rusty maroon Mirage Mitsubishi. Gracie was here, and although we'd reached an odd truce over Thanksgiving, suspicious thoughts jumped to the forefront of my mind. Like maybe she came out here to drink and smoke weed and plot her next goat-nabbing adventure.

Gravel crunched beneath my tires as I parked beside her car. I stepped outside to the rhythmic swoosh of waves crashing against the shore and brought my hand to my forehead, as if doing so might help me see through the night. I had never given Gracie a key, so unless she broke in again, she wasn't inside. And since we had new windows installed, the act of breaking in should have been more difficult than it had been back in August.

I spotted her in the light of the moon, which was muted but not obstructed by the clouds overhead. She lay back on a paint-chipped Adirondack chair on the pool deck, its empty twin beside her. There were another six in the pool shed. I'd been wanting to purchase two more, spray-paint them bright colors, and place one outside of each room on the ground level. But with Christmas closing in and a million things left to do, I hadn't gotten around to it yet. I made my way through the courtyard. If Gracie heard me coming, she didn't turn to look. She kept her gaze pinned on the sky above, her fingers wrapped around a can of RC Cola.

The new tarp we purchased to cover the empty pool rustled in the breeze as I stopped beside her. "What are you doing here?"

"Listening to the ocean."

"Do you come here often at night to listen to the ocean?"

She shrugged, then took a slurp of her Coke. "I like it here. It's a good place to be alone. To think."

I couldn't agree more. In fact, I'd done more thinking out here over the past three months than I'd done over the past three years. Something about the mixture of solitude and sweat and dirt and painfully sweet memories stirred up more thoughts of me and Ben and the turns life had taken than I knew what to do with. "Are you thinking about anything in particular?"

The breeze fluttered wisps of hair around Gracie's face. She peeled a few strands away. "I invited Elias and his mom to Christmas Eve today."

"Elias, as in Eli Banks, Ben's receiver?"

"That's the one."

I eased onto the chair beside her, sitting sideways to face Gracie as she reclined. "You two are friends?"

"I'm not sure what we are."

Curiosity begged me to pry, but fear of doing or saying something that would bring back the sullen, closed-off Gracie kept that curiosity in check. Getting unstuck from the mud on Thanksgiving may have hurdled us over a giant barricade, but I wasn't really sure what to do on this side of it. Every step I took came with extreme caution, lest it be the wrong one. "Well, Aunt Ingrid would say the more the merrier. Especially for Christmas."

Gracie took another sip of her RC Cola. "Do you think she'll remember me?"

"Ingrid?"

She nodded.

"It depends on what kind of day she's having." I hoped with every last ounce of hope I had that come Christmas Eve, Ingrid would be having a Gin Rummy 500 day. I wasn't brave enough to hope for Hearts. "If she's having a good day, then of course she will remember you."

Gracie's lips turned into a Mona Lisa smile. Just noticeable enough to soften her into someone younger and prettier than the scowling teenager I was used to living with.

"Is that all you were thinking about?" I asked. "Two extra guests for Christmas?"

"Sorta." She fiddled with the tab on her can, bending it up, down, up, down until it popped off with a clink.

I slid my hands between my knees, unsure if I should push or not. "How's the academic bowl team?"

"All right."

"Think you'll stick with it?"

"I probably won't make the final cut. They're pretty intense about making it to nationals."

"You shouldn't underestimate yourself."

Gracie flicked the tab from her thumb. It launched into the air and landed on the pool tarp. "Why did you come out here?"

"I wanted to check the sign. Make sure it's working." I looked toward the familiar shadowed marker growing up tall from the parking lot—barely visible through the dark. "It used to be one of my favorite things about this place when I was little. Seeing the neon lights when Dad I drove along the highway meant we were finally here."

Gracie sat up from her reclined position. She brought her knee to her chest and wrapped her arm around her shin.

"Aunt Ingrid used to tell me and my cousins that Neil Armstrong saw it all the way from the moon." I smiled at the memory.

"She told me that too."

"She did?"

"She also told me that there was a real pirate's treasure chest buried some-where in the courtyard." Gracie set her chin on top of her kneecap and gazed out toward the ocean.

Another wave crashed.

Not so far away, hotel lights off Navarre Beach twinkled like superficial stars.

"Gracie, why did you come to The Treasure Chest?"

"I already told you."

"I don't mean tonight. I mean when you left Apalachicola." Of all the places she could have come, why here? I'd asked the question before, but Gracie never answered. At least not seriously. Maybe tonight, in the absence of hostility, with memories surrounding us on all sides, she'd answer honestly.

"I don't know." Gracie lifted her chin off her knee. "Life was easier here. Not so heavy. Mom was always on her best behavior. And it was nice having somebody looking after me."

"You mean Ingrid?"

"Yeah."

The answer broke my heart. Gracie was right—what she said over Thanksgiving. I didn't know what it was like. Sure, I had grown up with Mom's dysfunction, but I never had to bear the full brunt of it. That had landed on Dad's shoulders, even if he did sweep her problems under the rug. Nobody had borne anything for Gracie. Certainly not me.

"And you always seemed happy here," she said. "At least that's how I remember it."

"I was."

"Why'd you let it get so run-down, then?"

Wispy clouds rolled across the sky, altering the moon's brightness like a dimming switch.

"I don't know. It just sort of happened." Natalie called it entropy. Nature's predisposition toward disorder. Unless we actively fought against it, things fell into disarray. Motels and marriages alike.

Gracie traced a line between two freckles on her knee. "I came here thinking Ingrid could give me a job. And maybe I could find happiness too."

As much as I didn't want to, I couldn't help but picture the scene. Gracie coming to The Treasure Chest in search of some stability, but finding an abandoned, run-down building instead. No wonder she had been so angry. "Maybe when we get this place running again, you can have that job you came for."

Her expression was equal parts hope and caution. I knew the mixture well. "I'd like that," she said.

"Me too." I placed my hands on my thighs and pushed up into standing. "Should we see if the sign still works?"

"Sure."

The two of us headed through the courtyard, into the front office. I found the power switch beneath the front desk and flipped it on. Electricity hummed through the line. Outside the window, the sign blinked like a strobe light, then remained steady, lighting up the night like a luminescent beacon for weary travelers.

I stepped into the opened doorway and set my hand against the door frame. The sign was every bit as glorious as I remembered—a bright display of an opened treasure chest filled with yellow, blue, and pink rubies casting their glow into the dark sky above and onto the green grass below. Like a bug attracted to the light, I stepped out from the doorway, past the protection of the awning, where a cold, barely there drizzle had begun to fall, taking me back in time. To the summer Gracie and Mom hadn't come and Ben and I had fallen in love.

The week before I returned to UVA, my last week with Ben, I had been unable to return the words he'd spoken to me on Aunt Ingrid's couch. Not because I didn't feel the same. In fact, I was breaking with love for him. I just didn't see any good in confessing my feelings, not when the confession wouldn't change our circumstances. For a few days after Ben's declaration, he waited. He never asked or pressured, but I could see the searching in his eyes. And when the words didn't come, he started to slip away.

The distance had already begun and we weren't even separated yet.

The night of our good-bye, Ben hugged me. I didn't want him to let go. Ever. I breathed in his scent and committed his warm skin to memory. My flight to Virginia was leaving early the next morning. I didn't dare ask him to drive me to the airport. Not when making a "clean break" was my idea. Besides, he had work now. Not motel work, but work work. At Bay Breeze High School. I stood on tiptoe and buried my face in the crook of his neck, and when his arms let go of me, I swallowed the growing knot in my throat and forced my arms to release him too.

He tucked a strand of hair behind my ear and looked into my eyes—one final search for what I had yet to say. When I didn't give him what he was looking for, he gave me a kiss that came and went like virga—the kind of rain so warm and light, it evaporated before it reached the ground.

"Good-bye, Carmen."

And just like that, he walked away.

I stood in the doorway of the front office, watching him disappear into the rain and the steam rising up from the hot cement, unable to breathe. Uncertain

I would ever be able to breathe again. I grasped the door frame with determined ferocity. We needed a clean break. It was easier this way.

Do not go after him.

But watching him walk away from me beneath the glow of The Chest's
sign was too much. I was coming undone. I needed a breath and after almost
two months of breathing in tune with him, I'd forgotten how to get one on my
own. My hand let go of the door frame. I stepped out into the rain after him.
"Ben!"

He stopped. And slowly, he turned around.

There was a moment—a second? an eternity?—in which neither of us
moved. We stared at one another with more voltage between us than the neon
sign above. And then, as though they could be contained no longer, the stifled
words burst out into the night with a vehemence that came when things were
pent up for too long. "I love you!"

His long, sure strides ate up the distance between us. He took hold of my
waist and he kissed me like I'd never been kissed before. He lifted me off the
ground, my body pressed against his. I dug my fingers into his wet hair. And
when the kiss ended and my feet were back on the cement, I looked up at Ben
through a sheen of tears. This time I was the one who did the searching. I
wanted an answer. I wanted hope. I wanted something to hold on to. "What
does this change?"

He swept wet curls off my neck. "Everything."

"Ben . . ."

"Carmen, I'll wait for you."

I bit my lip. Shook my head. I couldn't ask him to wait. Not when I didn't
know if I would be coming back. "You shouldn't."

"But I will." Gently, he clasped my hands together and set them over his
heart. "I'll always wait for you."

40

GRACIE

The run-down motel I ran to in August had morphed into a vintage Christmas wonderland. "The Little Drummer Boy" played from the speakers in the hospitality room. The smell of eggnog and gingerbread hung in the air. A pair of long tables draped in poinsettia-red tablecloths formed a right angle around the Christmas tree—a green-tinseled island in a sea of wrapped presents. One in particular kept drawing my attention, pulling the knots in my stomach tighter as I set forks on top of carefully folded cream-colored napkins.

When Carmen finished her table straightening, she looked up at me with a smile. "I really like your hair."

She wasn't talking about the tips, which I'd dyed tree-green yesterday afternoon in a rare but festive bout of Christmas cheer. My fingers moved to the bobby pin I'd used to pin my bangs back.

"You should wear it like that more often."

Carmen's compliment did not help with the stomach-knotting problem. The only thing worse than trying too hard was being caught trying too hard. Seriously, what had prompted me to invite Elias to our Christmas soiree? I mean, I was going to meet his mother. He was going to meet my mother. Our mothers were going to meet each other. I peeked at the present I'd wrapped in the midst of my dye job. What if he thought it was stupid?

Ben's mom hurried inside with a pitcher of iced tea and set it on the table and told us there was lots of work left to do. She stopped short of clapping her hands and saying "chop-chop," but the implication was there. I only met her last night and already I had her pegged. She was the kind of woman who delivered commands in a voice so sweet and southern, you'd never be able to call her out on it. The kind of woman whose "oh, bless her heart" was code for "what an idiot."

She rushed into the front office, where another long table had been set for the food. As soon as she was gone, I swear Carmen rolled her eyes a little. I set the final fork in place and wiped my hands on my ankle-length black cotton skirt.

"Are you nervous?" she asked.

"No." My answer came way too quick to be true. "Are you?"

"Terrified."

"Because of Ingrid?"

Carmen pulled at the hem of her blouse. "I just hope she'll be in a state of mind to appreciate all of this. I called Rayanna—her nurse—and she seems to be doing well, but you never know when the switch in her mind will turn off."

I tried to dredge up some comforting words, but the gift distracted me again, and then Mrs. Hart returned with a pitcher of water to set beside the tea. "Everyone will be here soon. Carmen, can you come help me with the last of the food?"

Daughter-in-law followed mother-in-law like an obedient puppy, and I made a beeline to the tree. A girl could only imagine the awkward scene that would unfold when she gave a boy a present and he had nothing for her so many times before she psyched herself out. I grabbed the gift, speed-walked to my car, and shut it inside the trunk. A long, slow breath leaked out into the air, and with it, my building anxiety.

I should have done that a long time ago.

Outside room 4, Mom sat in a lawn chair smoking a cigarette, watching Carmen's dad play a game of bags in the courtyard with Ben and his father and brother-in-law. They all arrived last night—Ben's parents, Ben's sister (Liz) and her husband and their hyperactive brood of children, Carmen's dad (Henry), and Mom. All of them were staying at the motel. I asked Carmen if it was weird for her—having her divorced parents in such close proximity. She said no. I was beginning to think it was more awkward for me. It wasn't exactly comfortable watching Mom work so hard to impress the man she lost all chances with the second she saw two lines on a stick. My baby bean of a self foiled her plans to win her ex-husband back. Seventeen years later and it seemed like she was taking another stab at it.

I crossed my arms to ward off the cold and joined her outside her motel room door. "Since when did you take up chain-smoking?"

"It's better than alcohol." She exhaled a stream of smoke.

"Same slow death. Just more coherent."

"Don't be so self-righteous, Gracie. It's not an attractive quality." Mom returned the cigarette to her lips and took another drag, her attention never leaving Henry. He was a good-looking man for his age. A bookish version of George Clooney. I could understand why Mom was attracted to him. This understanding, however, did not lessen the embarrassment that came with watching her gawk.

Henry and Ben laughed about something while Mr. Hart chewed on a cigar and tossed one of his bags. Every man but him had offered to help the women set up with the food. Mrs. Hart had shooed them all off, insisting it was women's work. I wanted to ask her if we should put on June Cleaver dresses and aprons and maybe strings of pearls while we were at it, but she probably would have laughed and said, "Oh, bless your heart." So I had refrained.

The crunch of gravel drew my attention away from the laughing men. A Honda Accord had pulled into the parking lot. It was in roughly the same shape as my Mirage. The sight of it had the short-lived relief I experienced upon shoving Elias's gift in my trunk whooshing away. "Mom, can you put out the cigarette?"

"Why, is this the boyfriend?" She stood from her lawn chair, the cigarette still lit.

"He's not my boyfriend."

She smiled, like my reaction amused her, then flicked some ash onto the ground.

The Honda came to a stop beside Liz's SUV. Elias stepped out first, wearing a navy-blue tie over an untucked white dress shirt, khaki pants, and his tried-and-true sneakers. No coat, despite the cold. His mother stepped out next, wearing a gray coat over a simple red dress. She had thin brown hair cut chin length and the kind of skin that looked like it was once tan, but she no longer had the time to maintain it.

The two of them walked toward us, Elias with a goofy grin.

The knots in my stomach tied double.

"You must be Gracie," his mom said when they reached us.

"And you're Mrs. Banks." She and Elias had the same eyes—same shape, same color—only hers were run-down. Not in the "I drink too much" sense, like my mom's so often were, but in the "I work too much and sleep too little" sense.

"Please, call me Leah. Elias talks about you enough, I feel like we've already met."

Elias tipped his chin. "Nice hair, Fisher."

My face flushed. Thanks to my stupid bobby pin, I had zero bangs to hide behind. I tugged at the sleeves of my sweater, newly grateful that I at least had the sense to shove his present in the trunk of my Mitsubishi. His hands were very empty.

His mom, however, held out a foil-wrapped plate. "I made fruitcake."

"Thank you." I took the plate, then motioned to my cigarette-smoking mother. "This is my mom, Evelyn. Mom, this is Elias and . . . Leah Banks."

Elias and my mom shook hands. His mom and my mom shook hands. There was a horrible moment of awkward silence, and then Ben called out to Eli and Leah across the parking lot. When he reached us, he gave Elias a full hug, Leah a side hug, and wished them both a Merry Christmas. Liz's husband and Henry came along with him. Ben's father remained in the courtyard, finishing up his cigar and the game all by his lonesome. I didn't miss the annoyed glance Ben gave his father before making introductions. When he finished, he cupped his hand on the back of Elias's neck. "You did a good job with this one, Leah."

"He's a keeper, all right." She slid her arm around Elias's waist and gave him a squeeze. The crown of her head was a good foot lower than his, which meant he must have gotten his height from his father. As the adults fell into conversation, Elias stood beside me with that unwavering grin of his.

"What has you so jolly?" I asked.

"It's the best time of the year." He leaned close. "And I really like your hair."

I would have perhaps slugged him in the arm if more crunching gravel hadn't distracted me. This time it was a Lincoln Navigator. A big black woman sat behind the wheel and a skinny old man with a white beard and a Santa Claus hat sat shotgun. As soon as the car stopped, St. Nick hopped out and opened the back door, and out stepped an older version of the woman who paid me for my seashells and drew me fake treasure maps. She had the same black hair (which I suspected she dyed), olive skin, and the ugliest Christmas sweater I'd ever seen.

Ingrid pressed her hand against her chest as she took in her surroundings. Her attention lingered on the large sign—bright even in the day—and when she finished examining every inch of the motel, her attention landed on me and my mother. "Evelyn Fisher and, oh my stars, little Gracie? Now if you aren't a sight for sore eyes."

I didn't know why it meant so much, hearing her say my name.

She wrapped her hand around St. Nick's elbow and walked toward us. "Put out that cigarette right now before you give us all cancer."

Mom dropped the cigarette and squished it with the ball of her shoe.

Henry hugged her first. Ingrid's fingers gripped the backside of his tweed jacket like she never wanted to let go. Then the door to the front office opened behind me and Carmen stood in the doorway.

"Carmen!" Aunt Ingrid let Henry go. "Look at my baby."

She didn't motion to the man she'd just hugged or Carmen in the doorway. She motioned to The Treasure Chest. It made my sister's eyes fill with tears.

41

CARMEN

Amidst the sound of ripping wrapping paper and the crooning of Bing Crosby, Aunt Ingrid passed out the presents with a glow in her cheeks. I made sure everyone had at least one present beneath the tree. Combine that with all the wrapped toys Liz and her husband brought with them from New Orleans, and there were plenty of gifts to be opened. Liz's Tasmanian devils had the process down to a hyperactive, assembly-line art form.

Eli and Gracie sat next to one another on the floor. He whispered something in her ear. She nodded once and the pair slipped out of the room. Unease settled into my stomach. They were hormonal teenagers, after all, and as much as I hated to admit it, I still didn't fully trust Gracie. I deferred to Leah. She paused from her conversation with Rayanna, taking note of her son's departure, but didn't object. I suppose if Leah trusted Eli, then so could I.

Aunt Ingrid picked up one of the few remaining gifts. "This one is for . . ." She flipped the box upside down to read the tag. "Nurse Ray."

Rayanna gave me a dubious look. "Girl, what you going and buying me presents for?"

I raised my glass of eggnog. "Merry Christmas."

She took the wrapped gift from Aunt Ingrid, clicking her tongue and shaking her head the entire way. I bought her a purple scarf from T.J. Maxx and, for fun, a gaudy headband with reindeer antlers. A laugh hissed through the gap in her teeth as she pulled it out from the box and put it on her head.

On the other side of the room, Mom flirted with Dad, and Ben's parents exchanged gifts with an unnatural stiffness that had accompanied their marriage since I'd known them. I told Ben once that I couldn't understand how they got to be that way—two polite strangers. My attention wandered to my husband, who watched his mother unwrap a pair of pendant earrings with the same furrowed brow he'd been wearing for most of the evening.

The final gift was from me to Earl. He tore it open with childlike enthusiasm and pulled out a stuffed penguin wearing a Santa hat like his own.

"Press the beak," I told him.

He did and the penguin lit up and started doing a funny dance to the tune of "Up on the Rooftop." Liz's children abandoned their toys and gathered around. Earl slapped his knee and let out a hoot. I couldn't tell who was more delighted with the gift—him or the kids. As soon as the penguin stopped dancing, Earl pressed the beak again while Liz stuffed balls of crumpled wrapping paper into a garbage bag. Once the floor was relatively wrapper free, Aunt Ingrid clapped her hands. "I have one last present."

My nieces and nephews looked up from the dancing penguin.

"Have you heard of the Christmas pickle?" she asked them.

My attention snapped to Ben. His lifted to me.

"I hate pickles," I heard Liz's oldest say.

"It's not a real pickle," Ingrid replied. "It's an ornament. And whoever finds it gets the final gift."

The kids' chatter fell away, and inside the charged connection of our gaze, Ben and I relived a Christmas Eve eight years ago. Gone were Earl and Rayanna and Leah, Liz and her husband and their pack of Tasmanian devils.

"Jingle Bell Rock" by Bobby Helms had been playing on the CD player. The motel guests had gone to their rooms for the evening. All who remained were my father, sipping the last of his eggnog; Uncle Gerald and Aunt Ingrid, engaged in a playful Lindy Hop; and me and Ben, sitting on the floor. I rested against his broad chest, relishing the feel of his arms around me, the lift and drop of each breath he took. He traced the lines on my palms, making my nerve endings tingle. The Christmas before, during my final year at UVA, had been miserable without him, and here I was now, living with Ingrid and Gerald at the Chest, working as Channel Three's newest weekend meteorologist. It was too good to be true, a hand-picked miracle from God. I still couldn't get over it.

"You haven't found the pickle yet," Aunt Ingrid said to me as Gerald spun her in a circle.

I chuckled. "Maybe the Lambert kids can look for it tomorrow before they hit the road." The Lamberts were staying in unit 3. They stopped at The Chest every Christmas Eve on their way to St. Augustine. They'd become like family.

Gerald pulled Ingrid close, pressed his cheek against hers as they swayed to the music.

"But the pickle is a Christmas Eve tradition and it's Christmas Eve."

"Better listen to her," Gerald said. "You know how this woman is about that pickle."

He was right, of course. Genevieve, Beau, and I had outgrown that pickle years and years ago. Ingrid refused to accept our aging.

Ben nudged me. "You should go look. I helped her hide it this year."

I turned around with raised eyebrows. "She never lets anyone hide that pickle but her."

He winked at me. "I told you. She likes me."

I left my comfortable spot on the floor in Ben's arms. As I searched, I didn't notice that behind me, Ingrid and Gerald had stopped dancing, or that Dad had put down his eggnog. I started low, working my way up the tinseled boughs, until I found it a foot or so from the top. I plucked it off the branch and turned around triumphantly. As I held it up, the pickle made a strange sound, like something was inside. Curious, I took off the top and turned it over, and a ring tumbled onto my palm. I looked up from my hand.

Ben was on one knee, smiling that crooked smile.

My hand fluttered to my chest.

"I love you madly, Carmen. I didn't stop last year when we were apart and I won't stop for the rest of my life." He looked up through his dark eyelashes, those blue eyes every bit as mesmerizing as they were when we first met. "I want you to be my wife. I want you to be the mother of my children. I want us to get gray hairs together, have grandchildren together. Who knows? Maybe someday, we can even follow in the footsteps of those two lovebirds over there and run this place together."

Tears blurred my vision. I looked over at Aunt Ingrid. She blinked them back too, with a smile that said nothing in the world would make her happier. Laughter bubbled up in my throat, so light I thought it might lift me into the air. I didn't know it was possible to feel so much joy in one single moment of time.

"Carmen, will you marry me?"

With the ring clutched in my fist, I nodded. Rapidly.

Ben jumped to his feet, wrapped me in his arms, and spun me in a circle. Then he kissed me. And as he slipped the ring onto my finger, I felt like a princess at the end of a fairy tale, heading into the sunset that was happily ever after.

"I found it!" Liz's oldest jolted me out of the memory. She jumped on the balls of her feet to the pouts and whines of her three younger siblings.

An alarming lump expanded inside my throat. It came without warning. It came without mercy. In light of such a happy memory, the brokenness around me glared. Aunt Ingrid and her ailing mind. Earl and his ailing heart. Ben's distant parents. My divorced ones. Gerald's absence. And most pronounced of all, the ghosts of my unborn children. They should have been here—at least one of them—toddling about after their older cousins, whining and complaining that they wanted the Christmas pickle too.

All of it had me scrambling from my seat and making a quick exit into the back room. I set my hands on either edge of the commercial sink and stared down into the drain. I should have been happy. Aunt Ingrid was doing great. More than great, actually. It was a Hearts day.

But what about tomorrow and the next?

If that memory proved anything, it was that moments didn't last. Moments weren't enough.

"Carmen—you back there?"

I wiped at my eyes and hurried into the front office.

Dad stood by the desk, peering past me as if the reason for my sudden escape could be found in the hallway. "Everything okay? You left pretty quickly."

"It's fine." I tucked a strand of hair behind my ear. I could have told him I needed to use the rest room or get a drink, but why was I in the back room, then? I walked to the table and refilled my eggnog. "Mom's in rare form."

"I'm glad she's doing well. I want her to be happy." His smile didn't reach his eyes. It was the same smile he'd been smiling all night. I assumed it was because he had to endure Mom's advances, but what if it was something else?

"Dad, is everything okay with you?"

He scratched the back of his neck. "The motel looks great."

"Thanks."

He paused. Cleared his throat. "Someone made an offer."

"What?" The news thumped me in the chest. Hard. I had no idea what shocked me more—his words or the bluntness with which he delivered them. "What do you mean an offer?"

He held up his hands, as if to calm me down. But I hadn't even gotten worked up yet. How could I when he'd just sucker-punched me in the gut? As far as I knew, we weren't putting The Treasure Chest on the market. That was why Gracie and I had been fixing it up.

"It came out of the blue, really. It's an older couple who've been searching for a mom-and-pop motel to purchase for the past two years now. They've never been able to find the right one. When they discovered The Treasure Chest online and saw that it had been shut down since last April, they started doing some research. According to the woman, they fell in love. He called me up a couple days ago with an offer."

"Did you accept?"

"I wanted to talk to you first."

"I thought we agreed we weren't going to sell it."

"We agreed we didn't want it knocked down. This couple has no intention of doing that."

"But what happens when they retire? What happens when they decide they don't want to be in the motel business anymore?"

"Honey . . ."

I shook my head, increasingly incensed. "They'll sell it to the CEO of Emerald Grande or some other luxury resort, and then a bulldozer will be here within a week. They'll knock The Treasure Chest to the ground, and it will be gone forever."

"Knock The Treasure Chest to the ground?"

The shocked question did not belong to my father. It belonged to Aunt Ingrid. She stood in the entryway between the hospitality room and the front office, the flush in her cheeks ebbing into a pallor that made her look every year her age and then some. She took a step back, the shock in her eyes morphing into a confusion that splintered my heart to pieces.

"What do you mean by knocking my motel down?" Her expression turned frantic. "Have you talked to Gerald about this?"

Dad took a slow step toward her. "Aunt Ingrid, please let me explain."

"There's nothing to explain. I want to speak with Gerald." She took another step back. "Where's my Gerald? He won't stand for this. And neither will I. This is our home! You can't knock down our home!"

Rayanna rushed into the room. "Ingrid, honey, why are you upset?"

She looked around the room—her movement wild, disoriented, frightened. Not a trace of coherency remained. "Please, where's Gerald? I want to know where my husband is."

Tears burned my eyes. Because I could give Ingrid a renovated Treasure Chest, but I could not resurrect her dead husband. And I could not bring her back from wherever she had gone.

42

GRACIE

Elias and I lay on the hood of my car, our backs resting against the windshield, our hands folded behind our heads, gazing up at the swollen sky. In the spaces between our words, all that could be heard was the soft whisper of the ocean and the faint hum of electricity that kept the sign bright. It lit up the parking lot and cast a pinkish-blue glow on the underbelly of blackish, purple clouds. It was a surreal moment. An "I can't believe I'm here with this boy on Christmas Eve" moment, with our breath escaping into the air like puffs of smoke. It was cold—enough that Elias had to grab a coat from the backseat of his mom's car.

"Do you think it will snow?" I asked.

"There's somebody we could ask."

I'd rather not defer to Carmen. No offense to her or anything, but I kind of wanted to stay out here with Elias forever.

He propped himself up onto his elbows. "I got you something."

"What?"

"A present."

"No, you didn't."

"Of course I did. It's Christmas." He hopped off the car.

I sat up, cross-legged, while Elias opened the back door of the Honda Accord and pulled out wrapped box that reminded me of the Twenty Questions game Mom and I used to play whenever we took a road trip. *"Is it bigger than a breadbox?"* For some reason, that was always the first question we asked. The gift Elias held in his hands was definitely bigger than a breadbox, and when he set it in front of me, it rattled like it was made of metal.

I scooted off the hood. "I got you something too."

"You did?"

I popped my trunk and removed the gift that had caused me so much anxiety earlier today. Now, the weight of it in my hands made me giddy. I handed it over and climbed back onto the car. My gift to him sat in his lap—

neatly covered in shiny blue paper with silver snowmen. His gift to me sat in mine, poorly wrapped in Star Wars birthday paper.

"It was all I could find," he said.

I laughed. "Who goes first?"

"We go at the same time."

"What?"

"It's more fun that way. Trust me." He positioned his hands over the wrapping paper, poised to tear. "Ready . . ."

I did the same.

"Set . . . Go!"

The tearing of paper drowned out the ocean waves and the humming sign. I peeled Darth Vader's head away and found a cardboard box beneath, the kind a person gets in the mail from Amazon. I lifted the lid and saw a six-pack of RC Cola, a tin of moon pies, and a Magic Eight Ball. My grin became uncontainable and so had Elias's, because he was holding up his new Erector set.

We both started laughing.

"You can defer the snow question to your new toy."

I picked up the Magic Eight Ball. "Will it snow tonight?"

Elias peeked over my shoulder, his body so close my skin tingled.

I shook, flipped.

It is decidedly so.

"This," I said, holding up the ball, "is officially the best Christmas present ever."

"I'm glad you like it."

I broke off an RC Cola for him and an RC Cola for me. We cracked open our drinks and clinked our cans together. "To the Bay Breeze General Store."

"And to snow on Christmas Eve," he added.

We took a drink and dug into the tin of moon pies.

Elias took a bite of his. Chewed and swallowed. "This place is pretty sweet."

"I would agree."

"Thanks for inviting us."

"Of course." I took a bite of my treat, the marshmallowy goodness enough to draw out a groan. Never in a million years would I have guessed that the boy

I met that first night on the dock would be here now—on Christmas Eve, at the motel I loved.

"Your mom seems to be doing well."

I rolled my eyes—not at his words, but at my mother's embarrassing behavior.

"You don't think so?"

"I think she's making a fool out of herself."

"With Henry?"

"You noticed."

"Maybe a little."

I finished off my moon pie and stuffed the wrapper into the tin container. "She's always carried a torch for him. I think she went to rehab that first time in an attempt to get him back. Unfortunately, I foiled her plans."

"What do you mean?"

I reached for the container. "I think we should have more moon pies."

Elias moved it out of reach. "No way."

"But it's Christmas. You're allowed to eat as many moon pies as you want on Christmas."

"You can't toss a comment like that out, then change the subject."

I waved my hand. "It's nothing. Really."

"Gracie."

"Fine. When Carmen was in seventh grade, she broke her collarbone in a car accident. Our mother was driving—drunk. I guess it was the straw that broke the camel's back, because Henry took Carmen and left. My mom checked into rehab, cleaned herself up, then rebounded with some military guy—AKA, my father—and whoops, hello me. Getting pregnant with another man's child pretty much put the kibosh on her Henry plans. And since she couldn't have him, there was no reason for her to remain sober."

Elias frowned.

"Aren't you glad you pushed?"

He spun his Coke can in a slow circle over his knee, his green-brown eyes shining with an intensity that made my heartbeat quicken. "We all got enough ugly in our stories, Gracie. No need to take on your mom's."

"Meaning?"

"Meaning her not remaining sober has nothing to do with you. That's her deal." Elias set the tin container in my lap and scooted closer. My heart did a quick *thud-thud*. I never realized until tonight how much security I took in my bangs. He rested his elbow on his raised knee and searched for something in my eyes. Permission, maybe? I had no idea. I only knew that the *thud-thud* of my heart had turned into a *flutter-flutter* and, despite the cold, my body was hot. Elias's attention dropped to my lips.

I sat statue still.

He leaned closer.

The door to the front office opened.

And the moment burst like a soap bubble.

Elias and I moved apart. Rayanna stepped outside with Ingrid, who cried hysterically. "I want my Gerald. I don't understand where he is. I don't understand why they're going to knock down my baby."

Carmen followed close behind, trying to comfort Ingrid by patting her on the shoulder. Except Ingrid looked at her like she was a stranger. Like she didn't know Carmen at all.

"It's okay, Miss Ingrid," Rayanna said. "It's okay. We're gonna get inside this car and work on settling ourselves down, all right?" Rayanna helped Ingrid into the backseat.

"Please bring me Gerald."

Elias and I looked at one another, our pupils too big for the night.

"Who's Gerald?" he asked.

"He was Ingrid's husband. He died four years ago." My attention moved to Carmen. She stood with her hand cupped over her mouth. And the strangest feeling wiggled its way inside my heart. It was a feeling I'd never felt before—compassion for my sister.

43

CARMEN

Ben's mother washed silverware in a sink of soapy water behind me. I wished she wouldn't. I wanted her to go away. Everyone else had, either home or to their respective motel rooms. In the apartment beside us, Liz attempted to put her children to bed. The whole ordeal sounded a lot like a calf-roping event at the rodeo. Her exasperated reprimands, muffled by the walls, wrapped around a heart that was already too raw.

The front door opened and shut. It was Ben, bringing up the rest of the pies. I opened up a gallon-sized freezer bag and placed leftover rolls inside.

"Mom," he said softly, "why don't you head to your room? Carmen and I can finish up."

"I'm not going to leave this mess behind."

I pressed my lips together and finished my roll bagging. If having more grandchildren was really so important to her, then why didn't she go next door and offer assistance to the ones she already had?

"I'm sure Dad would love the company." Ben paused. "Please?"

I thought, *No way.* She never left behind a mess. She never let the cleaning of that mess go unnoticed. And as far as I could tell, keeping her husband company had never been a priority. But miraculously, her scrubbing stopped. The door opened, closed, and just like that, Ben and I were alone. I zipped the freezer bag and put it inside the refrigerator. It already housed leftover ham, collard greens, stuffing, gravy.

He set a pie on the counter. "You okay?"

I shook my head. No, I wasn't. I was far from okay. I hated that Aunt Ingrid overheard what I'd said to my dad. I hated that he broached a topic so depressing during the party. And I hated that the news of tearing this place down was Ingrid's undoing.

Ben placed his hand on the edge of the counter.

I ripped off a piece of Saran wrap and covered the pie.

"What do you want to do with the motel, Carmen?"

I swallowed, as if doing so might loosen the knot in my throat, then Saran wrapped another pie. Tonight had been so perfect. But with a snap of a finger, it unraveled. "I just wanted this one night. One night for Aunt Ingrid."

"And what happens after this one night?"

I wiped my hands on a towel. "What do you mean?"

Ben's attention lingered on the couch.

I wondered if he was remembering like I had been remembering. Fixing this apartment—scrubbing from floor to ceiling, tearing up the carpet, battling layers of grime and dust—had resurrected memories from every nook and cranny. Laughing until we cried while playing late-night Monopoly games on the floor of the living room. Ben's disastrous attempt at making chocolate-chip pancakes in the kitchen on Aunt Ingrid's birthday. Stolen kisses in the hallway and the difficulty that came with stopping ourselves from going too far—a daily, desperate battle we had overcome together. All of them were his memories too.

"Tonight's just a night." He stepped closer, his blue eyes searching for the same something they searched for all those years ago, when I was too afraid to tell him what he wanted to hear. He tucked a strand of hair behind my ear. "I miss you."

Part of me wanted to withdraw, because it wasn't that easy. Another part of me craved his touch, the feel of his warm hand against my skin.

Ben lifted my chin, his searching eyes waiting for me to say that I missed him too.

"I miss the way we used to be," I offered. But we were a long way from that, and I wasn't sure it was possible to go back.

His hand fell away.

I turned to the sink, pushed the handle of the faucet to hot, squirted a blue ribbon of Dawn into the casserole dish, and watched it fill with suds. When the bubbles spilled over, Ben stepped behind me and shut the water off, standing so close that if I leaned back even an inch, his lips would be in my hair. He swept the curls off my neck, over my shoulder. "I don't want a marriage like my parents have."

The knot in my throat pulled tighter.

"There's no effort. No intimacy." Ben's breath tickled my ear. "No passion."

I closed my eyes, desire stirring in my belly, unearthing a whole host of sticky emotions that were best left undisturbed.

"My mom always used to say, 'Your father and I will never get a divorce.' That was her motto. Her safety net. She said it like Liz and I had nothing to worry about. But I realized something tonight." He ran his hand down the length of my arm, then turned me around. "The devil is every bit as satisfied with a dead marriage as he is with divorce."

The ache in my chest expanded.

"I don't want to be like my father, Carmen. I want to reach you. I want to fight for us, but you have to help me, because I don't know how anymore."

It was a question he asked once before. After our third loss—the worst of them all, when hopelessness won and my soul died. It was a question I left unanswered then. Because I hated that he didn't know. I hated that he had to ask. I hated even more that I didn't know the answer myself. I looked up at Ben, this man who was laying his heart bare, talking about things we didn't talk about, acknowledging the distance between us, and I knew I couldn't leave this one unanswered now.

There were a million words left to say. We had a million things to work on. But maybe one step was good enough for now. I leaned toward him—the subtlest of leans. Yet that was all it took. Ben's eyes went from searching to ravenous. His lips found mine and it was like flint against steel, igniting a latent passion I didn't know existed anymore. A latent passion that burned like fire— red hot and hungry. Ben lifted me off the ground like I weighed nothing at all. I wrapped my legs around his waist. Dug my fingers into his hair. With his lips on my neck, he carried me to the couch. And inside the motel where Ben and I began, the motel that had slowly come back to life, the motel I might still lose, we made the kind of love that honeymoons are made of.

Water crashed around me. It rose higher as I thrashed and flailed and gulped and sputtered. "Help! Somebody help!"

Ben reached for my flailing arms. "Carmen, take my hand."

But no matter how much I grasped it, it slipped away like a slippery eel, and I'd forgotten how to swim.

The waves rose over my chin.

Cold water filled my lungs.

And my eyes fluttered open.

I inhaled a deep breath—of air, not water—and lifted my head off of Ben's chest. I blinked away the confusion and the sleep and looked around. We were in the upstairs apartment, the one Aunt Ingrid used to call home, tangled up into a knot on the couch. No more bedtime battles through the walls. Liz's children were long asleep. The only sound was Ben's rhythmic breathing.

The counter light from the kitchen cast a dull glow into the living room. I looked at my husband—the dark fan of his eyelashes, his smooth brow, the strong line of his jaw, the fullness of his lips. He slept with one arm curled around his head, his palm turned up. Heat billowed deep inside of me as I thought about that hand on my body, those lips on my skin. Had that really happened? And what now? One moment of passion could not fix years of brokenness. A spoonful of sugar did not make everything better. No matter how much I wished it could.

I peered through the semi-dark at the clock on the wall: 12:45. It was already Christmas. I didn't have to work, but I did promise Dad before he retreated to his room that we could meet at Aurora's on Dock Street for their Christmas morning breakfast. "We need to talk," he'd said. And I agreed. Right now, Gracie was at home, all by herself. Someone needed to be there with her.

As surreptitiously as possible, I disentangled myself from Ben. He turned over and sighed but didn't wake. I got dressed, grabbed my purse, and walked to the door. We drove separately, so there was no reason to disturb him. Not when he was sleeping so peacefully. I stepped outside. Snowflakes fell from the clouds. So tiny they were barely bigger than specks of glitter.

44

CARMEN

I pulled into the parking lot of Aurora's, an oyster bar on Dock Street that served breakfast every Sunday and holiday. Last night when I arrived home, I had lain awake with my churning thoughts, Ben's side of the bed smooth and unrumpled. When I awoke this morning, I had one coherent thought. I needed to keep the motel—for Aunt Ingrid's sake, for Gracie's sake, for my own. Which meant I needed to convince my father to let me.

I stepped outside to a blast of wind that blew in from the bay and hurried toward the front doors. Dad was already there, standing in the entryway. I attempted to tamp down my irritation. Give him the benefit of the doubt as a friendly waitress wished us a Merry Christmas and led us through a crowd of holiday customers enjoying bacon and waffles and crab cake Benedict. She sat us at a booth and left us with two menus.

Dad kept his hands flat on the table. "I'm sorry."

"I don't understand why you brought it up yesterday."

"I never intended for Aunt Ingrid to hear."

"But me? You didn't think that would cast a giant shadow over the rest of my night?"

"I didn't know it would upset you. Last we talked, your concern was to keep The Treasure Chest up and running. If this couple purchased the motel, it would remain up and running."

He was right. Originally, that was what I cared about. But that was before all the hard work Gracie and I had put in, before I promised my sister a job. If I loved the motel before, I loved it even more now. The waitress returned with my coffee and Dad's water with lemon. He ordered the French toast. I ordered an oyster omelet. Once she was gone, he drummed his fingers on the tablecloth.

"Dad, I know you don't want to work in the motel business." My father grew up in it and couldn't wait to get out. But to me, it had been my place of respite. My escape from a dysfunctional world. The place where I met Ben. "But I might want to."

"What about meteorology?"

"I don't know." I loved the weather. Always had and always would. But lately, it had been getting to me. The expectations that came with being in broadcasting. The lack of privacy. The hours. Ben got home from work and I was off to bed. We didn't go to sleep together. We didn't wake up together.

"You should know, Carmen, that running the motel would be an entire lifestyle change. It's not like a regular job that you go to and then leave behind. Your life is your work and your work is your life. There's no separation."

"I know that." I grew up watching Aunt Ingrid and Gerald. Sure, the motel was their life and it came with a fair amount of stress, but at the end of the day, they loved the work. And they did it together. I realized Ben had his job and he was more than happy with it, but he had the summers off. And there was Gracie. "Dad, The Treasure Chest is part of our family. It's been part of our family for seventy-six years. Once you sell it, you'll never be able to take that decision back."

"I'm not trying to be callous, sweetheart. And I'm definitely not looking to make money off the place, but we can't let it drain Ingrid's bank account indefinitely. It doesn't seem like you're in a position to run the place right now, and we tried a manager before. If you remember, it didn't work."

"I know, but this time I'll be more hands-on. I'll make sure whoever is hired will do a good job."

Dad took off his glasses and rubbed his eyes.

"Please, Dad? After everything Aunt Ingrid has done for you and me, don't we owe it to her to at least respect her wishes?"

The waitress brought us our food, refilled Dad's water, asked if I'd like more coffee. I hadn't even touched what I already had. When she left, Dad put his glasses back on. "All right."

I sat up straighter. "Really?"

"*If* you can get the place ready to open, and *if* you can find a manager, and *if* it makes enough to pay for itself, then okay."

Relief washed over me.

"That's a lot of *ifs*, Carmen." Dad unwrapped his silverware. "I hope you know what you're getting yourself into."

"I'm not afraid of hard work."

"And Ben? Does he feel the same?"

I wasn't sure. I hadn't told him yet. I guess I'd find out when I got home.

Ben's car sat in the driveway behind Gracie's Mirage. I couldn't decide if I felt like a teenager, caught sneaking home after sneaking out, or if I felt like the girl meeting the boy the day after the first kiss, unsure how things would be on this side of the milestone. Last night changed things. I didn't know if they changed for the better or the worse or the different, but we took a step that couldn't be untaken. I pulled up beside his car and released an unsteady stream of air. Pretty soon, the driveway would be crowded. Mom, Dad, and Ben's family were coming over for Christmas lunch. I had to talk to him before the guests arrived.

As soon as I stepped inside, Ben stood from his spot on the couch, his brow no longer smoothed with peaceful slumber, but crumpled in confusion. Or maybe hurt. Judging by the state of his hair, he hadn't run a comb through it since last night.

On the TV, *A Christmas Story* ran its annual loop on TBS. Gracie sat with one knee pulled up to her chest, her bangs no longer pinned back, as she looked between us. She knew Ben had slept at the motel last night while I slept here. That had to say something. Surely nothing good. She set the remote on the cushion beside her and stood. "I'll, uh, give you two your privacy."

And so she did.

As soon as her bedroom door clicked shut upstairs, Ben ran both hands down his face, then back up through his hair. "Why'd you leave?"

"Someone had to be home with Gracie. I didn't want to wake you."

"Is that really why, Carmen?"

I hung my car keys on the hook above the antique storage bench. I could feel Ben staring at my back, waiting for an answer, but what answer could I give? The ground on which I stood felt so unfamiliar. With a shaky breath, I turned around. His wounded expression twisted my insides. "I'm sorry."

It was a paltry offering. Ben deserved better.

He shifted his weight. "How was breakfast?" he asked.

I clasped my hands together. Last night he asked how he could get to me.

I didn't have an answer then, but I did now. Here went nothing. "I asked him not to sell the motel."

"What did he say?"

"He said that if I can find a manager and open it soon, then he won't sell." Ben glanced down at the floor.

I wanted to know what he was thinking, but part of me was afraid to ask. Even with a manager, it was a big commitment. Another decision I went and made before discussing things with him first. I kept stepping out ahead of him. It wasn't intentional, but I couldn't seem to help myself.

He scratched the underside of his chin. "This is important to you?"

"Yes." Desperately so.

"Then tell me how I can help."

45

CARMEN

Mom returned to Apalachicola. Ben's family went back to New Orleans. And Dad flew home to Gainesville. Christmas had come and gone. The motel needed our attention. But first, I wanted to assure Aunt Ingrid that we were not selling it. Nobody would be knocking it over. It would stay in the family. I would make sure of it. I'd planned to visit on Christmas, but when I called, Rayanna explained that it wasn't a good day. Maybe tomorrow would be better. As I rapped on the door of Ingrid's room and took a tentative step inside, I hoped she was right. "Hello?"

Rayanna poked her head out of the bedroom and joined me in the living area with a tray of half-eaten food in hand.

"Is she doing any better?" I asked.

"It's been a rough couple of days."

"It's because of what she overheard at The Treasure Chest, isn't it?"

"Now don't you go on thinking that, Carmen. You know there's no rhyme or reason to this disease. If not that catalyst, there would have been another."

"Has she mentioned the motel at all? Do you think if I explained to her that we aren't selling it or knocking it down, it would help?"

"I think it would only confuse her. Right now she's grieving Gerald."

It pierced my heart. Grieving the man she loved was hard enough the first time. Did she really have to go through it over and over again—her pain on a recurring loop? All of it hit too close to home.

"Why don't you go visit with her? I'll bring up some dessert." Rayanna gave my elbow a reassuring squeeze, then left. Inside the bedroom, Aunt Ingrid sat in a rocking chair facing the window, a Bible opened in her lap, staring out at the live oaks on the lawn and the tall pines lining the cliffs along the horizon. "Ingrid?"

She turned at the sound of her name, her dark eyes filmy with moisture, and quickly dabbed at the corners with a crumpled pink tissue. She'd never been one to cry in front of others, and I could tell being caught now embarrassed her. There were some things, at least, that didn't change. These were the things I clung to like life rafts.

"Are you okay?" I asked, knowing even as I did that the answer was obvious. Of course she wasn't.

"My eyes are a bit soupy today, is all." She dabbed a few more times, then looked at me without a trace of recognition. "And you are?"

"Carmen."

She nodded. "Do you work here, Carmen?"

"I'm just visiting today. Would it be okay if I sat with you for a while?"

"I'm not sure I'll be good company."

I took a seat on the edge of her bed. "That's okay."

Her chin quivered as she returned her attention to the window. Down below, warblers and red-bellied woodpeckers and red-winged blackbirds flitted about from feeder to feeder. A few perched on the marble birdbath, dipping their beaks into the water. Many of the residents loved bird watching, especially during the colder months, when rarer species flew south for the winter.

Rayanna returned with two bowls of Jell-O. She set one on Ingrid's tray and handed one to me with another encouraging elbow squeeze before leaving us alone.

Ingrid dabbed once more at her eyes, then picked up her spoon and scooped off a bite. "I like Jell-O."

Yes, she did. So much in fact that a few months ago, my kindhearted aunt threw a spoon at a poor girl who tried taking the beloved dessert away. I held the bowl Rayanna had given me in my lap, watching Ingrid take small bites.

"Not all things are worth saving. But some are worth every ounce of fight you can throw at them. You just have to know the difference."

She'd spoken the words from a delusional mind about something as ridiculous as Jell-O, and while the context had been all wrong, the truth of them was no less profound. And as they echoed in my memory now, the same question that faced me then returned: *Is it worth saving?* Only this time the question wasn't about The Treasure Chest. It was about my marriage.

Aunt Ingrid finished the last of her dessert, wiped her lips with a napkin, and picked up the Bible from her lap. "Would you mind reading to me?"

I set my Jell-O aside and took the offering. The book was open to Isaiah—

one of Ingrid's longstanding favorites. Many of the verses were underlined. Tiny notes had been scrawled into the margin.

Ingrid closed her eyes and leaned her head against the backrest of the rocking chair.

I swallowed the lump in my throat and began at the top.

"Have you not known? Have you not heard?
The LORD is the everlasting God,
      the Creator of the ends of the earth.
He does not faint or grow weary;
      his understanding is unsearchable.
He gives power to the faint,
      and to him who has no might he increases strength.
Even youths shall faint and be weary,
      and young men shall fall exhausted;
but they who wait for the LORD shall renew their strength."

Aunt Ingrid, who did not remember me or the motel she'd loved for the entirety of her life, mouthed along with every word I read.

As December melted into January, Aunt Ingrid's sadness drifted away, but her wits did not return. She remained locked in the past, in a time before Gerald had his heart attack and The Treasure Chest shut down, before I existed at all. The longer she stayed there, the more frightened I became, increasingly convinced that the things she'd overheard on Christmas Eve had irreparably damaged her brain.

I begged Rayanna to let me take Ingrid to the motel again, so she could see with her own eyes that it was alive and well. In fact, it was looking better than ever. Ben solicited the help of the entire varsity football team to overhaul the landscaping, resurface all the bathtubs, and replace the toilets. They pounded nails and finished scrubbing out the pool. The most recent project was Natalie's brainchild—an ode to the motel's first financial investor, Charles Darrow. Ben was slowly and meticulously turning the square border around the swimming pool—made up of cement slabs—into a Monopoly board.

I was dying to show it to Aunt Ingrid, but her doctors didn't think taking her out of Pine Ridge was a good idea. They thought the disruption of routine had caused the dramatic decrease in function to begin with. So while her baby came back to life, I could do nothing but stand by and watch as she lost more and more of herself each day. We didn't play cards. We didn't visit the dining hall. Aunt Ingrid stayed in her room and asked me to read her the Bible. And as I read, whispers of doubt crept in. The kind I kept hidden in deep dark places.

What if none of it was true? What if this God we prayed to didn't exist at all?

Heaven knew I'd been trying to do the right thing by Ben. Every day the question that arose when Aunt Ingrid threw a fit over her Jell-O reverberated in my soul. Was my marriage worth saving? Yes, it was. I wanted to repair the broken parts. I wanted us to find wholeness again. But repairing a relationship wasn't as straightforward as repairing a motel. I had yet to find a magic cleaning solution that would remove the stains. For the first time in a long time, I was trying. But the harder I tried, the further into the depths I sank. Perhaps this was how my mother felt—desperate to win her battle with the bottle but unable to muster enough willpower.

Winter continued, colder than usual for the Florida Panhandle, and as January came to a close, I found myself stuck in a seemingly eternal wait. For Aunt Ingrid to come back. For the motel to open. For the social worker to call. For the lethargy in my soul to release its iron fist. For Ben to reach me—not just for a moment or two, but forever and always. I needed rescuing. And since I didn't know if God was there to do it anymore, I decided I'd just have to do it myself.

46

GRACIE

Elias's eighteenth birthday must have zapped my sanity, because at lunch on Friday, when I asked him what he wanted for a gift and he said he wanted me to come to church with him, I said yes. He told me he'd pick me up at nine. And, oh, by the way. I should probably wear a dress. I owned one black ankle-length skirt. I did not own a dress.

Courtesy of Carmen, I was wearing one—an A-line number the color of beet root with accordion pleats—on Sunday morning inside The Cross. It was my second time visiting, only this time I wasn't the only white girl. Elias's mom, Leah, was there too. We stood on either side of Elias, creating an inverse Oreo cookie that was more caramel than chocolate. The three of us walked into the sanctuary where an usher escorted us to a center pew. I pulled at the hem of my dress.

"You're fidgeting," Elias said.

"Probably because I feel awkward."

"Why?"

"Can you not see me?"

He tapped my knee with his bulletin. "You look good."

I probably would have blushed had the words typed on the front in big blue block lettering not caught my attention—*Baptism Sunday*. I plucked it from Elias's hand to get a closer look, but before I could investigate any further the choir on stage started clapping, and the congregation stood to their feet to sing some song about the battle being over. A large woman in front of us swayed with a rhythm I would never possess. To my left, an old man with Nelson Mandela hair (may he rest in peace) waved his hands over his head. Their voices rose like a shout, and I was the observer too afraid to join. After the fourth song, the congregation sat. I let out a relieved breath, and a familiar girl stepped apart from the choir to the front of the stage. It was Chanelle. When she started singing, I wasn't surprised. Everything about her was perfect. Why shouldn't she have a voice worthy of *American Idol* too?

"Amazing grace, how sweet the sound, that saved a wretch like me."
She sounded nothing like a wretch.

The lady in front of us must have resonated with the lyrics, though, because she nodded so fervently throughout the entirety of Chanelle's solo that her body rocked back and forth. I peeked at Elias. He watched Chanelle in a way that set off that annoying spark of jealousy Elias's reactions to Chanelle always seemed to spark. When the song ended and the choir exited the stage, Pastor Zeke stepped behind the pulpit—not dressed in his Sunday finest, but a pair of athletic shorts and a T-shirt—a splayed Bible resting across his large palm.

I leaned toward Elias's ear. "And you made me wear a dress?"

He smiled.

" 'Do you not know that all of us who have been baptized into Christ Jesus were baptized into his death? We were buried therefore with him by baptism into death, in order that, just as Christ was raised from the dead by the glory of the Father, we too might walk in newness of life.' Romans six, verses three and four." Pastor Zeke spread his arms wide. "Like our sister just sang, we once were lost, but now we're found."

Several churchgoers let loose some "amens" and some "mmm-hmms."

The woman in front of us started nodding again.

And as Pastor Zeke talked about the waters of baptism, I caught myself leaning forward in my seat, as if his words might answer all the questions that had accumulated since Mom first dunked herself in the creek. He finished more quickly than I anticipated. The choir returned to the stage to sing another song. Once they left, Pastor Zeke stood at the back of the stage inside a water tank, holding the hand of a skinny girl who couldn't be much older than I.

In a voice surprisingly loud for her small size, standing waist deep in the water, she told the congregation about her life before Christ and the freedom she found after Christ. When she was done, Pastor Zeke gripped her shoulders and she pinched her nose. "Based on your profession of faith in the Lord Jesus Christ, I now baptize you in the name of the Father and the Son and the Holy Ghost. Buried with Him in death. Raised with Him in the newness of life."

He dunked her under, and when he pulled her up—soaking wet, beaming from ear to ear—the congregation cheered and shouted out a chorus of "hallelujahs." After her, another person stepped inside the tank. He told his story and Pastor Zeke dunked him. Then another, and another, and another. And as I watched and listened, I couldn't decide if I wanted to dive in after them or call their bluff.

For the first time in my life, I was trying. Expending real effort. I joined the academic bowl team. My grades were better than they'd ever been. I had friends that teachers and guardians actually approved of. And yet somehow, my anxiety had only grown. The harder I tried, the worse the anxiety got. Ever mounting. Ever expanding. Because I knew the truth. No amount of spit and shine on the outside would change who I was on the inside—the same screwup, irritant-in-the-clamshell Gracie Fisher.

I folded Elias's bulletin into an accordion, then a paper airplane. I could feel him watching me, but I kept my eyes on my origami. When the service finally ended, I wanted to hightail it out of there. But Leah had to use the rest room and Elias wanted to say hi to Pastor Zeke in the lobby. Since it was his birthday, and since we couldn't exactly ditch his mother, I followed after him.

"Gracie Fisher," Pastor Zeke boomed. He had changed from his wet clothes into a coat and tie. "Back at The Cross for some more Jesus. Good to see you."

"Elias wanted me to come for his birthday."

"Baptism week is a mighty fine time to visit. We're all about celebrating new life here." Pastor Zeke gave Elias a fatherly clap on the shoulder. "Isn't that right, Eli?"

"Yes sir."

"You should invite Miss Fisher to dinner tonight. With your mama at work, we'll have an extra place at the table."

"Dinner?" I squeaked.

"We've been having a birthday dinner for this boy since he was in Pee Wee football. Chicken-fried steak with sausage gravy. Mm-mm-mm!"

Elias looked down at me. "Wanna come?"

"I'm not sure."

"Come on. Everyone should get to taste Mrs. Z's chicken-fried steak at least once in their lifetime." He gave me puppy-dog eyes. "Please?"

I had no idea why he cared. Why should somebody like Elias want me there? I eyed him, thinking about Christmas Eve on the hood of my car and the moment that passed between us before we were interrupted. I'd played it through my mind a thousand different times, a thousand different ways. If Ingrid had never come outside, would Elias have kissed me? And if he kissed me, would that have answered my question about his mysterious relationship with Chanelle? Several times I'd wanted to ask what they were to each other, but I couldn't figure out how to do it without sounding embarrassingly interested.

"One last birthday gift?" he added.

And just like I did in the cafeteria on Friday, I heard myself say yes.

47

GRACIE

Pastor Zeke lived in a coral-colored stucco home in one of Bay Breeze's more modest neighborhoods. A fence that had seen better days bordered a freshly mowed lawn. I took it all in from the safety of my car, more nervous now than I was before walking inside The Cross earlier this morning. I mean, it was one thing for Pastor Zeke and me to make small talk inside a church lobby. It was another to step inside his house and eat food at his dinner table—up close and personal. How long before he realized Elias was hanging out with the wrong girl?

Who cares if he doesn't like you? You don't need his approval.

The thoughts rose up inside of me like a pair of old friends. I grabbed for my key, still in the ignition, ready to turn the car back on and drive away, but I forced myself to stop. Take a deep breath. Resist the old Gracie urges. As much as I wanted to deny it, as much as I might even want to undo it, I did care what Pastor Zeke thought. His opinion mattered to me because Elias's friendship mattered to me. Probably too much.

I wiped my palms along the accordion pleats of my dress and picked up the plate of oatmeal-raisin cookies I made this afternoon. I stepped out into the nippy air and knocked on the front door. Elias answered so quickly, he had to have been watching from the window.

"You're still in your dress."

"You're still in your church clothes."

"True, but I wasn't the one acting like I wanted to be in anything but my church clothes."

"Well, I've never been to dinner at a pastor's house before. I don't know the dress code. When I tried searching for answers online, Google failed me. I even tried Bing. And nobody uses Bing."

Elias smiled and opened the door wider. "You could have called."

I stepped inside a small entryway with walls covered in rose-patterned wallpaper and framed photographs of what must be Pastor Zeke's family. The smell of southern fried cooking hung thick in the air.

"Aw, did you bake for me?" Elias asked.

I held the plate away from him. "These are for Pastor Zeke and his wife."

"Did someone say my name?" Pastor Zeke joined us in the entryway, making the already small space even smaller with his large presence. "Gracie Fisher, it's a pleasure to have you with us tonight."

"It's . . . um . . . a pleasure to be here."

"Oh, is Gracie here?" A woman stepped out from the kitchen wearing a plaid apron tried around her waist, possessing the kind of classic beauty reminiscent of Clair Huxtable.

"Gracie, this is my wife, Gloria. Gloria, this is Gracie."

I stuck out my hand to shake, but apparently Gloria was a hugger. When she let me go, she took my cookies with a warm "thank you" and then there was this super awkward moment where we all sort of stared at each other.

"The food smells wonderful." The overdose of nerves had turned me into Pollyanna.

"Thank you, Gracie. I hope it's as good as it smells."

"Your cooking is always as good as it smells, Mrs. Z."

Gloria turned her smile on Elias for a quick moment. "What can we get you to drink, Gracie? We have milk, iced tea. Eli says you're fond of RC Cola."

"Water's perfect. Thank you."

"Great. Eli, why don't you show our guest to the table while we finish up in the kitchen?"

Pastor Zeke took my coat, and I followed Elias through a small living area and into a dining room with wood-paneled wainscoting and more wallpaper. On one of the walls hung a large picture of Pastor Zeke, Gloria, three grown girls who looked exactly like Gloria, two men who didn't look like either Gloria or Pastor Zeke, and a happy baby on the pastor's knee.

Elias pulled out my chair. " 'Water's perfect, thank you'?"

"Shut up."

"You don't have to be nervous, you know."

"Easy for you to say." Pastor Zeke and Gloria loved him. He was already part of their family. And why shouldn't he be? He was like the male version of Chanelle. For all I knew, his solo would be next week.

He sat in the seat across from me and set his elbows on the table. "I keep waiting."

"For what?"

"You to wish me happy birthday."

"I already did."

"No, you didn't."

"I went to church with you. And I'm sitting here right now."

His dimples deepened. "Is it really that hard for you to say it?"

"Happy birthday."

"Why, thank you."

I rolled my eyes.

He laughed as Pastor Zeke brought out my water and a platter of chicken-fried steak. Gloria followed behind, a dish of turnip greens with ham hock in one hand, a plate of cornbread in the other. "Elbows off the table, Eli."

He removed them immediately.

I sat unnaturally straight and folded my hands in my lap.

Once the pastor and his wife were seated, Pastor Zeke blessed the food. It wasn't one of those standard, mechanical-sounding prayers I'd heard from Carmen either, but a heartfelt prayer spoken in his deep rumble of a voice. It was so mesmerizing I ended up watching him instead of bowing my head. When he said "amen," I glanced across the table and discovered Elias watching me, which didn't at all help with the sweaty palm situation.

"I'm glad you joined us, Gracie." Gloria passed me the cornbread.

"It's a pleasure to be here." As soon as it popped out, I wanted to bury my face in the cornbread. I'd already used that line in the entryway. It was painfully obvious, to me at least, that I had never been in the position of trying to get someone to like me before. It was sort of exhausting. I took the greens with what felt like a very awkward "thank you."

"We love when Eli brings a guest to dinner," she added.

I scooped food onto my plate, wondering how often he brought guests. Maybe this was a common occurrence. Maybe I was one of several girls he'd brought by and there was nothing special about our relationship at all. It wouldn't be the first time I'd misread a situation.

"We're empty nesters now, so the more the merrier."

I cleared my throat. "How . . . how many children do you have?"

"Three daughters," Gloria said. "Two sons-in-law. One grandson and another grandbaby on the way."

"The Lord has blessed us with a bounty of children." Pastor Zeke spooned a generous amount of sausage gravy on his plate and winked at Elias. "And not just biological."

"We're sad every time they leave. Like a mama bird watching her babies take flight."

Elias grinned at Gloria's heartfelt words. I focused on my meal, even if my nerves kept me from tasting the food. Thankfully, Pastor Zeke and his wife didn't give me the third degree. I mostly observed the conversation while they participated. We cleaned our plates and Gloria served us homemade pecan pie and the plate of my cookies. Elias brought up the academic bowl team.

"Are you enjoying yourself?" Pastor Zeke asked.

Part of me wanted to gush, because I was. My ability to retain large amounts of random information served me well. "We haven't done any competitions yet. Just practicing with each other. Next week they'll select the team that will compete for state."

"You'll make the team." There wasn't a hint of uncertainty in Elias's voice. "Malik's the captain, and according to him, you are irrefragably perspicacious."

Everyone at the table laughed. The words were one hundred percent Malik.

"I have no idea what that means," Gloria said.

Elias took a drink of his milk. "Don't feel bad. I had to look it up."

"I downloaded a dictionary app on my phone so I could carry on a conversation with him during practice."

Pastor Zeke laughed again.

It produced a warm, funny kind of feeling in my stomach.

"It means she's smart." Pastor Zeke shot me a wink. "Malik was paying our Gracie a compliment."

The warm feeling expanded. Not so much because of the wink, but because of the words. *Our Gracie.* I took a bite of pecan pie, my nerves slowly melting away.

48

CARMEN

"You need publicity." Natalie inched her chair closer to mine, her voice a whisper in the darkened room. "You can't just turn on the Vacancy sign and think people will start showing up."

I kept my attention trained on the TV at the front of the room. On the screen, a man with a Tom Selleck mustache collapsed to the ground and a woman with Dolly Parton hair let out an exaggerated gasp. I crossed my arms and leaned toward Natalie. "This acting is horrendous."

"It's a CPR training video. What do you expect?"

The gentleman sitting a row ahead of us shot us a look over his shoulder. Natalie and I shrunk back in our seats and watched as Dolly checked the man's vitals, then called for help. She pointed at a passerby and said, "You there, I need you to call 911 right away. This man isn't breathing."

She actually said "you there."

"What about getting the station to run a story?" Natalie whispered.

"On the motel?"

"Yes. You could send out press releases to the newspapers. Oh! Maybe you could call the historical society and have The Treasure Chest registered as a historical landmark. It's old enough, you know."

"First I need to hire a manager." Because without a reliable manager, The Treasure Chest couldn't open. Yesterday, I put an ad in the paper and on several online hiring sites. It made the whole thing feel very real. "Once we have a manager, then we can talk publicity."

"It's exciting though, isn't it?"

I nodded, but I wasn't so sure. The repairing part I could do. Ripping up carpet was all pretty clear-cut. This publicity stuff, on the other hand, intimidated me. Sure, I did some for Channel Three, but that was my job. Publicity for The Treasure Chest was a whole different ball game. The stakes felt so much higher. What if I found a manager and we opened the place and nobody showed up? Dad said we could keep the motel so long as it paid for itself. It wasn't going to do that without customers.

As soon as the video ended, the instructor moved us into another room of Bay Breeze's community center, where six CPR training mannequins lay spread out on the floor. Our instructor had us partner up and find a dummy. Today's two-hour training session would result in CPR certification—a necessity for Natalie if she wanted to begin in-home day care, a perk for me. Not only would *CPR certified* look good in our portfolio, it would give me an excuse to touch base with our social worker. We had been back on the waiting list for a few months now with no word and no phone call. There were moments, most often at night, when I literally wanted to crawl out of my skin with the waiting of it all.

"Since it's a full class today, we have to share the dummies. But don't worry, we won't share the germs." The instructor passed out packets of alcohol wipes, asked us to have a seat on the cold floor, then took his place at the front of the room. "This is the most important part of today's class. Hands-on training. If you ever find yourself in a CPR situation, I guarantee this, right here, is what you will recall."

He knelt behind his very own mannequin. "Somebody tell me, before you start administering CPR, what are you supposed to do first?"

Natalie raised her hand. "Ask someone to call 911."

"And then?"

"Try to rouse the victim and check to see if they're breathing."

"Good."

Natalie smiled at me. "See, I was listening to the video."

"If the person is unresponsive and is not breathing, you begin CPR. First, roll them on their back and start chest compressions." He showed us how to position our hands, with the heel of one palm on the victim's chest, the other hand on top of the first with fingers interlaced. "You compress the chest two inches for an adult, one and a half inches for a child, one hundred beats per minute. An easier way to keep track is to compress to the tune to "Stayin' Alive." "Another One Bites the Dust" works too, but that's a little morbid, don't you think?"

He gave us all a corny smile, then began singing the first song in a pitchy falsetto while compressing the dummy's chest. "Well, you can tell by the way I use my walk, I'm a woman's man. No time to talk."

Natalie and I exchanged high-browed looks.

"You want to press hard. You should hear your dummy make a rhythmic thudding click with each push. You want to do thirty compressions, then two breaths." He demonstrated how to tilt the victim's head and administer the breaths. "If your breath is too forceful, your dummy will make an impolite noise. Don't say I didn't warn you."

A nervous twitter rippled through the room.

"You should be able to hear a swish of air and see the chest rise."

He went through the process a few more times, then turned on the radio and invited us to try. The Bee Gees blasted from the speakers. I motioned for Natalie to go first. While she hummed along to the music, I found myself staring at the lifeless, half-bodied, plastic man in front of her. As its chest rose and fell with Natalie's breath, all I could think was that CPR wasn't something a person could administer to themselves. No matter how hard a person tried, she couldn't breathe life into her own lungs.

49

GRACIE

The moment Malik read my name off the list, an interesting progression of emotions tumbled through me like dominoes. A wave of disbelief knocked into elation, elation knocked into excitement, excitement knocked into anxiety, anxiety knocked into fear. The kind that went well with a barf bag. I was officially on the academic bowl team—not just the after-school practice team, but the team that would compete. The team that went all the way to nationals last year and expected to do the same this year.

A sophomore gave me a congratulatory pat on the back.

Our practice group had been whittled from ten to four—Malik, Veronica, me, and a kid with a rat face and horrible acne but a mind capacity the size of China. Seriously, he was like a walking database for Wikipedia, only everything was accurate. His name was Fred and his biggest dream was to have the longest winning streak on *Jeopardy,* which I had no doubt he would one day accomplish. I was the only new person to make the competition team, replacing a girl who graduated last year. There were also two alternates, should one of us fall suddenly ill or die unexpectedly.

Malik started the meeting. "If nobody objects, we will employ the same strategy as last year. 'If it ain't broke, don't fix it' may not be a grammatical gem, but I happen to think it's an infallible philosophy. Fred, last year you were our reigning expert in all things history and current events. How do you feel about taking a shovel to that expertise this year?"

With his hand in the shape of a gun, Fred flicked his wrist at Malik. It was Fred's way of saying "You got it." I imagined him doing the same thing one day to Alex Trebek, should Alex live long enough for the encounter.

"V, you ready and willing to resume your role as our science and geography aficionada?"

Veronica gave him a double thumbs-up.

"That leaves me quarterbacking literature and art, and Gracie Fisher, that leaves you with RMP." Malik looked up from his clipboard. "I can be of assistance with the R, as I happen to be a longstanding connoisseur of religious matters, but the M and the P will be all you."

RMP stood for religion, mythology, and philosophy. I couldn't be happier with the assignment if I chose it for myself. I found all three topics interesting. "Sounds good."

"Welcome aboard, Fisher. I'd say do us proud, but I know you will."

Malik went on to explain the new practice schedule now that our first competition was around the corner, stop number one on the road to nationals. His words set a kaleidoscope of butterflies free in my stomach. This whole extracurricular endeavor just got very real. As soon as our team captain wrapped up and dismissed us for the day, Veronica offered me a warm, official welcome and Elias knocked on the classroom door. He walked inside and slapped hands with Malik. I had no idea why he was still at school.

"Competitions are a blast." Veronica pulled the strap of her bag over her shoulder while the rest of the team dispersed. "We all pile into Malik's van and cram the entire way there. Then afterward, we look for the most random restaurant we can find. Last year, we found this hilarious pirate ship–themed family eatery in Seagrove. The waitress made Malik walk the plank."

"Into a ball pit," Elias added from a few desks away.

I raised one of my eyebrows. "You were there?"

"Unfortunately, no. But I've heard the story a few times." He smiled at me. "Congrats on making the team. I knew you would."

"It's not a big deal." Never mind that I may need a prescription for Xanax.

"What are you talking about, 'not a big deal'? Leave that heresy at the door." Malik set his hands over his chest in classic Malik fashion. "You are an official member of Bay Breeze's academic bowl team, the reigning state champions. It is a triumph worth lionizing."

I laughed. "Lionizing?"

Somewhere in the middle of Malik's speech, Veronica started nodding. "I agree. We should celebrate." She looked between Malik, the wordsmith, and Elias, the beanie-wearing football star. "We should go the Sadie Hawkins dance."

Both boys pointed to their chests.

I was as confused as them. "*Who* should go to the Sadie Hawkins dance?"

"All four of us. Malik and I can go together. And you and Eli can go together. We can double."

I glanced at Elias, who seemed entertained by the suggestion.

Malik pushed his black-framed glasses up the bridge of his nose. I discovered a while back that they were all for show. They didn't actually have prescription lenses. "Woman, are you inviting me to the dance?"

"I guess I am." Veronica shrugged good naturedly. "Come on, it'll be fun."

"That's some kind of delayed celebration," Malik said. "The dance isn't until the end of February."

"Fine. We can go to The Barbeque Pit tonight, and the dance in a few weeks." She turned to me with excitement in her eyes. "What do you think?"

"Gracie doesn't like dances," Elias said.

"Even if I did like them, we couldn't go."

"Why not?"

And here was the perfect opportunity to figure out what Elias and Chanelle were exactly, without sounding overly interested. "Wouldn't Chanelle object?"

"Chanelle?"

"Yes, Chanelle." I curled my thumbs beneath the straps of my backpack and focused every ounce of energy on not blushing. "Aren't you two . . . ?"

"Aren't we what?"

"Together?"

Elias shook his head.

I tilted my head. "Come on. All that touchy-feely, snuggly stuff you two are doing?"

He choked back a laugh. "Chanelle and I have known each other forever. She's like a sister."

"Perfect," Veronica quipped. "Then let's all go."

Despite my best efforts, heat crept into my cheeks. It even flushed up into my hairline. My ankles bowed outward so that I stood on the edges of my boots. "If that's how you want to celebrate, then I guess I'd go." I looked at Elias. "If you want to."

His left cheek pulled in with the makings of a smile. "Did you just ask me to the dance?"

Malik slapped him on the chest. "In an offensive sort of way, I believe she did."

50

GRACIE

I stared wide-eyed at the impostor in the mirror while Carmen stuck the last of the bobby pins in my hair. Yesterday, she kidnapped me after bowl practice and not only took me dress shopping at Cordova Mall, she paid for manicures and a visit to some fancy hair salon. Since my mousy-brown roots had grown out quite a bit and the tips that I dyed green over Christmas had turned the color of wilted asparagus, I didn't protest. I mean, if she wanted to drop a hundred dollars for what I could accomplish with an eight-dollar box of Garnier Nutrisse, that was her decision. If I'd known the hairdresser would make such a strong case for a rich mahogany brown, maybe I would have protested. "It will make your eyes absolutely pop," she had said.

Now, with my hair pinned up and my black eyeliner replaced with a soft smoky shadow, I didn't recognize the girl staring back at me at all.

Carmen and I made eye contact in the mirror's reflection. "What do you think?"

I twisted my mood ring around my finger. Thanks to the manicure, I didn't even have hangnails or cuticles to pick. "I look weird."

"You look great."

Yeah, like a great phony.

Carmen held up the dress we bought at Dillard's—knee length, halter neckline, vibrant turquoise. It was a color that combined the tranquility of blue with a hint of yellow's energy. I could have done without the yellow at the moment. Carmen handed it over with an excited flourish, set a pair of nylons and high heels on the chest at the end of the bed, and left so I could have some privacy. I stepped into the dress and bypassed Carmen's accessories for black calf-length leggings and a pair of laceless Chuck Taylor All Stars. They made me feel a lot less glamour girl and lots more Gracie.

The doorbell rang.

Show time.

Shaking out my cold hands, I stepped into the hallway and made my way down the stairs. On the third step, the conversation between Ben and Elias faded into silence. All three of them stared, Carmen with her eyebrows pulled together (no doubt at my legging-shoe combination), Ben with his mouth hanging open like a fish, and Elias . . . well, he slid his hands into his pockets and let out a low whistle. "Gracie Fisher, lookin' fine."

His compliment made my ears burn.

When I reached the bottom of the stairs—the center of all the attention—I wished more than anything that Elias would have let me pick him up. But he had remained resolute. I might have asked him to the dance, he still insisted on picking me up for it. I stole a glance as nonchalantly as possible. He was wearing an outfit similar to the one he wore on Christmas Eve, only his dress shirt was tucked in and instead of a navy-blue tie, he'd chosen slate gray.

Carmen clasped her hands beneath her chin. "Where are you two going for dinner?"

"We're meeting Veronica and Malik at the Hot Dog Hut," Elias answered.

"The Hot Dog Hut?"

I could practically see the romantic bubble she'd created in her head (candlelight dinner for two complete with a violin serenade) pop with Elias's news. She hadn't asked what was going on between Elias and me when we were shopping at the mall yesterday, but her running commentary made it clear she'd jumped to some inaccurate conclusions. "Why wait an hour at some overpriced restaurant in Pensacola when we have the world's best chili dogs at our fingertips?"

She wrinkled her nose.

"No corsage?" Ben asked.

"Gracie made me promise not to get her one." Elias wore his smile when he said it, like my insistence amused him. Seriously though—corsages and boutonnieres? Cheesy high school dance pictures? I had to draw the line somewhere. And if Elias could be stubborn about picking me up, I could be stubborn about this.

"Well, you didn't make me promise no pictures." Carmen held up her phone.

I groaned, but a tiny speck of reluctant appreciation blipped inside of me. This was as close to a doting mother as I'd ever had.

Elias placed his hand around my waist and tipped his lips to my ear. "No scowling at the camera."

The tickle of his breath turned my stomach into a Tilt-A-Whirl.

Carmen snapped her picture. Ben kissed my cheek and told me I was beautiful (not at all helpful for the ear burning). And Elias and I were off, driving to the Hot Dog Hut in his mom's Honda Accord.

The student council had transformed Bay Breeze's cafeteria into a dance hall that was all balloons and streamers and lights, complete with a photographer in the back corner who wore a black fedora and took pictures against a gossamer backdrop. A D.J. played some awful mix of teen pop while girls in dresses of every color and boys in ties moved in a giant mass on the dance floor. Even though it was pretty much the antithesis of everything I stood for, a giddy feeling had gone and glued itself to my person. I couldn't get rid of the flush in my cheeks if I tried.

Elias looked at me.

I started shaking my head before he could ask.

"But Fisher, it's called a *dance*, not a stand."

"My feet don't dance."

Elias attempted to recruit Malik and Veronica to his side, as if taking away the two people I'd *stand with* would make my feet reconsider. It turned out, Malik's feet had no more interest in the dance floor than mine. Veronica looked tempted but followed us to a table near the back while Elias gazed at the dance floor longingly.

"You don't need to stay here with us." I waved toward the crowd. "You're more than welcome to go bust a move."

"You don't care?"

"No." But there was a ping—of jealousy? of longing? I wasn't sure.

"All right. One dance. Maybe two. Then I'll come back and see if you've changed your mind." Elias flashed me his smile, then weaved his way toward the mass of bodies. I watched him go, trying not to think about who he'd dance with.

Malik cleared his throat, extra loud, and folded his hands over the table. He'd opted for a black bowtie, matching suspenders, a white dress shirt, and jeans. He pulled the outfit off in typical Malik-style. "What's up with you and Banks?"

"What do you mean?"

"What do I mean? Woman, you know exactly what I mean."

Veronica leaned over the table. "For the past month he's been eating lunch with you most days in the cafeteria. He was totally flirting with you at dinner. And this is the first time he's ever partnered off to go to a dance. Every other time, he's gone in a group."

"That's because you put him on the spot with your impromptu suggestion."

"A suggestion that found him exorbitantly compliant."

I shook my head at Malik's comment in an attempt to brush it off. Elias had plenty of opportunities to ask me out. So far, we remained friends. Sure, there was the almost-kiss moment on Christmas Eve and he *had* been extra flirty tonight, but I didn't want to be one of those girls who read into things that weren't there. I didn't want to be the girl I was last year in Apalachicola, when I thought Chris Nanning actually liked me. Song one ended. Song two began. I glanced at the dance floor, then back at my teammates. "Do you think we're ready for semis next week?"

"Evasively played."

"Seriously, Malik. How good is Lake City?"

"Good enough to make it to the semis," Veronica said.

Florida broke their high school academic bowl competition into four regions: South Florida, Central Florida, North Florida, and the Panhandle. The regional winners faced off in the semis: South versus Central, and North versus the Panhandle. If we beat Lake City, we would either compete against Coral Gables (South Florida regional champs) or Kissimmee (Central Florida regional champs). Whichever team had the best point record got "home court" advantage in the finals. Of the four teams remaining, our overall point total was the highest, which meant should we make it to the academic bowl state championship, it would take place in Bay Breeze. Anytime I pictured this scenario, I lost my appetite. According to Malik and Veronica, people actually came to watch the finals, and if it were in Bay Breeze, I imagined the crowd would be substantial.

While Malik and Veronica broke down the strengths and weaknesses of our upcoming opponents, I tried not to think too hard about what lay ahead. Somewhere in the middle of my trying, a familiar song started playing from the speakers. The Euro-symphonic rock had my jaw dropping a little. The D.J. had Delaine on his playlist?

"You can thank me on the dance floor."

I jumped at the sound of Elias's voice in my ear and turned my head to find him smiling smugly. Before I could ask any questions, he grabbed my hand and pulled me toward the clot of teenagers jamming to music they didn't know, let alone appreciate. Halfway there, my shock wore off and panic kicked in. I dug in my heels, but I was no match for Elias. He might not act like a meatheaded football player, but at the end of the day, he had the strength of one. And thanks to that strength, he had gotten his way. We were standing inside a hot horde of bodies, my heart thudding harder than the beat of the music.

"I don't have rhythm!" I yelled over the noise.

"Don't worry, I have enough for both of us."

He wasn't exaggerating. While I stood there lamely, not at all sure what to do with my hands, Elias proved that he not only had rhythm, he had rhythm with a sense of humor—this slick combination that had me laughing—and before I could remain self-conscious for too much longer, the song melted into something slow. His dancing stopped. My standing continued. Students paired up. Elias scratched the back of his neck. I rolled my eyes and turned to walk away, but he snagged my wrist, pulled me toward him, and wrapped my hands around his neck.

"Come on, Fisher. All you have to do is sway."

Yeah, sway. An easy task, if the nearness of his body wasn't making blood *glug-glug* in my ears. "You do realize that slow dancing is about as lame as corsages, don't you?"

"Lucky for me, you didn't forbid slow dancing."

"I'll have to remember to add that to the list next time."

"Next time?" He quirked one of his eyebrows. "Are you asking me to prom?"

"Never."

Elias chuckled.

I tried ignoring the smell of his cologne, the feel of his large hands on the small of my back. *Friends, Gracie. You two are friends. Friends, friends, friends.*

I focused on taking calm, even breaths and pinned my attention on all things not Elias. The streamers hanging from the ceiling. The balloons taped on the support beams. Classmates swaying back and forth, some couples closer than others. Seriously, how long was this song?

"Coach was right, you know."

I looked up at him. "About?"

"You *are* beautiful."

There was a pause. A hitch. A small stretch of electrified silence where I looked up at him and he looked down at me and it was like we were back on the hood of my car on Christmas Eve. Beautiful? Elias thought that I—Gracie May Fisher—was beautiful? That was a word that had only ever belonged to my mother and Carmen. The compliment turned me into reckless Gracie, the girl who acted first and thought later. The girl who stood on her tiptoes and pressed her lips against his.

Only Elias didn't kiss me back.

He leaned away.

The flush drained from my cheeks. And with it, every good and happy feeling the night had brought. Vanished in one fell swoop. I was Gracie the Schmuck all over again. At a high school dance. Swaying to an incredibly lame song. Surrounded by classmates. All of whom had just witnessed Elias's rejection.

With a sick feeling in my gut, I removed my hands from around his neck and hurried away. Outside and straight for Elias's car. I didn't pay attention to the chill in the air or the stars up above. And I didn't look back, not even when I heard his footsteps closing in behind me.

"Hold up a second." He touched my elbow.

I shrugged him off and kept going.

"Can you stop, please?"

"Why?"

"So we can talk."

"I'd rather not." I was too preoccupied with the deep, incessant need to burrow inside the earth until I passed through the core and came out some-place near Singapore.

"Come on."

I pivoted on the heels of my Chucks. "Am I a pity project to you?"

Elias stopped. "What?"

I thought about Parker's warning at the party, all the way back in the fall. At the time, I'd chalked it up to drunken idiocy. Whenever suspicion crept in, I did my best to shove it aside. Elias had never treated me like a project, and forget Parker. But now? "Do you get extra points with the big guy upstairs for befriending the loser new girl at school or something?"

"What are you talking about?"

"I'm talking about this." I motioned from him to me. "Us. What am I to you?"

"You're my friend."

"Your friend?"

"Yes."

"Well, guess what, Elias. Friends don't call friends beautiful. And friends don't flirt the way you flirt with me. Even Malik and Veronica noticed it." I shook my head. He was a tease. And I was an idiot. I could dye my hair and join as many teams as I wanted, the old me was alive and kicking.

"You're right." He massaged the bridge of his nose. "I'm confused. I'm conflicted. I'm leaving for Mississippi State in June."

His confession took a needle to the heated bubble ballooning inside of my chest. It popped and whirled away, leaving me empty and deflated in the Bay Breeze parking lot.

"Gracie, we're a couple of high school kids. I don't do casual. And you're not even a believer."

"What's *that* supposed to mean?"

"No, wait—that didn't come out right." He folded his hands on the crown of his head and glanced up at the stars. "I like you. A lot, actually. More than I probably should. But all I can be right now is friends."

Heat stung my cheeks. Maybe his confession should ease some of the sting, but it didn't. Rejection was rejection was rejection. I was so tired of it. "I wish you would have told me that before the entire school watched me make a fool out of myself."

"The entire school is not at that dance."

"Enough that everyone is going to know on Monday." I stared off into the dark, a heavy weight gathering on my shoulders. How was it possible that a half hour ago, I thought I'd float off the ground? "Can you drive me home?"

"Gracie—"

"I'm too embarrassed to be your friend right now, Elias."

His eyes were sad, conflicted. He looked like he wanted to say something more, argue or ask a question. But he shifted his weight and nodded. "All right. I'll drive you home."

51

GRACIE

We crushed Lake City in the semis. Malik, Veronica, and Fred were thrilled. I was getting an ulcer. Today, on this day after our victory, Malik decided to give us the afternoon off. Revel in our triumph and hit practice hard on Monday. They invited me to The Barbeque Pit to continue the celebrating from last night, but I opted out. I'd rather help Carmen spray-paint the last of the Adirondack chairs. Plus, I was pretty sure Elias was going to join Malik at The Barbeque Pit too.

Squinting against the sun, I walked between Carmen's car and a white F-150 with splatters of mud on the hatch. A gust of briny wind swept across the beach and hit my side, tangling and twisting mahogany hair around my face. I peeled the strands from my cheek and headed into the front office, where conversation sounded from the hospitality room. Inside, a gentleman dressed in a suit, a shoestring necktie, and a cowboy hat gestured with his hands to Carmen, who sat across from him.

She caught a glimpse of me in the doorway and nodded at the man. "Thank you for stopping in for an interview, and for bringing a copy of your résumé." She held up the sheet of paper. "I'll be getting back with you shortly."

He thanked her, tipped his hat at us both, and made his exit. As soon as he was gone, Carmen buried her face in her hands. She had interviewed at least five people now, and so far she found something wrong with each applicant.

"Not a good interview?" I asked.

"He worked on a dude ranch for five years." Her palms muffled the words.

"Which means he has experience in the hospitality industry."

"The place shut down three months ago."

I snagged the empty seat the cowboy left behind. "So what—you think he's jinxed?"

She looked at me over her fingers. "I don't know."

"Why don't you just run the motel yourself?"

"Because I have a job." She tucked a strand of curly hair behind her ear, her posture perking. "Hey, congratulations on making it to the state finals."

"You congratulated me last night."

"Not in person." Carmen asked me to call her as soon as the match was over. So I did. By the time we made the long drive home in Malik's van, Carmen was long asleep. "Does this mean I finally get to come watch you compete?"

I drummed my fingers against the table. Veronica had already invited her entire family, extended relatives included, as well as the whole of Bay Breeze's marching band. Fred even invited his dermatologist. Malik planned on inviting everyone from youth group, which included Elias. My stomach twisted at the thought. I'd been avoiding him since the kissing fiasco on Saturday.

Carmen raised her eyebrows, waiting for my response.

"Yes, you can come."

The smile on her face erased some of the tiredness around her eyes. "You know who else I think you should invite?"

"Who?"

"Mom."

My lips pursed. A reflex reaction, I guess, when it came to our mother.

"She misses you, Gracie."

"She misses drinking."

"She's trying."

She'd tried before, and I'd let myself hope before. A girl could only be let down by her mother so many times before that hope shriveled up and died. But even I had to admit that Mom was making an effort. She continued calling, anyway. No longer every night, but at least once a week—asking about my schoolwork, the motel, my job, the academic bowl team, Elias. Lately the conversations had been different. Filled with more silence. As if Mom was—as my sister insisted—missing me and no longer knew what to say. Carmen had given me another chance back in November. Could I give my mother the same?

Everything in me resisted the pull toward stupidity. Warned me not to put myself out there again. Still, the tiniest sliver of hope remained. One I could not extract. And that tiny sliver of hope asked a very loud question. What if this time, Mom really had changed? I sighed. "I guess I can make a surprise visit to Apalachicola."

Carmen smiled. "She would love that."

My car needed a new muffler. The engine grew increasingly louder the farther east I drove on Highway 98. "Come on, girl," I said, patting the dashboard. "We're almost there."

Several weeks ago, Elias named my car Wanda, which had somehow led to me referring to an inanimate object in the feminine. My attention wandered to my phone sitting in the console. No, I would not call him or text him or stalk him on social media. I refused to be that girl. Absolutely one hundred percent refused.

I flicked my blinker and turned onto Twenty-fourth Avenue, appeasing the worst of Wanda's grumbling. Five minutes later, I idled in the driveway of my old home. After all these months, it was weird, being here. Except for the long grass and some unwieldy weeds in the flower beds, everything looked the same. I gave my keychain a twirl around my finger and stepped outside, trying to decide whether or not to knock. I'd never knocked before, but I also hadn't told Mom I was coming.

I raised my fist and gave the door a self-conscious tap. She didn't answer. Maybe she wasn't even home. For all I knew, she was out running errands. Or maybe working a Saturday shift at her new job. I tried again, harder this time. Still nothing. I stuck the house key on my key chain into the lock, gave it a twist, and stepped inside a dark house with shades drawn.

"Hello?"

A bottle of wine and an empty wine glass sat abandoned on the coffee table. I was so used to seeing them in our home that they didn't register—not at first. Then Mom appeared in the living room dressed in pajamas, her hair a tangled mess, as if she'd just woken up.

It was almost lunchtime.

Her hands moved to her hair in an attempt to cover what I'd already seen. "Gracie? What are you doing here?"

I stood there in shock, unsure why I should be. This was my mother, after all. "We won the semis. I came to invite you to the state finals."

"Really? That's wonderful. Here, come on in." She removed the crumpled blanket from the couch cushions and waved me inside. "It's so good to see you."

My muscles recoiled from the invitation, the feigned nonchalance of it, as though nothing at all was wrong with this situation. I told myself to turn around and walk away. Go back to Wanda and her loud motor and pretend today hadn't happened, but there was that desperate, stupid sliver inside of me that wanted to be wrong. That said not to jump to conclusions. Maybe she had a friend over last night and that wine glass didn't belong to her, even if the guilty way she picked it up and hurried it into the kitchen, out of sight, said otherwise.

I didn't move from my spot in the entryway. Not when she was in the kitchen clunking around, not when she fumbled around inside the bathroom, and not when she returned and wrapped me in a trembling hug.

"I'm so glad you came."

She reeked of alcohol and mouthwash.

A lump of revulsion built in the back of my throat.

She let go and fiddled with the hem of her pajama top. When she looked up, tears swam in her bloodshot eyes. "Please don't tell Carmen."

No "I'm sorry." No "Don't be mad." All she cared about was hiding her secret from my sister.

"She'll be upset," Mom said.

"And what about me?" The question shot from my mouth like a missile—a fiery accusation that made her flinch. "Don't you care if *I'm* upset?"

"I was fired a couple weeks ago, for no good reason at all. And I miss you, Gracie. It's hard being alone here."

"Don't." I shook my head. The phone calls that had changed? The bouts of silence I mistook for sadness? That hadn't been sadness at all. That had been my mother trying to sound sober. Or pausing to take another drink of her wine. "Don't you dare put your drinking on me."

She cupped her hand over her mouth, the glossy sheen in her eyes thickening. "I'm sorry. I don't know how it happened. After I was fired, I went to the grocery store and I came home with one bottle. I was just going to have—"

"One drink? Really, Mom?" How much more cliché could she get? "Save your story for somebody who cares. I've heard it enough."

"You don't understand, Gracie. My life is hard."

"Join the club." I spat the bitter words at her feet, then walked outside and slammed the door, disgust blistering under my skin—more toward myself than her. I knew better by now. The sliver of hope needed a date with the tweezers. My mother could try all she wanted. It didn't change a thing.

52

CARMEN

The mixture of raw meat, egg, onion, and breadcrumbs squished between my fingers as stray thoughts bounced around inside my mind. I couldn't pin one of them down long enough to form anything cohesive. They hop, hop, hopped like a jar full of bouncy balls dumped onto a concrete slab. The unfilled manager position at The Treasure Chest, Aunt Ingrid's steady decline, my producer's continued pressure to build my platform on social media, Gracie gone for the night in Apalachicola, Ben and I alone for the night for the first time since August, and the phone call from our social worker that never came. When I called her about my CPR certification, she congratulated me, added it to our profile, and that was that. I hadn't heard from her since.

The front door slammed shut.

Ben was at Brandon's, helping him put on a new roof. By my watch, he wasn't due home for another forty-five minutes. I removed my hands from the bowl and leaned back on my heels to see into the living room. It was Gracie. She kicked off her boots and marched upstairs. No "Hello." No "Hi, I'm home early." Did she even go to Apalachicola at all? A seven-hour round-trip drive wasn't easily done in one day.

I quickly washed and dried my hands so I could go upstairs to check on her. When I reached her bedroom, I found her lying on her stomach in the middle of her bed, earbuds in, chin resting on her fist, eyes closed. We'd gone to the hair salon a week ago, and I still couldn't get over how much better she looked without the black locks trimmed in green.

"Gracie?" I took a tentative step inside.

Nothing.

"Gracie?" I said, a little louder this time.

She opened her eyes and removed one of the earbuds.

"Is everything okay?"

"Peachy."

"I thought you weren't coming home until tomorrow?"

"Plans change."

"Do you want to tell me what happened?"

"Not particularly."

Her short, dry tone set off an unwelcome combination of irritation and fear. Irritation, because it brought back unpleasant memories of our relationship before our Thanksgiving breakthrough. Fear, because I'd been secretly anticipating this moment of reversion—bracing for it—as though the last several months had been a strange fluke and at any moment the tenuous relationship we'd established would be cut in half. I swallowed the emotions down and took a more definitive step inside. We'd come too far to revert to our old ways. I wouldn't let her shut down now. "Did you invite Mom to the match?"

"Yes."

"Is she coming?"

"She has to work."

"What?" That was ludicrous. Gracie was her daughter, for crying out loud. This was exactly why a person was given personal days. "Did you tell her it was the state championship?"

"It's not a big deal."

Having Gracie in my house had taught me a few things. Namely, the more she acted like she didn't care, the more she actually cared. I was compelled to call Mom up myself right now and demand she take the day off. It didn't make any sense, her not coming. And seeing as I was the one who encouraged Gracie to put herself out there and invite Mom, I felt personally responsible for her disappointment now. "I'm going to call her."

She scrambled up into sitting. "Don't do that."

"Gracie, you made it all the way to the state finals. I don't care what you say, that is a big deal. Mom should be there."

Gracie picked at a loose thread on the down comforter.

"It's a big accomplishment. You should be really proud of yourself." I took another step inside. "Ben and I are. You know that, right?"

A soft blush crept into her cheeks.

There were moments like these—more and more of them—that endeared me to my sister in a way I never expected. This thing I was doing—taking care of Gracie? Somewhere along the way, it had turned into something so much more than obligation. "Are you sure you don't want me to call her?"

"Positive."

"Well, if Mom isn't coming because she has to work, that's her loss. I will be there—front and center. I'll even wear bells if you want me to."

Although Gracie looked down at her lap, her cheek swelled in a way that lifted my spirits. I'd made my sister smile. "I don't think bells will be necessary, but thanks."

"You bet." I turned to leave before remembering something. "Hey, I almost forgot. Eli stopped by earlier."

She looked up. "When?"

"A couple hours ago. I told him you weren't going to be home until tomorrow."

"What did he want?"

"I'm not sure. To hang out, I guess."

"Oh." Gracie resumed her thread picking.

"Is everything okay between you two?" Gracie had come home earlier than expected last Saturday. I'd wanted to ask why, and about a million other questions too, but I showed some restraint. Another thing I'd learned about my sister these past few months? The more I asked, the less she said. I waited for Gracie to brush the question off. To tell me yeah, everything was fine. Instead, she twisted the ring on her finger, her eyes transforming from unsure to resolute. And just as she opened her mouth to say something, my phone rang.

I ignored it, silently cursing the interruption.

On the third ring, Gracie plugged the earbud back into her ear. "You better get that."

With a sigh, I pulled the interrupter from my back pocket. The second I caught sight of the number on the screen, my breathing stopped. It was our social worker. Our social worker was calling. On a Saturday. My heartbeat quickened into a full-throttle gallop. One that pounded in my throat and in my ears and in the back of my knees. I stood there for one hopeful, terrifying second, then stepped out into the hallway with all the uncertainty in the world gathering in my chest. I swiped at my screen with numb fingers and pressed the phone against my ear. "This is Carmen."

"Carmen, hello! It's Sandy Booth. How are you?"

"I'm okay." More like having a heart attack. More like unable to breathe.

More like one hundred percent freaking out, because why was she calling me on a Saturday to ask how I was?

"Good, good. So I have some promising news."

I held my breath.

"A birth mother saw your portfolio this morning." There was an infinitesimal pause. An eternal pause. An outside-of-time pause. "She'd like to schedule an interview."

It was the phone call I'd been waiting for. The phone call I thought would never come. And suddenly, it was here. This was really happening. At some point today, while I was lost in my helter-skelter, bouncy thoughts, a birth mother saw our portfolio and called our social worker, and now our social worker was calling me. She explained that the birth mother would like to schedule an interview with us this Wednesday. I answered Sandy's questions as coherently as possible. And when I hung up the phone, I slid down the wall and cried.

53

CARMEN

Ben pulled into an empty parking stall and turned off the car. I wiped my palms along the thighs of my pants. I'd changed my outfit twenty times before settling on a nice pair of jeans and a lilac-colored blouse. I hoped the casual confidence of the ensemble would hide my growing sense of desperation for a baby and put the birth mother at ease. But what if I was wrong? What if she took one look at my jeans and assumed I didn't care enough? Dress to Impress, that was my producer's motto.

Drops of rain spat at our windshield. I peered up at the gray sky with mounting disconcertion, trying not to take the drizzle as a bad omen. I had been absolutely meticulous about pinning down the initial weather conditions earlier this morning. My meticulousness was one of the reasons I was so good at what I did. The rain wasn't supposed to begin until after midnight. I'd said so myself on this morning's forecast.

"You okay?" Ben asked, his hands still on the steering wheel.

No, I wasn't. Ever since our social worker's phone call, I'd been tossing and turning at night, catching twenty-minute snatches of sleep between long lulls of staring at the ceiling. I should have been exhausted by now, but so much adrenaline coursed through my veins, I could probably go another forty-eight hours without any sleep at all. My teeth began chattering. It had nothing to do with being cold.

"Carmen?"

"She has to like us, Ben."

He let out a long breath and pulled at his jaw. There wasn't a whisker in sight and it was Wednesday. Ben never shaved on Wednesdays. Today, however, was not a normal Wednesday. Today was so far from a normal Wednesday—so packed full of consequence—that I couldn't get a grip. "I'd like to pray for us before we go in."

I blinked at the suggestion. It had been a long, long time since he'd suggested it.

Ben reached across the seat and took my clammy hand. I didn't understand how his could be so dry, so steady. "Lord, thank You for this opportunity. We're both nervous . . ."

The rest of Ben's prayer slipped away. I couldn't hear his words over the pounding of my heart or my own frantic, *Please, God . . . Please, God . . . Please, God.* It had been so long since I'd let myself hope, and now that it was knocking, I was flat-out terrified to answer.

If You are really up there, please.

When the prayer ended, we stepped out into the afternoon drizzle that wasn't supposed to be, took the elevator to the third floor, and entered suite 301, an office we were well acquainted with. Sandy glanced out her open door and stepped out to greet us with a handshake. She had a chin dimple, a pixie haircut, and a calm demeanor I was sure she'd learned throughout her years as a social worker. "Come on in," she said, leading us into her office and motioning to a round table in the corner. "How are you two doing? I know this can be nerve-racking."

Can be? As in, some people's nerves weren't racked at this point in the process?

"We're hanging in there." Ben pulled out one of the chairs for me.

"That's good." Sandy sat at the table too. "I want to remind you that an interview doesn't always result in a match. The birth mother is interested in your portfolio and would like to get to know you a little better. The best thing to do is to just be yourself."

I nodded, but in all honesty, I wasn't sure what that meant anymore. *Be myself.* Who was that? The Carmen everybody thought they knew on the television screen each morning? The Carmen who smiled at church on Sunday? Or the Carmen who, at one point or another, started feeling disillusioned by it all? Ben gave my hand a reassuring squeeze beneath the table.

A soft knock sounded on the opened door.

Ben and I stood. And there she was—the birth mother, a small slip of a girl with dark hair, freckles, pale arms, and a bulging belly. She couldn't be any older than Gracie. Sandy greeted her with a warm hug and introduced us. Missy offered us a shy "hello" with a thick Alabama drawl and took the last of the four chairs at the table. I had an almost irrepressible urge to wrap her in a hug, but I mashed my hands together in my lap. Hugging her would be odd.

"This can be as long or as short as we'd like," Sandy said. "It's nothing formal. It's simply a chance for you to get to know one another and ask some questions."

I couldn't take my eyes off Missy's belly. There was a little baby in there, a baby that might become a Hart. A baby I might hold in my arms and call mine. A baby we'd been waiting so long for. A deep and irrepressible longing swelled in my chest, and with that longing came the hope I was terrified to let in. I forced my attention away from her belly and noticed that Missy was looking at me. My heart skipped a few beats. *Say something!* But nothing came. I was completely tongue-tied.

"How are you feeling?" Ben asked.

"Besides the heartburn, the pregnancy has been pretty easy."

Ben smiled that smile of his—the extra charming one. I'd never been more grateful for it. Maybe it would win us points with her like it did with all the booster club moms.

Missy smiled back, then pulled a folded piece of paper from her pocket. It was the kind of sheet one tears out from a spiral-bound notebook. "I wrote some questions down."

"That's great, Missy," Sandy encouraged. "Why don't we start with those?"

"I really liked your portfolio." The paper crinkled as she unfolded it and looked at Ben. "You're a high school teacher?"

"Yes. I teach ceramics and I coach football."

"They're two-time state champs." The second the words jumped from my mouth, I cringed inside. What relevance was that?

"You must be good, then." Missy turned to me. "And you're a meteorologist?"

"For now, but we've always talked about me staying home once we have a child." My thoughts wandered to The Treasure Chest. Aunt Ingrid was able to run the motel with Gerald and raise Dad and Patrick at the same time. What if I did the same? I imagined living there. Gracie too. Running the motel alongside my sister with a little baby in my arms.

"And y'all don't have any children yet?"

"That's correct."

"Carmen's younger sister is living with us temporarily," Ben said.

"She's around your age. Her name's Gracie. She's a great kid."

Missy looked down at her paper. I didn't miss the way it trembled in her hand. Seeing the tremor eased some of my anxiety, made me feel a bond to the girl. I wanted to assure her that I was nervous too. We could be nervous together, and then maybe we could laugh about it together too. But I kept the words inside. "Why haven't you had any biological children?" she asked.

Ben glanced at me. "We've had some miscarriages."

"That must have been hard."

"It was, but we're excited to be here now," Ben said.

"God had a purpose for it." I cringed again, because did I really just say that? How many times had people offered that same sentiment to me after our first miscarriage, and how many times had I wanted to crumple it into a ball and light it on fire? It might be true, I may have once believed it, I might even believe it still. But that didn't make it helpful.

Missy shifted in her chair. "Your portfolio mentioned that y'all are Christians. Is your religion a big part of your life?"

I held my breath, unsure where to step. This entire conversation felt like a land mine. We learned, during all our classes and meetings with Sandy, that sometimes a mother will choose a family because of a particular answer, sometimes they will reject a family because of a particular answer, and sometimes the answers matter very little. Faith was a hot-button topic. The best thing we could do, according to Sandy, was answer honestly. Easy for her to say, since she wasn't the one with everything to lose.

"Yes, it's a big part of our life," Ben said. "Or at least we want it to be."

Missy nodded, as though she approved, and like a baby bird flapping its wings for the first time, hope fluttered. This time, I didn't fight it. I didn't attempt to tamp it down. As the interview continued, Missy seemed to grow more comfortable. The paper in her hand stopped shaking. She became more generous with her smile. We even shared some laughter. And my fluttering hope took flight. Sandy was there in case things got uncomfortable or stilted, but she barely had to say a word. Missy asked us how we met. Ben shared the story, and even Sandy seemed to get caught up in the romance of it. When he finished, Missy folded up her paper. The interview had come to an end. I was desperate to know if we passed.

"Are you all finished?" Sandy asked.

"I have one more question." Missy set her hand over her swollen abdomen. "Would you like to be in the delivery room when the baby is born?"

Tears pricked my eyes. Yes, yes, yes. A thousand times yes. I blinked quickly, to dry the tears before they formed. "We'd love to, but only if you're comfortable."

Sandy turned to us. "Do either of you have any questions for Missy?"

Ben and I exchanged a look. We didn't have any questions, but maybe we should. According to Sandy, the father wasn't involved, nor did he wish to be involved. I didn't want to bring up a sore topic, but it felt like I should say something. A million things. About how long we'd waited. How desperate I was to be a mother. How much we would love her child. But I couldn't gush. I couldn't beg. Those were things I could not do. So I smiled a smile I hoped conveyed everything I was feeling. "You are very brave," I said, "for giving this child life."

Ben took my hand and echoed my sentiments.

On the walk to the car, I wavered between elation, because I was positive this was it, and the worst kind of dread, because what if it wasn't? The winged hope inside me alternated between soaring and plummeting. It was enough to give me a stomachache. As soon as we were in the car and buckled up, all the nervous energy I'd been holding in tumbled out. I gave my husband a play-by-play of the interview with commentary as if he hadn't been there. He pulled out onto the road and drove us home. By the time I finished, we'd already crossed the Three-Mile Bridge.

"What did you think?" I asked.

He shot me a quick glance, then returned his attention to the road. "I think it went okay."

His response set my hope into a nosedive. "Just okay?" Were we not in the same interview? "She asked if we wanted to be in the delivery room. That has to mean something."

"How do you know she doesn't ask that for every interview?"

My defenses flared.

"I just don't want you to get your hopes up."

"My hopes up? Ben, this is the first time I've felt any hope at all."

A muscle worked in his jaw.

I wanted to scream. "Is it really too much to ask for you to be hopeful with me?"

"That's not fair."

"*Fair? Fair!* None of this is *fair*. We did everything right, Ben. We played by God's rules. Natalie and Brandon didn't. My mother didn't. Neither did your sister. Yet God still gave them kids. Tell me where the fairness is in that."

Ben had no response.

The only noise was the *pitter-patter* of rain and rhythmic *woosh-swoosh* of the windshield wipers. I pressed my lips together and stared out the window as water painted streaks across the glass and my eyes blurred with heated emotion. Neither of us said a word. Not when we turned down our street. Not when familiar houses slid past the window. And not when we were parked in the driveway with an engine that clicked and clinked into rest.

He twisted the car key around his keychain. "Will a baby fix everything that's broken, Carmen?"

The whispered question slunk into my ear, chafing against my heart, my nerves, my mind.

"Because I have to tell you. I am terrified it won't."

Unable to sit beneath the weight of his fear for even a second, I grabbed the door handle and let myself into the rain.

54

CARMEN

I rinsed off a green pepper and began dicing it on the wooden cutting board Ben's mom had given me for Christmas. Quesadillas were about as complicated a meal as I could prepare in the kitchen right now, what with Ben's question running laps in my mind.

"Will a baby fix everything that's broken?"

I wanted to reach inside my soul, grab the question by the neck, and yank it out. Yes, it would. Because once we had a baby, the waiting would be over. The winter season would be a thing of the past. And this distance Ben and I kept trying to bridge would float away like mist. I rotated the pepper and brushed away some of the seeds. Gracie came into the kitchen. She grabbed a carrot stick from the bowl I set out and crunched into it. I scooped the diced peppers onto a plate, then removed a can of Mexicorn from the pantry and dug through a drawer for the can opener.

"Where's Ben?"

"Downstairs, I think."

"On the pottery wheel?"

I shrugged listlessly. Ever since Sandy called on Saturday, Ben had changed up his routine. Instead of going to his man garage before dinner to throw darts or lift weights, he'd taken to going downstairs to work on the once-dusty pottery wheel we shoved aside years ago.

Gracie took another crunch of carrot.

I opened the can of corn.

"How did your thing go today?" she asked.

"Good." Not okay. Good. I had been sure of it, at least until Ben had his say. I mixed the corn and the peppers, then pulled out leftover chicken, a pack of tortillas, and shredded cheese from the refrigerator.

"I have to get to work."

"Okay." Usually I'd ask if she'd had any dinner, or if she needed some cash to pick some up on the way to the theater. Tonight the questions slipped through the cracks in my mind.

She took another carrot stick from the bowl. "You'll be at the match to-morrow, right?"

"Yeah, of course." My attention wandered to my cell phone on the counter. Sandy said that sometimes a birth mother decided right away and sometimes she had to think about it for a few days. So here I was, faced with more waiting. The worst kind of waiting too, like I'd swallowed a ticking time bomb and I had no idea if the explosion would bring celebration or despair.

The front door opened and shut.

Gracie was gone.

I turned on a stove burner and poured olive oil into a pan, replaying the interview, dissecting Missy's body language, her questions, her tone, trying to convince myself that Ben was wrong. Urging my hope to take flight once again. When the oil began to crackle, I set a flour tortilla into the pan, covered it with cheese, chicken, the vegetable mixture, another tortilla. Ben came into the kitchen and grabbed a drink. I waited for him to return the juice carton to the refrigerator and leave, but he remained. I flipped the quesadilla, wondering if he was going to stand there and watch me.

"I think we should talk."

We didn't need to talk. We needed Sandy to call. I glanced at my phone. Once Sandy called with news that Missy had chosen us, we could start getting the nursery ready. I always thought Gracie's room would be the nursery, but the room on the other side of the hallway would work just as well. Missy was due at the end of April. That was only a little over a month away. Ben and I could start talking about names again, like we did all those years ago. We could ask Gracie to be the godmother.

I moved the first quesadilla from the pan onto a plate and got to work on the second. As I sprinkled the bubbling tortilla with cheese, a sound like a drill filled the kitchen. I turned toward the noise. My cell phone buzzed against the counter. Even from here, I could see Sandy Booth's number on the screen.

For a millisecond, my heart stopped beating. My lungs stopped breathing. My thoughts stopped churning. Ben stepped toward my buzzing phone and answered it. I turned around. Plugged my ears. Squeezed my eyes shut because

I didn't want to hear or see. My heart beat frantically—a violent *thud-thud* that punched bruises against my chest. I stood in the center of the kitchen, my body going hot, then cold, hot, then cold like a broken thermostat, and resumed the prayer I prayed earlier. The only prayer I'd been able to pray for days now.

Please, God . . . Please, God . . . Please, God . . .

Ben touched my arm.

When I turned around, his blue eyes didn't sparkle. They didn't dance. They didn't smile. Tears gathered in them, but they were not happy tears. "I'm sorry, Carmen."

No. This wasn't happening.

He wrapped his arms around me, but I drifted away to someplace numb, to someplace cold, while dinner burned on the stove.

Rain pounded the pavement of the parking lot outside and fell like pennies against the awning overhead. I gripped the armrests of the Adirondack chair— the one Gracie spray-painted fire-engine red last week—and stared into the onslaught. It came early, it was staying late, and it was much heavier than it was supposed to be. I was sure somebody, or several somebodies, would have something to say about my miscalculation tomorrow morning.

After Sandy's phone call, I'd told Ben that I needed to be alone. The house and its empty rooms felt too suffocating to bear. Ben understood. He gave me my space. I packed a small bag and drove out here to collect my thoughts, as if they could possibly be collected when they poured through my mind as heavy as the rain.

I asked Ben if Sandy had given him a reason why. Where did we go wrong? Why did Missy reject us? Sandy told him it wasn't personal. Missy was simply looking for a couple who was less religious. The irony was too rich for words. Not only was God not answering my prayer, being affiliated with Him was directly preventing me from getting what I'd been begging Him for.

I glared up into the angry heavens—a cloak of rain-soaked darkness and rumbling thunder—and told God what I'd been too afraid to tell Him.

"You aren't real." I leaned forward in my seat and let the thought fly. "Do You hear me?"

The shout returned on an echo.

And the tiniest of cracks fissured through the numb wall around my heart. What good did believing in God do, anyway? Aunt Ingrid devoted her life to Him, and look at her now. She didn't know who she was half the time. I was sitting at the motel she loved more than life, the one that should be ready to open in time for the bulk of tourist season, and Aunt Ingrid didn't even know. She devoted her life to God, and I followed in her footsteps. I didn't pass through any wild, rebellious years like so many of my friends did. I truly believed that living His way was best. And yet, look what I'd become now. A barren womb. A bag of dry bones.

My fingers dug into the painted wood. "I don't believe in You anymore!"

I wasn't so far gone that I missed the incongruity of the moment, or the inherent fallacy of my declaration. If what I said were true, if I no longer believed in God, then why did I need to say it at all? *Who* was I talking to?

55

CARMEN

Ben reached for me. "Carmen, take my hand."

But I couldn't reach him. And he couldn't reach me.

I thrashed and I flailed. I fought with every ounce of strength in my body—to save myself, to swim, to breathe. But the waves were too strong. They crashed over me. Again and again until I was choking on salt water. I had nothing left. No strength to spare. So I let myself sink. And somehow, in the sinking, I could breathe again.

A loud *beep-beep-beep* sliced through my shocking moment.

My eyelids fluttered.

I inhaled air, not water. Awake. I was not drowning in the ocean. I was at The Treasure Chest, sleeping in one of the motel units. I was here because of Sandy's phone call last night. I rolled over and slapped at my phone. Outside, the rain had stopped. Inside, the numb wall around my heart stood strong and sturdy.

As usual, I was one of the first to arrive at the station. I went through the motions. I did my due diligence, checking radars and satellites, pinning down the weather's initial conditions. But what was the point? I'd done the same thing yesterday and I couldn't have been more wrong. The weather didn't do what it was supposed to do.

Slowly, the station came to life. More people shuffled in the doors. More lights turned on. I did my best to avoid eye contact while analyzing the last of the data, then recorded some sound bites for local radio stations in one of the editing bays. The falsely chipper tone of my voice as I talked about the stormy day ahead scraped against my nerves. I couldn't have been any more sick of myself if I tried.

Back inside the studio, the two morning news anchors sat behind the anchor desk. Jason, the male half of the duo, held up a mirror with one hand and messed with his hair with the other. "Hey, Hart," he said as I passed. "I left my car windows open yesterday evening. Should I bill you for the water damage?" His voice was lighthearted, teasing.

I laughed an empty laugh.

The cameraman adjusted one of the cameras. "Thirty seconds!"

I uncapped a bottle of water and took a swig. Attempted to rally. Don my Carmen Hart with Channel Three News persona so I could give a few forecasts and leave. Survival mode, that's what this was. I'd been here before. I could be here again. Let the numbness carry me through today and the next until time dulled the pain. Carmen the Pill Bug.

"Ten seconds."

The cameraman counted down.

The anchors slapped on straight, white-toothed smiles.

And Jason began reading from the teleprompter—something about petroleum and gas prices. Nancy caught sight of me across the way and hurried over with an appalled expression.

"Carmen," she whispered, "you look awful."

"I didn't sleep the best."

"Are you okay to go on air?"

"I'm fine," I said, watching Jason.

"A sailor disappeared after a navy helicopter crashed into the ocean Wednesday morning during a routine training exercise. Four of the five crew members were hospitalized immediately after the crash. One remains in critical condition. Rescue crews have been searching for the missing sailor since Wednesday." Jason turned to his female counterpart. "Our thoughts and prayers go out to the families."

"Yes, they do, Jason." She picked up where he left off. "Unfortunately, this isn't the only sad story we have this morning. A two-month-old baby was found dead in an apartment building in Pensacola last night. Police found the child in his crib, after a concerned phone call from another resident in the complex. The mother was apprehended shortly after. Police have stated that the woman was high on methamphetamine."

A picture filled the screen—of a strung-out mother who'd killed her own baby.

The story was like a sledgehammer to the numb wall around my heart. There was a giant *thwack* that created a spider web of cracks upon impact.

"Come find me after the show." Nancy patted my shoulder. "I want to talk to you about a blog series idea I had last night. And maybe touch up your makeup." She walked around the set, leaving me standing alone in front of the green screen.

"And now," Jason said, "to Carmen Hart with our weather forecast."

Here was where I needed to smile at the camera and give the weather report. A substantial storm system was supposed to be moving up from the Gulf, scheduled to arrive this evening and produce strong gusts of wind, along with some scattered precipitation. But the truth was, I didn't know. I couldn't predict the future, especially when that future was a constantly changing thing.

Jason cleared his throat.

The cameraman waved his hand.

I was on the air. I'd been on the air, for a few seconds now, staring off into space. I needed to pull myself together. Recite the forecast I'd prepared in advance like a professional. But when I opened my mouth, that wasn't what came out. That wasn't what came out at all.

"I don't know."

Stillness filled the studio.

"I could tell you there will be storms, but I don't know." A squeak of laughter escaped—deranged in its pitch. "Nobody really knows, and if they say they do, they're lying. It's all a crapshoot."

The stillness gave way to a flurry of panic. The cameraman pounced into action, panning back to the morning anchors, who attempted to recover my horrendous fumble. I stood there, in front of the screen, every bit as shocked as the rest of them. Because what had I done? What in the world did I just say?

Nancy's eyes met mine.

Before she could reach me, I snagged my purse and ran out of the station.

As soon as I walked inside the house, Ben came out of his seat like a jack-in-the-box, his hair sticking up every which way as though he'd pushed his hands through it too many times to count. Apparently, he either heard about or watched my unraveling on air, since he should have been at work.

"Where have you been?"

"Driving."

"All day?"

I set my purse on the bench.

"I've been calling you every five minutes."

"I'm sorry." I couldn't answer Ben's phone calls. I couldn't answer my producer's phone calls or Natalie's phone calls, either. All I could do was keep both hands on the wheel and my foot on the gas pedal and drive, as if enough distance might erase everything that had happened. I didn't ease off until I reached Baton Rouge.

"You're sorry?"

"What else do you want me to say?"

"I don't know—that we should talk?"

"I don't want to talk." I'd be happy never to talk again. I turned away from Ben's distress and climbed the stairs.

He followed.

I pulled my suitcase out from our closet and laid it open on the bed.

"What are you doing?"

"Packing."

"For where?"

"The Treasure Chest." I began snagging tops off hangers, stuffing them inside. I didn't even bother folding them. The wrinkles could be dealt with later. "I can't be here anymore."

Not here, in this house, where life unraveled. Not here, in Bay Breeze, where everyone would whisper about the weather girl and her second public meltdown—this one all the worse, since it wasn't on YouTube but live television. I lost it on live television and then I walked out of the station in the middle of the newscast. I didn't even know who'd covered for me the rest of the morning.

Ben stood there for a long moment, unmoving in the doorway, watching as I dropped a couple pairs of jeans inside the suitcase. This was it, I thought. He was done fighting. I was done fighting. We'd reached our end, with nothing left to hold on to except broken dreams and a whole world of hurt feelings. I grabbed a pair of sweatpants from the bottom drawer of my dresser. And then Ben retrieved a suitcase of his own and set it on the bed next to mine.

"What are you doing?"

"Packing for The Treasure Chest."

I shook my head. "I need some space."

"No."

"What do you mean 'no'?"

"You asked for space after each miscarriage and I gave it to you. You asked for space last night and I gave it to you. I'm done giving you space, Carmen. We don't need any more space."

I continued my head shaking and stepped away.

"You are my wife." With a single stride, he ate up the distance I created. He stood so close, it chipped away at more of the wall—the one I wanted left intact, even thought it was already damaged. I was afraid of what I'd find behind it. He placed his hand along my jaw and curled his fingers around the back of my neck. "I'm not going to let you drown."

The declaration undid me, because how could he know? How could he know about my dreams when I'd never told him? "You shouldn't have waited."

"What do you mean?"

"I told you not to wait for me—when I left for UVA." Maybe if he wouldn't have waited, we could have avoided all this pain and heartache. No broken marriage. No miscarriages. No dying dreams. "You should have listened."

"You regret marrying me?" Ben's hand fell to his side.

A tear rolled down my cheek. Followed by another, then another. I stepped away. Looked away. "We're never going to have children, Ben. This house is empty. It's always going to be empty." The certainty I felt squeezed my lungs. Ravaged my heart. Burned my eyes. "I can't give you babies!"

He picked up my suitcase and hurled it against the wall, his eyes blazing like blue fire. "I don't want babies!"

I flinched.

The luggage fell to the ground with a thud.

"I want my wife."

His words reached down deep inside and smashed into the wall, crumbling enough of it to expose the ache behind. No matter how hard I scrambled, I couldn't hold it up anymore. I couldn't rebuild it. And my tears were no longer tears but a sob. "But I do!"

Oh, God, I do.

With every single pregnancy, the desire had grown stronger. With every single loss, the ache had grown larger. I wanted to be a mother more than I wanted anything. I wanted it more than I wanted The Treasure Chest. I wanted it more than I wanted Aunt Ingrid to return. I wanted it more than I wanted Gracie to get through this year.

I wanted it more than I wanted my husband.

Do you want it more than Me, beloved?

The question was not even a whisper, but a silent query straight from God that stretched up from the depths of my soul and slapped me into stillness. The truth fell from my deadened, desperate heart.

Yes, God, more than You.

The realization collapsed what was left. I crumbled. But Ben caught me. He cradled me against his chest as I cried tears long overdue. I grieved a grief that turned me inside out. I grieved for the ways I hoped our life would go, but didn't. I grieved for the six babies that took root in my womb but would not stay. I grieved the easy road that so many traveled not even realizing they traveled it—getting married and having babies and watching those babies grow. And when I was wrung dry and the tears were no more, I sat in the stillness and listened to the steady thrum of Ben's heart.

I sniffed and wiped at my tears. "Why does it have to be so hard?"

"I don't know."

"We did everything right." But even as the oft-repeated words escaped, they sounded paltry. Right according to whom? I knew the Bible. Did I really believe that God somehow owed me one for good behavior? Somewhere along the line, I made a bargain with the Lord that He never made with me. I'd love Him, I'd do what He said, so long as He gave me what I wanted. I reduced Him to nothing more than my personal genie. "Ben, what if we never have kids?"

"Then God will give us the grace we need to live with that."

They were scary words. Uncertain words. Words that came unattached to a promise. Words without a clear ending. Words that required everything and nothing but trust in a sovereign God who was wholly good, despite the circumstances of the moment that might say otherwise. I wasn't sure I was there yet.

"Carmen, I think we should go back to Dr. Rafferty."

"Once Sandy gets wind of my meltdown, we probably won't have a choice."

"Not for the adoption. For us."

My gut reaction was no. We didn't need counseling. We needed a child.

But I was so weary of needing something that might not ever come. I was so sick of being in a constant state of longing. Perhaps it was time to set it down and attend to what I had in front of me, instead of what I didn't. Right now, I had Ben. At one time in my life, that hadn't been just enough; it had been everything. Maybe if we could find a way back to each other, stronger than we were before, then maybe there was grace to be found in this after all. "Okay."

He cupped my face with his hands and wiped my tears with his thumbs.

"I think I lost my job today," I said.

"And if you didn't?"

I'd like to hang up my Carmen Hart Channel Three News persona for good. "I want to resign."

56

CARMEN

I walked inside Pine Ridge, a strange mixture of frightened and free. When I signed in as a guest, I avoided eye contact with the gal behind the desk and made my way to Aunt Ingrid's room on the second floor. I'd stopped hoping to find her in the dining hall weeks ago. The closer I got, the louder the ruckus. It appeared that Dorothy had turned her TV volume to the max. Her hacking cough mixed with the TV noise, as did Rayanna's calm, southern drawl, politely yet firmly insisting Dorothy turn the volume down.

"But I can't hear it if I turn it down. What's the point of having a TV if I can't hear it?"

"Now Miss Dorothy, every single person in Pensacola can hear that TV."

I stepped inside Ingrid's room and found her in a familiar position—sitting in the rocking chair facing the window, her arthritic hands resting on top of the Bible in her lap. A gust of wind swayed the trees outside and set the barren bird feeders to swaying.

I cleared my throat and knocked on her opened bedroom door to announce myself, wondering who I would be today. A stranger. Evelyn. Myself? Confusion and recognition went to battle in the brown of her irises. I rooted for recognition to win, but confusion came out victorious.

"Hello," I said from my spot in the doorway.

"Hello," she said back. "Have you seen the sky?"

I nodded.

"It looks like a storm is coming." She smiled at the dark, swollen clouds blowing in from the south. "I like storms."

Even though she didn't recognize me, she was in a pleasant mood. Most days, her forgetfulness, her inability to remember, her constant state of confusion agitated her. Today was not one of those days. It was a small sort of victory, I guess.

"Do you mind if I visit for a while?" I asked.

"That would be nice."

I took a seat on the edge of her bed as another gust of wind swept through Pine Ridge's lawn below. They had several wind chimes hanging in their courtyard. I could almost hear the loud tinkling notes they made as they knocked together.

Aunt Ingrid rocked back and forth.

"I got fired today," I said, still unable to fully believe it.

Ingrid raised her sparse eyebrows at my confession. "What kind of job did you have?"

"I'm a meteorologist."

This seemed to delight Aunt Ingrid. "On the news?"

"Yes."

"Then you know all about the storm that's coming."

In theory.

"Why were you fired?"

"I made too many mistakes." Or more like two big ones. They'd extended grace back in August. This time there was no grace to be had. Not when I broke down on air and then walked out of the station, leaving them high and dry.

"Do you know what you will do now?"

I shook my head, because I had no idea. Would I work at The Treasure Chest? Would Ben and I sell our home and move into one of the upstairs apartments? Would Gracie join us? I wished I could tell my aunt about all we'd done with the place. I wished I could ask for advice, but she was lost in a world where The Treasure Chest did not exist.

Ingrid rocked a little longer while the wind blew outside, then picked up the Bible from her lap. "Would you mind reading to me? The words get all jumbled in my mind when I try."

I leaned away from her offering. I told God I didn't believe in Him, yet it was like He had me by the scruff of the neck and wouldn't let go. She held her Bible out farther, giving me no choice but to take it. So I did. I opened it up to her bookmark and found Job. The two most depressing books of the Bible had to be a toss-up between Lamentations and Job. It figured she'd ask for one of them.

I began reading, disturbed by all the suffering. I glanced at Aunt Ingrid a time or two, worried the story might disturb her as well. But she rested her head against the back of the rocker, eyes closed, listening with a serene expression on her face.

"'Then Job arose and tore his robe and shaved his head and fell on the ground and worshiped. And he said, "Naked I came from my mother's womb, and naked shall I return. The LORD gave, and the LORD has taken away; blessed be the name of the LORD." In all this Job did not sin or charge God with wrong.'"

Aunt Ingrid had underlined the passage in blue ink and scrawled a familiar date in the margin. It was the day Gerald died of a heart attack. I blinked down at the note, overwhelmed by all my aunt had lost. Her parents, every one of her siblings, and her husband too. As if that weren't enough, now she'd lost herself. Dementia had stolen her memories. Her relationships. Her wits.

But it had not stolen her faith.

The thought struck me, profound in its truth. That was the one thing dementia had been unable to steal. And even if it did, even if she ended up forgetting every word she underlined, she couldn't really lose it. Ingrid was sealed. She was secure. This world could take every last thing from her, yet God would not let her be plucked from His hand. It was a promise straight from the book I held in my lap.

"The LORD gave, and the LORD has taken away; blessed be the name of the LORD."

Inside Aunt Ingrid's room at the Pine Ridge Retirement Facility, a place where age won every battle, I came face to face with the fact that He was God. Who was I to say He couldn't take away what He had given? Who was I to think He owed me anything? Especially when He already had given me everything—on that cross and in that empty tomb, He'd given it all. Anything else—my marriage to Ben, my friendship with Natalie, my budding relationship with Gracie—was extra.

The realization of it all unearthed a seed in my heart—a seed of entitlement and bitterness. A seed that had sown nothing but death. I didn't want to let the seed remain, but after all this time, I wasn't sure how to pluck it out.

"Knock, knock! It's time for dinner." Rayanna stood in the doorway.

"Is it dinnertime already?" Ingrid asked. "I'm not even hungry."

The news came as a jolt. I looked at the clock on Ingrid's nightstand. Gracie's academic bowl started in ten minutes. I'd come much too close to forgetting. Leaving the Bible on the bed, I said good-bye and hurried out to my car. With light traffic, the commute from Pensacola to Bay Breeze took fifteen minutes. I was trying to get there during rush hour, with dark-as-night clouds swirling overhead.

Taking the route least traveled, hoping to avoid as many stoplights as possible, I picked up my phone. I needed to call Gracie and let her know that even though I was running a little late, I'd be there. I promised I'd be there, and I was not going to break that promise. But when I tried powering up my phone, there was no power to be had.

Between not charging it last night and the copious phone calls coming in today, the battery had died. I tapped the wheel, glancing at the clock, muttering, "Come on, come on, come on!" the entire way. Then I reached the Pensacola Bay Bridge and my stomach dropped. Traffic was at a complete standstill. I tried craning my neck to figure out why, as if the why might get it moving again. All I could see was a long line of bumper-to-bumper cars. The bridge was gridlocked.

Forget late. I'd be lucky to make it at all.

57

GRACIE

I squinted into the auditorium from the back of the stage, scanning the audience row by row. So far, no Carmen. Behind me, my teammates went over last-minute notes. Every single one of them had somebody visit backstage—Malik's parents, Fred's older brothers, Veronica's new boyfriend. The only person who didn't have anyone visit? Me.

Malik called me over to the group.

My stomach cramped with nerves.

"All right, today's victory depends on quick hands. Coral Gables is lightning fast with the buzzer. We can't let them lock us out." There was no poetic vernacular today. This was showtime. Whoever won would move on to the national academic bowl in Chicago. Last year, it was held in St. Louis. The team made it all the way into the quarterfinals. This year, Malik thought we had a shot at becoming national champs. "Don't forget your area of expertise. If we zero in on the topics we've been studying, we should be fine. Our next stop will be Chi-town."

My nerves switched into panic mode.

"Hands in the middle. On the count of three, *focus*. One . . . two . . . three . . ."

Malik, Veronica, and Fred lifted their hands and shouted the word. I lifted my hand too, but the dryness in my throat kept me silent.

Bay Breeze's principal wished us good luck and shuffled us onto the stage. The crowd applauded. There were even a few hoots and hollers. The moderator—a severe-looking woman who was all sharp points and bony edges—introduced us one by one and invited us to take our places behind a long table. Across the stage, our opponents sat at a table like ours, wearing matching red shirts with *Cavaliers* stitched in gray on the front. There was a buzzer and a desktop microphone in front of every seat.

I twisted my mood ring around my sweaty finger. The stone was a bluish green, which couldn't be further from the truth. I was not feeling at all calm or relaxed. The moderator explained the rules of the game for the audience's sake, not ours. I spotted Elias sitting in the center of the auditorium, a few aisles back. Chanelle sat beside him. No Ben. No Mom. And for all her talk about being proud, about being there front and center with bells on, no Carmen either.

I tried shaking out my hands beneath the table, as if the movement might get blood flowing into them again. They were freezing cold. The moderator told us to move into position. We each placed one palm flat in front of our buzzers and our opposing hands behind us.

"For ten points," the moderator said from behind her podium, "identify the metric equivalent of the U.S. unit of horse—"

Veronica slapped the buzzer and leaned toward her microphone. "Watt."

"That is correct."

The audience cheered. Malik and Fred gave Veronica an encouraging pat on the back.

I thought about my mother, lying on the couch in our dark living room, surrounded by cheap wine boxes. I couldn't count on her. But I had counted on Carmen. I'd trusted her when she promised to be here.

"For ten points, which eleven-letter adjective is used before the word *mark* to refer to—"

Malik and a pudgy kid from Coral Gables hit their buzzer with Malik ahead by what could only be a fraction of a second.

"Diacritical."

"That is correct."

More cheering. More encouraging back pats.

One of the doors at the back of the auditorium opened. I peered through the dark, attempting to bring substance to the person walking down the aisle. Was it Carmen? Or Ben?

"For ten points, which philosopher argued against innate ideas, holding that the mind is a tabula rasa—"

I lifted my hand off the table, but not quickly enough. A team member from Coral Gables had already buzzed. "John Locke."

"Correct."

My teammates stirred beside me, because that was my topic. I was supposed to know that answer, yet I hadn't even hit the buzzer. I couldn't relax. I couldn't focus. As the questions continued, I kept glancing into the crowd, waiting for Carmen to materialize. I didn't understand how she could forget. I reminded her last night. She said she'd be here.

We entered into the next round, where questions were worth twenty points instead of ten.

"The masculine half of this deity is known as Purusha, while this figure's female form is called Satrap."

Malik shifted his weight and gave me a slight nudge, as if to say, *Here's mythology. Your turn, Gracie Fisher.* But my brain had become a tabula rasa.

"Among the objects is his arms are a water jug—"

Veronica slapped the buzzer too late. Someone on the other team had already locked us out. "Brahma."

Twenty points to them.

My confidence wilted.

I may have fooled Elias and my teammates and Pastor Zeke, but I never fooled myself. I didn't belong up here, in this position where others depended on me. I wasn't sure how I let myself get up here at all. Veronica made eye contact, a question in her eyes, as if to ask whether or not I was okay. No, I wanted to say. I wasn't. I needed to get off the stage. I needed everyone to stop staring at me.

"During World War II, his nickname was 'Old Blood and—'"

Fred buzzed in and won our team twenty points with George S. Patton. The second round melted into the final. Still no Carmen. The points were neck and neck. Malik, Veronica, and Fred fulfilled their roles. They answered the questions they were supposed to answer. I, however, kept messing up. Every time an RMP question arose, I was either distracted with movement in the audience, too slow to the buzzer, or unable to think of the correct answer. Malik came to my rescue with some of the religious questions, but I was supposed to have mythology and philosophy covered. By the time we reached the end of the match, we were up by ten and everyone in the audience had come to the edge of their seat.

Behind the podium, the moderator flipped to the last question.

I squeezed my eyes shut and prayed it did not belong to me.

"The blood of this deity created a plant that could be turned into an ointment that gave its wearer invincibility."

My palm broke free from the table and slammed the buzzer, because the question was mythology and mythology was mine. I needed to answer this question if we were going to advance to nationals. *Come on, Gracie—invincibility. You read about this two nights ago.* I knew this answer. It was lodged somewhere inside my brain. The moderator looked at me. My teammates looked at me. Everybody in the audience looked at me.

Absolutely nothing came.

"I'm sorry, you have run out of time." The moderator turned to Coral Gables, and the same team member who knew the Brahma question leaned toward her microphone.

"Prometheus?"

"That is correct."

His team went nuts. They fell into a huddled-up hug, jumping in unison while their small cheering section cheered and the rest of the audience clapped politely. I stood there feeling sick. I lost the match. I lost the match and Carmen never showed. I thought she cared. I thought I mattered to her. But once again, I misread the cues. She didn't care about me, at least not as much as she cared about getting a baby. That was her obsession. That was all that mattered. For all her talk, I was still an afterthought.

Unable to face the teammates I'd failed, I hurried off the stage. I grabbed my backpack and made a mad dash toward an obscure exit backstage when somebody grabbed my arm. "Gracie, wait."

It was Elias.

We hadn't spoken in nearly two weeks. I still didn't know why he stopped by the house last Saturday. I never asked and he never offered. Seeing him now, knowing he witnessed my failure while Chanelle most likely held on to his arm, set my entire face on fire.

"Are you okay?" he asked.

"Not really." I pulled one strap of my bag over my shoulder and pushed open the door.

"Hey, do you want to grab something to eat?"

I shook my head. No, I didn't want to grab something to eat. "I need to be alone right now." Away from anyone and everyone who knew me.

If only I could get away from myself.

Strong waves curled up onto white sand. The clouds were dark purple bruises that stretched to the horizon and met the white-capped sea. Unlike the dock where Elias and I used to sit, there was nothing hemming this body of water in. No shore across the bay. No hotel lights glittering on a stretch of island in the distance. It was a vastness that seemed to stretch into eternity—miles and miles of angry ocean and injured sky.

I came to The Treasure Chest to think and somehow ended up on the shore. A gust of wind rocked me back onto my heels. I closed my eyes against the invisible force, pictures forming a confusing kaleidoscope in my mind. My mother with a hangover. Carmen chopping green peppers with a catatonic expression on her face. Chanelle in her choir robe, singing *"Amazing grace, how sweet the sound, that saved a wretch like me."* Elias's youth group raising their hands high, whatever problems they had melting away as they lost themselves in the music. Pastor Zeke dunking full-grown adults into a tub of water, then lifting them out while an entire church celebrated. My mother walking into the creek. The canvas hanging in my room.

Behold, I make all things new.

Standing there on that beach, I only knew one thing with certainty. I didn't want to be Gracie Fisher anymore. I was done being the inconvenience, the burden, the screwup. Even when I tried my hardest, I still wasn't enough. If tonight's match proved anything, it was that. I had studied harder for that match than I'd ever studied in my life, and yet when it came down to it, all I did was mess up. Another gust of wind knocked into me. A wave reached the toes of my boots. The air smelled like rain. Like Elias. And his question came with the wind, the one he asked in the parking lot of The Cross.

"Who do you say Jesus is, Gracie Fisher?"

I didn't know. Not really. But I knew who I wanted Him to be. And I knew who I didn't want to be. I took off my boots. Left them in the sand. And walked out into the water.

Make me new. Please, make me new.

58

CARMEN

As soon as I pulled into the parking lot, I knew I was too late. People were already getting in their cars. The parking lot was clearing. My heart sank. I messed up, royally. I made a promise to Gracie, and in the midst of my own turmoil, I broke that promise. Sure, I couldn't control the traffic jam, but I should have never been in a position to get caught in the traffic jam to begin with. Up until ten minutes before the match, I'd forgotten all about the girl who'd been counting on me.

I unbuckled my seat belt and made my way inside the school. Like a salmon swimming upstream, I headed toward the auditorium while everybody else headed away, keeping an eye out for Ben or Gracie. I pushed through the heavy double doors. Pockets of students remained. I rose up onto my tiptoes and spotted Eli leaning against the stage with a small group of classmates. I made my way down the aisle. Eli saw me coming before I arrived.

"Hey, Mrs. Hart. Did you just get here?"

"Unfortunately, yes." I glanced around at the others, giving them a distracted smile. "Do you know where Gracie is?"

"No. I asked if she wanted to hang out after the match, but she said she wanted to be alone."

"They didn't win?"

Eli shook his head. "It was close, though."

I cupped my hand over my eyes. Gracie and I may have made giant strides over the last several months, but our relationship wasn't what I'd call stable. We were still in the trust-building phase. "Have you seen Ben?"

"No, sorry."

The pit in my stomach grew. "Could I borrow your phone? My battery's dead."

"Sure." Eli took his out from his back pocket and handed it over.

I dialed Gracie, then stuck my thumbnail between my front teeth. No answer. I tried Ben next. He answered on the third ring.

"Hello—Eli?"

"Please tell me you're here somewhere at the school. Please tell me you didn't miss it too."

"Carmen?" There was a pause, and then a light bulb must have gone on, because Ben let out an audible groan. "The academic bowl."

"Yeah."

"I am such a schmuck. With everything that happened . . . I totally forgot. I'm at home, making dinner."

"Gracie's not there?"

"No. So you missed it too?"

"There was an accident on the bridge. Traffic was at a standstill. I would have called you, but my phone died. I just got here. Eli said they lost and that she wanted to be alone. I have no idea where she is." But even as I said it, a memory wiggled its way to the forefront of my mind—a night several days before Christmas, when I drove out to The Treasure Chest to check on the sign and found Gracie sitting by the pool with a can of RC Cola. *"I like it here,"* she had said. *"It's a good place to be alone."* "Never mind. I know where she is."

"Where?"

"The Treasure Chest." Of course she'd go there. She ran there once, she'd run there again.

I hung up with Ben, gave Eli his phone back, said "thank you," and hurried out of the auditorium, my worry gathering and swirling like the storm outside. It was a much different kind than the worry I felt that very first Friday, when I came home from the football game and discovered Gracie wasn't there. Much different, even, than the worry I felt later, when Eli brought Gracie home drunk and stoned well past midnight. That was the indignant kind of worry. The "how could you be so ungrateful" worry. The kind of worry that was more anger than concern. The worry I experienced now was of the "squeeze your heart" variety, the "Lord, please help me find her" variety.

I stepped outside into the dark and the wind, climbed into my car, and drove east. Up above, the sky was a mass of angry black that tied my frazzled nerves into knots. By the time I reached Highway 399, the wind was so strong, I had to wrestle with the steering wheel to keep the car on the road. I didn't release my tight grip until I turned into the parking lot and spotted Gracie's Mirage parked near the front office. I pulled up beside it and rushed out into a wind that turned me into Dorothy from *The Wizard of Oz,* only instead of shouting "Auntie Em, Auntie Em!" I was shouting Gracie's name. She didn't have a key to get inside, which meant she must be outside. I headed through the courtyard, toward the pool, where some of the chairs had toppled onto their sides. Palm trees bent at odd angles in the distance, a storm siren wailed.

I turned in a three-sixty and spotted someone on the beach, walking into the water. My heart leaped into my throat. What in the world was she doing— trying to drown herself? I ran as fast as I could, into the wind, past the line of palm trees, across the beach, straight into the storm. I didn't stop until I reached the waves, kicked off my shoes, and ran in after her. "Gracie, stop!"

If she heard me, she didn't turn around.

"Gracie!" I yelled again.

A wave tossed me about like a buoy, but I didn't stop until I reached her. "What do you think you are doing?" I had to shout to be heard above the wind and the waves.

She stared at the horizon.

The water rose to my middle. I wasn't sure if we were drifting out, or if the violent waves made the ocean swell. I grabbed her arm. "We need to get back to the shore."

Gracie jerked away. "You lied."

"I'm so sorry for missing the match. I was an idiot. I let you down. But Gracie, we need to get out of the water." Not only was it dangerous; it was freezing.

She shook her head, like she wasn't at all alarmed that the ocean had risen to our chests. "You're no better than she is."

I didn't have to ask who she meant. I knew exactly who Gracie was talking about. I'd let her down just like our mother. But we couldn't have this conversation now. The siren wailed and the wind roared. We needed to move to safety. Right now. "I know. I'm sorry. I want to make it up to you, but we can't stay out here."

"I screwed up the match. We lost because of me."

Desperation rose along with the water. How could I get Gracie back to shore? "So you came out here to drown yourself?"

"No, I don't want to drown myself. I want to baptize myself."

"Baptize yourself?"

"I want to be a new person." A wave knocked us about. "I don't want to be me anymore."

"Gracie, you can dunk yourself in this water until kingdom come. It won't change anything."

"So it's hopeless, then?"

"I didn't say that." I grappled for a response. Anything that might get her moving. The wind was so fierce, I could barely hear myself think, let alone talk, and I swore the distance between us and the shore had grown, even though our feet had not moved. "I just mean we're powerless to change ourselves. That's something only God can do."

I grabbed Gracie's arm. If I had to drag her to shore, I would. But before I could take even a step, a wave crashed over us. It swept my feet out from under me. I clamped tighter onto Gracie and held my breath. Tried to break through to the air, but I didn't even know which way was up, and by the time we surfaced, my lungs burned and the shore was much farther away than it ought to have been. Beside me, Gracie panicked. The kind of panic that threatened to pull us both under.

Her arms flailed. Her legs kicked.

It was exactly like my dream, only Gracie was me.

"I don't know how to swim!" she screamed. "Help!"

Another wave crashed, pulling us under and flipping us about. We were going to die. Out in the sea—my sister and I were going to die. Fear like I'd never known gripped my entire body. I swam against the current with all my might. Gracie did everything she could to keep her head above water. But no matter how hard we fought our way to the shore, it grew more and more distant. Another wave crashed over us. I gulped for air. And as Gracie thrashed beside me, clawing her way through the water, I heard Earl's voice.

"You'll never escape a riptide by fighting against the current."

The wave broke, and I held on to my sister with a grip that was not mine. "Gracie, we have to swim parallel with the shore!" I screamed, changing my course, pulling her along with me. No longer did I fight the current. I let it carry us out to sea while swimming sideways. The waves continued to crash. Salt water stung my lungs. I swam and swam until I could swim no more. My strength gave way. We weren't going to make it. We were sinking. I wasn't strong enough.

Help us, Lord. I can't do it on my own!

Another wave swept past, but something in the current shifted. Changed. And all of a sudden, instead of pulling us out toward the horizon, the waves were carrying us inland. I focused every ounce of energy that remained on holding on to my sister's arm, keeping my head above water. And somehow, someway, we reached the sand. I pulled Gracie onto the beach. Exhausted, exhilarated. Relieved.

"We made it. Gracie, we're okay."

Gracie did not respond. She lay on her back, eyes shut, lips blue. I shook her shoulder. Nothing. I shook her harder. No response. I bent my ear to her lips, but she was not breathing. I fumbled around for her pulse, but there was no pulse to be found.

No. No, no, no . . .

I spun around on my knees, but nobody was there and my phone was dead in my car. I shook Gracie again. She was as unresponsive as the plastic mannequins at Bay Breeze's community center.

"If you ever find yourself in a CPR situation, I guarantee this, right here, is what you will recall."

I placed the heel of my palm against Gracie's sternum and began chest compressions. One, two, three, four, five. To the beat of "Staying Alive." "Come on, Gracie, wake up!" Sixteen, seventeen, eighteen . . . "Somebody help!"

One of Gracie's ribs cracked, but I kept going. Twenty-eight, twenty-nine, thirty. I tilted her chin back, plugged her nose, covered her lips with my mouth, and blew two breaths into her lungs. Her chest lifted, but she did not wake up.

Please, God . . . Please, God . . .

"Come on, Gracie. Wake up!"

My sister could not die. I could not watch her die, not when we finally made it to the shore. I started the chest compressions over. Another bone cracked. Gracie's head lolled. Tears swam in my eyes. Wind blew in my face. I looked around, well past the point of frantic, and saw Ben racing toward us on the beach.

"Call 911!" I screamed at him.

I tilted her chin back again. Breathed once. Prepared to breathe twice, but astoundingly, miraculously, Gracie coughed. A stream of water gushed past her icy blue lips. She rolled onto her side and gulped for air. I wrapped my arms around her and I didn't let go.

59

GRACIE

My eyelids fluttered open to pristine white—white walls, white floors, white sheets. It was a color that contained an equal balance of every other color in the spectrum. One that signified wholeness and new beginnings. Why, then, did I feel like death? A groan pushed past my parched lips. Everything hurt. My muscles. My face. My arms and my legs. My tongue. My ribs.

Oh, my ribs.

I groaned again, and someone gripped my hand.

It was Carmen. She sat by my bedside, her hair a tangled mess, looking every bit as horrendous as I felt. "How are you feeling?" she asked.

"I've been better."

She laughed a little.

I did too. But it made me grimace. "What happened?"

"You don't remember?"

I closed my eyes, bits and pieces of memory gathering together like a puzzle. Losing the match. Driving to The Treasure Chest. Walking out into the ocean. Carmen coming after me. Being carried out to sea. Crying out for help, thinking that we were surely going to die, and then nothing. "How did we make it back?"

"I'm still not entirely sure." A shudder rippled through Carmen's body. "I had to give you CPR. I didn't think you were going to make it."

I blinked up at the ceiling, astounded that I was here. That I was alive.

"Gracie, I am really sorry that I missed the match. I know I let you down. There was this accident on the bridge." She shook her head. "But that doesn't even matter. I should have—"

"I forgive you." It came without effort. It came without hesitation. Because there was something else I remembered too. Carmen didn't let go. Even when I was pulling her under the water with me, she didn't let go.

She gave my hand a squeeze.

We sat for a while in the silence, neither of us speaking.

Carmen broke it first. "You have a visitor."

"Who?"

"Eli's been waiting outside with Ben. I think he's pretty eager to see you." She slid her hand away from mine. "I'll go get him."

"Wait."

Carmen stopped in the doorway and set her hand on the door frame.

"Thank you."

"For what?"

"For holding on."

Tears welled in her eyes. "Always."

We exchanged a smile, and a few minutes later, Elias rapped on the opened door. If I wasn't so terribly sore, I might have pulled the pillow over my head. I must look awful. But he came to my bedside flashing his deep dimples, like he didn't care how I looked at all.

"What are you doing here?" I asked.

"I could ask you the same thing."

I rolled my eyes. Even that hurt.

"I was worried about you, so I called up Coach. Imagine my surprise when he said he was following an ambulance to the hospital. One with you in it." He pulled up a seat and folded his arms on the edge of my bed. "Can you please tell me something?"

"I can try."

"What were you thinking, going out into the ocean in the middle of a storm?"

"I'm not entirely sure I was thinking."

Elias shook his head—partially baffled, partially amused. "Never a dull moment with you, is there, Fisher?"

"Haven't you missed me?"

"Yes, actually. I have." He took my hand, threaded my fingers with his.

My heart gave a *blip*. Poor thing was probably tired of blips by now.

"So what's the deal—you ready to be friends again?"

"Friends, huh?" I ran my free hand over my bottom lip, which was dry and cracked. "I don't know. I might have to consult the Magic Eight Ball on that one."

He chuckled.

It was a sound I'd missed. A sound that warmed my heart. I closed my eyes, feeling as though I could sleep for a year. And as I drifted off, with my hand in his, I thought once again about the question he asked in the parking lot of The Cross. The question I couldn't answer on the beach before I waded into the ocean.

"Who do you say Jesus is, Gracie Fisher?"

I still wasn't entirely sure, but I did know that if Carmen hadn't found me when she did, I never would have made it back alive. And I did know that when I cried out for help, He didn't let us drown.

I guess I could start there.

CARMEN

I drove out to The Treasure Chest with the radio playing a song by Tenth Avenue North. We brought Gracie home yesterday. This morning, Eli Banks came over with Funyuns and a movie—*Little Shop of Horrors,* of all things. I thought it was a little strange. Gracie seemed delighted. I still couldn't believe she was alive. I couldn't stop replaying the events of Thursday.

At what point did coincidence stop being coincidence and turn into something else altogether?

A few days before Christmas, I had an illogical urge to check The Treasure Chest's sign. If I hadn't had that urge, I wouldn't have known that Gracie went to The Treasure Chest to be alone and I might not have been as quick to go there. Long before that, Aunt Ingrid had a Hearts kind of day. She talked about a nightmare she had, and Earl shared a random fact about escaping riptides. Natalie's youngest son went to kindergarten this year. His sad mama wanted to occupy her days with in-home day care and I wanted my portfolio to look good. So we ended up taking a CPR training class. Years ago, that same mama started taking CrossFit classes and convinced me to exercise with her. It gave me a stamina and a strength that kept my head above the water.

Literally. And when we were sinking in the ocean, with no strength left and nobody around to hear, it wasn't until I cried out for help that the current changed.

Coincidence?

Or evidence of a God who orchestrated even the most mundane details for our good? A God who never lifted His hand from my life. Not when I doubted. Not when I lost hope. Not even when I looked up into the heavens and told Him He didn't exist. He was there, through it all. On that beach as I breathed life into Gracie's lungs, He breathed life into mine.

I wasn't sure it was something I would ever get over.

Tenth Avenue North melted into Matthew West. I pressed a little harder on the gas pedal and pulled my visor down. The sun was bright. The storm has passed. All across Bay Breeze, there were tree limbs down, even a power line or two. There had barely been any rain, but the winds had been hurricane force. I was anxious to see how The Chest fared at the end of it all.

Earlier this morning, Ben left to run errands. I hadn't seen him since. But when I turned into the parking lot, it was not empty. His car was parked in one of the stalls. I pulled up beside it, turned off the ignition, and took in the damage with a growing sense of dismay. Chairs had blown every which way. Flowers and greenery had been ripped apart in the courtyard. The pool tarp had twisted its way around the trunk of a palm tree. Branches and shingles and broken bits of who knows what decorated the parking lot.

Ben stepped out of the front office with a garbage bag in hand and stopped when he saw me sitting behind the wheel of my car. I opened my door and joined him beneath the bright sun.

"I thought I'd get a head start on the cleanup," he said, holding up the bag.

Tears pricked my eyes. "There's a lot of damage."

He closed the gap between us and took my hand. "We'll fix it."

"Hurricane season is coming." I looked around at all the work that a simple storm had undone. "What if this keeps happening?"

"Then we'll keep on fixing it." Ben wrapped his arm around my waist and pulled me to his side. "However many times it takes. For however long it takes. We'll fix it together."

Then he said to me, "Prophesy over these bones, and say to them, O dry bones, hear the word of the LORD. Thus says the Lord GOD to these bones: Behold, I will cause breath to enter you, and you shall live. And I will lay sinews upon you, and will cause flesh to come upon you, and cover you with skin, and put breath in you, and you shall live, and you shall know that I am the LORD."

EZEKIEL 37:4–6

READERS GUIDE

1. Whose story did you enjoy more—Carmen's or Gracie's? Why?
2. This novel was inspired by the valley of dry bones in Ezekiel. A couple times during the story, Carmen feels like she's nothing more than dry bones. Have you ever felt this way? Has God ever resuscitated an area of your life you thought was past the point of resuscitation? Share with the group.
3. Carmen suffers from a recurring nightmare that changes slightly each time. How does the nightmare start? How does it change? What shocking thing happens in the last nightmare? How do these nightmares reflect Carmen's waking hours? Can you relate? How so?
4. At the end of the novel, Carmen wonders at what point coincidence stops being coincidence. Do you believe in coincidence? Why or why not?
5. Ben describes a process called wedging, wherein clay must be broken apart and kneaded back together in order to survive the kiln. How might this analogy relate to Carmen's and Gracie's lives? What about your own?
6. Entropy is the gradual decline into disorder, the idea that without regular upkeep, things fall into disrepair. What things in this story suffer the effects of entropy? In what ways do you combat entropy in your own life?
7. Carmen believes that a baby will solve her problems. Do you think this is realistic? Why or why not? Have you ever fallen into this same way of thinking? Please share with the group.
8. Gracie and Carmen cope very differently with their mother's alcoholism. How does Carmen cope? How does Gracie cope? As the story opens, how have their past experiences shaped who they are?
9. Carmen thinks God owes her for good behavior, that He has intentionally withheld something good from her life. Has there ever been a point in your life when you felt the same sense of entitlement? Do you think God intentionally withholds good things from our lives?
10. Who is your favorite secondary character? Why?

11. Gracie calls Carmen a hypocrite. In what ways is Carmen hypocritical throughout the novel? How does social media play into Carmen's struggles? Do you feel like the person you project to the world is an honest depiction of who you really are? How can we get better at being real?

12. In what ways do Gracie and Carmen help each other throughout the novel? Whom do you think ends up being the most helpful?

13. What do you think the title of this novel, *The Art of Losing Yourself,* means? How do various characters lose themselves throughout this story?

ACKNOWLEDGMENTS

I have a different relationship with every novel I've written. There are those I fall in love with immediately. Those that begin with a vague sense of fondness. And then there is this one . . .

For a long while, I did not have happy feelings toward *The Art of Losing Yourself*. It seemed to bring out a whole host of unpleasant emotions, with insecurity, frustration, and weariness leading the way. It's hard, when you're in the midst of a waiting season, to write a story about a character in a waiting season too.

If not for these champions cheering me on and offering support, I might never have pushed through the "pull out my hair, grappling in the dark, I have no idea how to make this story better" stage to the place we find ourselves in now. It's funny how, sometimes, the most stubborn of stories can end up being favorites.

Big thanks go to . . .

Ryan, for not only being my husband but my best friend. Every writer needs a spouse like you. Unfortunately for the others, you're all mine.

Melissa Gilroy, for not only reminding me of the things I so easily forget when I'm in the thick of a writerly crisis, but for every other single thing you are in my life. I'd say you don't know how much you mean to me, but something tells me that you do.

My family, for your ceaseless support. Without you, I couldn't do this thing I love.

Jill Kemerer, Beth Vogt, Becky Wade, Carla Laureano, Laurie Tomlinson, and any other writer friend who helped me turn a vague idea into a full-grown story.

Hillary Manton Lodge, for providing the perfect idea when I was scrambling. The goat came at just the right time and did wonders to lighten up the story line. Abby Van Gerpen, for sharing a funny story, which led to conspiracy theorist Jimmy. My cousin, Travis McGivern, and the Bettendorf High School debate team, for answering all of my silly questions and letting me sit in on a practice.

James Zahara, chief meteorologist for Storm Team 8, for sharing with me the ins and outs of weather broadcasting. Any inaccuracies in the story are all mine.

Shannon Marchese, as always, for your brilliance and for seeing what isn't there. It's a pretty amazing gift. You have this way of pulling out the potential until it's not just potential but, as Malik would say, kinetic. Thank you for believing in me and this story.

Lissa Halls Johnson, for walking beside me and holding my hand when I was all wrung dry with no more brain cells left to spare. Your specific feedback was the perfect amount of light I needed to pull this story apart and put it back together again.

Laura Wright, for your amazing attention to detail. The entire team at WaterBrook Multnomah, for the enthusiasm, energy, and hard work you've all poured into my writing career. I've got nothing but love for all of you.

Rachelle Gardner, agent extraordinaire, for all you do to get my work out there.

My readers, for being the best in all the land. Your notes of encouragement—whether they be through e-mail, Facebook, or Twitter—come at the perfect time, every time, just when I need them. I pray this story ministers to you.

And, of course, to my Lord and Savior, Jesus Christ—the giver of every good gift, the only one who can breathe life when there is none. As the title of this story suggests, there is an art to losing ourselves. My prayer is that I would lose myself more and more each day in the all-encompassing glory that is knowing You.

ABOUT THE AUTHOR

KATIE GANSHERT is a Midwest gal who's passionate about Jesus, her family, adoption, writing, grace, Africa, and all things romance. When she's not plotting her next novel, she enjoys going on ice-cream dates with her husband, playing make-believe with her son, and chatting with her girlfriends over coffee and bagels. She could talk books all day and absolutely loves connecting with her readers.

You can connect with Katie at
katie@katieganshert.com
www.katieganshert.com
Twitter: @KatieGanshert
Facebook: www.facebook.com/AuthorKatieGanshert
Pinterest: http://pinterest.com/katieganshert

Grief like winter may have its day,
but life comes back in springtime.

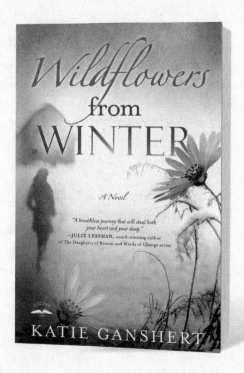

Architect Bethany Quinn is comfortable being the creator, but not acknowledging one. So when tragedy takes her back home, can she keep avoiding the God of her childhood?

Sometimes everything you ever learned about yourself is wrong

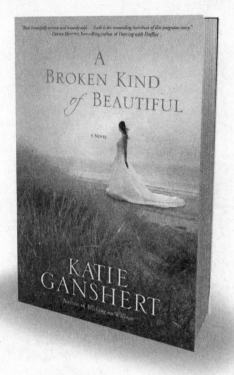

Ivy Clark sums up her worth by looking at the past, but a humble photographer seeks to show her a God who turns brokenness into beauty.

Read an excerpt from this book and more at www.WaterBrookMultnomah.com!

A local widow, an out-of-town charmer,
and a town caught between them.

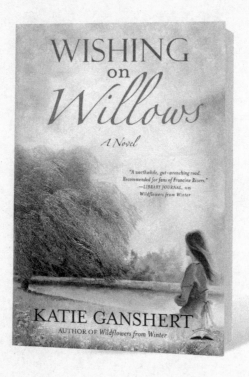

Widow and single mom Robin Price has worked hard to
get her business and life in order. Will the handsome Ian
McKay undo all her plans?

Read an excerpt from this book and more at
www.WaterBrookMultnomah.com!